THE
INVENTION
OF THE
WORLD

THE INVENTION OF THE WORLD

A NOVEL BY
JACK HODGINS

Macmillan of Canada / Toronto

Canadian Cataloguing in Publication Data

Hodgins, Jack, 1938–
    The invention of the world

ISBN 0-7705-1518-5

I. Title.

PS8565.034I58   C813'.5'4
PR9199.3.H63I58   C77-001100-4

*The author wishes to acknowledge, with gratitude, that this
novel was begun with the aid of a Canada Council Grant.*

Printed in Canada for
The Macmillan Company of Canada Limited
70 Bond Street, Toronto M5B 1X3.

this story is for my parents

for Shannon
and Gavin
and Tyler

for David Arnason

Becker, the first time you see him, is at the mainland terminus waving your car down the ramp onto the government ferry and singing to your headlights and to the salt air and to the long line of traffic behind you that he'd rather be a sparrow than a snail. Yes he would if he could, he loudly sings, he surely would. In his orange life-jacket and fluorescent gloves, he waves his arms to direct traffic down that ramp the way someone else might conduct a great important orchestra — a round little man with a sloppy wool cap riding his head and a huge bushy beard hiding all of his face except the long turned-down weather-reddened nose. He'd rather be a forest, he sings, than a street.

Follow him home.

Ride the ferry with him on its two-hour trip across the Strait of Georgia, while the long backbone ridge of the island's mountains sharpens into blue and ragged shades of green, and the coastline shadows shape themselves into rocky cliffs and driftwood-cluttered bays; then follow him up the ramp, the end of his shift, as he sets out through the waiting lines of traffic and gusts of rushing passengers on foot. No longer the serenading conductor, he is a short stump of a man walking the full length of the waterfront parking lot and then up the long slow hill towards the town, his black overcoat hanging down past the top of his rubber boots suggesting the shape of a squat crockery jug. He stops to explore the rain water running through the limp grass in the ditch, and to talk for a while with someone leaning over a front-porch ledge, and to buy a pocketful of candy in a corner store. But eventually he gets into his old fenderless green Hillman parked in one corner of the shopping-centre lot, and drives down the long slope to the beach again, and along past the bay, and north beyond town altogether on a road that twists around rock bluffs and dips through farm valleys and humps through second-growth timber until he turns off suddenly and rattles downhill on a gravel lane to his log cabin where it stands with others near the water's edge.

And now, Strabo Becker poised on his front step looks back down the strait where the ferry he has just left is nosing its way out again into the open water beyond stony islands and buoys and floating debris. Away, he sings, I'd rather sail a-wa-a-ay. His only song, it is half mumbled this time, or chewed; he's no golden-voiced crooner. He is only a man, he says, and that's more than enough for anyone to be.

And yet this man, this bushy raccoon of a man, with his long narrow red-rimmed eyes calmly filming the world, and his large bent-forward ears silently recording all that the world might say, this man has pretensions. He has chosen to nest on a certain piece of this world and to make a few years of its history his own. The debris of that history is around him and he will reel it all in, he will store it in his head, he will control it; there will be no need, eventually, for anything else to exist; all of it will be inside, all of it will belong only to him. Becker wants to be God.

Inside the moss-roofed cabin, amongst his god-hoardings, he is inclined to strut for you, to pull it all out where it can be touched, and seen. He hauls scrapbooks and shoeboxes of newspaper clippings and cardboard boxes of old photographs out from under the little cot and from behind the bedroom door and down from the dusty boards that lie across the ceiling beams. He pulls crates of cassette tapes out of the closet. He takes dozens of notebooks down from the shelf over the fireplace. He gathers all of it, collects it around him, he lays it out on the table, on the chairs, on the floor around his feet. Touching, brooding, gloating, he thinks that what he has here is at least the equal of all that exists outside his walls.

Sometimes this god-man almost believes that he owns this island, that he has perhaps invented it. He expects that he should be able to conjure it up for you out of the thick air above his kitchen table: twelve thousand square miles of rugged stone mountains and timber stands and logged-off slopes and deep green valleys, sprinkled with fishing villages around rotting wharves, with logging camps of tarpaper huts on skids, with towns and resorts and hobby farms, with snag-spiked lakes and long crooked green rivers. In words, if you let him, he will decorate the tree-furry coastline with used-car lots, rotting hay barns, smoke-blooming pulp mills, weedy estuaries, log-booming grounds, and brand new subdivisions, with old beached freighters painted up for restaurants and rusted wartime destroyers sunk for breakwaters, with mountains of gleaming white shells growing right up out of bays and topped with tiny shacks selling oysters. He will even take the credit, now, for the single grey highway that stretches from the bottom tip two-thirds of the way up the eastern coast, and for leaving all the rest to be found by narrow snaking roads designed for logging trucks. And he will act as if he himself had set all this down in the ocean, amidst foamy rocks and other smaller islands where sea lions sunbathe and cormorants nest and stunted trees are bent horizontal from the steady force of the Pacific wind.

It is not necessary, of course, for him to invent the centre of his stage, which is all around outside the little cabin: a wide shaggy swell of land that thrusts out from the eastern shore and curves tightly south around a shallow bay, announced far up the slope at the open gate by a thick and handsome signboard painted green: *Revelations Trailer Park*. The long shiny trailers, which are owned by American tourists who spend their time out on the strait catching salmon to take home with them, are tucked away out of sight behind a strip of fir and hemlock and thick salal. Between him and the pale sea, directly across the little stone wellhead which is the exact centre of this circle of buildings, is the House of Revelations itself, that tall old brown house out on the promontory in a confusion of pink arbutus trees. Its high gables are as sharp and varied and apparently unplanned as the mainland mountains beyond: its verandahs sag under the weight of honeysuckle and morning glory which have over the years become intertwined and thick with possessiveness. A door opens, closes; a window shivers; a voice somewhere inside calls crookedly, a question.

But don't ask Becker to answer questions. He is a shy man, who knows only this much: that the tale which exists somewhere at the centre of his gathered hoard, in the confusion of tales and lies and protests and legends and exaggerations, has a certain agreed-upon beginning:

Donal Keneally's mother started it all, a hundred and fifteen years ago and thousands of miles away. When she was told in a dream that her child would be fathered by a black bull from the sky, she fell off the side of her bed in alarm and knocked all memory right out of her skull. Countrymen, frightened by the wild look in her eyes as she wandered from village to village, waved her on, kept her moving, and mumbled prayers to their Blessed Virgin until she was out of sight. "Bad luck to her so," they said, for all their piety, and spat on the ground. "Isn't it trouble enough we have in this world, without inviting tragedy in to sit at the fire?"

Indeed they were probably right, says Becker among his boxes and books, but consider the difference it would have made to us here if one of those Connemara farmers had taken her in.

Becker the caretaker-god sits deep into night, every night, in his nest of deliberate clutter. He touches, he listens, he reads, he worries. He will absorb all this chaos, he will confront it and absorb it, and eventually he will begin to tell, and by telling release it, make it finally his own. Becker, on this day that you've met him, is singing, though broodingly, that he'd rather be a sparrow than a snail.

MAGGIE

1

On the day of the Loggers' Sports, on that day in July, a mighty uproar broke out in the beer parlour of the Coal-Tyee Hotel, which is an old but respectable five-storey building directly above the harbour and only a block or two from the main shopping area of town. To the people out on the sidewalk, to Maggie Kyle stopping to mail a letter at the corner post office and to others coming out of the stone courthouse at the top of the grassy slope across the street, the fight seemed no different at first from what they might have overheard outside any one of the town's twenty-seven beer parlours on a Saturday morning like this, just the loud clash of voice attacking voice, bass and treble. But a fight is still a fight wherever it is found, and not to be lightly dismissed: like Maggie they all discovered reasons to hang around for a while, talking to strangers or reading a newspaper or watching pigeons, to see what would happen next.

What happened next was this: the door banged open and a woman black as a Zulu in a pair of lumpy jeans and a flowered blouse rushed out onto the sidewalk yowling insults over her shoulder. That son of a bitch behind her was worse than a savage animal, she said, and oh how she'd like to cut his throat. She stopped and swung a terrible scowl around at her startled audience and loudly offered to do the same for any one of them who got close enough to reach. They were all the same to her, she said, she was a stranger in this dump. Bronze hair fell for a moment across a furious eye, then was flicked back by a ring-cluttered hand. This was no one Maggie Kyle had ever seen before.

Though the same could not be said of her friend, who stepped out of the hotel and ducked neatly to miss the beer glass the Zulu hurled. This was Danny Holland, down again from a bunkhouse camp deep in the north-island woods to take part in the annual Loggers' Sports: three times axe-throwing champion of the island, twice of the whole Pacific Coast. A celebrity. He was dressed for work or play, it made no difference: a pair of low-crotched blue jeans hacked off above his boots and held up by wide elastic braces, a white T-shirt stretched over his thickened middle, and a shiny new aluminum hat sitting level on his head catching sunlight like a warrior's shield. He roared, "Blast you woman for your donkey nature!" and whipped off the hat to scratch around in his hair.

Then, quickly, the Zulu was down inside the green sedan at the curb. "I love you, you stupid jerk," she threw at him, then drove off, snarling something inaudible at the street gawkers, and disappeared around the bend behind the town's one and only highrise apartment building. "Me too!" he shouted after her, and leaping into his pickup truck, made a tire-squealing U-turn and drove off down the slope in the opposite direction, past the post office and the customs house and the boat basin. The spectators breathed again, sighed; you could always count on a good show when the up-island people were in town. Straight out of the bush, they didn't know any better, half of them were crazy.

The safest thing perhaps, thought Maggie Kyle, was just to ignore them.

But ignoring them would not be possible for long. From around the curve beneath the highrise the Zulu's sedan soon reappeared. And from somewhere down beyond the customs house Danny Holland's pickup returned, roaring and bouncing up the slope. They rushed towards each other from either end of the street. In front of the coffee-shop windows of the Coal-Tyee Hotel their brakes squealed, both vehicles slid sideways and whipped back again; their noses met with a harsh grinding crash. Headlights shattered and fell in pieces to the pavement, grills collapsed, fenders folded back. In the terrible silence that followed, both drivers' heads were wooden-rigid; from behind the glass they glared at one another.

It was amazing, someone near Maggie said, what love could do.

Then both reversed and backed away from the scene of the crash in opposite directions down the street. The woman's sedan dragged a squealing piece of its own bumper along the blacktop. Danny Holland's pickup sprinkled a trail of broken glass; the upright exhaust pipe behind his cab threw up clouds of smoke, plumes of challenge. They stopped, changed gears noisily, and roared ahead again. This time there were no brakes applied; they nearly missed, sideswiped each other, and bounced away. Doors sank in, windows clouded up and laced themselves like crazy cobwebs. Something dropped out of the bottom of the sedan and clattered across the pavement towards Maggie's feet.

They turned again and once more came at each other, cautiously, this time hitting directly nose to nose, barely hard enough to scratch. Engines stalled. Something heavy dropped from under the sedan and the back end settled like a tired bull. A moment before the quiet impact the woman's door had opened and she leapt free, rolled over twice towards the hotel, and righted herself in a sitting position against a light pole. She held an arm hugged close against her waist, nursing it, rocking. A small stream of blood glistened on her cheek.

Danny Holland, as Maggie Kyle and anyone else who knew him would expect, sat behind the wheel of his pickup and laughed. He spat snoose out the broken window onto the pavement and wiped an arm across his mouth. If the rather vigorous demonstration of his feelings had caused him any pain he wasn't about to show it here. He laughed again. When he opened his door it squealed and popped and sagged. Standing on his step, he hauled a red-and-white handkerchief out of the back pocket of his big loose jeans and blew his nose, as if he'd waited days for just this opportunity. Then, shoving the handkerchief back down inside the pocket, he looked at the long-legged black woman at the curb. "Well?" he said.

"You're still a jerk," she said, but with less conviction.

Before he could step down from the pickup to prove her right or wrong, the wail of a police siren came clearly on the air from somewhere deep in town. Danny Holland dropped back inside his truck, leaned into his starter button until his engine finally caught, backed off, and drove whining and sputtering away without so much as a see-you-hon to his woman. By the time the police arrived he was long gone and the woman was left to protest in a loud and insolent voice that it had only been a friendly fight and nobody's business but their own.

"He's a son of a bitch all the same," she told the RCMP officer who helped her to her feet. What she lacked in variety of language she made up for in sincerity of tone. "When I see him again I'll cut his stinkin' throat."

"When you see him again," the officer said, "you'll both be talking to a judge." He winked at someone on the curb, to show that he understood the craziness of bush people as well as anyone else.

"Don't count on it,"she said, and put a hand over the bleeding side of her face. "There's a long line of people want to get their hands on Danny Holland's throat but none of them ever seem to manage it."

And this is one of them here, said Maggie Kyle to herself. Let me at the man, I'll rip out his gizzard and feed him to pigs.

A perfect sense of timing, she thought. He couldn't have picked a worse day to arrive. If he had written her a note saying *Of all the days in the year, which one would it upset you the most for me to land in town*? she could not have thought of another day. This was it. This was the worst one. Of course she should have known, she should have thought about it, it only made sense. Danny Holland was made for spoiling things, you couldn't expect him to turn down a chance like this.

So she could hardly hold back a good hoot at the sight of the Zulu being carted away in the purple police car. She'd been bush herself once, and hadn't forgotten the shocks and humiliations that met you when you came out. She even waved at the silly woman, who could not have known who she was, or guessed all that they had in common.

She'd been bush herself once, and there were people who said Maggie Kyle had the smell of pitch and the mountains on her yet for all her moving down to civilization, to the coast; but others claimed it was because she hadn't moved all the way in to town the way you'd expect a forest refugee to do, she'd settled into that sagging old house out north a ways, surrounded by second-growth fir. And a good thing, too, they said, until she learned to laugh like a lady instead of like a chokerman stomping on a snake.

But it only took a single glance to see how little she cared for anyone's opinion. When a tow truck pulled up in front of the hotel to haul the crumpled green sedan away she stepped out and told the driver he could thank an empty-headed axe-man for this mess, but he could send his bill to the moon for all the hope he had of getting paid by *him*. Then she went inside the hotel and came out with a broom to sweep up the broken glass herself.

Though what else could you expect? one ancient lady said. Because wasn't Holland ... ? A carefully pencilled eyebrow implied all that Holland had and hadn't been to Maggie Kyle. There was knowledge here, invisible as air and just as certain, and puzzles had a way of falling into place all by themselves.

"If that Zulu would do what she threatens to do," she said, "I'd be the first in line to hand her a prize." She might have been talking to the broom, or the tires of the towing truck.

But the driver answered, pulling heavy chain off his winch. "There's plenty more like him to take his place. They're all the same. They get drinking," he said, ducking under the car, "and there's no telling how much damage they'll do. Some people ought to be locked up at birth."

Amen to that, said Maggie Kyle. Amen to locking, amen to chopping, amen to anything you could think of so long as it stopped the inevitable. She'd never vote for hanging but she was beginning to understand why people committed crimes of passion.

What she couldn't understand was how the crowd had lost interest so fast. People drifted away. Only the waitress was left, keeping an eye on her broom and teasing a pimple. "You'd think some of them would want to help," she said, and pushed at some glass.

The driver ducked out, his face red from the exertion, and looked at the street. "You won't have no trouble finding people to watch you smash yourself to pieces," he said, and flopped over onto his back. "But they don't find cleaning up the mess so fascinating." His head and the hand holding the hook at the end of the chain disappeared again under the car, levered forward by one hingeing leg.

One other person who hadn't left, of course, was Cora Manson, who was sitting in Maggie's van palming the horn to death. When Maggie looked and looked away again as if she didn't exist, she gave up honking and got out of the van to come down to the scene of the action. Poor Cora was suffering, it was obvious; the world never failed to live up to her worst expectations. She was in no mood for dawdling, or finding entertainment in a street brawl.

"On days like this they ought to close down the beer parlours,"
Cora said, "like election days." Now that she was in front of the
hotel she gave it a look that put most of the blame right in the lap of
its owners. She herself of course had been sipping a glass of diet
cola when Maggie had arrived at the bake shop to pick her up for
the Loggers' Sports. "Straight out of the bush. They think nothing
of making fools of themselves."

"Or of the rest of us either," Maggie said.

"And if that was who I think it was ... "

"It was."

Cora bridled. "Then this wedding tonight will be even wilder
than I expected."

"Expect again," said Maggie Kyle, "because I'll drive over his
neck with a bulldozer before I let him set a foot inside to spoil a
thing."

Poor Cora groaned. The world never failed her, never. "Who was
the woman?"

The driver shrugged. He was wiping his hands on a piece of old
rag he'd hauled out of his coveralls pocket. His job was this car,
nothing else.

"Never seen her before," Maggie said, lowering her voice. "His
taste is as consistent as his bad manners, he still likes long legs.
Long legs and big boobs, he used to say. They drive him crazy."

Cora whimpered and jammed a cigarette between her lips.
She'd been cursed with short doughy stumps for legs and no
chest at all, and the mere mention of such things was a knife
thrust. Cora was a woman with an infinite capacity for suffering
over the foolishness of others, and Maggie knew the only reason
she ever left her bake shop to go along to things like the Loggers'
Sports was just to get her mind off sex. A short thick chain-
smoking little lady, she had startling dyed-red hair so thin it no
longer hid her scalp and a putty-coloured face that puffed up
around her eyes and drooped through half a dozen chins before
disappearing in her dress. She stood on her aching feet all day in
her bake shop, staring at the gooey pieces of cream-covered cakes
she'd baked and thinking of all the men she'd never had: approximately one half the population of the earth. She'd reached the
age of forty and not a man in the world had shown a spark of
interest in her. Though she'd developed an enormous contempt
for the whole pack of thoughtless clods, she'd confided to Maggie

that she could think of nothing else so long as she was in her shop. Being out among them on the other hand, she said, seeing their thick insensitive necks full of dirty pores and smelling their sweaty armpits knocked all fantasies of romance right out of her head.

That was why Maggie had rescued her from the bake shop this morning. "If it's dirty pores and sweaty armpits you want then I know just the place we can go." A purple-haired matron, undecided at that moment between cream-puffs and jam tarts, wheeled around and left the shop without either. Before the little bell over the slammed door had stopped tinkling, Cora had her shoes back on and was ready to go. She was in no mood, now, evidently, for prolonged conversation with drivers of tow trucks.

"Maggie's son is getting married tonight," she told him. Then she grabbed the broom out of Maggie's hand and took it back to the waitress. "There are people who are paid to clean up this kind of mess. Let's go, your van is overparked."

It was an old grey Ford, a delivery van, which had been driven nearly to death by the pest-exterminating company that had owned it before. On either side, Maggie had painted out the name of the company but had left its trademark, a picture of a resentful black bug that lay curled and gracelessly dying with a look in its eye that could stop you dead in your tracks, though Maggie doubted it could scare off any cop who might catch sight of the expired meter.

"That's all I need," she told Cora, as they drove up through town. The wired-shut hood rattled and bounced in front of them. "Danny Holland showing up to wreck everything. And to flap my business in everyone's face while he's at it."

Cora fanned the air in front of her as if that might help to brush his memory away. "Everybody in this town already knows all your business," she said, perhaps with envy. "You have that effect on people, they make a point of finding out all they can."

Maggie couldn't deny that they tried. She was used to having people think they knew all there was to know about her; they thought everything about her was as obvious as this red-and-black plaid shirt she liked to wear. Some people's lives, they said, were written on their faces and in their gestures and into the air that surrounded them as clear as any newspaper account.

Let them think it. Because what did they really know? Nothing important. They knew about her childhood, spent in one shabby gyppo logging camp after another, up north and on the west coast and in among the mountain lakes, with parents whose fighting and boozing drove her more and more often down under the shacks they lived in, to play in the lifeless dust with her cat, or the lizards she found there. They knew about the whole series of men from the camps and fish boats who left their wives and children to live with her for as long as it took their families to come to their senses and demand a hasty return. They knew about the four surprise children who were left inside her by some of those grateful men like thank-you notes — Forbes, and the twins, and Carla—who'd learned so young to fend for themselves that they'd been able to discard her just as easily as their fathers had before them. And about a husband once, a Mr. Somebody Kyle (they wouldn't know his first name, it was George, she called him Shorty) who stayed a year with her, winter to winter, and then snuck out of her house in the middle of the night leaving twenty hundred-dollar bills on the bedside table and was never heard of again, good riddance. Until he died, somewhere, and left her a nice fat pile of insurance money. All of this was public knowledge and happened long ago and far from here, it didn't matter to anyone except as gossip, or when some of it caught up with her and turned into a kind of joke: the oldest of those surprises was Danny Holland's kid, a skinny adolescent who was getting married tonight after the Loggers' Sports to his pregnant girlfriend. But the real joke, they knew, was this: tall and gorgeous Maggie Kyle at thirty-three would be escorted down the aisle of that church tonight as mother-of-the-groom, all alone, wearing a corsage she'd probably have to pay for herself. And like it or not there was practically nothing she could do to stop the father-of-the-groom from showing up and raising Cain. If the boy hadn't wanted him there why would he pick this date? Maggie could hear them laughing.

"Wouldn't you know it'd be a hot day," Cora said. She suffered from heat too, along with everything else, and checked her armpits for the spreading stain.

There were sprinklers sowing curved sprays of water on all the lawns down the left-hand side of the street. The stucco high-staired houses looked dry and blank and quiet. Dark windows revealed only faint impressions of bowls of flowers and furniture and mirrors, and the flashing movement of themselves going by: the Bug Wagon, grey and old and loose, with its patches of rust and its mean-eyed dying insect. There were no people in sight.

Maggie Kyle eight years ago had got tired of dirt roads and two-room shacks and the habit people had of disappearing. She moved down out of the bush — an end-of-the-road mountain place called Hed that even the logging company had abandoned years before she got around to it — moved down here with her insurance money and bought up everything that was left of the famous Revelations Colony of Truth a few miles north of town — a house, a circle of leaning cabins made of logs, a few caved-in barns, and all the gone-back land that hadn't been already chopped up for subdivisions. She turned it into a trailer park and lived out there on the cliff, above the strait, in the old House of Revelations itself which the leader of the colony had built for his first wife in nineteen-oh-three and used as his headquarters until the colony fell apart. It had proved to be a good place to live, once she'd scoured it out and burned all the rotting mouldy furniture, and done a few repairs. She had twenty American families paying for the privilege of parking their long awkward trailers on her land while they stacked their bedrooms full of the salmon they caught out in the strait and canned on their Coleman camp stoves in the dark of night. What difference did it make to them if the place was crawling with ghosts? They could take a little history with their fish. Even those people in town would have to consider twenty American trailers harmless enough, since they stayed out of sight behind trees, and since the Americans themselves were far too busy catching salmon to bother anyone.

What probably convinced them that she'd left whatever sense she'd been born with behind her in the bush was the collection of people she'd gathered around her in the House, and in the cabins behind it. She'd hardly got the place cleared out and the junk all burned when sour old skinny Julius Champney arrived, from the prairies, and set himself up in one of the cabins. She hadn't advertised, he'd just arrived, and it seemed like a good idea. He paid his rent. He didn't want to live in town, he said, he hated crowds. Once a week he caught the bus in to do a bit of shopping and to sneer around a bit and let people know how much contempt he had for salt water and coast dwellers. He spent most of his days, when the weather was good, wrapped up in several sweaters down on her wharf watching out of his old yellow eyes while the tide came in and went out. No matter how long he stayed here, he said, he'd never trust a body of water whose edges were capable of creeping up on you like that.

And then Becker had appeared one day out of nowhere like a nervous raccoon at her door to ask for a place to live. A funny little man. At least he found work, he didn't go on welfare the way she half-expected from the looks of him, and directing cars off and onto ferries meant a regular government cheque to pay his room and board. All he wanted from her was the food and the place to sleep and the right to be left alone to play with his tape recorder. He'd quit a job in a university Back East, to do his own kind of research. He was digging into the history of the colony, he said, and liked to go around the district sticking his microphone into people's faces: *What do you remember about Donal Keneally? Weren't you related to the murdered boy?* Maggie got phone calls, telling her to call him off, to send him packing so he wouldn't bother people any more. But it had nothing to do with her, she said, he was only a boarder. He paid.

Anna Sterner didn't pay. She lived right in the House and helped. She'd run away from a pair of wealthy parents to live in a commune somewhere up in the mountains, an End-of-the-World religious group, and then had run away from that too when it turned out to be more than she could handle. Her parents said *Sorry, you made your bed, now lie in it*, and she came running for refuge. A fat high-complexioned girl, she dragged around in long skirts and bare feet, but she did her job.

What Lily Hayworth did, however, was complain. The naïveté of the Kyle woman, people said, was reaching madness when she opened her door to that one. Maggie could almost have agreed. But ancient failing Lily was filthy-rich. She was the third wife and widow of the lunatic Irishman who'd run the colony, but she'd had the good sense to marry money the second time, lumber money, and had moved with her husband down to Victoria where lumber money was nearly as good as any other kind. But old Hayworth in his retirement senility decided to transfer himself and half his tree-fortune to a villa full of Polynesian servants down in Fiji, and to leave the other half of the fortune in the arthritic hands of his abandoned wife to do with as she pleased. What she pleased was to high-tail up-island as fast as her creaky bones and a blue-striped taxi could take her, straight to the house where she'd once been chatelaine, to pay through the nose for the privilege of being waited on like a decaying dowager. She was waiting, she said, for her husband to come for her. Whether she meant Hayworth from Fiji or Keneally from his grave Maggie wasn't sure. She'd go off, likely, with whoever arrived for her first.

They were called Kyle's Krazies, sometimes. And the Revelations Colony of Kooks. By people who never stopped to think. Maggie didn't much care what kind of names they made up, it only showed their ignorance. There was something else about her that no one knew but herself, and it was even more preposterous than what was known. She had schemes, she had plans for the unspeakable, she had decided that the only appropriate direction for her life from now on was *up*, she intended to rise somehow until she could see right down into the centre of things. Nothing less. But let the people who scoffed find that out about her and there was no telling what they'd have to say about it. She'd keep it, thank you, to herself. For now at least.

Cora would consider it a betrayal at least, a personal slight, if not a calculated madness.

Though no more, perhaps, than this rough, pot-holed, narrow road they were following. The van shuddered with every jolt of tire along the broken-away edge of blacktop, and Cora, braced against the dashboard, was clearly looking for someone to blame. But she still hadn't found a culprit when they pulled up into the dusty parking lot of the Sportsman Grounds. And Maggie didn't offer help. Cora, for all her loneliness, did not need encouragement.

Nor did the sun. It had risen well above the high wall of long-trunked firs that completely surrounded the field, and shone down out of a clear sky, hot, on everything. In the parking lot, which like the field itself had been bulldozed out of raw forest without any attempt at seeding or gravelling or paving, dust lifted from the powdery dirt and settled on the cars and the leaves of the salal bushes around the edge, and even high up on the green fir branches themselves. Everything, including the long sagging hall where the sportsmen held their meetings and dances, wore a dead grey coat of dust.

But it was bush, true bush, without a square inch of pavement or concrete in sight! Maggie could have shouted out her relief. Even the taste of dust in your mouth, dry and unpleasant as it was, had more life to it than the sour odour of tar. She stepped out of the van, smiling, as if the trees had been asking when would she get here, as if the loggers who had come from all over the island to this spot had been waiting for her arrival before they began it.

They were on the dusty bottom of a round clearing which had been scooped out of timber; the area was alive already with the sounds of chain saws snarling through logs and the smell of sawdust and woodchips and sweat in the air and the sight of blue exhaust smoke rising like the dust into the branches of the trees and the sky.

Yahoo she nearly yelled, but "Oh no" was what she said, and ducked. "Look who's here before us. Madmother Thomas!"

And farther along the row of parked cars a little old woman climbed down out of a wooden contraption on steel-rimmed wheels and walked around to unhitch a donkey from the front of it. Patting its neck and chanting some kind of verse, she led the animal into the shade and tied him to a tree. Then she looked up and checked the sky, brushed dust from her hands. Sunlight flashed in her eyeglasses.

"Madmother Thomas." Cora Manson sagged under the weight of her dismay. Days, for her, began in torment and steadily went downhill.

"Yes," Maggie said, who put annoyances in the same category as turnips: something to be swallowed quickly and forgotten. "That's her all right."

That manure-spreader of hers was not something you made a mistake about. Behind the kitchen chair she perched on when she got tired of standing up to drive her donkey, an old pointed-roof shack sat on the bed of the wagon, covered with unevenly-nailed-on cedar shakes. It was just big enough for a cot and a tiny heater, someone's old tool shed perhaps, or a deluxe-size privy.

Madmother Thomas herself was no less conspicuous than her rig. A tiny, round old woman with floating hair like a handful of white cloud, she kept her dainty feet in fur-trimmed rubbers and left her muscled arms exposed in sleeveless dresses all year round. She turned up, in Maggie's life, two or three times a year, and always at some kind of event like today's. She was drawn to competition, and always walked away with trophies she had no room to store.

She spent her time riding from place to place all over the island, standing up at the front of that donkey-pulled manure-spreader while the rusted row of spreading-teeth turned constantly at the back end, stirring up nothing but air. She travelled in no particular pattern, picking up whatever prize money there might be lying around for nail-driving or women's bucksawing. All this, however, was a far cry from the real purpose of her movements. Madmother Thomas, like someone in an ancient book, was looking for the place where she'd been born. It was so blasted long ago, she'd told Maggie once, that the name of the village or town or whatever it was had been knocked right out of her head. She didn't even know for sure that it had ever had a name. But she'd find it some day anyway, she was confident she'd find it some day if she just kept moving; there were only so many places it could be on an island, though she hoped to hell it wouldn't take forever because her idea was to have herself buried there.

"You'd think she'd've died by now," said Cora Manson, who preferred mourning to the irritation of people's presence. "Or found whatever it is she's looking for."

"Looking for attention maybe is all," Maggie said. "The old rip." Though she admitted to a tiny hope that this year for a change the old woman wouldn't notice her at all. In some of the books Maggie had read, a person as strange as Madmother Thomas would have ridden in for just a short while and then disappeared, like a sign of some truth that had managed to escape you, but in real life this old lady had a habit of hanging around to make a nuisance of herself. She had a way of getting you involved, of dragging you in on responsibilities that were none of your business. "But hold your step a minute, hold back until she's had time to get herself lost in the crowd."

"Well look out then, and duck, because here she comes and now she's seen you!"

The old woman hurried down the row of cars, stirring up dust with her tiny rubber boots. She grabbed one of Maggie's hands between both of hers and grinned up at her face, eyes snapping. "Maggie," she said, as if Maggie were a special surprise someone had arranged just for her. She looked at Cora Manson, a stranger to her selective memory, flicked a tiny pick tongue across her bottom lip, and laughed. It was the kind of laugh that came down like a blow from the top of the head, and she stamped one foot to shake it loose. "The sweat's already just pouring out of me, I swear I'll dissolve in a puddle. But listen ..." her tongue flicked again, her eyes slid sideways to surprise eavesdroppers, "did you hear them announce the nail-driving?"

"Haven't heard anything yet," Maggie said. "We just got here."

"Hah?"

"I said, we just got out of the van. We haven't been here only a minute."

"Son of a gun," the lady said, and spat out dust. "And so did I. One of the damn shakes fell off my shed and started a whole row dropping. I had to go back as far as God-knows-where to pick them up. Strung out along the road like shit behind a cow." She stopped, blinked off towards the noise and smoke, then turned and drove an index finger into Maggie's arm. "What's this I hear?"

Some people expected you to be a mind-reader. "About what?"

"About a wedding." The little eyes scrunched up to nail a crime. "I heard about a wedding I never got invited to. Tonight."

Maggie laughed, and stepped back. Short people made her do that, want to step back a pace to see them right. "That's Forbes," she said.

"Hah?"

"Forbes. My boy. He's getting married."

It took a minute to register. "Son of a gun," she said, and spat out dust again. "I thought it was you."

Cora moaned.

"Well I did so. I thought it was Maggie. I said to myself ain't that nice, Maggie Maclean's got herself someone permanent this time, I wish her luck, she deserves it. Your *kid*?" The tongue flicked.

"Yes." They would make her feel old yet, if they kept this up. "I've had my turn once at that business," she said. "You won't catch this gal jumping in a second time in a hurry. There are other things."

The old woman considered the other things a while, then shook her head. "You'll be singing another song some day, I'll tell you that right now."

"I've been singing it for years," Cora Manson said, "but look at all the good it's done me." She almost smiled, but it turned into more of a wince. "I'm as single as the day I was born."

Madmother Thomas considered Cora's shoes, coated in dust. "We all are, girlie," she said, letting her gaze slide up. "Even those of us who walk the aisle, we're still single all our lives, you can

only be one person at a time. But tell me this, Maggie Maclean,
Maggie Kyle, or whatever you call yourself now, what happened
to that little girl I met the first time, how many years ago —
twenty-five? She told me she had places she had to go. That was a
girl with plans." She let out a *hsst* then, suddenly, and threw back
her head to listen. "I knew it I knew it, that was the lady's
nail-driving they just announced, I've got to get a move on." She
threw Maggie a wink. "Never let it be said this old thing missed out
on a prize because of standing around talking. I'll see you ladies
later."

She hurried across the parking lot to join the crowd, where
power saws roared and blue smoke drifted. The little black rubbers slapped up puffs of dust.

Cora Manson fell back against the van. "She must be seventy if
she's a day. How long can that woman keep it up?"

"She's as old as the century," Maggie said. "Her old lady was on
that boatload that came out to set up the Colony but she took off
the minute they landed and had her baby somewhere else before
they found her. Nobody knows where, not Madmother, not even
the government."

"Time she quit then, and acted normal."

She'd drive you nuts all right, Maggie had to admit, but you
couldn't help but hope you'd be as alive as she was when you got
to that age.

The old woman had already begun her wanderings as far back
as when Maggie was a small girl on the west coast. She'd ridden
into the village on her manure-spreader one late summer day —
pulled by what must have been an earlier donkey—and had come
right down to the wharf where Maggie was catching bullheads on
a piece of old fishing line. She hadn't looked nearly so old then, of
course, but she'd already been widowed and done enough to earn
herself a reputation among the coast people. "What's the name of
that mountain over there, girl?" she said, pointing across the inlet.
"That one that looks like a big hairy pyramid."

"That's Lone Cone Mountain."

"And what's that string of shacks laid out across its base? At the
water's edge?"

"Indian houses, I guess."

"Any white people ever live there?"

Maggie had shrugged her shoulders. At that age what did she

care who lived where? It was more important to hide the tear in her hand-me-down dress.

"Then tell me where I can find somebody to take me across."

In the hotel beer parlour up the slope she found someone who owned a small boat and had nothing better to do with his day. She tied her donkey to the railing and climbed into the boat as if riding on water was something she did every day of her life, but when she climbed back out of it again much later, when Maggie had already had three calls home for supper and the threat of a good tanning if she didn't hurry up, she held on tightly to the railings and rubbed her rump. "This blasted island is enough to drive you bats," she said. "Every time you turn a corner there's some place else you never heard of before." She put a thick hand on the top of Maggie's head. "If you've any sense, child, you'll just stay put."

Maggie had no intention, even then, of staying put. Not in that village. Water on three sides and mountain behind. And not in that tarpaper shack. The only good thing about it was that she could crawl underneath and still be in daylight, among the rusted cans and broken toys and brood hens and dry lifeless dirt. Sitting with her back against one of the rough posts that rested on flat stones she could listen to Ma and the Old Man fight until dark, if necessary, or until one of them stomped out, slamming the screen door, and headed down to the village centre and the beer parlour. Under the shack, Margaret Patricia Maclean could hatch her plans. And read, what was it? Some book. Not even the long chilling sound of her mother's "Maggeeeeeeee!" could bring her out until she was ready.

But the day she met Madmother Thomas she did not crawl under the shack. After supper she walked out on the road south of the settlement, following the direction people told her the old woman had gone, and found her camped under a shelter of driftwood logs right down on the sand on the Pacific side of the strip. There was a small fire burning behind a big log out of the wind, and the woman in her shelter was chewing on what looked like a leg of chicken.

"See that there?" she said, waving the chicken bone in the direction of the open sea. "Nothing between us and Japan, except that water."

Maggie had heard all that a hundred times before and wasn't impressed. She was more interested in the forest and mountains at her back. Take me up into those, she wanted to tell the woman. Take me climbing up, rising up to the very centre of whatever there is behind us. So that I can see.

But she had to shout to be heard above the constant roar of the sea. "Did you find it?"

"Find what?"

"Whatever you were after at Lone Cone Mountain."

The woman laughed. "If I did, I didn't recognize it," she said.

"Are you going away again tonight?"

"If you ever been on that goat trail through them mountains you'd know that nobody coming down here one day is gonna be heading back the same. I'll hang around as long as it takes to catch my breath, and take a few more boat rides while I'm at it maybe."

"Will you take me with you when you go?"

"No, madam, I will not. No one travels with this old boot but Jenny here and God, and there are days when I swear that even the Old Gentleman has got himself lost in a gully somewhere or wandered off up a draw."

"But I want to get out of this place, I want to see more."

The old woman's tiny eyes squeezed shut. "You will child, you will soon enough." Then she grunted up onto her feet. "But the where of a life don't matter at all, it's the how of your life that'll count."

The day she went down to the beach and discovered that the old woman had pulled up camp she walked deep into the wind-stunted pines and sitka spruce, determined that if she was doomed to be left behind in this place she may as well get herself lost in the bush. An appropriate end. But the flashing of the brilliant blue jays in the branches over her head had distracted her from her purpose so that eventually she was content to let the roar of the ocean be her guide and lead her out again to safety and the dullness of an ordinary life.

Now, twenty-five years later, while Madmother Thomas with her tongue tucked outside one end of her mouth threw all her tiny weight into the nail-driving contest, Maggie Kyle who had already escaped the tarpaper shack, and many others after it, was more interested in the newer faces in the crowd. There were plenty she knew, they'd come here from every corner, she could trace her whole life through them if she wished. Holland was nowhere in sight, thank God, maybe he'd been scared off. If she was lucky he'd be fleeing north from police back into his faraway bunk-house and be only a faint memory before the wedding began.

And another face was absent: Wade Powers, who never missed these things, he always turned up to lose the tree-climbing contest. Down from that silly museum he'd built, he never failed to put on a good show for them, never failed to come last no matter how greenhorn the competition. And she wanted him today for more than a laugh. There were favours to be asked that only a relative could bestow. Or an almost-relative like Wade.

Another familiar face: Forbes, her son. The bridegroom. Slouching around in his narrow mean-faced way, alone. He was a throw-back, she was sure, to some sneaky weasel on his father's side. There were no men like that in her family. He slid around among the knots of spectators with his hands buried deep in his pockets, pushed down nearly to his knees, occasionally picking at his chin, his eyes nervous. When he saw Maggie he came closer, then suddenly veered away and lost himself in the crowd. She couldn't blame him, there was no telling what the sight of a mother like her might jar loose in his wedding-day mind.

For Maggie Kyle, despite her extravagant intentions, had no illusions whatsoever about her success as a mother. She was a flop. She had never in her life met anyone else who'd been quite so much a flop as a mother.

But then, she said, she didn't know anyone else who started so young. Or so ignorant. They ought to be grateful she hadn't drowned them by accident or forgotten them in a stranger's car. They were lucky she hadn't starved them when they were too small to feed themselves.

Cora Manson didn't stay to watch the nail-driving. Hammering nails in public was no business for a woman, she said, the sight of those ugly muscles in a woman's arm made her want to throw up. So she wandered off along the yellow rope that divided the public from the contestant area, to stare at the idle loggers and look for people to criticize. There was no problem keeping track of her, Maggie knew; in any crowd you could pick out that head of hair, the violent unnatural colour of an open wound. Nor was there any chance that Cora wouldn't keep coming back to her, to report the atrocities she'd seen and to slander half the population of the island. "That big broad who comes down every year from Beaver Cove's got a fatter arse on her than a D-8 cat. They say she's slept with the whole Nimkish Valley including the elk, which shows you what kind of taste they have up there. If I see that Holland arrive I'll drag him over here to you.''

"Don't," Maggie said. But she knew that not only would Cora do as she promised, she'd also have told him all of Maggie's business and a piece of her own mind besides by the time she got him here. If he had the cheek to show up at all.

In that crowd Maggie Kyle felt at home; even in this artificial scooped-out dust bowl there was something *home* about it all. The loggers were younger than they used to be, of course, but they quickly took on the shapes and attitudes of the older men. Boys a year out of high school had already got themselves sagging beer bellies and sway backs and sunburnt throats. They swaggered in their work clothes like kids who'd just discovered a basement dress-up trunk: hard hat, torn T-shirt or undershirt, jeans too large and held up by the regulation wide braces, caulk boots. She could swagger with them, it made her feel that way just being here. In this place they were lords, and knew it; the world beyond the stockade-rim of trees did not exist.

Oh she could go back, easily, and that was the thing that scared her. The pull of the bush was strong. Sometimes she saw herself giving everything up with a giant whoop of relief and heading back. The fuss they'd make would be exciting. She could cook in a camp, or run a hotel, she could even drive a truck if they offered, there'd be no trouble fitting back in. She'd be treated like a queen. But it wasn't what she wanted, despite the queer sensation in her gut, it had nothing to do with what she really wanted. Sometimes it scared her to realize how easy it would be, and how fatal, for her.

"Maggie Kyle!" they screamed, the women, when they saw her. They broke loose from the crowd to greet her, half scared she'd have changed, half hoping. Was she coming up in the hunting season this year? Was she really doing as well as they'd heard? They were dying, they said, to see what kind of a house she was living in now.

"Well, Jesus Christ, it's Maggie Kyle," the men said, and sometimes slapped her on the back. But after the initial burst of enthusiasm they developed half-grins and looked away as they talked. They couldn't be sure she was still what she'd been and that a slap on the back wasn't a blunder.

Yes, I've changed, she wanted to tell them, I want *more*. No, I haven't changed, she wanted to say. I love the smell of the woods still, and the grease on your hands, and I want you to slap me on the back. I want other things too, as they were.

Just keep Danny Holland away from me, she thought. Of them all, only he could shake her resolve. Only that one wild madman could spoil the whole blessed works without even trying.

The rest of them were still her kind of people. When she'd left the bush behind she hadn't meant to turn her back on *them*. So Maggie Kyle cheered as loud as anyone else when little Mad-mother Thomas drove every one of her six-inch spikes into the solid block of fir in half the time those younger babes could manage it. And roared along with the rest at the enormous fat-quivering woman from Cowichan who held her hammer right down at the head and couldn't even get her nails to stand upright while she swatted at them. She elbowed her way up through kids and gossiping women in house dresses and warm grease-smelling husbands to the yellow rope to get a good look at the long line of men, surrounded by smoke and pale flying sawdust, who carved two-minute chairs and stools with snubby-blade chain saws out of their standing posts of peeled fir. In the ear-ringing silence that followed, when the results were all set out for judging — three-legged stools and highbacked children's chairs and fancy diamond-shaped seats with knobby legs — she wanted to yell out her approval, she wanted to leap into the sawdust bed with them and throw her arms around the whole sweaty lot. Maggie Kyle, if they let her, would be having the time of her life.

But time of her life did not include Cora Manson, who was muttering and scowling and threading her way in Maggie's direction among dangerous elbows and unpredictable feet.

Poor Cora, this race of giants had been bred specifically to burden her. Puffing, she confronted Maggie's chest, another source of pain. "It's time."

"For what?"

Cora frowned around at the others, as if she suspected Maggie of forcing her to say it out loud just to embarrass her. "The weigh-in."

She was right, too. It was time. One o'clock. And the ladies expected promptness, there were no excuses, they ran that dieting club like an army. One o'clock every Saturday or else. Maggie would have forgotten, would forget every week if it weren't for Cora's reminders.

"But wait," she said. "There's Wade." The face she'd been looking for was here after all, black wild hair and white teeth, down at the other end of the rope where he was waiting for the tree-climbing race. Telling a dirty joke, probably. He was leaning back against a tree as if it were there just to prop him up. A relative, or nearly, he could save her.

"He'll keep," Cora said. "He won't go away. Don't you dare make us late."

But he'd seen her, too, and she could hardly ignore him now. "Well!" he said, coming out of a long laugh that had nearly doubled him over. "It's Maggie Maclean herself." He looked at the other men as if he expected their congratulations. "Don't we know each other from somewhere?" Smiling, he was all teeth. Teeth and that wild black hair.

She could play his kind of games. "We do. Yours was the first dink I ever saw." Cora's gasp had more resignation in it than shock. "You pulled down your pants behind my grandfather's dairy. I think," she told his audience, who were slack-jawed with surprise, "I was seven years old and thought he had some ugly growth between his legs."

One of the men, laughing, nearly choked. He had to walk away a few feet and come back, a string of spit hanging from his mouth.

"Lord, Maggie, you're rough." Wade came under the rope, grinning, and hugged her. "Do you have to speak *every* thought that passes through your head?" He turned to look at his friends, running his hand inside his shirt to scratch his chest. "And look, you've made these gentlemen blush."

That wasn't blush in those faces. In the fat man it was the high colour of blood pressure and wine. In the other it was the rosy flush of pleasure. She'd made loggers blush before now and knew it took more than a dirty joke or an unexpected revelation.

Wade Powers, of course, was no logger. At least not any more. He'd worked in the bush for a while once, surveying logging roads just as he'd later tried selling real estate and peddling insurance and building rowboats, but for the past few years he'd been sitting back on his own piece of land a few miles north of here and letting the tourists put their money in his hand just for the privilege of walking through a phoney fort he'd built and filled up with a lot of rusted pioneer relics. But he'd taken up tree-climbing just as a hobby, he said, to keep himself in shape, though he'd never in his life topped a spar tree or gone up to hang the rigging. "I'm a gentleman logger," he'd told Maggie, by which he meant that when he went up a tree it was an act of love rather than of violence. Those others, the real timber men, he explained, made the climb with the cold passion of a rapist. It came from their attitude to trees.

Attitude or no attitude, it had never helped him win a race that Maggie knew of. He showed up at these things, came last every time, and went home looking as if he'd done everyone a big favour.

"You didn't bring your mother," Cora said, who could bring people down, if they needed it.

No, he hadn't brought his mother, he said. To Maggie. He'd left the old woman home in her wheelchair counting tourists. She hated these things, she hated to see him take part in them. Virginia Kerr on the other hand, that redheaded beauty over by the concession stand, didn't mind seeing him here at all and was just waiting for the climbing race to be over so they could go off for a beer together.

"And a good idea, too," Maggie said, "though I wonder if your red-haired friend has plans for tonight."

"I hope she has," he said. And cast her a sly look. "I hope she has. But if I know that voice at all I'd guess you had some plans yourself. What is it, Maggie? What are you up to now?"

He knew her. Had known her too well since they'd both been kids and he'd attached himself to her grandparents. She'd never been able to hide much from him.

"Of course we'll be late," Cora said.

Wade frowned. Even frowning, this bugger could look amused.

"Walk with us over to the hall," Maggie said. "We have a date with a set of feed-store scales."

He walked, intrigued. He was her match, in height, or maybe had an inch on her. The two of them were taller, likely, than most of the people here.

"That is," she said, "if your redhead won't object."

He looked as if it didn't matter. Nothing mattered, you sometimes suspected, to Wade Powers. He had that look, that look of someone peering through branches and leaves he is pushing aside, to get somewhere, until he smiled as if you were what those branches were screening. It had never done him any lasting good, Maggie thought, to have that handsome face, or that surprised look. But it gave you a shock of delight sometimes, just to be the cause of that display of teeth.

Wade Powers was not, of course, in the costume of the day. No baggy low-crotched pants for him, or braces over T-shirt. He wore a shirt he could leave unbuttoned halfway down, and jeans washed tight and faded, nearly white in mottled patches around the fly, and a thick leather belt. Any stranger walking in would know he was only playing at this business, yet took it seriously.

"Emma Dickson who's president of the club was offered the concession stand for this thing," Maggie said. "She nearly turned it down until she hit on the idea of having the weigh-in right here where she'd be close."

The name of Emma Dickson was enough to inspire terror in Cora Manson. "Come on," she whined, and hurried ahead.

But: "Where you going?" It was Forbes, slouching by. He always got friendlier when he saw the way others were pleased to see her. He'd been watching, she knew; out of his little shifty red eyes he'd measured her popularity.

"Weigh-in," she said. She couldn't hide her distaste for it.

Forbes sneered. "You know what I bet?" he said. "I bet you haven't lost an ounce. I bet you weigh the same as you did last Saturday. I bet you have to wear the pig."

She knew he was teasing, of course. Not even Forbes could be cruel enough to mean a thing like that. Any woman in the group who didn't manage to lose at least an ounce in a week was given a plastic pig to wear around her neck day and night until the following Saturday.

"And what would you do if I had to wear it to your wedding tonight?"

"I'd laugh."

"You wouldn't laugh. You'd die of embarrassment."

It was Wade who laughed, and took her arm to encourage her towards the hall.

She'd never have to wear it, of course. Even though there wasn't a thing wrong with her figure and it was only for Cora's sake she belonged to the club, she still managed somehow to lose that ounce every week. Sometimes, though, she liked the idea of starting out fat. It would be exciting to drop off pounds of lard, to peel the fat off layer by layer, and get so thin eventually that they would have to wire you to the earth to keep you from ascending to the sky, floating right up out of sight because there wasn't enough of you left for gravity to get hold of. She could see herself, going up in the air like a slow rocket, ascending perpendicular, and all encircled in light like one of those saint-people, pure spirit, while flesh and bones lay heavy on the ground like discarded clothes.

For Cora Manson, of course, it was a different matter. She worried so much about losing weight that she ate to comfort herself and had to starve the last three days of every week in order to avoid the pig. On Saturdays, she told Maggie, she took a long bath to get all the dirt off, even sweat and dust weighed, and wore the lightest underwear she owned. She shaved her legs. She even clipped her toenails and trimmed her corns.

When they'd gone through the empty echoing hall to the cluttered little kitchen at the back, Emma Dickson turned from her paperwork and said she'd nearly given up on the two of them, everyone else had already weighed in. The half-dozen other women sighed their relief. The place smelled of sour dishrags and oilcloth.

"And all of us have lost," chirped Hilda Smith, who didn't really need to lose weight any more than Maggie did, but couldn't stand being left out of anything.

"Congratulations," Cora said, and skulked around the room kicking off her shoes and pulling off her rings to get ready.

"Of course we can't have a man," Emma Dickson said, looking at Maggie; *get him out of here* was what she meant.

And Wade, who didn't know which way to look anyway, was happy to bow out, and turn his back at the door.

Maggie stepped up onto the scales and saw that she'd lost her ounce. "Too bad," she said, stepping down. "I kind of liked the idea of marching into that church with a plastic pig around my neck."

Everyone laughed except Cora, who suddenly panicked. She pulled her dress up over her head inside out, and threw it over Maggie's arm while she yanked down the slip that had ridden up her dimpled thighs.

Emma Dickson, who took her presidential duties seriously, turned frowning eyes on everyone, stared them into stillness. "Well, Cora, are you ready?" She drummed her fingers on the slanted linoleum-covered drainboard.

"Just a minute," Cora said, and rushed for the bathroom.

Hilda snickered. "No sense carrying added liquid onto that machine."

When Cora came out again she was holding her girdle and nylons, which she hung with her dress over Maggie's arm. "How do I ever get myself into these things?" she asked the ceiling, though it was clear from the look she gave Maggie that she knew exactly whose fault it was.

She looked so dismayed when she stepped up onto the scales that she didn't even need to change the expression on her face when they told her she hadn't lost a thing, she'd actually gained a pound this week. "Fourteen ounces, to be exact," Emma said.

"I was going to that wedding tonight," Cora told the wall. "I was going with the mother of the groom."

Emma Dickson moved closer. "You are also the Pig of the Week."

"Fourteen ounces? You call me that for fourteen ounces? It isn't fair."

Maggie handed Cora her underthings and dress and stepped back. She wished they'd never come today, she wished she'd never talked Cora into joining this stupid club.

Cora slipped the dress over her head, wriggled it down over her body, and pulled the zipper closed at her hip. "Well?" she said. She might have been looking for where they'd hidden the cross, or the nails.

Emma Dickson took the plastic pig out of the cardboard box. It was big and ugly, no cute little Disney pig. Its stomach was grotesquely fat, its face was ugly, its body was covered with bristles like an old rooting sow in somebody's muddy sty.

Maggie said, "Well, maybe since tonight's the wedding, maybe it would be good enough if ... "

All the ladies started talking at once. Yes, yes. Exactly what they were going to say. They were all thinking the same thing. What difference did one night make? After all, a wedding is a wedding and Cora Manson was a friend of the groom's mother.

"Just take it home," Emma said, uneasy at her own weakness. "Put it on tomorrow morning."

But Cora snatched the pig out of Emma's hand, hung it around her own neck and let it slap against her chest. "When I belong to something I don't bend the rules to suit myself. A rule is a rule." She shoved her feet into her shoes and headed for the door.

Oh no, they started to say. Oh no, Cora, you mustn't. Tomorrow is soon enough. Oh, Cora, don't let it spoil tonight, don't let it. It's not meant to be taken that seriously.

Like a hen house, Maggie thought, stirred up by a weasel.

But Cora turned in the doorway. "Not meant to be taken seriously?" she said. "Just see how seriously I take it."

Maggie followed her outside the hall. Nothing, nothing on earth would stop her now from the full pleasure of her suffering.

Wade, standing in grass and mustardy paper napkins, was confused.

"I can thank you for this," Cora told Maggie. "Pig of the Week. Just don't think I'm going to let it keep me home." Suddenly her voice went up higher, as if out of control, caught in a flywheel. If she'd only thought about it, she said, she'd have known this was exactly what would happen to her today, that even though she'd never been the one to wear it before, it was only natural that on a day when whe wanted to go out and have a good time at somebody else's expense for a change she'd end up with a plastic pig around her neck, that was the way life was. She wanted to know how they could be sure those other babes had actually weighed themselves before they got there and hadn't cheated. Emma Dickson wasn't above such things you could tell by her little eyes, nor was silly Hilda Smith the old fart and it wouldn't surprise her a bit to find out they'd cooked it all up among themselves before she got there just to be mean because they knew there was no one else in this town who'd suffer the way Cora Manson would suffer from it, though God knows she ought to be used to the dirty tricks of the world by now. Oh, it really made you feel important, she said. A thing like this happening to you really made you feel you were an important part of the universe.

The voice went up higher, completely out of control, and faltered. Cora discovered she'd been singing her song to a circle of strangers who were staring at the pig on her chest.

Maggie, walking with Wade, couldn't resist a hoot as soon as they were out of earshot. They headed back across the dust to join the crowds. Let Cora wind down on her own. There were limits, even to friendship.

But there were no limits to Wade, no limits to what you could ask, or expect. "Well!" he said, "I think you had something you wanted to ask me. Before all this."

"It's time for your event, Powers," someone yelled. "Get in there."

He went back under the yellow rope and began putting on his gear. Shin guards and spikes that went down the inner side of each boot. A safety belt.

"The wedding," Maggie said.

"Oh hell. I forgot about that until we saw Forbes back there." He kicked at dirt as if the fault could be found in earth.

"It's an easy thing to forget. Forbes is an easy person to forget. I forget about him for months at a time myself and I'm his mother."

"But people remember weddings. How come the Old Lady didn't remind me?"

"Your mother doesn't approve of pregnant brides."

"Neither do I," he said. "I think they should have their babies first, to see what they get. Then if they're not satisfied they can try again, to see if a new combination has better results."

She threw him a look meant to wither. "It doesn't work, I tried it. Four times. If I'd kept looking for the right combination I'd have had enough kids to populate a good-sized reform school and still be as single as the day I was born."

The man with the microphone came closer and checked Wade's equipment, then checked his opponent's equipment. He spoke into the microphone. "A hundred feet up, ladies and gentlemen. A hundred feet up, see those bells at the top of each pole. The contestants will climb up, ring the bell, and come down."

"I need your help," Maggie said.

"What?"

"In this first heat we have two old hands at this type of thing. Jacques Monet up from Jordan River, twice champion of the island! And Wade Powers, who hasn't missed a race in seven years!"

Wade and the other man, a serious-faced French Canadian, stepped up to their separate poles, threw their ropes around the base and strapped them to their belts. Then they leaned back and dug their feet in.

"I'm not going in that church alone," Maggie said. "I'd rather stay home."

Wade looked surprised. "That doesn't sound like you, Maggie." He bounced a few times, to test the rope.

The man with the microphone waved Maggie back.

"Will you take me?"

Wade laughed, to show people it was all a big joke they were hearing. "Sure," he said. "There isn't a man here who wouldn't take you anywhere you want to go. Even to church. I'd be a fool not to."

There was no time to enjoy the relief, for Madmother Thomas came up beside her and elbowed her in the waist. "They don't have a woman's contest in this or I'd win that too," she said, and let out one of her foot-stomping laughs. "Gawd it's hot. Who's that you were talking to? He's black and hairy, like my husband was."

The man with the microphone stepped back and leaned forward. "Timer ready?" he said. "Contestants ready? One ... two ... go!" His starter gun cracked the air.

Going up, for a while, the two men kept abreast. They found some kind of rhythm and followed it, the rope slapping against the backs of the poles, spikes crunching in wood, though Wade's left foot slipped once and he missed a beat that kept him back a little behind the other. Together their rhythms slowed as they neared the top. But they hit the bell almost simultaneously with their heads and started down. Wade descended almost as he'd gone up, slapping rope, leaping back, but the French Canadian leaned in, somehow dropped down the pole barely touching it with anything but the inside leather of his boots, and skidded the last twenty feet to the ground. The crowd, which let out one long "awww" while Monet plummeted, had already finished cheering him by the time Wade reached the ground and let out his war-whoop.

But the war-whoop was drowned out for Maggie by a screech from Madmother Thomas at her side. The old woman, red in the face and dancing on her dainty boots, had seen something that was stirrring up the crowd farther down.

"My donkey!" she cried, and whirled around as if looking for something to lay her hands on. She ducked under the rope and picked up a double-bitted axe, but one of the loggers pulled it out of her hands. She whirled again and threw Maggie a black scowl. "It's that damn Holland fool."

Maggie didn't believe it. In her mind she'd already followed him north to the end of pavement, then on through twisted gravel roads past mountains to his inlet and the shabby bunkhouse. She'd disposed of him. A sudden reappearance was not an easy thing to believe in.

But someone in the crowd raised the yellow rope high enough

and Danny Holland rode the old woman's donkey out into the contest area. One arm held his aluminum hat straight up in the air, his head was thrown back as if the loud *haw haw* of his laugh was aimed at an audience hidden in the tops of the firs, his caulk boots ploughed dust-raising furrows in the dirt. The little donkey trotted ahead, stopped, then trotted ahead again confused, its jerky motion setting the long trunk of his rider into a slow exaggerated swaying like a mast.

You idiot, she thought. *Danny Holland.* Not enough brains in his stupid head to tell him *run*.

"Keep going, donkey!" he roared, and kneed its stomach. He spat snoose and laughed, nearly fell off the back when the animal burst ahead. "Keep going, donkey! I've ridden plenty of jackasses before but never one with four legs!"

The crowd cheered its approval. He rode once around the bucksaw log before Madmother Thomas caught up to him.

"This time the jackass is on top, Holland. Get down off of that animal."

He feigned surprise. Dropped his hat on his head, tipped it to her. "Madam Thomas!" he said. "What are you doing out here in this heat? You'll get sunstroke." He tried to put his hat on her head but she knocked it away and it spun across the ground to clang up against a power saw.

"Get down off that animal, you stupid man, get down."

She lunged at his leg to pull him off, but he kicked out with his boot and knocked her back onto her behind in the dirt. When she rose up again, coated with dust, she spat once and whirled away. Even Holland was quiet while she waddled over to the birling pool and came back with a peavey held in front of her like a lance.

"All right everybody," the man with the microphone said, trying not to laugh. "Let's break it up. The fun is over. Waddaya say, Danny?

Holland scowled down, laughed suddenly, then scowled again. "I say the old biddy's as nutty as a fruitcake. I say to hell with the whole stinkin' lot of you."

Maggie, whose lungs burned from her held breath, broke at last: "No!"

But no one heard. The old woman held the peavey aimed at Holland's belly while he rode that donkey in a full circle around her. "What do you think I've got to lose?" she said.

Holland aimed a kick again, at the peavey, and sent her spinning away. But she came back at him and slid its steel point up his chest to his Adam's apple and stopped his movement dead. The curled-back side hook rested on his shirt. People held their breaths, though they continued to smile.

Maggie moved along the yellow rope, closer. You couldn't stand back and watch a thing like that. Not like these others, who acted as if it were all part of the programme, clowns for comic relief.

Sweat ran down the dust on the old woman's face. Her glasses had fallen off and the little eyes blinked rapidly, squinted. Something wheezed in her chest. Then, defeated, she stood back and drove the point of the peavey into the ground between her feet.

Holland's head leapt back, laughing, laughing. Maggie could kill him for his laughing. His laugh filled the sports ground, bounced from side to side in the tree-rimmed circle. It was all she could hear.

She ran.

Maggie Kyle ran. People stepped aside. Friends reached out to stop her. Faces noses mouths blurred. She headed for the van, the Bug Wagon. But his voice, louder behind her even than his laugh, halted her: "Maggieeeeeeeeee!"

She turned around, nearly falling against someone's parked car. Dust rose up to make her cough. Danny Holland was standing on the back of the donkey now, facing her, his hands cupped around his mouth. Everyone, everyone was staring at her.

"Maggie Maclean!" he yelled. Her old name, she hated it. "Maggie Maclean, where are you going?"

"Screw off," she said. Not very loud, but they heard it. They laughed. Holland nearly fell off the donkey laughing.

Break your neck, she thought. *Fall off and break your neck*.

"We'll see you at the wedding," he yelled. "See you at the boy's wedding!"

His laugh drowned out the only reply she could think of: "Over my dead body." She got into the Bug Wagon as fast as she could and drove out of that parking lot. A red and yellow figure thumping down the road meant nothing to her at first, until it dawned that she was leaving poor Cora Manson behind.

But Cora, once rescued, still sang the same tune as before, her hideous plastic pig riding the waves of her heaving chest. If it weren't for the business, she said, she'd up and leave this place, head over to the mainland where people might not be so mean, where maybe plastic pigs hadn't been invented yet or put to such cruel use. Oh, it made you feel important, she said, that pile of horse manure at the side of the road was more important than she was.

Important? Maggie thought.

What did anyone know about important?

What did any of these people know about the way it felt to be important?

2

Seventy miles from here a narrow gravel road left the highway and twisted for miles through second-growth fir and cedar swamps, right back inland almost to the base of the closest mountain. She could remember every turn, sometimes every inch of it. Near the end, the road swung suddenly and crossed the river on a high bridge without railings, where the loose planks of varying thickness thumped and shuddered under cars. Beyond the river the road straightened out and cut through a half-dozen small farms, past the Jimmy Jimmy Arts and Crafts Commune, and an old water tower. This place was called Hed, and Maggie Maclean lived in that little grey shack right up at the end, in the dying orchard. Until eight years ago.

Not one of her children was with her that final summer. Forbes had gone off to a camp. The twins, Albert and Veronica, had moved out when their father left, and lived with him and his wife in their split-level house in Campbell River. Her baby, her Carla, whom Old Man Schmidt had left like a gift in her just before he died, was staying with a friend out on the highway. Maggie was twenty-four. It was the year Shorty's insurance money came through.

Every day that summer, about two o'clock in the afternoon, she had gone for her walk. First she tied a kerchief over her head, because although it may be all right to have rollers in her hair all day long in her own house, it didn't seem proper to go out on the road with them showing. She put lipstick on, too, because sometimes strangers drove through, lost perhaps or looking for some place that didn't exist. She picked up all the empty beer bottles in her living room and put them in the cardboard boxes out in the back room, in case she met someone who wanted to come back to the house for a while. She closed the door and walked down the slatted boardwalk through the long grass, then lifted the picket gate up out of her way, went through, and leaned it back into place.

She loved walking. Every day that summer she had gone past the little farms, two of them abandoned, and had waved to Manson Hed, who lived in the old water tower he'd converted. She'd tried to imagine what went on in the Jimmy Jimmy Arts and Crafts Commune, what those strange people she'd never talked to might be doing down there. But most of all she had enjoyed the sounds and the smells: the clicking of the grasshoppers in the weeds, the hum of the telephone wires, the high sweet odour of hay uncut and dying in the fields.

It started to happen, of course, by the river, the thing that spoiled it all. She was just walking up to the bridge when the car approached. She liked the bridge best of any place on her walk, she liked to stand on the dusty planks and look down into the green slow-moving river. Sometimes she even climbed down the bank and stood on the edge to watch for fish, though all she ever saw was minnows, darting this way and that like a handful of black needles.

The car, a long blue sedan, came across the bridge so fast she held her breath expecting to see it slide off the edge and drop. But it bounced down onto the gravel again and skidded to a stop beside her. A cloud of dust moved up around them, so thick she had to close her eyes and mouth until it settled. When she could see again, a middle-aged man was leaning out the window and looking at her.

"Where's the commune?" he shouted at her. "Jimmy Jimmy Arts and Crafts."

He wore a dress shirt and a tie, loosened at his throat. She pointed. "Keep going. Another hundred yards and you're there."

He squinted. "You from there?"

"Not me," she laughed. "Not this kid."

So he ducked back into his car and leapt ahead, spraying gravel out from behind his tires. Maggie hoped that she would never have to be in such a hurry to get anywhere.

A few minutes later, maybe ten minutes later, she was down under the bridge watching a water snake when the car went back. It rumbled over the planks above her and shook pieces of dirt down over her head, then roared off up the gravel road through the trees. Dust hung in the air for a long time afterwards.

Heading home, she heard the screams a good distance away. She stopped walking and listened. Through the trees it was impossible to hear any words to the sounds but she could tell someone was in real trouble. Hurrying, she got to the commune gate at the same time as Manson Hed, and neither one of them knew what to do with the girl.

She was splattered with blood. Her hands were red. Her face and throat were streaked and smeared. Her long cotton dress was soaked through in patches. And yet none of the blood seemed to be her own. Maggie couldn't see any wounds.

"It's Jimmy Jimmy," she said, and pounded her fist on the gate post. She ran back and forth across the driveway, as if she couldn't see. "He's killed Jimmy Jimmy!"

No one had ever been killed in Hed before. People had been drunk and deserted and beaten up and even carved up a little with a knife. Once there had even been a rape, though everyone agreed the girl had asked for it. But there had never before been a killing, and Maggie Maclean didn't know what to do about this one.

Nor did Manson Hed. Through his silly round glasses he looked from Maggie to the girl and back again. He spat on the ground. He was a salesman and should have been at work, but Maggie supposed he had been going through another one of his sick spells. Finally he said, "We better call the police."

But the girl wouldn't go back into the commune buildings, and she wouldn't let them go in either. She held onto Manson's arm and begged him to phone the police from his own place. "You can't do nothing for Jimmy," she said. "And the whole place is blood."

"But I should try," Manson said. "Just in case."

"He's dead," the girl said. "You can't do a thing."

"Where's the rest of them?" Maggie demanded.

"Town," she said. She started to cry. "Everybody's in town but me'n Jimmy Jimmy. He came here looking for Warner, but chopped up Jimmy."

Maggie, though she would never admit it to anyone, would have loved to go in and have a look. She had never seen a murdered person. But she knew that the minute she saw him she would be sorry; this wasn't a television programme. She took the girl's arm and started walking down the road. Manson Hed threw up his hands and followed.

Walking, the girl told them what had happened. The man in the fancy car was the father of Warner Bolt, one of the young people living in the colony. He'd hunted halfway across the country for his son, swearing that he'd kill the son of a bitch who got his boy mixed up in this kind of life. When he found out it was Jimmy Jimmy who'd talked Warner into coming to live in the colony to do his painting the man grabbed the little axe from behind the wood stove and brought it down on top of Jimmy's skull. Then he went wild and chopped at Jimmy another dozen times before he dropped the axe and got out of there. He was heading in to town, he said, to look for his son.

"Good heavens," Manson said. "We'd better hurry."

Once they were up the ladder and in Manson's water tower the girl threw herself onto the little bed and buried her face in the pillow. Manson paced up and down in front of his telephone. "Do *you* want to phone?" he said.

"Just do it," Maggie said. She sat down on a bench and looked out the window Manson had cut in the wooden staves of the curved wall. All of Hed was quiet. From up here she could see every building in the settlement and not one person stirred. No one else even knew there had been a murder right in their midst. Her own little house, up at the end, sagged as if the afternoon sun were sucking all its strength.

She felt the same. Droopy.

When Manson Hed put down his telephone he said this: "You might as well go home now. The police will look after everything."

"Don't be silly," she said.

"There's nothing more you can do," he said. His round eyes behind those glasses blinked rapidly. She could tell he enjoyed saying that.

She could tell, because Manson Hed never missed a chance to annoy her. Because his grandparents had been the first family to settle in Hed just after the First World War he thought this gave him the right to argue over everything under the sun. Maggie and Manson were the only members of their families living in Hed now, and they didn't argue about very many things at all. But Manson, who had faithfully mourned the death of his wife for eight years, never missed a chance to let her know he disapproved of the way she lived her life. And treated her, always, as if the world could do just as well without her in it.

"Listen," she said. "You know you always get tongue-tied around cops. If I don't go down there you'll get everything all mixed up and tell it wrong."

"Tell *what* wrong?" he said. "You and I didn't see a thing. It's this little girl here who has the story to tell."

The girl did not look up. She squirmed her body harder into the soft bed and moaned.

"Besides," Maggie said. "I'm the one who saw the man's face. Close up."

And added, in case he had any doubts, that when the bastard was brought to trial they were bound to call on Maggie Maclean to testify. She would be in the witness box but where would Manson Hed be? At work where he belonged, or in the visitor's gallery if he was lucky. How many lawyers would there be asking for *his* opinion?

Manson said he hoped there was a lawyer smart enough to ask questions about her past. *Then* see if they believe anything she says, a person like her.

"My God," the girl said from the bed, without turning to face them. "Jimmy's down there hacked up and listen to you two."

"You want to stay here with Manson and rest?" Maggie said. "Or do you want to walk back to your place with me and wait for the police to get there?"

"You're crazy," Manson said.

"Be quiet," Maggie said. She leaned over and put a hand on the girl's forehead. "Don't you think you should at least wash up?" she said.

The girl turned over, suddenly, and sobbed against Maggie's arm.

Going back down the road her heart sang. Manson with his silly shuffle soon dropped behind, and the girl leaned most of her weight against Maggie's shoulder. When was the last time anyone had been jealous of Maggie Maclean? When was the last time anyone needed her shoulder to lean against? Oh Carla, she thought, if you could see your old lady now.

"When you get there don't touch that body," Manson shouted. "You know they don't want nobody monkeying with things."

Maggie didn't even answer. She tightened the grip of her arm across the girl's back.

"And don't forget, if them cops want to know what kind of witness you'll make, just send them to me for a character reference. I'll tell them."

"I bet."

"There ain't nothing I haven't seen from up my place."

Maggie sniffed. "Pity the man with nothing better to do," she said. "Must be a lonely life." And felt good, in her heart, to know that back there Manson was turning green.

At the gateway to the commune she wasn't sure what to do next. Manson had stopped a hundred feet back down the road and sat in the ditch, pulling heads off the long grass that had gone to seed. The girl seemed in no hurry to go in, and neither, to tell the truth, was Maggie, though she would like a peek, perhaps just a glimpse through the window.

"Go ahead in," Manson said. "You didn't come down here for a suntan."

But the police arrived before she could do anything. The RCMP car drove in past them and pulled up in the yard. Then the commune truck swung in behind and stopped with its front bumper right up against the house. When the people got out, the girl ran down the driveway and threw herself into a young man's arms.

"Well now, Maggie," Manson said. "Don't keep them waiting."

One of the policemen had gone inside and the other was trying to make some sense out of what the girl was saying. "Excuse me," Maggie said. "I live just a ways down the road."

The policeman turned two grey eyes on her. "Look," he said, gently. "Let's not have any neighbours in right now."

"I saw him," she said.

"Saw who?"

"Saw him, the man that did it."

One of the young men walked over to Maggie. "He turned himself in," he said. "I heard he confessed it all."

Maggie tried to keep her chin from trembling. "Well, won't they want a statement from me?"

"Not right now, ma'am," the policeman said. "You say you live down here? Well, we'll get in touch if we need you. Right now there are other things."

An ambulance pulled into the yard but the policeman took the time to copy Maggie's name down in his book. Then he snapped it shut and turned to go inside. Maggie looked for the girl, but she had gone inside too, with her friends. In a moment there wasn't anyone left outside but Maggie and a half-dozen black hens that came around the corner of the house, pecking in the dust. One of the hens stopped to look at her, cocked its head, then dismissed her as being of no consequence, and went on with its business of finding bugs.

Manson was still in the ditch, pulling hay apart. "Well," he said, as she approached.

"Well what?"

"Is he really dead?"

Maggie stopped to look at him. "Am I a doctor? Do I know these things?"

"Did you make a statement?" he said, standing up and coming out of the ditch. "Will you be called on to be a witness?"

Maggie tossed her head. "They took my name," she said.

"Well that's something," Manson said.

It was something but it wasn't enough. That night Maggie Maclean didn't sleep very much. Up near the end of the road in her little grey house she lay awake and thought about her children and their fathers, thought about Manson Hed and that girl and the whole lot of them down at Jimmy Jimmy Arts and Crafts. It was a warm night and she kept only a sheet over her. She would have opened a window but she knew that if she did she would start hearing sounds from out in the bush.

And the next day when she went for her walk she was glad to see that Manson's car was gone, that he was at work where he belonged, that she would not have to talk to him or even wave. When she passed the gateway to the silent commune, however, and felt a strange sad sickness tighten up in her chest, she knew that her walks had been spoiled. She knew that she didn't want to walk down past here any more, even though it meant cutting herself off from the river and the bridge, that it just wouldn't be any pleasure any more. The trouble was—and she hated to think of this — in the other direction from her house the road very quickly came to a dead end and all there was beyond that was the steep rocky side of the mountain.

She would move. She would get out of there.

3

It was only natural that on the day of the wedding Lily Hayworth would throw one of her fits and go into what looked like a final decline. That was exactly the type of thing Maggie expected the old woman to do, she never missed a chance to spoil everything she could. Her greatest pleasure would be to have Maggie stay home from the wedding to sit by her bed and listen to her scratchy breathing; she would even die, deliberately and cheerfully, if she could be sure it would spoil something important enough.

The only reason Maggie knew she wasn't plotting to die today was that she'd made it clear she didn't for a minute believe in the wedding. "You can't be the mother of the groom," she said, "you've only just turned thirty." A little more, a little more, a year or so past that, said Maggie Kyle. "And anyway," sang out the goat-faced woman, who had her lucid moments still and plenty of spirit left, "If there really was a son we'd have met him by now, he'd have pushed himself into the house to ask for money if nothing else."

True, unless you knew that Maggie Kyle mailed cheques to help him out. To keep him safely distant in his downtown basement suite. Coffee in his lunch hour once a month, on plastic swivel stools, was the full extent of son-and-mother bond between them now.

But to give the Hayworth woman her due, she didn't spoil the entire day. She had a better sense of timing than that. She waited until they'd finished eating an early supper, when it was time for Maggie and the others to start getting dressed. She waited until it was too late for anyone to think of a calm and rational solution, then she hit them when they were all off guard. Up until that time she behaved more or less in a normal manner and spent the

afternoon doing a paint-by-numbers picture, in the living room
where Maggie could keep an eye on her, heaving sighs thick with
meaning in the direction of the clear-blue strait beyond the windows.

"I can't imagine why you bought me one with dogs," she said.
"I've always hated dogs." She could make the simplest complaint
sound as if she suspected a plot. Her nose wrinkled, ready to track
it down.

But Maggie Kyle was one jump ahead, she'd had practice. "You
asked for dogs," she said. "And you're doing all right. Finish it and
if you still don't like it you can give it away." To the garbage
collector, maybe, like so many of the others.

"My first husband had a dog. A great big ugly thing with yellow
teeth, he called it Thunderbird." She kicked at a pile of magazines
near her feet, as if the animal were hiding there. "He used to
follow my husband wherever he went and snarled back his lip at
anyone he didn't like, he thought he was put on earth to scare the
pants off human beings. The stupid animal trusted me, he never
guessed my feelings, he didn't know how much I hated the sight
of him. Where's that number seven? What happened to the
number seven jar? How can a person ever find anything in this
mess?"

"It's behind you. You put it on the coffee table."

Not that it would make much difference whether the old
woman used the right colour. The picture would look horrible
anyway. Lily Hayworth couldn't stay within the lines to save her
life. Her hands were steady enough, even at her age they were
steady, and there was nothing wrong with her eyesight, but she
got so carried away with talking or watching the strait or day-
dreaming that she sometimes smeared the gobs of oil paint on the
canvas just wherever her brush happened to push them.

"The dog died," she said, "in your kitchen." She could deliver
lines, like that, the way some could shove food at you.

"What?"

"That snarling old hound, Thunderbird. Keneally sicced him
on Paddy O'Mahony and he would've eaten out the man's throat
if Paddy hadn't had hands like steel clamps. Right in your kitchen,
inside the back door."

Maggie didn't like to think of the things that had happened
inside this house before it was hers. She didn't want to hear about

them. She loved the place now and didn't want to be reminded of anything that might spoil it. As far as she was concerned the past had been rubbed out when she went through the whole place top to bottom with a bucket of lye and a scrubbing brush, Keneally and his crazy colony were erased when she set a match to the furniture; the flames reminded her of a slash fire, burning off the nuisance debris to make room for newer growth.

And it was her house now, to grow in. When Maggie Kyle took possession of a house she absorbed it, it entered her bloodstream and was fed from the same sources as her legs were, or her hands. It breathed with her, and reflected her state of mind. Bedrooms, she said, you'll be restful places; and every room on the second floor became a place of quiet and softness, where even the crazy angles of the ceiling-roof leaned in as if to offer comfort. When she had the huge kitchen remodelled it was for convenience and speed: this is a service-centre, she said, things go out from here to keep the rest alive. She kept the old wooden table in the very centre of the room, the only piece of furniture salvaged from the mouldy remains, a place to stop and sit and think. In her dining room, which jutted out so close to the cliff's edge and the water that there was a danger of forgetting all about the land, she hung two of her favourite prints, forest scenes, to remind them of the trees at their backs. It was her house now, she'd created it out of an ugly old abandoned monster, it inhabited her as certainly as she inhabited it.

More than any other part of the house she loved this living-room, this giant old parlour the colony had crowded into long ago for its meetings and which Keneally had used for his raving speeches and his vulgar shows of magic. Visitors were shocked by the chaos now, they backed out again thinking they'd stumbled into a storage room she would rather have kept hidden from them. But only if they didn't know Maggie Kyle. She liked it that way, especially the confusion of mismatched auction-sale furniture and the random styles of collected things. Besides Lily's easel, which was always set up there in the clearest light, with the latest paint-by-number naked to every eye, there was the old wooden loom taking up half one wall with a nearly-finished bedspread still on it, exactly as it had been when the old woman lost interest a year ago. A chicken house would have used less space, Maggie said. Books and magazines were spilled all over the floor, almost burying the braided rugs and the kangaroo hide that Julius had bought in Australia.

In front of the big fireplace you had your choice of the sagging chesterfield draped over with a red plaid blanket to hide its cotton stuffing or the tall green reading chair that had recipes and newspaper clippings and snapshots shoved under its cushion. Between them a round cut-down dining table hid beneath a jumbled load: a vase of dying peonies, books of photographs, clay ashtrays, folded maps, bowls of coloured pebbles off the beach, and a battered globe that advertised the expanse of the British Empire. Leaning against the fireplace were two old faller-springboards Maggie had found out in the bush behind the house; they were pitted by the spikes of logger boots and bleached and worn by weather, with brown stains running in the wood from the rusted steel ends. And everywhere, of course, no matter where you were in the room, there was the sharp awareness of the sea, so close, and on a day like this the blue and jagged mountains of the mainland.

On the long wall, where the others wanted her to hang a framed painting or a gilt-edged mirror to reflect the moods of the strait, Maggie had pinned up an assortment of creased and wrinkled maps. A row of pale brown nautical charts told her the depths of the strait and outlined the coasts of islands and marked the perils of the shoals and narrows for a hundred miles in either direction. Gas-station maps of the island, a brilliant unnatural green, were mutilated by red and black and broken lines twisting everywhere like spreading vines, and black fly-speck dots to show the settlements of men. Four grey timber survey maps of the mountains told her just exactly how the crown land had been divided up among the logging companies and then divided once again into different lots and settings. Maggie kept track of all their progress, they needn't think that no one knew what they were up to; she added a big black X wherever she knew another stand of timber had been cleared away. There wasn't all that much of it left: they'd crept up the mountains to the edge of stone and alpine meadows, they'd spread out along the nearly-impossible slopes of the western coast, they'd met themselves from either end of giant valleys. She hated the maps, or what they showed her, and yet she could not have done without them, she occupied herself for hours on end with contemplating them. Sometimes she could dissolve right into one of the offensive lines and go rushing off to disappear in unmarked regions of green, or spring up full and alive in the centre of some remembered dot behind a hill. But it was the nature of a map to fix limits, she knew, and certainly not to open up the range of freedom; that was what mapmaking was all about. The surveyors and the land-developers were there to create borders and to try to change the nature of the land, and there was something in her that found the business foul.

So foul in fact it sometimes invaded Maggie Kyle in dreams. Walking across landscapes, she climbed grid lines as if they were fences and knocked on the edges of the black spots asking to be let in. And always, always from behind a mileage number or a boundary line an upright man-like shadow would appear and pursue her running down the broken lines and twisting roads, down blue-vein streams and narrow inlets, his laugh a thunderous roar that made the paper ripple beneath her feet.

"If there really is a wedding I should think you'd have more than enough to do, you should be running around cooking something or polishing your nails or soaking in a bath."

Old Lily sometimes forgot she wasn't mistress any longer of this place. She barked orders and cut criticism at people as if Keneally were still alive and she the House of Revelations's mistress. It was because she didn't believe in Maggie yet, even after all this time. She could believe in her if she came across her sweeping out a bunkhouse somewhere, Maggie knew, or slinging hash in a run-down village hotel, but she could not believe in her as the soul of the house she was living in.

And yet she'd been glad enough to come back and park her old self on Maggie. Banging on the front door as if she'd just gone out for a minute and the wind had slammed it shut behind her. Impatient, after forty-two years. Angry. When Maggie had opened the door she thought it was some kind of joke, some kind of costume, people that old didn't just turn up on your front verandah uninvited and without an escort. The blue-striped taxi was fleeing already, up the driveway; it seemed that there wasn't going to be any choice in the matter. But this wasn't just any dry old yellow-skinned woman, this was Lily Hayworth. Lily Keneally, who'd left this place in nineteen twenty-eight along with all the other people of the colony, and promptly found herself a millionaire to pamper her all the remaining years of her life. Or most of them, until he found other distractions. This was no ordinary person, this was Lily Hayworth, and she was willing to hand over her half of that timber fortune for the chance to pretend in the few remaining years of her life that it was nineteen twenty-eight again, or earlier, and that her hollered orders were still as valid as they had been then. A tall old goat-faced woman, white and grey and pale yellow, banging on the door. All she wanted, she said, was someone to look after her, she'd heard Maggie did that kind of thing. "No, I don't," Maggie had said. "This isn't a Home." But she pushed her way inside, and walked through all the rooms of the ground floor, sniffing, until she found the old wooden table in the kitchen, a survivor like herself. She sat down at it, creaked down into a chair, and laid her big hands out on the gold grain of the wood. "The taxi driver left my cases at the bottom of the steps," she said.

And settled, just like that, into Maggie's life.

"Stand out of the light," she said, "and quit your breathing on me."

Though Maggie could clout her or give her big fleshy ears a yank, she'd never send her away, even without the fortune. She'd keep the old girl alive as long as she could, and laugh at her bullying.

The thing was, Maggie knew she had a perfect set-up. She had this land, opened up to the whole wide strait along this edge as if there were no real borders on her world at all, and grown up thick with alder and second-growth fir behind the buildings to hide the caved-in barns of the colony and the brand new houses of the subdivisions that surrounded her. She had this house, bigger than anything she'd ever lived in before, and full of surprises and possibilities, so interesting she never tired of prowling through it or pushing things around inside to see what differences she could make. And she had her people: Lily Hayworth, and sour Julius and little Strabo Becker and Anna Sterner. If she'd gone wandering the world for them she couldn't have picked a more irritating cantankerous lot, and yet could never find another group so sure to make her feel that this was the way for things to be. Not even the bush could compete. Not even the urge that came over her every once in a while to chuck it all and head back up into the hills to settle into some camp somewhere. This was what she wanted for herself, she said, a solid base from which to rise, a life that had some purpose in it.

What she didn't want was Danny Holland showing up to wreck it all. As he could. As he would love to do. A plague of locusts would be more welcome.

As long as she'd stayed up in Hed she'd seen him often, there was no escape. She'd seen him on the sidewalk of the riverside town where she did her Saturday shopping. She'd seen him always at a street corner talking with a group of men who waited for their wives to come out of stores and passed the time by talking about their bosses and machinery and the company men they held in such contempt. She knew them all, by name some of them, or by reputation; in their weekend mackinaws and wash-faded jeans, they tipped forward from an aching hip or leaned back against a wall or put their weight on one thrust-forward leg, frizzled jaws working over a wad of snoose, each of them paying attention to the others only while he talked himself, then coming out of a sudden laugh to sweep the street with unseeing eyes while the others talked, or watched the *Men's Entrance* to the Riverside Hotel. She knew the weather-coarsened skin of their faces, loosening up in age, sagging just a little, the hard black-lined creases of their hands, and their smell, of grease and a harsh and gritty soap. She knew, too, the lazy hesitant way they had of breaking away from the group when a wife coming out of a grocery store signalled for help, and the strange suspended silence that followed each departure. Holland never broke away until the last, unless it was to cross the street and try to talk her into a beer or two at the Riverside; he stayed until there was only himself and another man left and then he threw his arm across the other fellow's shoulders and led him in through the *Men's Entrance* door where they would spend whatever was left of the afternoon.

As long as he was out on the street, though, she was aware of his busy eyes. He chewed gum then with his mouth open a little, always grinning, always flushed up and waiting for the next laugh, his eyes unlike the others' always busy, always scouring up and down the street, casually running up legs, idly following a pair of shifting hips, flickering across store signs, estimating the value of parked cars, sliding up to identify a passing bird or plane. Pleasure, always pleasure, he always looked as if the next good joke was only seconds away, so that when he spotted her there was no surprise, merely the broadening-out of his grin — the joke was even better than he'd expected — and a slow straightening of his shoulders. He broke away from the others without a word of explanation, looked both ways as if he intended traffic to part for him, and—when it did—walked his long strides casually across to her. "Maggie," he said. "Son of a bitch, you look good."

And that was supposed to make her throw everything into reverse. *Son of a bitch, you look good.* He thought that all he had to do was show up wherever she happened to be, and say a thing like that; he thought even now that all he had to do was show up wherever she may be living and throw her a line like that and she should be glad to abandon the direction of her life and slide back down to where she'd been so many years before. For him.

Son of a bitch, you look good.

Sure she looked good. She knew it. She was one hell of a good-looking woman. And she felt good, too, why shouldn't she? She enjoyed her life. She liked herself. She liked the people around her. The only thing she didn't like was his loud quick shadowy presence, turning up here and turning up there wherever you didn't need him, laughing, threatening to spoil everything. Sometimes she suspected he wasn't real at all, but some kind of vision conjured up by her worst imaginings to keep her always on edge.

He belonged to her all right, but not in any way he wanted it to be.

If she had to endure this wedding—and there was no way she could imagine avoiding it, it was the one thing a mother had to do even if she failed to do everything else—she intended to endure it like a lady and get all she could out of the experience, but she didn't see how she could stop Holland from showing up and wrecking everything.

"I've seen him at weddings before," she told Lily Hayworth. "I've seen what he can do to a wedding. Forbes will be humiliated, he'll never get over it. The place will be a shambles, the people will be stirred up like a hornet's nest."

"But that's not what you're really worried about," the old woman said. She screwed up her face and moved in closer to the canvas to jam a daub of white paint into the dog's left eye. "You're scared he'll crook his finger once too often and you'll go running."

"If I broke his leg," she said, "wouldn't he have to stay in the hospital at least overnight before they'd let him out to walk around on a cast?"

Maggie was so preoccupied with plotting roadblocks for Danny Holland after she got home from the Loggers' Sports that she was only half aware of what was going on around her. When Anna Sterner tried to get her attention through the living-room window she was absent-mindedly jabbing a fingernail into all the dots on the centre map and only the sudden banging on the glass and Lily's bark ("Maggie wake up or that girl will bring the house down!") pulled her away from a plot to have someone steal his clothes.

"He'd go naked anyway," she said. "What do you want, Anna? What does that girl want?"

"Ask her," Lily said. "What does she ever want? Maybe she wants to break the glass."

"She could come inside and ask, like other people."

But Anna never came inside the house if she could help it, except to eat or do specific jobs that Maggie lined up for her. She stayed outside as much as she could, she liked to work in the garden, or skittered in the back door and up the staircase to her bedroom when she was driven in by dark or the weather. Houses seemed to hold some kind of threat in them for her, she'd pull you out of them if she could, or stand on the verandah for any talking that needed to be done.

When Maggie went out onto the verandah the girl slid along the wall, a little closer to her, her eyes running down along the railing. She was a big girl, with a round high-coloured face and bones that seemed to push her eyes slanted up against her forehead. She grinned, twisted her pale dimpled hands into the coarse weave of her ankle-length dress, all she ever wore. "Have you ever heard of a Mr. Horseman?" she shouted.

She had a soft eager voice when she wanted to use it, but she had a habit when nervous of gasping first to get a hold on things and then shouting it out.

"What is it, Anna? What's the matter?"

The eyes ran up a post and followed the eavestrough back, her bare foot twisting on the verandah boards. Maggie nearly told her to watch out, she'd get slivers, but it would only make her twist and grimace even more. "Ever heard of a Mr. Horseman?"

"What's that, a new make of car?"

Because Anna liked to be teased. Sometimes it was the only way Maggie could get through.

"Naw!" She could hardly force herself to look at Maggie, she was so disgusted, so pleased. "Naw-w-w!" she told the wall she leaned on, the floor, the railings. "Horseman is a *man*!"

"Where is this man? Where is this Horseman?" There was no one in sight but old Julius, down on the wharf soaking up sun.

Anna's mouth twitched as if something was alive in there and trying to get out. "In the barn," she said. "In the chicken barn. I was feeding my chickens and this man came in out of the bush."

"Horseman?"

The girl nodded.

"Never heard of the man. Why didn't he come to the house with you? What did he say? Is he still there?"

The girl shook her head this time, as if saddened to bring such news. "He left. He stepped out of the bush and right into the barn, I nearly screamed when I turned around and saw him, the sun coming through the roof made him striped across with wide bars."

"And he said? Was he a salesman? What?"

"He said 'Is this where Maggie Kyle lives?' and I said 'Yes' and he left."

"Left?"

"Stepped back into the bush and disappeared."

"Horseman. I never heard of a Horseman. And that's all he asked?"

"He just went off tramping through the bush towards the road. Before I could think, he was gone."

There was some kind of relief in having delivered the message. Anna sagged, nearly allowed herself to sit on the wooden bench. She was the daughter of a pediatrician and all her life she'd been nagged at to stand up straight. Whenever she could relax enough she just let her shoulders drop as if they were made of boneless flesh.

The pediatrician and his wife had nagged about more than posture, had gone on about this and that until at seventeen she ran off with a boy named Joel who'd come up from the States to start a commune. He was a religious enthusiast of some sort and had calculated the exact date of the second coming. He moved his little community up into the mountains to wait for it, camped in an abandoned copper-mine where they could see far enough in every direction to have plenty of warning. But when the second coming was postponed for some reason or other, or had happened in a quiet manner somewhere else escaping Joel's notice, they came down out of the mountain and Anna left them. She showed up at Maggie's door and begged for the chance to earn her keep.

That was nearly the last bit of information she ever gave away about herself. In two years she'd told them no more than what was necessary to get her through each day without serious mis-understandings. She worked as hard as you wanted, or harder, and only asked to be left alone.

But a man named Horseman, evidently, was enough to shake something loose. "At first I thought it was that friend of yours, Wade — that cousin or whatever he is that comes around. Could've been his twin. But he had a soft, nearly whispering voice."

There was nothing so very strange about it, Maggie told her. There were always people coming in and poking around, she knew that. People who used to live here, maybe, but wouldn't admit it, or people who'd heard about the colony and couldn't believe the things that were said.

But still, she said, it was beginning to look like an invasion.

She walked out to the barn with Anna, as much to get her back to work and out of the way as to sniff around for answers. The chickens, a dozen Rhode Island Reds Anna looked after for their eggs, were penned up in one corner of the nearest barn, the only one of the barns still safe enough to walk into. It was up a trail that set off behind Becker's cabin, through grass and wild sweet pea, skirted the base of the grown-over pyramid of earth high as a house that some early excavations had left behind, then cut through brush to a clearing thick with alders and blooming fireweed. The barn was little more than a skeleton of peeled poles hung with sun-bleached patterns of nail-stained boards. Butter-cups spotted the long grass growing around its base. Inside there was plenty of dry manure dust to walk around on, and cobwebs to catch at hair, and old tubes of vaseline and salves along a ledge, and the ammonia smell of the chickens in the air, but there were no traces of this Mr. Horseman, whoever he was.

"He just said is this where Maggie Kyle lives and I said yes and he left."

"He could've learned as much from a phone book," Maggie said.

Later, when Maggie went down onto the float to gather Julius

Champney in for an early supper, her annoyance at Holland's appearance had turned into anger, and the plots against him had already included locking him in sheds and phoning the police. "Do you think Becker could be persuaded to shanghai him onto a government ferry? Two hours over, two hours back. He'd be a dangerous man when he returned, but at least the wedding would be finished."

The old man stood at the very end of the float, his toes only inches above the water. He looked as if he'd been designed by a child playing around with a length of wire: all long narrow stems and sharp angles.

"I was at a wedding, once, where the bride's father was so drunk he passed out halfway down the aisle. It wasn't, I might add, a pleasant sight." When Julius talked he looked as if he were measuring his sentences and laying them out before him like an unrolled blueprint to be studied. "When he came to, they'd propped him up in the front pew."

Maggie had heard it before, he'd told it before. "Yes, he stood up, looked out over all the people in the church, and said, 'What the eff are you all starin' at?'"

His yellowed droopy eyes turned from the water and looked her over suspiciously. She'd stolen his line. "Needless to say, I left immediately. It was too painful to see that man standing there. And his wife."

"It's not the church I'm worried about. Like most of them he's scared enough of the inside of a church to behave. He'll tell a joke in a loud voice or shout across the pews to somebody he recognizes, just to show he's no sissy, but he'll shut up and go red in the face the minute the preacher comes out. It's not the church, though I'd give a lot to keep him out of it."

Julius sniffed at the salt air. Clearly it was all the fault of the coast. "Typical behaviour for this island," he said. "They are, you see, embarrassed by anything that resembles civilization."

Maggie could only laugh. For a man with so much contempt for salt water and rain and for people who liked it here, he spent an awful lot of his time on this float by himself.

From down here, looking back up the cliff, she could see only the top half of her house, a number of gables in the crowns of trees. "I've made us a bite to eat," she said. "So there'll be time enough to get ourselves ready. The mother of the groom has got to look gorgeous." In that mixture of tree tops, the arbutus leaves were the only things broad enough or shiny enough to catch the sun's light. She could believe there were trees in there that were hung with a thousand pocket mirrors, bushes which chose to bloom light instead of flowers.

"Maggie," he said, his long face pulling down grimmer even than usual. "You'd be gorgeous if you went in Becker's coveralls."

Old Julius, for all his crankiness, could offer a compliment now and then. Unlike most of the men she knew, he was not afraid of women, or her. Maybe it was something that happened when you grew up on the prairies. Or maybe just because he was old.

Danny Holland's idea of a compliment was a jarring thump on the back.

Wade Powers had never tried either kind, though he treated her, at least, like someone with a brain in her head. And usually looked pleased to see her, made her feel like a pleasant surprise.

"And speaking of our friend Becker," Julius Champney said. He let his bony chin complete the thought, pointing at the grey crescent of beach that rimmed the bay. Short squat Becker was out there, in his black overcoat, walking towards them. He didn't see them, though, he prodded with a stick under driftwood logs, turned over rocks, stirred in the tide pools. Like a kid, she thought, hoping for prizes, or people's lost valuables.

"I expect," Julius said, with only the hint of a smile, "he is looking for an ancient crab with a memory. So he can ask for an interview, with his tape recorder, and discover even darker secrets about the past. He won't be satisfied, I suppose, until he's uncovered a second murder."

"Or caused one," Maggie said, thinking of the calls she'd had. "But at least the crabs have no way of complaining about his intrusion."

"Or if they do," he said, "we have learned how to avoid listening."

The tide was out; the float they stood on, all but this farthest end, lay on the damp stinking sand. The pilings it was chained to, and which it would ride up when the tide lifted it, were covered with barnacles and slime. The sun, heading west, still had a way to go before the tree shadows would be laid out here on the beach like cool darkened spears.

Becker turned landward, without seeing them there, and went up out of sight behind the bluff. Whenever she saw him like that, alone, Maggie thought there ought to be a dog following him, he was that kind. But she would never mention it to him, in case he liked the idea; she didn't need a dog around the place.

And Julius could look, even now, as if there were dog odours offending his nostrils. Sometimes the whole place affected him that way.

"I can't imagine," he said, "what he thinks he will have accomplished. You can't pretend there is any history on this island, this is still the frontier."

Julius Champney had travelled and knew what it was like to walk on streets that thousands of people had been killed on, over and over again, down through centuries. Maggie hadn't been any place like that, she couldn't imagine it. When he talked about visiting the Tower of London it was only words. She couldn't get her fingers into words, the way she could into this gravelly beach, or that water. When she opened her hand and placed the palm against the trunk of a tree she could feel bark the way those words could never make you feel stone, or the thatched roofs of fugitives, or dungeon floors. And what was the good of travel, she would like to say to him, if it only made you come back and sneer at your home? And make people around you feel they've missed out on something important?

"The best he can dig up," he said, still looking out where Becker had been, "will be little more than gossip. You can't turn that into history, no matter how hard you try. Not in a place like this. You are inheritors of a failed paradise. This island is littered with failed utopias."

But time was flying. Maggie couldn't stand here and listen. "Come on up to the house," she said. "We'll eat."

"Then tell me," he said, "about this man who has you all stirred up. What is he like? What is the nature of his power over you?"

But Maggie didn't answer. There was no need. The old man was preoccupied already with sizing up the long steep series of steps he had yet to climb. With hulking Anna Sterner there at the top, looking down on them from beside the pile of rotting seaweed she'd hauled up to spread on her garden.

By the time they sat down to supper Maggie had run out of imaginary plots against Danny Holland and realized her anger had turned to panic. She wouldn't go, she thought. She couldn't trust herself. She'd stay home from the damn wedding and pretend it meant nothing at all to her. If that man showed his face she was liable to scratch his eyes out, or worse; they were better off if she didn't go. Panic uncoiled in her chest like a snake looking for escape.

"I won't go," she said.

But no one heard. Lily Hayworth sniffed at the bowl in front of her. "What's this?"

Julius stirred with his spoon. "Clam chowder in July?" he said. "In this heat?"

Hayworth shuddered. "Did you cut off their heads? The green bellies are hard enough to take but those necks ... "

"Where's Becker?" Maggie said. "Why isn't Becker here? Maybe he could tell me what to do. Becker is always a help."

"You scared him off," Anna said. "He got wind of your state and headed for his cabin. He won't come out."

"It seems to me," Julius said, and levelled his sad yellow eyes at Maggie Kyle, "that you should take a closer look at your reasons."

"Julius is a great believer in reason," Lily said. "An unusual thing. For a poet."

The old man snorted. He'd liked pushing words around on paper, Maggie knew, in the same way he liked making lines on blueprint. He'd been a town planner on the prairies and saw making patterns out of words as part of the same kind of business. Ordering things. He wrote a twenty-page poem expressing his hatred for salt water and mountains and it was accepted by a literary magazine in the East. But when he got his three free copies, all he was ever paid, and saw that they'd printed only the first eight lines, he swore he'd never submit anything again, to anyone. The editor of the magazine, answering Julius's insulting letter, explained that hatred was only effective in short doses, after eight lines the rest was only monotonous repetition and made it all look silly. But Julius had never been accused of silliness before in his whole life and sulked for so long that Maggie burned all three copies of the magazine.

"Julius is not a poet," Maggie said. "He swore off poetry. Nobody reads poetry anyway around here, and just think of the trees whose lives are being saved if he never publishes another poem."

"If you were only worried," Julius said, "that this Holland will make a fool of *himself*, you wouldn't be getting yourself so worked up."

"Worked up?" she said. "I'm scared stiff."

"Then admit why."

"She knows why," Lily said, and gulped chowder. "And so do you."

"But I haven't heard her say it."

Lily's face snorted back from her spoon. "Do people always *say* everything? For all your chasing around the world didn't you learn anything better than that?" Her hand clutched at the lapels of her dress. "Julius went chasing off to Australia once," she told Anna. "To worship at a rock."

Anna would believe anything, only didn't want to hear it. Her face ducked.

"People go there to climb it, to see it," Julius said. There was no hiding his distaste for anyone who couldn't understand a thing like that.

"A big orange rock glowing out in the middle of the desert. He used to tell us about it, about how big it was, how there are smears of human blood, how the aborigines had stories about it, but he doesn't talk about it any more, he only likes to give advice. It turned out, after all, to be only a rock."

"It makes as much sense as any other pilgrimage," Maggie said.

"Or that woman," Lily said, pointing her spoon at the painting opposite her, "with her trees."

There was a print on either side of the room—she could hardly afford the originals. A cathedral grove of long blue plasticine trunks soaring up to a dark ceiling, and across from it, a brown corridor between thick trunks under draped hanging sheets of green.

"Well of course she was mad," Julius said.

And for once Lily agreed with him. "The only painter I ever heard of who could make a forest look like it's made of satin sheets, folded and draped and hung and propped up like the display window of a yard-goods store. From what I've heard she would have felt right at home in this house, she lived in chaos herself. Animals and boarders and mess, she couldn't see dust and dropped clothing for following her visions into the bush."

"And good for her!" said Maggie Kyle. And wondered how the painter would have liked to have *these* in her collection of boarders. Their disapproval would be enough by itself to keep her painting. "At least," she said, "when she painted things she left them upright and didn't reduce them to lines and squares laid flat out on a table."

Julius drew back, she could hear his gasp. He would sulk now, there was no telling how long he would sulk.

"Why don't we all get into a rip-roaring fight?" Lily asked the ceiling. "Maggie is edgy enough for it, she'll bite heads off before this day is through. And Julius is always as ready to take offense as he is to dish it out. Maybe we could get worked up enough to throw things at each other. That ought to make us all feel grown up and civilized."

Poor Anna became so agitated she had to leave the table and pretend all the tea mugs needed refilling.

"Becker," Maggie said. "Why isn't Becker here?"

But Becker still hadn't come in, and Maggie still had no answers when they'd finished eating and it was time to get dressed for the wedding. Lily wouldn't be going, of course, and Anna — who'd never considered going — had offered to keep her eye on her so that Julius and Becker and Maggie could have a good time with a clear conscience. But the old woman, who went into the living room to work on her dog picture so she'd be out of the way while they dressed, suddenly dropped to the floor in a faint and had to be lifted up onto the chesterfield. When she opened her eyes again she groaned and thrashed around and hollered things until Maggie was ready to scream. She'd seen Keneally, she screeched at them, she'd seen Keneally coming to get her, she'd seen him coming up the path from the driveway. Back from the dead, she said, she'd seen him, heading for the house. He'd get her, he'd get her before the night was over, she'd be dead as a doornail by morning.

What she'd seen coming up the path to the front step was only Wade Powers dressed in his best suit, and when Maggie opened the door to him she couldn't help hollering in his face: "Now what? Now what? The old woman's gone off her head and all because of you!"

"Now what?" he said. He came into the house, as into everything, as though there were branches to part, and leaves. He looked for a moment as if he were expecting to be ambushed.

"Screaming and yelling, I can't leave her, I'll have to stay."

"Because of me?"

Then Maggie laughed, she couldn't help it. Here she was, all dressed up, or nearly, looking gorgeous as hell in this long pink sexy dress with its low neck and slit-open sleeves, yelling like a fishwife at this guy, at Wade, when she'd give — what? — just to curl up against him. "Congratulations," she said, "she thought you were a dead man. She thought you were that madman-devil himself, the one she married, come back to get her."

"Well, I'm sorry to hear I'm dead," he said, "because I was hoping to give you these." And brought out a florist's box from behind his back. White rosebuds, she discovered.

"White for virginity," she said, and made him help her pin them on. "In society weddings I think the groom's the one buys all the flowers, but this one's looking more and more like a do-it-yourself affair every minute. Too bad I won't be there to see it, it ought to be a riot."

"Oh you'll be there, Maggie, one way or the other. Because if you don't go with me there's another gentleman who has plans to take you. Coming down your driveway now."

"What?"

"Danny Holland in his pickup. Here he comes."

Anna came out of the living room, panic-stricken. "You can't leave her with me. You can't let me stay alone with her. I don't know what to do."

"Get Becker," Maggie snapped. "Get Strabo Becker, he always knows what to do."

"He won't come out. He's locked himself in his cabin. He won't come out, you know what Becker's like."

"Then tell her to shut up, just tell her she has to shut up! Tell her we can't afford to have people throwing fits today. Look at that son of a bitch out there, grinning in his bloody pickup. Wade, you go tell her to shut up, tell her, slap her face if you have to. Tell her I've got enough ... Look at him parking right there in front of the steps. Wipe that smile off your face, Danny Holland, wipe it off."

"Maggie," Wade said, and put a hand on her arm. "Maggie."

"The bastard's blocked my van, I can't get out."

"Maggie, you're going in my car, not in yours. Don't get so mad."

Oh, she was mad all right. You bet she was mad. "He could've gone back," she said. "He could've crawled back into that hole he came out of."

"But he didn't," Wade said. "Because his son is getting married tonight."

But Maggie pushed past him and went out onto the verandah. Holland's twisted smashed-up pickup was parked on the narrow road that squeezed between the steps and the fence along the edge of the cliff, blocking off her Bug Wagon which she'd backed down under a tree. Holland, leaning out his window, his big red hand hanging down the outside of his door, grinned at her as if this were more of a welcome than he'd even dared to hope for.

"Son of a bitch, Maggie, you look terrific!" His hand swung up to take hold of the handle. He was in a dress suit, a red tie tight at his famous throat.

She wished she were in pants, this dress made her feel like a made-up clown. "Don't get out, Danny. Just please go away."

He threw back his head and laughed. He couldn't believe it. "It's nearly time for the wedding. I thought you'd give me a beer or something before we left."

She hoisted up her skirt and went down a step—pink, what the hell was she doing in pink? Squeezed between the house and the fence like that he could almost have touched her. "Where's your Zulu? What'd you do with her?" she said. "Have you even gone back to see what the cops have done with that woman? Why isn't she in the truck, going with you?"

Without his hardhat he looked naked, and must have felt it— his fingers combed back through his thinning slicked-down hair. "Who? Stell? She's nobody. Hell, Maggie what would she want to go to a wedding for, she'd rather play poker and drink everybody under the table."

"Then go play with her, go on back, don't spoil this day for Forbes."

There was no grin left on his mouth now, it had sobered out to a frown. His face flushed up even redder than before, white patches appeared in his cheeks as if someone had pressed thumbs against them. "That's my kid, Maggie. I'm going to my kid's wedding."

"The hell it is."

"That's my kid, Maggie."

"The hell it is."

"You bloody bitch standing there like a goddam queen all dressed up like there wasn't nobody good enough for you, Jesus do you think you're any different than you ever were? Do you think you're any better?"

"Prick!" She swiped a hand at him and missed when he ducked

inside the cab. "You useless arrogant prick. Get out of my way. Get your bloody crate out of my yard."

"Maggie," he said, and grinned again. He just would not believe it.

But she had to get him out. She had to make him believe. She had to get out of here herself. If she turned, if she even glanced around there would be Wade and Anna, there would be Julius looking at her. She had to get out of here. Her head would split wide open. She'd say things, she'd yell things at him even worse than she had, she couldn't stay here. His eyes, those pinked-up mocking eyes, could have belonged to a part of herself, an old mirror somewhere, she couldn't stand to be looking at them. The smell of the beer, the whole day's consumption stinking on his breath, could have been her own, too, coming back at her to choke her, she could smell it even stronger than the salt smell of the strait, stronger far stronger than her roses, her goddam flapping corsage.

She ran. Again running from him, a second time in the same day. But she discovered she wasn't going to run away from him at all, she was going to get rid of him. She got into the Bug Wagon, hauled the long skirt up onto her lap to free her legs, and started the motor, roared ahead. She would bulldoze him right off the cliff if she could.

Holland, surprised, thought it was a joke. Laughing as she approached, he threw open his arms in mock alarm. Rolled his head back in ecstasy as if what he was doing was gathering her in, as if she were driving ahead not to hit him but to join him, to throw herself into his embrace.

"Yahoo!" he yelled.

But his head snapped rigid, his face jumped, when she collided with his front bumper. Her own body leapt at the jolt, her jaw trembled with the shock that ran up her bones.

"What the hell?" he hollered.

She pushed the Bug Wagon gas pedal to the floor, heard oyster shells and gravel fly back from under her, and pushed the pickup backwards past the house. Holland's face, in the cracked windshield opposite her, glared back, unbelieving. This was not what he'd intended.

But he recovered soon enough. Evidently he thought she was playing his kind of game after all. The broad grin returned, joy leapt into his face. He fumbled down at the ignition switch.

She pushed him back a hundred feet or so before he got his engine started, let out his clutch, and dug in. Nose to nose the two engines roared up to a high whine. Back tires flung gravel and shells and dirt, churned up clouds of dust. Exhaust smoke boiled up around them.

He put his head out the window, hollered something at her, but she couldn't hear.

"You can't get at me!" she yelled back. "You can't get at me!"

His face, rigid in a grim smile, reminded her of someone else. There was someone other than Danny Holland sitting in behind those eyes. Someone else was looking out at her from behind those pinked-up glaring eyes.

Manson Hed.

Manson Hed, in the ditch, pulling hay apart. Sneering.

Did you make a statement? Will you be called in to be a witness?

They took my name.

Well, that's something.

Manson Hed, who had looked at her in just the same way that chicken had before dismissing her and going on about its own business.

Alarmed by the sudden memory, she released the accelerator, and Holland's truck began to push her back a little, to push her front end twisting sideways. Steel scraped against steel, screeching. She would find herself going over the edge of that cliff in a minute.

To shift into reverse, to get out of here before she got herself killed, she had to push in the clutch pedal. The second she did that, her van went shooting back under the pressure of Holland's push, swung sharply in time to miss the fence, went back swerving past the house, scraping along the verandah steps, and ended up where she'd come from. Holland's truck stopped where it had been before and he sat there leaning over his steering wheel, looking puzzled.

The others were on the verandah, watching. Wade, scratching inside his shirt, looked ready to leap, ready to help, but he didn't understand what was going on, he couldn't. Anna hunched back against the wall of the house, hardly daring to look. Julius Champney, wiry old Julius, stood upright and sober, contemptuous of them all, gloating perhaps that they had turned out to be no better after all than he'd expected.

What am I doing? she thought. What are you doing to me, Danny Holland?

Those people on the verandah had seen what he could do to her. They'd seen.

She would roar ahead again, while he was stopped, she would drive the Bug Wagon as fast as it would go, straight into the front of that truck, snapping his neck, crumpling her own van up, smashing her face against the window glass. She would go that one step further than the stupid Zulu had, he wouldn't leave her at that level, she'd go that one step further and show him this was no game. Maybe if she smashed them both, maybe if she broke bones and lay bleeding, he would believe.

But along the verandah, those people were watching. They'd seen what he could do to her. Wade and Anna and Julius. Becker no doubt was watching, too, from some hidden place. They'd all seen. She was the Zulu, there was no difference. They'd seen her.

Except for Lily Hayworth.

He'd made her abandon Lily. The old woman was in the house, alone, he'd caused her to do that.

They took my name.

Well that's something.

But it hadn't been enough. Danny Holland had made a fool of her. And worse than a fool. Lily Hayworth was in that house *unattended*. The old woman could be dead, or dying.

She got out of the Bug Wagon and slammed the door and headed back towards the house. Holland, too, climbed down out of his truck and stood between her and the steps. He wasn't laughing now, he wasn't glaring. He held out his hands, his arms, as if after all he would gather her in.

And she walked in, walked in to him, put her forehead lightly touching against his chest, his cleaners-smelling suit, acknowledged him.

Then she stepped back, away from him, away from that red knotted tie too tight around his red neck, the throat. "I've got to go to Lily," she said. "You made me forget her."

But I acknowledge you, she thought, and touched the tie. Straightened it. He always wore his ties too tight, as if to demonstrate his hatred of them.

"It's all right," Wade said, from the door. "Becker's with her. It's all right."

But they didn't dismiss her, those people on the verandah. They didn't look at her the way that chicken had, that hen. There was something else in their faces. Not just the confusion or the fear or the contempt she thought she'd seen from the van, there was something else. There was a feeling there of some kind, it mattered to them that she was acting the fool, it *mattered*. They had thought that she had left them.

"Jesus, Maggie," Holland said, and would have gathered her back.

But she'd seen the faces.

"There's beer in the fridge if you want it," she said, stepping around him. "Help yourself if you want, it doesn't matter. Go on in and help yourself."

He looked confused. That uncertain grin started up again, as if he were looking for the joke. He didn't know where to put his hands.

"I don't have time to wait on you," she said. "Help yourself if you want, if you want the beer, I've got to check on Lily, I've got to do something about this goddam dress, and my hair. But you can hang around if you want, until it's time to go to the wedding. You can ride with us in Wade's car if you like, it doesn't matter."

He would be there, in the same pew as she was. He'd get even drunker than he was now, and noisier, and wreck furniture before the night was out; he'd break noses and insult people, he'd stir up the guests and probably make his own son hate him. Just as he would always be there, somewhere, showing up here, showing up there, wherever he wasn't wanted, she wouldn't escape him. She couldn't. He was alive, he was real. But she wouldn't, any longer, have to care. That was his own business. He could drag around behind her like a shadow now and then if that was what he wanted, she couldn't stop him, but she didn't have to be afraid of him or give him any more importance than he earned. She was free, now, to choose her own direction.

"Is she all right?" she said, from the living-room door.

Becker stood in the middle of the room, his feet buried in books and magazines, his nervous hands kneading each other. "She's asleep," he said. "She's all right. I'll stay with her, I'll watch her tonight."

"But you'll ... "

"But I'll call you if anything ... I'll call you if she gets worse, if I've had to telephone a doctor."

"You'll call me home."

"Yes."

Maggie went over to the chesterfield and saw that Becker or someone had pulled a blanket up to the old woman's chin. Her face was yellow-white, but no worse than it often was. She had her spells like this, they scared you but she came out of them. She was an old woman, after all, this Lily Hayworth, but she'd live to keep their lives on edge for quite a while longer yet.

Through the window she saw a taxi emerge from the bush, follow her driveway along the beach, then come up the hill to the house. When she went out onto the verandah to see who it was, Cora Manson was already out, paying the driver. She wore a bright red dress, something Maggie had never seen before, but it was too tight and the ridges of her girdle could be seen through the material. When she straightened up and turned to them, the big flat plastic pig which had been hanging free slapped back against her chest and shivered. Her hand went up to stroke it into place.

"I waited," she said, "I thought, well, any minute now they'll come and pick me up for the wedding, I'm a friend after all, and I don't have a car of my own. I nearly phoned but I thought, no, I'm a friend and I don't need to beg, I'm an important enough friend to take certain things for granted."

Holland was still down on the oyster-shell driveway, leaning against his truck. He looked at Cora, then up at Maggie, then back again.

"But then of course I thought, what makes you think you're so important as all that, they've probably gone off without you and never given you a passing thought, they could sail right through the wedding and never notice you haven't showed up. So here I am." She cut Holland a look and walked past him up the steps. "But I'm not riding in that thing."

Maggie laughed. "We'll go in Wade's car, Cora. We'll go in Wade's car. Nobody has to ride in Danny Holland's truck, right now it's on the wanted list by the RCMP and shouldn't be on the road at all."

"Or anywhere else," Cora said.

"Cora's afraid of me," Holland said. He looked as if he rather liked the idea: one hand stroked the scratched paint of his door. "Cora Manson is afraid of me."

"No one is afraid of you," said Maggie Kyle.

"Son of a bitch," he said, and reached to whip off the aluminum hat which wasn't there.

Cora Manson went inside the house, sighing, and Anna and Julius followed her. "It's nearly time," Julius said, and almost touched her arm. "If you're going to fix your hair."

Wade Powers said, "I wouldn't want to get married on a warm night like this. It's no kind of weather for a wedding."

Holland dry-laughed and looked at the sky. "One time is as bad as the next for that kind of thing."

"But nobody," Wade said, "likes to be cooped up in a stuffy church on a summer evening."

"Is there really beer in the fridge?" Holland said, his eyes scooping down to Maggie. "I don't know whether I ought to go now by myself, or take the time for a quick one."

"It doesn't matter," Maggie said.

"What does that mean?" Holland said.

"Nothing," Maggie said. "There's beer in the fridge if you want it. Have one if you like, but it doesn't matter."

The Eden Swindle

Becker tells you this:

Trust me or not, believe what you want, by now the story exists
without us in air. I am not its creator, nor is any one man; I did not
invent it, only gathered its shreds and fragments together from the
half-aware conversations of people around me, from the tales and
hints and gossip and whispered threats and elaborate curses that
float in the air like dust. Listen. Donal Keneally is dead. He built
this island colony for his own reasons and lived out his life in his
own way and then, by burrowing himself into earth, released
those who remained on its surface to find their own manner of
suffering. The force of his death-cry sent shivers through earth as
far away as the town, and there were those who believed a god had
been slain. Donal Keneally is dead. Believe what you want.

It was Keneally's mother who started the whole deception, one
hundred and fifteen years ago and thousands of miles away.
When the ghost of Cathleen ni Houlihan appeared in a dream to
predict that her child would be fathered by a bull-god from the
sky, the poor girl was so alarmed at the prospect that she got all
tangled up in her blankets, fell off the side of her bed onto the
stone floor, and knocked every trace of memory right out of her
pretty skull. She could not remember a thing: not her name, not
the cause of the long white scar down the side of her throat, not
even the nature of the dream which had caused her to lose her
memory. She did not recognize her mother, a fat sharp-eyed
woman who claimed an ancestry including the warrior-king Brian
Boru, and who locked herself in a shed of stones rather than face
the shame of a simple-minded daughter. Nor did she recognize
her father, a man whose peasant instincts ran to less dramatic

gestures than his wife's: he simply showed his daughter the road and started her on its winding way down out of the stony hills towards the green water of Galway Bay. The least she could do for him, he said, was drown herself in a place where she had no name. "What kind of life is it at all," the girl asked everyone she encountered on her subsequent travels, "where a soul cannot remember what it is she is fleeing and has no notion of what she seeks?" Countrymen, frightened by the wild look in her eyes, waved her on, kept her moving, and mumbled prayers to their Blessed Virgin until she was well out of sight. "Bad luck to her so," they said, for all their piety, and spat on the ground. "Isn't it trouble enough we have in this world without inviting tragedy in to sit at the fire?"

Though it could not be denied, they admitted as they eyed her retreating backside, that she had hips on her surely that were made for the bearing of Finn MacCool.

It is not known which village she came from, though it is fairly certain she was raised somewhere in Connemara among the rocks, for after she'd wandered the countryside for a few weeks she took up with a tinker family who taught her to beg on the narrow streets of Galway. With a baby borrowed from the tinkers and a blanket wrapped around the two of them against the weather, she wandered barefoot on the streets of the merchant city shaking her little box in people's faces and saying "Somethin' for the baby's breakfast, sor? God bless you, sor" until the dark of every evening sent her back to the caravan camp on the edge of town. A tall square-headed police officer, who led her down behind Spanish Arch on the pretext that he was taking her in to the station, knocked out two of her teeth when she indicated a reluctance to lie down by the river bank and throw her skirt up over her head for him. With the gaps in her mouth bleeding and her arm nearly wrenched from its socket, she was persuaded to show considerably less reluctance and even to feign enjoyment. She was so surprised at the ease with which she could bestow such pleasure, in fact, and so impressed with the kind of gratitude it seemed to create, that within a few weeks she was throwing her skirt up over her head for the entire police force of Galway, and might have gone on doing so for a good many years afterward, if the original officer hadn't misunderstood the nature of her generosity and knocked out all that were left of her teeth.

Fortunately, she had just enough sense left in her head to see that this was no place for the likes of her. A girl from the country could get herself killed having too much to do with uniforms. What she needed was a place with less law to protect herself from, she announced, and handed the tinker baby back to its parents before she set off on the road, heading south. She didn't know where she came from, she didn't know where she was going, but by the time she got as far as Limerick she knew she was in trouble: the sores in her mouth had begun to swell up and fester painfully, and she was continually having to spit on the road in order to avoid swallowing the pus. An old Limerick woman with a pointed face half-hidden beneath a thick black shawl found the girl beating her head against the stones of a fence at the side of the road, brought her home to her cottage, and put her to bed in the cow shed behind. But this old woman, whose name was Grania Flynn, was a noscy sort of a woman. For the rest of her life she would insist that she went out to the shed in the night to check on the girl and found her mounted by a monstrous black bull with eyes that shone like red lanterns and a scrotum that hung like a sack of turnips. In the morning there was no trace of the bull at all and of course the girl had no memory of her extraordinary experience, but old lady Flynn said a decent woman couldn't have that kind of thing going on in her shed every night of the week, and sent the girl on her way. The next night, however, the child who had been conceived in that cow-shed mating appeared in the shape of a burning eye and told the old lady that the only reason she'd been allowed to live to such an unbelievable age, an ugly deformed old hag like her, was that she was destined to nurse-maid a god. So the old woman, who never questioned a dream, set off with her walking stick and her long black shawl to follow the girl down the winding road to wherever it was she was heading.

Keneally's mother, it is said, had forgotten not only her own name, and the name of her village, and the episode with the bull, she had already forgotten the old woman who had taken her in for the night, so she was not at all disturbed that the whole way down the road to the city of Cork, and then down the pink country road to the town of Bantry, and around the rugged head of Bantry Bay, she was followed by a bent-over limping black figure whose grey hair, in that time, grew at an alarming rate down to her waist and to her knees and eventually to her ankles like a bridal veil. They slept under the hedges, a hundred yards apart, or in gaps in the high wall of shrub that lined the road; they begged, separately, at the open doors of the cottagers who couldn't afford to give away anything at all but fed them anyway, so they could tell their neighbours without shame of the girl with the swollen red face and the long-haired old woman who'd come to the door, a few minutes apart, and threatened identical forms of damnation to anyone who refused.

At the tiny village of Kealkill, a few miles inland from the head of the bay, when the labour pains began like knife stabs in her belly, the girl left people behind and headed up towards the nearest mountain. She went up the steep hill behind the village, followed the road up, up, past field and farm, up between hedges of fuchsias that dropped their red blossoms at her feet, up, steeply up (whimpering now in her torment) past trees and stones all the long way to the top where the world levelled out at last to green boggy plateau and the wind came howling across in a cold steady blast that threatened to lift her right off the face of the earth. She paused a moment, just long enough to fix the four lonely directions in her eye, and set out with squelching steps across the ground towards the falling sun.

At the very edge of the hill, within a shredded circle of low scraggy furze and stunted, nearly leafless twigs of sally, the neolithic stones were grey and rainy-wet and silent in the grass where hands had set them unknown thousands of years before: two tall rough mottled slabs broader than doors standing up to twice the height of men, broadside to the sunset and casting shadows like two parallel and nearly endless spirit roads laid out across the green plateau. Beneath them lay an oval bed of small white rocks where prehistoric cooking fires had burned, or vigil flames to keep the spirits at a distance; and twenty feet to the left, a tight muddy circle of squat square-cornered boulders the size of altars, where ancient men had come to pray or offer up their sacrifices to whatever gods they spoke to in the sky.

She stood crouched over in the centre of the circle as if mesmerized, shivering from the steady cold of the wind, and between waves of pain looked panting out across the deep narrow valley she'd just left: the silver inlets of the bay to the south, the mountains on her right folded harsh and rolling into one another, fading green into blue and out of blue into hazy sky, and directly ahead the cold light of the sunken sun slicing in white rays through layers of cloud and mist and blinding her to all the wide dark space of farm-patched hillside opposite. When the final sudden urge drove her to her knees she released a scream that could be heard as far away as County Clare, a long and terrible sound that forced even the old woman who was struggling up the mountain road to fall to the ground and cover her ears in order not to be deafened. It was a scream, she told people later, that dropped rabbits dead in their tracks and tore blooms off all the fuchsias so that you'd think the road had become a river of blood.

"There'll be no good come from this day," the old woman said, and tried to stand up. But a sudden shifting of the earth, like a rug pulled out from under her, dropped her to her knees again. Deep below her, stones ground against stones, gas bubbled and ran shuddering, the bowels of earth shifted and settled. A great noise went slapping off from cloud to cloud above her, and wind howled down the slope like keening spirits. Grania Flynn's bladder, most unreliable of all her ancient organs, spilled a sudden flood of scalding urine down her legs.

But it would take more than dancing earth and stinking bloomers to keep her from reaching the top of that hill. She crawled. Rocks and bony knees dug at each other. When she finally arrived at the giant stones, however, there was no sign of the girl. Apparently the earth had opened up to swallow her. Lips of soil were closing together to form a narrow crease across the circle of stones. Mouth of earth or whatever, it had just disgorged a child.

And such a child, she thought. Or was it a child at all? Blood-smeared from his birth-struggle, he sat up like a little old man, with a face that was purple with rage, and glared at her out of eyes that had clearly taken in all he could see of the world and had already decided to condemn it. He opened his toothless mouth to protest, or cry out his victory. This is all impossible, said the old woman to herself, but as her whole lifetime had been a series of impossibilities from the beginning, she merely stooped to pick him up and hold him to the dry warmth of her withered dugs. That was when she noticed he had on him the enormous scrotum of an adult bull.

"God save us all!" she gasped, and nearly dropped him. For she couldn't help but think that the kindest thing might be to bash his brains out now against the ancient stones. And years later, when she was being buried alive in a bog by that same child grown to man, she would curse herself for not following the impulse. Hundreds of years from now, perhaps, when some turf-cutter drives his slean into the peat in that desolate valley he will find the old woman's body perfectly preserved and completely wrapped in the hair which had grown during her journey south, her face no doubt still registering her dismay.

She carried the ugly child in her arms down the steep mountain boreen to the village, where she stopped just long enough to steal a shirt off a laurel bush where it had been hung out to dry, and to wrap the shirt around the child in order to hide its deformity. Normal babies were offensive enough; abnormal ones were frightening. Then she went on down the valley to the bay, where the stink of rotting seaweed made her nostrils flare and tears spring stinging to her eyes. It was her intention to head home to Limerick and escape this salty place, though she dreaded having to face the other women on the street when they discovered what she'd inherited. But, curled up to sleep behind a tall stone in the Bantry cemetery, she dreamed that the dead girl told her not to go home at all, but to take a certain road south down a rocky peninsula until she came to a village called Carrigdhoun where a man without hands or legs was expecting them. Grania Flynn awoke to a terrible morning, with rain slashing at her like scythes and wind threatening to rip the baby right out of her arms, but she set out with her blackthorn stick and her new ward in the direction she'd been given and did not stop to eat or speak the whole way down through mountains and valleys and barren heaths to the appointed village. "If I live to see this child a man," she told herself, "I'll be one hundred and twenty years old or maybe more." She couldn't help but wonder why some younger soul hadn't been chosen for all this chasing around the countryside.

Her armless legless man was Jerry Quirke, who waited for them on his donkey cart out on the narrow road. He'd been a teacher for a few short years in his youth and a travelling singer after that, and a farmhand, a baker, and an amateur magician as well, and now that he was unable to follow any of these careers because of an unexpected encounter with an English landlord in the bedroom of the English landlord's mistress, he spent his days on that cart, in the middle of the village road, entertaining any children who happened by and working a magic trick or two for any gentleman who brought a pint of porter out from Moriarty's Bar. A nephew carried him out to the cart every morning and carried him back in at night to his tiny stone cottage where he slept in the main room by the open turf fire, wrapped up in a quilt like a round lumpy sack of belongings someone might throw over his shoulder to go on a journey. He'd learned long ago that things like arms and legs were only machines to make life simpler for a man and that anything worth while could be done without them, by voice or vision or the concentrated exercise of will. Boys years before, it was claimed, had often tipped him over onto his back so that they could have the fun of watching him try to get upright again, but that all stopped when he made fat pink worms come crawling out of one boy's ears and told another that he would live exactly one minute after doing such a thing again. "Never mistake him for a fool or a toy," people warned their children, "for he could turn your tongue into a lizard that would crawl backwards down your throat until it choked you dead." His family, like every other family in Carrigdhoun, went back beyond anyone's memory or record, and on fair days when all the farmers brought their cows and sheep and goats and vegetables in to the village centre to sell or trade or simply show them off, he was as important to it all as anyone else, set up like that in the centre of everything; he put on a show of magic tricks and ballad singing and poetry reciting that made the people wonder at their good fortune. "But ye needn't think I was put on earth to paint smiles on yer ugly gobs," he told them often. "There's another coming here one day that'll need my teaching, and when that happens the rest of ye can burn your feet on the doorstep of hell for all the attention ye'll be getting out of me." The smell of his breath, when he got himself all in an uproar like that, was enough to knock you flat. He suffered from stomach.

"We came," the old woman told him, when she stood facing him in the street "because we had no choice." She looked around at the village as if she'd just found herself at the bottom of a sewer ditch and was looking for a quick way out. Her eyelids beat the rhythm of her dismay.

But when Jerry Quirke learned that she intended to stay right where she was and help him raise the child, he precipitated a commotion unparalleled in all the long history of Carrigdhoun. He rolled around on his donkey cart, his face red as a radish, and sang out a list of curses that should have reduced her to a trembling twig of fear. He threatened to turn the stones into slobbering wolves and sic them on her. He called the villagers around him and told them to stone the witch to death before she gave their unborn children the snouts of pigs and the fins of salmon, but they went back to their own business without picking up a single rock and only laughed at the spectacle he was making of himself. He brought a thousand more curses down on her head in a voice that made the mountain shudder, and ordered his nephew to boil up a pot of water to toss the old hag in. But when he had exhausted himself and lay panting on his back, his poor upset stomach raising the old Cain inside him, she was calmly sitting on a chair in his dooryard, unperturbed by anything that had happened, watching him as if he were merely an interesting mechanical invention that was bound to run down sooner or later. The only words she used were the ones she had already spoken to him and repeated now: "We came because we had no choice."

His was a two-room cottage which the nephew kept whitewashed inside and out and she was given the tiny bedroom to sleep in, while Quirke and the nephew and the baby slept in the main room near the fire. There was very little in the room, only a wooden table and chairs standing on the bare stone floor, and a settle bench, a cupboard of dishes against one wall, and a heap of turf bricks at the end, ready to be added to the heap of embers. The old woman, whose breasts had been dry as fireside peat for seventy years, fed the child on milk from a goat that came inside the kitchen once a day. Like a young couple with a precious first child, they were eager to give him a name and fought over every villager's suggestion until someone came up with Donal, which they both liked for its sound.

But the dead girl pushed her way into a dream and said that like it or not the baby's name was to be Brendan Keneally: Brendan because like the saint he would reach America, and Keneally because she had got some of her memory back and remembered that Keneally was the name of the policeman she'd liked the best of them all in Galway. The exasperated old woman told the girl if she intended to make a nuisance of herself, telling them what to do every time they turned around, she might as well have stayed alive and done it all herself. Wisha, she said, they're better off when they're dead, it seems, they get to give all the orders and do none of the work at all. The mother promised to keep her nose out of it, however, and to invade only the baby's dreams from then on, so long as they did everything he told them to when he learned to talk.

The child talked, it seemed, almost immediately, and one of the first things he told them was that he intended to be called Donal despite his witless mother. He said from what he'd heard of St. Brendan there wasn't all that much to rave about, and from this day on no one was to pay any attention to the silly slut of a dead girl, no matter how often she disturbed his sleep or how much trouble she tried to cause. Jerry Quirke was so delighted at the kind of child he'd inherited that he nearly toppled over laughing and decided to invite the whole village to a party to show him off. They came in from all over the mountain to Quirke's place that Saturday night, ate and sang and danced on the road in front of his cottage and agreed afterwards that it was a better time they'd had than ever before, even better than Bridget Ryan's marriage to Liam the one-eye Burke or the wake they had for Padraic Murphy the oldest man to die in Carrigdhoun. For how often any more did you see Conal O'Sullivan at his age and disposition put down the half-door on the ground and dance on it so fierce and loud that the brood hen came out of her nest in the thatch to see what was going on in the world of men? And how often were you invited to a party where a child hardly more than a baby stood up in its sleeping box and told Molly O'Bryne if she didn't watch her step with the drink she took she'd be in the way of starting another fatherless baby before the night was out? And how many times in this life did you hear a child like that recite the whole of "The Cattle Raid of Cooley" from beginning to end in Irish and then proceed to explain to them all what it's true meaning was? He'd be nine feet tall like Finn MacCool, they said, and do miraculous things like Cuchulain and save his people like Brian Boru who drove the Vikings out. "Wisha!" Jerry Quirke hissed at them. "Be careful not to insult the lad with your poor comparisons! 'Tis certain when he's a man he'll be the master of them all, and they only a crowd of ancient weaklings!"

It seemed perfectly natural to them that the village of Carrigdhoun should produce a giant of a man after all, because in all its long history up to now it had produced nothing at all to boast of but a couple of accidental saints and Stuttering Paddy Kerr back in the seventeenth century, who could tell your whole future for you down to your great-grandchildren from the shape of your ears

if you had the patience to let him spit it out. They were a fine class
of failures altogether, they admitted, and it was all because since
the founding of the village there was never a man in it or in the
farms around it who knew the meaning of fear. It was like a disease
they'd all inherited from the founders, or a curse put over the
mountain by some ancient witch.

The absence of fear. It denied them any kind of success, of
course, because they had no fear of failure, and no one had
thought of any other reason yet for putting effort into his work. It
denied them the pleasure of stealing from each other or murder-
ing each other because they were not afraid of letting their
neighbour appear more prosperous than themselves and had no
fear at all of looking like a fool. They were denied, too, the delights
of drunkenness because unlike their countrymen they were afraid
of neither Englishmen nor the threat of hell, and so had never felt
the need to cultivate the habits of escape.

There was a beautiful stone church in the centre of the village,
of course, with a steeple tall enough to be seen for twenty miles,
but the priests had never had any success in getting people to
attend and had withdrawn long ago, sending in only the most
indifferent clerics who'd become an embarrassment somewhere
else and needed a place to retire. The last one locked up the
church and did his preaching in the streets, in the homes, using
the Bible to prove that the way to heaven was through relaxation.
Since God had created them in His own image, he said, why not let
Him do the worrying? Sit back and trust. And he sat back and
trusted while the entire population allowed itself to be converted
to Protestantism right under his nose, content in the certainty that
they would treat their new religion with as much indifference as
they had their old. The Dear knows it will not make one bit of
difference at all, he said, sucking at his pipe. And indeed he was
perfectly right; while he sat back and trusted in salvation through
relaxation he saw the walls of the new Protestant church abandoned before they reached the top of the windows, and eventually assisted every man woman and child of the village in a private
return to at least the formalities and rituals of their previous faith.
Not that they mean a thing to a one of them, he shrugged, but it's
always wiser to play it safe. Each successive invader — the Viking
raiders, the Norman soldiers, the Spanish merchants, the English
landlords — learned early enough there was little point in trying

to stir up trouble in Carrigdhoun, and were content to let a few of their men wander in and marry someone and stay to add a drop or two of foreign blood to all that had come before. Officials from Dublin or Cork, passing through, told them they could hardly call themselves Irishmen when they kept themselves so isolated from the business of the country, but the villagers only laughed. "Sure the rest of them are as Irish as we are," they said, "and when the last foreign conqueror has gone back home to where he belongs you'll find they were only pretending all the while and underneath we're all the same!"

As the child Keneally had been conceived and born in the outside world, the villagers watched him anxiously in the first few years of his life for some evidence that he shared their affliction, this fearlessness, and were delighted to discover that he had it worse than the whole lot of them together. The O'Sullivan family reported that they'd seen him, at the age of three, marching across their bottom field where their meanest bull was kept out of the way of mischief, to give the snorting beast a crack across his nose. And Moriarty in his bar reported less than a year later that he'd seen the boy give Jerry Quirke a good kick that set him rolling on his back. "Oh he's a bold child, that one," they all agreed. Old Grania Flynn said if she'd known he was going to become such a holy terror she'd have drowned him at his birth, and threatened daily to go back to Limerick. "Leave us so!" Quirke shouted at her. "Couldn't we do just fine without ye?"

But she stayed on, sleeping in the damp bedroom and cooking meals of potatoes and limp cabbage and pig's trotters. She hadn't even suspected such places existed on God's earth, she said. Where she came from there were fine green farms with fields of hay, and low rolling hills, but here there was nothing but a mountain strewn with stones, where a cow would starve to death if it weren't willing to wander for miles after a decent mouthful, or climb the tops of fences to crop the weeds. And the mist, too, was enough to drive her mad, creeping down the mountain every day and filling the air around them so that she didn't know if she was still on the earth or living in the sky. "The men who founded Carrigdhoun were a pack of idiots," she said, "and gave birth to an idiot pack of offspring too stupid to get out." Not only that, she said, but the white mist had soaked their brains like pieces of bread dropped in water. And the greatest fool of all, she was forced to admit, was an old hag of a woman who came from the outside and stayed for the sake of a devilish brat when she could have gone home any time she wished. But she stayed because she suspected that at her age she was still alive only on sufferance, that if she gave up the only job that was expected of her she'd be dead before she got as far as Cork. She forced the priest to open the church and to say mass every morning for her and to pray for her soul and for the soul of Donal Keneally if he had one, but the old priest had by this time got so far away from his original training that he could only do a half-hearted job of it, and she was sure it was all quite useless. But she kept him at it, anyway, so he wouldn't think she was someone you could ignore like an old toothless dog.

While the old woman looked after the boy's stomach and at least attempted to care for his soul, Jerry Quirke was busy providing him with his education. "I don't know why it is I bother," he said, "for there's nothing you can do with an education in this village except sit on it like a sore boil on the arse. But 'tis a fact there's something in me wants to share what I found out for myself and maybe a teacher is always a teacher, as they say. Besides it is a fact that the boy needs me." Perhaps he was fooling himself, perhaps he wasn't, but the boy was the easiest pupil he'd ever taught. All that was necessary in order for him to learn to read was to be shown the alphabet, and have a few words read aloud to give him the general idea. Within a few months he'd read through all of Quirke's small library of books and sent out for more. All the principles of mathematics and geometry and economics were mastered in a single afternoon of mending a fence that had fallen down at the rear of O'Sullivan's lower field. Quirke went along and sat on his cart while the boy helped O'Sullivan lift rocks up off the grass and put them back in the broken wall. "Look up along the moor there, Donal," Quirke said. "Now count those rocks." Within minutes the boy had discovered the concept of infinity. Within hours he'd learned how to add stones together into fences, subtract them from the fields, divide them among the farmers, and multiply them with a hammer. He went on, then, to learn about shapes and sizes and angles and strength from them, and finally even discovered how to turn them to a profit, though this part of the lesson was the least successful of all and tended to be highly theoretical. Digging peat in the bog, he learned all he

needed to know about geography: that even nature's most ludi-
crous accidents could be valuable to man if he treats them with
respect. And in the evenings he sat in his sleeping box in the warm
glow of the little heap of burning turf while Quirke on the settle
showed him — with the nephew's help — how to find rabbits in
your back pocket and make coats look as if they can go for a walk
all by themselves and cause stones to bleat like sheep.

When people stopped by the cabin to compliment Quirke on
the progress of his student, his face coloured up with pleasure
and he said, "A good teacher tries not to hinder his student's
education" and looked modest about it all, but the fact was that
he was confused. The boy had in what seemed like no time at all
gone on learning far past anything that Quirke could have taught,
and this gnawed at the teacher-soul in him which liked to see
students rising up from below but hated to see them soaring off
above. When he asked the boy where he was learning all these
things his only answer was "Ideas are in the air", and "Knowledge
just is, it doesn't have to be dug out like potatoes", but this didn't
satisfy Quirke at all. If ideas were in the air and so easy to pick up,
why hadn't he become the smartest man in Ireland long ago and
been invited up to teach in the Dublin university?

While Quirke, who refused to be rendered useless, racked his
brains for new things to teach the boy, and the old woman prayed
for all their souls, Donal Keneally absorbed knowledge as if it
came down the mountain in the mist and clung to him like the
moisture to his hair. By the age of twelve he was able to tell
everyone in Moriarty's Bar of fifty different ways you could come
at a word like "truth" and arrive at a separate meaning every time.
On his thirteenth birthday he invited the whole village into the
square and delivered a lecture on astronomy which was so clear
and direct that everyone went home certain he'd understood it all
and yet so profoundly complex that they wondered if they'd been
hit on the head with a boulder. On another occasion he hyp-
notized them all into believing they were a herd of cows and sent
them mooing down the road tossing their heads at flies, but when
they came back an hour later to the square expecting to be milked
Quirke told him he'd gone too far and ought to be beaten like a
dog. Through some act of magic even Quirke had never heard of,
the boy caused a whip to materialize in the air and gave each of
them one good crack with it, including Quirke and the old woman,

before making it disappear. The villagers said that though they had as healthy a respect for learning as anyone else in the world, there was a limit to how much knowledge was good for you and Keneally had just passed it. They asked the old woman if she hadn't made a mistake about her dream in the cemetery, if the dead girl hadn't mentioned the name of a different village which only sounded like Carrigdhoun. They wanted to know if a man as clever as Quirke, who was so good at teaching people to be smarter and smarter, might know of a process of reverse teaching which could make a person stupider. But Quirke had to admit that contrary to all the evidence being turned out by the schools of the country, and of the world, there was no proof that such a process existed and they would just have to get used to having a genius around.

"Bad luck to your genius!" said Con O'Sullivan. "For in some matters he's as ignorant as the next man and twice as dangerous. This minute he's up back of my farm showin' off for my second daughter Nora!"

"And what way is he showing off to your second daughter Nora, Con O'Sullivan?"

"By lifting my milk cows one by one and putting them across the wall to the next field."

"And what is it you're afraid of losing, Con O'Sullivan, your second daughter Nora or a day's milk gone sour?"

Conal O'Sullivan said that like everyone on this mountain he was afraid of nothing at all, but he had a hard feeling inside of him that they'd all some day regret they hadn't wrung the boy's neck for him when he was too small to know the difference.

But it wasn't only Nora he was after, Quirke explained. The boy was chasing every girl who caught his eye, teasing them into distraction with his promises, insulting and delighting them with his outrageous demands, tempting and amazing them with his display of unequalled equipment and unparalleled performance. There wasn't a daughter on the mountain who'd not been approached at least. He'd devoted a whole month of his life exclusively to the pursuit of the unwilling Kitty O'Mahony, a pretty black-haired girl who lived near the top of the hill by Carriganass Stream, stalking and ambushing her until the poor girl, confused and desperate from the need for constant vigilance, lost her wits completely and was sent off to an asylum in the Midlands so that she wouldn't do herself any damage, and her family would be spared the need to see her in the corner every day, blubbering and drooling and playing with herself. There were farmers, too, who claimed that their sheep and donkeys were no safer than their daughters. But that was only a small part, Quirke said, of the enormous appetites which were working to build him up to a giant of a man. Didn't he drink poteen to the equal of any four men on the mountain and not feel the effect of it at all? And hadn't he broken an arm or a leg of every other boy in the place, not out of any meanness but only out of a love for the sports of wrestling and tumbling about? And wouldn't old Grania Flynn be the first to tell you he put inside him every day enough food to keep ten men alive and only asked for more? Potatoes and cabbage went down that throat as if there was a roaring fire below that had to be kept supplied.

"I would not begrudge him his share of food," the old woman said, "or, God knows, ten times his share if he were only willing now and then to spend some of that energy on the growing of it."

"This is no ordinary boy," Quirke said, who never left a thought unspoken no matter how obvious it might be. "Yerra, this is a boy apart."

In his eagerness to remain of some use as a teacher and at the same time give the boy something else to do besides glut his appetites, Quirke dug far back into his past and dredged up all he could recall of hypnotism and illusion-making from his days as a travelling magician. He discovered soon enough that it was a terrible mistake, for Keneally with his usual capacity for not only learning all there was to teach, but also going on from there to every possible logical extreme, immediately turned himself into a pair of twins. Quirke was never able to discover how it was done, though he understood it had something to do with disturbing the sense of time in every person in Carrigdhoun. Thus one of the twins, a rather docile lunk of a boy who insisted on being called Brendan, was home nearly the whole time endearing himself to Grania Flynn by carrying out her every wish. He worked long hours in the bog, bringing home creel after creel of turf on the donkey's back to store it in the shed. He milked the goat every morning before untying it and leading it out of the house. He mended fences where the stones had been knocked down, and brought fish from the stream, and took such good care of the garden that he went regularly with Quirke's cart all the way to the sea for a load of seaweed to manure the ground. When he stripped all the thatch off the roof and replaced it with new, he did it so gently and so well that the hens who nested in it hardly noticed the difference. Unwilling to let the old woman be the only one to benefit from his good nature, Brendan Keneally could be seen in his evenings helping the widow Donahue bring in her turf and helping Con O'Sullivan nurse his ailing cattle and helping Moriarty serve the drinks in his bar. He was such a fine lovely boy, they said, that they could see now that the whole history of Carrigdhoun had been nothing more than a waiting for his arrival. If there was one of him in every village of the country the life of an Irishman would be a much easier thing for sure. Brendan Keneally blushed at the praise, and ducked his great head with its big red ears, and told himself he was a fine lad altogether.

At the same moment, of course, his twin brother Donal was tearing the skirt off Brigid Moriarty behind her father's house or lifting O'Sullivan's cows across the fence to O'Mahony's bull or taking the whip to a passing stranger who had no money he wanted to spend on Keneally's enormous thirst. Once, in a blind and roaring rage at a Kerryman who refused to give him a florin for crossing the bridge over the stream, he pulled down the bridge stone by stone and rebuilt it higher up the hill where it was no use to anyone at all. It was left to his brother Brendan, the only one who equalled his strength, to move the bridge back where it belonged.

The villagers became so angry at the boy's nonsense that instead of complaining to Quirke as they had done in the past they came in a group to Brendan, and tried to persuade him that for the good of the whole mountain he should strangle his brother in his sleep, or at the very least persuade him to move away. Poor Quirke, alarmed by the success of the illusion, told them it had been nothing but a magician's trick from the beginning, but they refused to believe him. Perhaps that was the way it had begun, they said, but widow Donahue had seen the two of them talking by the bridge in the light of noon and everyone knew she had the best pair of eyes in the village since Padraic Ceillaigh in the twelfth century who had seen people walking on the moon naked as Adam. Quirke, who never before had reason to suspect his own sanity, could only tell them weakly that perhaps the day would come when they'd be glad enough to have the roaring twin as well as the docile, and maybe they would thank old Quirke for having the sense to bring up the two where another man would have been satisfied to bring up only the one. But he was no more convinced of it than the rest of them, and entered a period of decline in health so serious that even Grania Flynn found it in her heart to be kind to him once in a while, and the nephew began to panic at the thought of his own useless future if the limbless man should die. Quirke seldom left the settle now, and spent his time staring into space and searching himself for an explanation of the world-gone-mad, and he refused to speak to either Brendan or Donal Keneally until they came to him together, and standing side by side asked what they could do to help. They could both drop dead, he said. But Grania Flynn, whose view of life had improved considerably since the sudden appearance of the helpful twin, told Quirke to shut his gob or she'd dispatch him to a workhouse somewhere to rot with the rest of the poor and useless. There was no real harm in the lively one, she said, and a lot of good in the other.

When the twins had grown to their full height, which was considerably less than the height of the great Finn MacCool though tall enough and hefty enough for any man to be, and had reached an age where some of their contemporaries had settled down to married life with the girls who were long exhausted from either fleeing or submitting to Donal Keneally's pursuit, they considered throwing the whole mountain into confusion by multiplying even further into four or eight. They would become a whole army, Donal said, and toss the English back across the water to their own and proper island; but Brendan told him not to forget one half of them would be pacifists like him and not much use in any battle. "'The devil break your neck for saying so!'" said Donal Keneally, and gave his brother such a hefty clout across the side of his head that the spell was broken immediately and there was only one of them after all, a furious lout of a lad with a burning sore ear for a souvenir.

This was the time of the Land League. The villagers, like the rest of the country, had been hearing a good deal of talk about the man Charles Stewart Parnell and his plans, and of his friend Mr. Michael Davitt, and now they began to hear rumours of their latest scheme. Tenant farmers all over the country were joining together to refuse rent payments to any landlord who would not lower his rent; and they were punishing any family that dared to replace an evicted farmer by refusing to have anything at all to do with them. The farmers on the mountain around Carrigdhoun had poor land and a poor existence, and the man named Robert Horgan was a decent enough landlord, but the rent was high all the same, and they thought that if this was the way the world was headed they may as well go along with it. The next time a bailiff arrived to collect the rent, they sent him home again with a statement of exactly how much they were willing to pay. The world, they said, was changing.

What they had not stopped to consider was the nature of this particular bailiff, who was not much interested in what was happening all over the country and had no respect at all for the inevitability of history. It is unlikely that he even reported the farmers' absurd demands to Robert Horgan. He simply returned the following day with a gun and a pair of snarling dogs, and told them any man who refused to pay the demanded rent would be camped on the bog by sundown or floating face down on the stream. The farmers, faced with the guns and the dogs, agreed that if there was any good at all in this new scheme of the politicians it would eventually be made into a universal law they could benefit from without having to become martyrs in the meantime, and cursed themselves for having forgotten the generosity of their own particular landlord. If the world was changing anyway, they said, they could wait until the change had been completed.

But Donal Keneally, who was never very far away whenever a crowd had gathered, stepped up to the bailiff and told him they would deal with the landlord directly, please, and to send him along tomorrow to collect exactly the amount of rent the farmers had agreed upon. The enraged bailiff released the dogs, which, snarling and slobbering, leapt together for the throat. Keneally plunged both hands down into open jaws and ripped out the canine tongues. Then he snapped the necks of both dogs, as if they were little more than hens, and tossed their bodies in Carriganass Stream. The bailiff, who seemed to have forgotten he'd brought a rifle with him, swung his horse around and galloped down the mountain in the direction of Robert Horgan's estate.

The devil break your leg! the farmers shouted at Keneally. Was he mad or only simple-witted, for now he'd be bringing the wrath of the whole British Empire down on their heads and causing them no end of trouble. "It's a strong man surely that can tear out the tongues of beasts," said Con O'Sullivan, "but now it's an honourable man you must be as well, to take on yourself the blame for what you have done." The witch who had caused the disease of fearlessness to affect the people of the mountain, he said, had not cursed them with stupidity as well, and a good thing, too, or they'd all be dead and buried long before and there'd not be a village here at all for him to do his knavish growing in. It is to his credit perhaps that he did not laugh at their timidity, and it is certainly to his credit that he agreed to take on himself the whole responsibility for the angry bailiff, though there is some question that there was anything admirable in the way he released a sudden eruption of gas so potent that it knocked two men over and sent the rest scurrying for home and cover.

The bailiff was a man named Spindal, a tall hunched-over hairy sort of a man with pale burning eyes, and it was rumoured of him purely on the basis of his appearance that he had been raised in a cave by a mother whose family had withdrawn from the evolutionary chain five hundred thousand years before. Despite his background, or the rumours of his background which were so widely believed that he must have accepted them himself by now like someone acting out a role in a legend, he was a proud man and in no hurry to report his failure to the master. Nor was he likely to forgive the loss of his dogs. He set out in the dark of that night to the village of Carrigdhoun, armed with his gun and a pocket full of rocks, determined that when the morning came the big-eared brute who'd killed the dogs would be following their carcasses down the mountain stream to the lake below and perhaps all the way to the sea.

But Donal Brendan Keneally, who had read the legends himself and remembered them well, waited for him under the bridge, and leapt up to challenge his approach. The bailiff raised the gun to shoot, but before he could pull the trigger he found it ripped from his hands and flung off into the darkness. "Bastard traitor!" Keneally shouted, and grabbed the bailiff by the throat. What followed was a mighty battle which has been told and retold in every house on the mountain and down through the families to this day in many parts of the world, and with every telling it has gained a little more colour, a little more noise, a little more blood,

until you'd think Carrigdhoun was a battle ground for two clash-
ing armies that fought to the death for a year and half at the bridge
over Carriganass Stream.

The truth of it was simpler. Keneally drove the bailiff down onto
his back and began to choke the life out of him, but the bailiff
lifted a foot and kicked his attacker in his famous crotch, causing
him to let go of his hold on the throat. In a moment they were both
on their feet again, and the bailiff with his head tucked down
drove fist after fist into Keneally's belly, backing him down the
road past two or three farmhouses and the houses of the village.
Then Kencally, roaring, clamped both hands on the bailiff's
shoulders and lifted him into the air. He set him down on the top
of Widow Donahue's wall and twisted his arm until it came out of
its socket, crunching like a bone bitten through by a dog, and came
away from the body altogether. The loud howls of the bailiff woke
every sleeping person on the mountain and sent those who were
listening at their windows back to their beds to hide. But the
terrible cry was followed by another and another and another as
the hunched and dying bailiff staggered down across the mountain fields into the valley leaving a trail of blood behind him that
scorched the grass and melted stones. Cooled and hardened,
these stones formed a paved red trail from field to field the
women would use whenever they went out to gather furze. They
called it The Bailiff's Retreat and convinced the priest to bless it so
the dead man's ghost would never haunt them.

There was nothing more than that to the battle, for all the
boasting that's been done about it, and brave Keneally took his
countrymen's advice and hid for three days in Con O'Sullivan's
house while they waited to see what would happen next. He
discovered, quite by accident, that the hiding place which was the
safest and the most comfortable in Con O'Sullivan's house was
under the covers of Nora O'Sullivan's bed, where she clamped
herself around him like a lobster all night long and paid him
several visits in the day. At the end of three days, however, when
no word at all had come up the mountain from the landlord's
estate or from the police, the men of the village persuaded him for
the safety of them all to go away somewhere and let them pay their
rent as they'd always done before.

Keneally, for all his intelligence, did not know where to go.
Since his arrival as a baby he had never once left the mountain or

felt any desire to do so or had any real need to give serious thought to the outside world. So when he'd been escorted down off the mountain in the middle of the night by one hundred percent of the population of Carrigdhoun — all of them singing ancient songs with meaningless words and beating on pots and pans as if they were performing an exorcism — he had no idea whatsoever where to go or what to do. "Go anywhere you wish," the Widow Donahue cried, "only don't come back here." She had nine growing children and was glad to see the end of that imperfect model. Moriarty shouted, "Here the choice is simple. Go anywhere but north and you'll end up in the sea." He laughed and repeated himself to several of his neighbours, because of course it is a great relief to see the tail end of a wild child like that one, and it is even more of a relief to discover a sliver of stupidity in one whose cleverness has been a source of awe. Old Grania Flynn, who'd packed a bit of food for the boy to take with him, looked hard at the miserable face of Jerry Quirke, hunched down on his chest and scowling at the back end of his donkey as if answers could be found there that he'd never be able to find anywhere else, and then she hobbled forward to put a hand on the arm of the creature she had raised. If he were to have any life ahead of him at all, she whispered, it would be a necessary thing for him to go back and start again at the beginning.

When Keneally had crossed the bog alone, his feet squeaking on the soggy ground, he looked back and saw the silent villagers as motionless and dark as a cluster of trees at the foot of the hill, and above them in the village and all along the mountain road not a light was burning in any home that he might use as a memory-hook when thoughts of home would be needed in a strange and foreign place.

He found a road that appeared to be heading north and followed along until it suddenly veered off to the east and twisted in and out of farms, then he cut across fields and bog until he found another road, but it took him higher and higher into a mountain until he was completely surrounded in mist and could see nothing at all but the one foot at a time in front of him. At the very peak of the hill the road suddenly ended and it was necessary for him to find his own way down the other side — sliding down steep slopes, climbing hedges, passing through herds of sleeping sheep, wading through streams — until he arrived at a sudden drop to the sea and had to follow the edge of the headland north. Travelling at night in what seemed like random directions and sleeping in the daytime in the hedgerows, he worked his way through moors and valleys and villages and towns all the way up to the mountain which had been the place of his birth. Waking that evening in a pile of ruins at the edge of the village, he saw the tallest stone high up at the summit reflecting the last light of the sun among the shadows and followed the same narrow road up the slope which his mother had taken years before with the old woman behind her. Like his mother, too, he walked across the spongy plateau at the top, stepped through the row of wind-ravaged brush that encircled the sacred spot and stood in the centre of the circle of giant stones, the muddy intersection of two sloppy cow trails that crossed the grass. All the valley was there below him, from the mountains in the north to the bay in the south, and the last light of the sinking sun came, it seemed, in harsh level slices and horizontal bands through the lower clouds. At his back, a cold wind began suddenly, a steady force that bent the bushes down and howled around the grey and heavy stones. When he looked behind, a herd of black cattle had moved in and stood looking at him from just beyond the circle of trees. The bull lowered his head and shook his horns, bawling menacingly. Suddenly and inexplicably terrified, he turned again and felt as if he were about to fall from the peak, or be blown away by the wind. He stepped to the glowing side of the tallest upright slab, where the wind was broken, and discovered that not only the light of the sun but the whole day's heat was preserved in it as well. Touching it, running his hands over its rippled worn surface, he could have believed the secrets of centuries were absorbed in the stone, to be unlocked if only he knew how it were done. Fear, this new thing in him, ran like water in wave after wave down his chest and sent icy streams out his arms. It cramped in a sudden fist in his stomach and hammered him down onto his knees. Then a blow to the back of his head pushed his face into the wet ground. He saw deep, deep into the darkness of the earth and some time in the course of that long night he heard the soft voice of his mother laying out for him the direction of his life like a complicated map of roads. In the morning when he awoke it was a day of driving rain, and his clothes lay in shreds on the ground around the base of the stone. The herd of cows had gone, except for the bull, who stood just outside the circle and watched him until he had walked to the edge of the hill and started down.

When the people of the village below laughed at his reported revelation and finally chased him out of their midst, he found the nearest estate, with its miles and miles of high wall and its iron gates, and, dressed in clothing stolen out of housewives' yards along the road, charmed his way to the old master himself who sat on a chestnut gelding ready to set off across his fields on a round of good-will inspections. But the mounted landowner only laughed at Keneally's crazy scheme and told him to leave. Keneally left, but not until he'd spent the night explaining his grand plans in whispers under the sheets to the youngest helper of the cook, a red-faced Kerry girl named Eileen, and not until he'd filled the pockets of his rags with enough money to buy him a new suit of clothes and passage to North America. The girl Eileen, more red-faced than ever and speechless as well, received a good flogging when the missing money was noticed, and was sent home to her people in Killarney, where she was to spend the rest of her life trying to struggle back out of the cloudy dream world of her night with Donal Keneally. The master, who was a kind enough man normally and had been caught at a moment when he was worrying about the stomach pains which would kill him, made reference to the ragged thief at least four times in the remaining month of his life, and marvelled every time at how similar the young man's dream had been to his own as a youth when his uncle had died and left him this enormous property. His widow, who shared none of his confidences and knew nothing of the incident beyond the grumblings of a cook who must find a new helper, was only a little interested and mildly puzzled when a sum of money was delivered to her door twenty-three years later with a short note signed *The Revelations Colony of Truth*.

Keneally, however, did not give a passing thought to the gentleman on horseback or to the Kerry girl with the ruddy face and eager limbs or to the landowner's wife whom he hadn't seen, for while in his wake they were sorting out their destinies he was sailing by steam from the port of Queenstown to the city of Halifax in North America. If he were to be Moses and saviour to this nation soon, it was necessary first that he find the Promised Land his mother had told him about on the mountain top. For three years he worked as a hired hand in a western Nova Scotia apple orchard and in all that time did nothing notable at all except the work he was paid to do. He moved on to Toronto for a while, working on the docks, and then caught the newly-completed railway west. But there was nothing he saw out of any window that reminded him of home and there was no sign at all to show him that he'd arrived at the place that he was looking for. He strained eagerly at the window day after day, for over the next hill, around the next corner, there may be the sign his mother's voice had promised. But he stayed on the train all the way to its end and got off in the harbour noise of Burrard Inlet. There was a city being built here, of some sort. "Is that all?" he asked the conductor as he stepped down off the train.

"It is." The conductor was a Dubliner by birth, and had taken a special interest in Keneally.

"And that water I'm seeing here is the Pacific Ocean itself?"

"It is."

"Devil me arse, then there's no more to the country than I've seen?"

"There is not," the conductor said, and turned away. But he came back and pulled at Keneally's sleeve. "There is no more to the country than you've seen, young man, except a long strip of an island out there about thirty miles."

When Keneally learned from the conductor that the island was nearly the size of Ireland, he caught the earliest ship across the strait, eager to see the rolling hills and green fields which would remind him of his home. But he saw soon enough that the mountains were higher and harsher than he'd hoped, and that there were no rolling green fields at all, only miles and miles of tall thick forest. The heart sank in him. But while he stood on the ship's forward deck, watching the island grow larger as they approached, he heard his mother's voice again, and knew that he'd arrived. He stepped off the boat in the centre of the little town, and said to the first person he saw, "My name is Donal Brendan Keneally."

But the townsman was a Chinese who had only recently arrived from Hong Kong and didn't know the language. He sang out an alarmed string of sounds and hurried away. Keneally, who had been warned on the boat that the town was made up almost entirely of Englishmen, marvelled at the length to which the bastards would go, in dress and language and even in appearance, in order to assume mastery over a foreign land. When he saw an Indian, however, leaning over the railing of a sea-edge boardwalk, he knew exactly what he was looking at, for the books of Quirke's library had included one or two in which there were pictures of redskins biting the dust. He walked over and stuck out his hand and said, "Thon amon dieul! If that is the manner of Englishman you're after suffering 'tis no great wonder at all that you cut off the scalps when you can and eat the flesh of their babes." But the Indian, who was a fisherman from a nearby tribe, only shrugged. He was lost in his daily contemplation of the uncontrolled chain of disasters his chief had precipitated upon himself and upon his tribe and upon this whole part of the island when he'd taken a walk along this beach in the days of the trading post and noticed a chunk of a black shiny rock the whiteman called coal. Out of pity for his people and for his ageing chief, he spent a part of every day walking down to the beach and contemplating the terrible mistake.

The town, like other towns along the coast, had been a trading post of the Hudson's Bay and still had the little white bastion to prove it, just as it still had more beer parlours than churches to prove it was as tough as any other western town, and still had a wooden gallows sitting at the entrance to its harbour to prove it was a decent Christian community that loved justice. But the Indian chief had taken one walk too many along that beach and changed everything. A casual remark in a blacksmith's shop, where he'd seen the same black substance burning, though it had been shipped all the way around Cape Horn from England, ignited a spark of greed in a thousand hearts and launched a rush of immigration, a chaos of growth, a blaze of competition, and a mad tunnelling in every direction under the ground that made the countryside as precarious as a field riddled with groundhog burrows. It was to the chief's credit that some of the townsmen would go on to become wealthy politicians with castles in Victoria and offices in San Francisco, and it was equally to his credit that others in the town were able to spend a lifetime underground like moles and die of lung diseases and mine explosions without ever having to worry about a useless old age. Of course, the people of this busy town stopped their busyness as often as they could to think with gratitude of the Indian whose casual observation had put money in their pockets and ambition in their hearts. And so that all the world could see the extent of their regard they erected a huge lump of coal in the town square where other towns had statues or flower gardens; they named their most elegant hotel after him (though his people were to be barred from entering its doors for another fifty years); and they settled his tribe on an attractive reserve with a view of the harbour where they could be watched over with gentle concern and only a minimum amount of the necessary condescension. When Keneally arrived, the Indian chief, who had lived a long and satisfying life except for his one questionable deed, was within a few months of his death and this conscientious fisherman had taken it on himself to convince the One Spirit that the old man deserved the happy hunting ground as much as anyone, and needed it more than all of them put together. So he hardly noticed the crazy Irishman's arrival.

Despite his three-year stay in Nova Scotia and his time in To-ronto and the railway journey across the country, Keneally did not find it easy to get used to this frontier town. It was like no town or village or city he had ever seen. Instead of a quay or a pier, there were a number of wooden wharves stuck out into the water, some floating and tied to pilings, others up on posts with narrow rickety railings. The stores, of course, were built of wood, with fancy-work verandahs and high elaborate false fronts and outside benches for people to sit on when they felt the need of a rest. Most amazing of all was the cluster of buildings where the people with strange eyes and braids looked out at him from behind the win-dows, or ran from door to door in the oddest kind of clothes he'd ever seen. Sure, he'd found himself a fine sort of a place to start his colony in, he thought, surrounded by savages and moonmen and more bastard English than you'd find admitting it in the whole county of Cork. A place where the trees were as thick as the stones at home, and you'd break your neck before you'd find a herd of sheep on the hills, and where they told you there was no mist at all except sometimes in the month of November, if the weather was just exactly right for it.

But it was November when he arrived and on his second day there was rain. When a storekeeper said "Don't be surprised if it rains from now right through until May," he knew at last that he'd made no mistake, he'd found his land, and immediately got him-self a job in the mines so he could save enough money to put a down payment on the property he wanted and to pay for his passage home when he went to collect his followers.

Though he stayed only long enough to earn the necessary money, there were plenty of people on the island who had reason to talk about him, or think about him, or curse him, until he returned. It took Peter Krup eight years to find husbands for his five beautiful daughters because Keneally's regular Sunday visits to the Krup home had stirred the girls up so thoroughly they were content to risk the lives of old maids in order to wait on the slight chance he might make one of them his wife on his return. Gunnar Nelson, who had been a foreman in the mines until he was fired for lack of interest, became even more of a drunk than his father had been before him and spent all of his wife's school-teacher salary on beer in the Paradise Beer Parlour where he nearly ruined the business by insisting on telling every customer who stepped in the door the whole long story of the mine collapse. He had been trapped behind a wall of fallen stone with the air fast running out until Keneally the Irishman tore a hole through that debris with his bare hands from the other side and raised a collapsed ceiling beam up with his back long enough for Nelson to crawl out. Gladys Featherstonehaugh, the sallow hunchbacked sister of a mining company director who had brought her out from England for the sake of her health and his parents' sanity, sat on an ache so devastatingly painful that she knew if it ever diminished it would mean she was dead. Two years later when it began to fade she paid a fisherman to take her out to the little island across the harbour entrance, where she hanged herself on the public gallows. Her irrational behaviour and unfortunate death touched off a debate among the town officials concerning the gallows that lasted without any resolution until the structure collapsed under the weight of its age and the force of a heavy storm several years later, but not before the mayor delivered his famous farewell speech in which he condemned the town as a stinking snake-hole full of abnormalities, aberrations, deviations, abortions, miscreations, monstrosities, and monsters. The mayor, who was a lover of words, had not (as his speech clearly indicated to all his audience) been his old optimistic self since the visit of Keneally to his town, and he'd resigned his post in order to take an extended vacation with his family in California, where he hoped with the aid of a soothing sun to erase from his memory the image of a wild Irishman springing up surprised from the mayor's bed, roaring like a bull, and pulling the ceiling and two walls down on their heads before the mayor's poor alarmed wife had time to scramble back into her flannel nightgown. And he wanted to erase the image, too, of that same crazy Irishman the very next day coming down the main street of town, on both sides at the same time, wishing him a fine fine day out of two identical mouths moving simultaneously.

So violent and apparently unnatural was the final confrontation between Keneally and the mayor down at the wharves on the day of the ship's departure for San Fransciso that no townsman could ever be persuaded to tell of it. A prospector, down from the mountains a week afterwards, recorded in his diary that he found the town a complete shambles. When he walked down the length of the main street, which curved from a high crest of rock in a double-S down to the harbour docks, he thought there had been an earthquake, or a siege. An old-timer, he even wondered for a moment whether the Haidas had come south again for a new supply of slaves from the local tribe and somehow got themselves into a battle with the white people of the mining town. On the cobbled street the stinking bodies of dead dogfish lay amongst the dried green shreds of seaweed, the bloated bodies of cats hung draped over the front verandah railings, and ravens croaked from rooftops. The front windows of every beer parlour he passed were broken, the splinters of glass sprayed out across the street like glittering seeds. He was able to follow a trail of clothes from door to door down the slope, dresses and coats and shirts and boots. He could smell the high bitter stench of burning indignation. He heard a low menacing hiss that seemed to be coming from the buildings themselves, the ugly sound of a nursed grudge. Furniture lay broken and scattered; groceries lay spread out for the scrounging gulls. And all down the street the people, the survivors, sat out on their verandahs on wooden chairs and benches, silently watching him out of stunned expressionless faces. From person to person the prospector went, staring into the alarmed and dreaming eyes, grasping the rigid shoulders asking "What happened here? What happened?" and from person after person down that curved and cluttered street he received nothing more than the same unsatisfying answer, over and over: "Keneally." This of course explained nothing at all, he wrote in his diary, and by the time he'd reached the foot of the street and found himself looking out over a harbour strewn with the floating debris of splintered docks, the man in question had already departed, like his opponent, and begun his journey back to his home.

Keneally gave no thought to the mayor or the mayor's bony wife or to the insatiable Gladys Featherstonehaugh or to the five beautiful daughters of Peter Krup or to the shocked and damaged town he'd left behind. Once he'd put his foot back on Irish soil all his energies were channelled into his plans for gathering people willing to be his chattels for the opportunity to follow him into the Promised Land. In the city of Cork he stood at the foot of the brand new statue of Father Matthew the temperance preacher and, facing St. Patrick's Bridge and the River Lee, made his very first public speech. He promised to lead them out of this land of repression and poverty into a brand new land of opportunity, he promised the safety and security of a close-knit colony carefully protected by himself, he promised wealth and comfort and freedom from fear; but the people coming off the bridge or passing by on either side of the wide street of shops paid him no more attention than if he'd been an Arab selling sand. He rented the second floor of an old building down a side alley where for the five people who attended he put on a display of levitation, hypnotism, illusion, and preaching, intended to knock their eyes out, but which interested them only slightly and was forgotten immediately. "The English bastards have taken away your imaginations and your courage along with your freedom," he shouted at their departing backs. "Seven hundred years of robbery." But one of the five spectators was a deacon in the Church of Ireland who sent a policeman around to arrest Keneally and throw him in jail for attempting to disturb the complacency of the people of Cork. Keneally left the policeman wrapped up in forty yards of cotton from the storeroom and, deciding that the people who dwelt in cities had been dulled in their brains by such close living, he set off into the country to look for more appreciative converts.

"Converts to what?" a farmer in Mallow demanded. " 'Tis nothing at all you offer but the exchange of one madman master for another." By the time he reached Macroom he'd realized that he'd need to offer them more than a pale imitation of heaven if he wanted their attention. The priests had been offering them that for centuries, and they'd bought it long ago. What more had he to offer?

For a while in Kilorglin he thought he'd discovered what he had to offer. Dressed as a Turkish sultan he rode in to town on a grey ass on Gathering Day when people were arriving from all over the country for the famous yearly Puck Fair. In a bar he told the men that he and his harem had just arrived from his palace in Madagascar, but that a doltish country boy had turned his whole harem of thirty-six wives loose, and they were wandering freely now through the fair dressed as ordinary Irish lasses. When the wild puck goat was led through the street and crowned king of the fair and raised high onto his platform forty feet in the air, he told the men at his shoulders that before the fair was over he intended to steal that goat from right before everyone's eyes. In the middle of the night, drinking home-made whiskey in the back of a bar run by a skinny youth named Jems the Cripple, he confided to the men who'd gathered around that he'd only come to town to capture a few dozen more slaves and boost the number in his harem to seventy-three.

By the noon of the second day there was no doubt that every eye in the place was watching him: the farmers got no kind of price at all for their milk cows or for their sheep, for the buyers standing ankle deep in the yellow manure that covered the street could not keep their minds on the job; the parents of the small children who did reels and stepdances on the platform under the goat were unable to enjoy the delicious pride of parenthood for watching to see what the sultan was up to now; the bars did a poorer business than they had ever feared in their darkest dreams because as long as the sultan was outside in the square no one wanted to be inside drinking, and whenever he went inside they all wanted to be in the same bar as he was, or as close as possible. Like every other man, woman, and child in town Jems the Cripple knew that the sultan was the biggest liar they'd ever encountered, but that fact only increased their desire to find out why. When the sultan finally climbed up onto the platform beneath the goat, Jems the Cripple abandoned his bar and pushed himself through to the very front of the crowd.

Later, and for the rest of his life, Jems the Cripple was to tell how the man stood there with his feet planted wide apart, glaring out over their heads until everything was so quiet you could hear the River Laune flowing by at the foot of the street. When the three heifers tied to the door of MacMahon's Butcher Shop began to bawl, someone turned them loose and chased them out of town where they wouldn't be a disturbance. "If you think you are free to do whatever you please," the sultan told them, "if you think you are not slaves, you need only walk up to stand on this platform beside me to prove it and I will ride out of this town immediately." But no one moved. Jems the Cripple was to say later that they looked as if they'd been clouted between the eyes with a hurling stick. "Since you've agreed by your silence that you are slaves, slaves to history and to man and to yourselves, and that now you are slaves to me, I will show you the road to freedom." And without changing the expression on his face he rose off the platform, ascended slowly to the level of the goat, whose crown he removed to put on his own head, and descended again to the platform. No one moved. Out of this pocket and that pocket and out of his sleeves he pulled wheels and rods and cylinders and boxes until he had assembled before him a large complicated machine which he told them was God. The priests had probably told them that God was a fart-ridden cranky old man who looked down on them from the sky, he said, but the fact was that God was a machine which he carried around in his pocket. God was his slave too, just as all of them had become his slaves, and he would show them what he thought of God his slave. He aimed a good kick at the side of the machine and brought it crashing down in pieces to the platform. One wheel rolled across the boards and dropped off the edge into Jems the Cripple's hands, which immediately turned black and began to smoke, until the terrified little man tossed the wheel of God back onto the platform. Within seconds the sultan had put all the pieces back together and promised to show them proof that he had made God his slave. He put both hands on the top of the machine while he closed his eyes, then he raised the hands, smoking and black, high above his head. With his eyes still closed and his hands smoking like knots of pitch, he commanded the machine to suspend the law of gravity, and at once the people felt themselves floating in the air in front of him like pieces of weed in water. Then he commanded the machine to strike fear into the heart of the most guilty sinner in the crowd, and far far back a terrified cry went up and an old woman beating her fists on her head went wailing off across the bridge and disappeared down the road that led to Tralee.

For his last proof, he told them, he would command God to

destroy himself. The hands, still smoking, though nothing seemed to burn, cut arcs across the top of his head and then fell suddenly to his sides. The machine collapsed, fell apart in an ear-splitting clatter, and lay in pieces at his feet. "There is no God," he told them. "I've made God a machine, and now at my command he's destroyed himself and ceases to exist. I am all there is." Certainly at any other time these same people would have torn him apart for mouthing such things in public, but caught in his spell they only nodded vacantly and waited to hear what he said to them next. What he said, as he stuffed the pieces of his broken machine back into his pockets, was that he was prepared to lead them away from this place, to set up a civilization of their own where the fear of God would be a forgotten thing and living a satisfying life the only goal. He spoke on and on, while the crowd watched him pick up one piece at a time, polish it with his sash, and put it into his pocket or up his sleeve, and as he talked he painted a word-picture of an existence so ideal and glorious that they should have been falling over each other to promise him their undying loyalty.

But they did not. When he'd finished all he had to say and had released them from the spell of his voice and his powers, they only drifted silently away to their homes. The memory of that day was never mentioned by any of them to another and was not even passed on to the following generations, so that when the youngest child there, a Miss Kitty Daly, drowned in the tide at Rossbeigh as a lady of seventy-three in nineteen hundred and sixty-one, the final trace of the day's memory was completely erased. Only Jems the Cripple out of all that crowd, his hands still searing from the feel of God, stayed to pledge his support and follow the disappointed Keneally out of town on a cart, his bad leg coiled like a thick rope under him, his wide eyes burning with hope. When Keneally stopped a few miles down the river and waited for him to catch up, he promised to follow to the ends of the earth or to hell if necessary for just one glimpse of this Eden he was promising. And from that day on, in every village or town where Keneally preached, Jems the Cripple could be seen at the front edge of the crowd, his eyes bulging with eagerness to see the machine, his hands itching to touch its parts, his mouth drooling uncontrollably with the passion of his hope.

Now this great giant of a man, for all his magic and his promises and his God-in-my-pocket, could see by the manner of man he had attracted that there was something wrong with his delivery, and when the same performance in a dozen more villages brought not one additional person to his cause, he stopped at the town of Cahirciveen on the Iveragh Peninsula to examine the nature of his failure. In the narrow strip of town he found lodgings one block from the main street in the house of a certain lady named Mrs. Delaney whose men had fished the waters of Dingle Bay for centuries until the very last of them had been drowned at sea in a terrible storm. She had a two-storey house, one room wide, in a long row of identical houses slapped up against one another. Like them all she had one half-door open to the street most of the day, and one window covered by a piece of old and dirty lace, and a staircase to his bedroom that went up the side wall of her kitchen so the heat of her fire could warm both floors at once. Mrs. Delaney was a wide woman with a flushed face and three missing teeth. "Hee, hee," she said. "We got word of your coming from the people up the way, hee hee, but a wee bit of magickry and carrying on never put me off if the man himself is fine enough looking!" She told him the neighbours thought she'd dropped her wits over the pier when she agreed to take him in, but a great lot she cared what they thought or didn't think. For it was a sure thing there was none that wasn't jealous that old Meg Delaney had got the man with God in his pocket sleeping under her very roof. "Now if you'll only show me what it is you keep hidden in your trousers," she said, sliding one pudgy hand down his belly, "I'll know the face of God when I see him after this day sure." It wasn't the face of God he showed her, or anything else she'd hoped for, only the back side of him going out the door. He rode to the end of the meandering street of shops on a beautiful stallion left fortuitously unattended by Meg Delaney's neighbour, and then out across the flat land and along the bottom of a long green shelf of mountain-side, until he was stopped by a young woman who stepped out of the bog where men were cutting turf and stood facing him in the middle of the road.

"Is it Donal Brendan Keneally?" she said.

"It is."

"Do you travel alone?"

"I do, yes."

He did not, of course, because Jems the Cripple was never very far away, but the two of them scarcely spoke to each other and the cripple preferred to maintain a certain distance from which to worship the man he followed.

"And are you off to America still, as you're after promising the people?" she said. She had the bluest eyes, he saw, and there was a spark of liveliness in them that appealed to him.

"I am, for I've a piece of land there waiting for me now, and the will to go, but I'm wearied out from searching for the folk to share it with me."

" 'Tis a certain thing you're telling it to them wrong, then. For there isn't a cottage in Ireland that hasn't heard of Donal Keneally or talked of his deeds across the fire at night or given some thought to the idea of following him."

"Talk and thought won't take us there, and I'm near to saying farewell to the whole nation and going all alone."

"Not alone," she said. "For here's one that will go along, and has waited many a day to say it."

"Do you tell me so?"

"I do. And my name is Nell McGuire."

"Devil you say. And you're telling me true, that it's off to the island with me that you plan?"

" 'Tis, yes. I've a strong back and a keen wit and I'm not so willful that I'll not take orders from another. Lead the way, Donal Keneally, and I'll do your bidding. Say this and I'll this, say that and I'll that, and tell me to die and I'm dead."

Her mother had everything ready for her, she told him, and had kept the priest a prisoner in the house so he'd be close at hand when the moment came. Within twenty-four hours Donal Keneally was a married man, his general disappointment overshadowed by the strange new feelings that bloomed in him when he was with this Nell. Then together they travelled east, moving daily closer to the ship that would take them west, though not forgetting to plan a farewell visit to the village of Carrigdhoun.

When the villagers at Carrigdhoun heard of Keneally's approach, a mighty alarm went out and children hurried off in every direction along the mountain to spread the word. The legless-armless Jerry Quirke was brought out into the middle of the street where he sat on his cart and waited for Keneally to get close enough to be greeted by the words he'd said a thousand times over in his head: " 'Tis a long long time we're after waiting for ye, Donal Keneally, but ye've come at last and we're all packed and ready for the journey." But the shock of the promised land was more than old Quirke could endure, for he'd waited far too long and got himself much too excited; the words were barely out of his mouth when he keeled over onto his face, dead on the spot. It was left to the rest of the villagers and the countrymen to explain that they'd got word of his speeches, despite their isolation, and had voted right down to the last man of them to follow him to his far-off island. They could be ready to leave, they said, in a matter of a few hours if he wished.

Keneally, alarmed by the sudden shift in his fortune, told them they hadn't heard correctly what he'd been telling all those people in the other places, maybe they didn't know that the only people who could follow him were those who were willing to accept him as leader and devote all their energies to serving him. Daniel Doherty the blacksmith stepped forward from the gathering crowd in the road and told him they'd line up once a day, every man of them, and kiss his rear end if only he'd take them off this godforsaken mountain. Grania Flynn, the old black-shawled woman, held back, however, and watched the goings-on from her open doorway with a great frown on her face, for she was a hundred and thirty years old by now, at least, and unlikely to survive the crossing of the Atlantic, and she'd had another one of her well-timed dreams in which she'd been shown a mind-jolting vision of herself at the bottom of that boghole. She didn't know if there were bogs in the land where the boy was taking them, but she had a suspicion there were not, and that she'd never live to see the ship that took them there.

A fine lot of fools they were then, he told them all, if they thought he was a rich enough man to put them all on the boat at Queenstown. Was it a fortune they thought he was out collecting all these years on the road? But they assured him they'd have the money for the fare and plenty more besides, the night before they started on the trip, if he'd only tell them when. There was a terrible mean bastard of a landlord who'd bought out Robert Horgan, who rode his coal-black stallion through these hills and had the finest home you'd want to see behind Scully's Hill, and Peter Scully himself had told them all a hundred times it wouldn't break his heart at all to sneak into that English lair one night and ride off with all his wealth.

Daniel Doherty the blacksmith spoke up again and said they'd line up and kiss his rear end for him one at a time if he wanted, but they'd heard of the things he was after doing to knock the eyes out of those other villages, and wasn't it time now that he put some of that power into proper use to raise old Quirke from the dead before he was too far away from his body to come back? It was a shame, he said, if the old fella's excitement did him out of an Atlantic ride. Keneally's face reddened and he rose up on the toes of his boots. "I'll do better than that," he roared, "You all know that Quirke was parent to me and teacher in my childhood and that I loved him well. You all know that the sight of my poor man dead on his face is the saddest sight in all the world to me. And you all know that bringing him back to share the journey with us would be as easy for me as milking a lazy cow. But it would be a selfish thing for me to do, to bring a man back from his reward and only because I miss him so. My demonstration to you will not be that, my demonstration will be to call on all the powers of the universe to help me resist the easy temptation to bring poor old Quirke back to this miserable life." And furthermore, he added, if they were so almighty eager to kiss his arse, they could start right now to show their gratitude to him by addressing the wife at his side as the Lady Nell. She'd been sent to him by the gods, he said, to help him lead his people justly and with wisdom.

"The devil break your leg!" shouted someone deep in the crowd. "She don't look much like a Lady to me, but she does look like a fine addition to a bed, and we'll honour her for that!" It was a fat apple-faced nephew of Daniel Doherty who spoke, and it was for the looseness of his tongue that he became the only villager, aside from Grania Flynn, that Donal Keneally refused to take along with him on the exodus. He was ordered to stay behind and take the full blame on himself for the murder of the landlord. He did exactly that, a few months later, and did such a fine job of it, too, that no one thought of bringing back the boatload of emigrants for questioning, and no one ever thought to investigate the possibility of a fortune's being stolen. The night before he was executed he wrote a letter in his prison cell, addressed to Donal Brendan Keneally, Canada, in which he said, simply *I done it and now the curse of all the Devils on You ta tu leat fein*, but the jailor, who saw no point in sending off a letter written by a dead man, tossed it in his fire that night in his home without bothering to open it first or even to read the name and address on the envelope. There was a good deal of executing going on that week, and though it never hurts a man to humour the condemned a bit, you couldn't spend your whole life doing favours.

In all the mountain the only person who showed any resistance to his plan was old lady Flynn, who was beginning to wonder if she were going to be left alive forever without knowing what her purpose here on earth was meant to be. But she knew, after looking once into the eyes of the returned Keneally, that in the years of his absence the trickster child in him had been nurtured into meanness, the unnatural strength of him had developed into a danger, the immense knowledge of him had twisted itself into a cynicism. The fiery glow in his eyes was more the light of a fanaticism than of the god-qualities in his bull-father she'd seen in her shed all those years before. In the days after their return, while Keneally sat in the cottage drawing up his plans and his bride turned the dooryard into a place of worship where people could tiptoe in, take a peek at the musing genius, and pay tribute to his pretty wife, the old woman travelled around the village and up and down the mountain roads trying to talk everyone out of the crazy venture. She could hardly walk now, even with her two crooked sticks, and her head was bowed down so low it made her eyes ache to look at anyone above the knees, so she took her time about it, and eventually spoke to every single person on the mountain. Yet she had no success at all, because in the years of Keneally's absence the one thing had happened to the people of Carrigdhoun that had never happened before and that no one had ever dreamed could happen to them: they began to be afraid. The only village in the world that had never known fear from the day of its beginning had been transformed into a trembling collection of cowards.

It began during the Year of Mist. On a morning soon after Keneally's departure the fog did not lift from around the village houses at its usual time, nor did it do so all that day. Day after day it stayed, and thickened, until it became impossible to set foot outside the house without bumping into something, until it was necessary even inside to keep the lamps burning all day in order to see. It was as damp as living at the bottom of the ocean, they said, only worse, because under water it was at least possible to see where you were going. It became so thick that people stopped farming and kept animals inside the house. No one went any-

where, except to the garden for the mouldy water-logged vegetables or—when the turf was low—down to the bog with the slean,
tied to the end of a long series of ropes and sheets fed out by
someone in the house like a long fishing line. It was now impossible, they discovered, to see what the real world looked like, and
before the year was over they'd learned to create worlds for
themselves out of their imaginations. Moriarty, for instance, became convinced that since no one else existed in the world but
himself and his family (all he ever saw) there was really nothing
now to hold him back from treating his wife and daughters in a
manner more consistent with his feelings about them: he began to
beat them regularly, and to torture them with stories of the evil
that swam about in the fog waiting to swallow them up. The first
wife of Scully the schoolteacher, who lived on a part of the
mountain where the fog was so thick it was impossible to see
anything beyond their own bodies, became so preoccupied with
her skin that she developed a rash which spread from her head to
her toes and eventually drove her mad. On the edge of the village
where she lived alone, the old mother of Conal and Bridget Ryan,
whose eyesight had never been very good at the best of times, got
the notion into her head that she was made of clay and sticks.
Recalling the fate of an old clay pot which had dropped to her
stone floor and broken into a thousand pieces and been trampled
into dust by her children before she could sweep it out the door,
she panicked and began to run crazily about the house bumping
into things and eventually, true to her own expectations, dropped
down dead in the middle of her kitchen floor. By the end of the
year, when the mist lifted at last and they were able to see the
world again — which they dimly suspected was only the pale
counterfeit of the world they remembered seeing before — the
fear-disease had taken root.

The first one to fall victim to this new disease in this new and
illusive world had been Nora O'Sullivan, whose bed had once
been Keneally's hiding place. Soon after Keneally's departure she
discovered that whatever he had planted in her with his enormous plough had started something growing, though she didn't
know what it was. Her mother had no trouble at all identifying the
growth and clouted her across the side of the head with a milk can
for it. Then one night Nora woke up in the dark, heard the foxes
barking far up in the mountain mist and the sheep bleating on the

slope, and realized suddenly that she was terrified of dying. Within a few days the thing that was growing in her went out of control and ate out her insides like a ravenous hyena, killing her before she had time to tell anyone about the terrible pain. Soon after the lifting of the mist, Con O'Sullivan, her father, began to fear that his cows might get out of the fields and find themselves on someone else's dinner table, so he started getting up every hour of the night to check on them and never again got a good night's sleep. Moriarty discovered that he was afraid he'd never become a rich man if he left his prices low and continued being so friendly with the customers that they didn't feel they should have to pay, so he raised his prices and started acting the way he thought a city bartender would act. It made an enemy of every man in the village, though they continued out of necessity to buy his porter and his ale. But they never bought another glass of whiskey from him, for Liam the one-eye Burke, who was afraid that Brian O'Connell's still would bring in more money than his own, had stepped up production to a point where there were some who felt they had to drink it steadily every day to keep Liam the one-eye Burke from having to throw some of his poteen away. Not long before Keneally returned, O'Sullivan's oldest son, Sean, killed Billy Murphy in a fight over a girl both were afraid of losing, and was taken away by the law authorities to be punished in the city. This made everyone realize that Carrigdhoun for all its history of isolation was just as vulnerable to outside control as any other village, and from that day on no one ever saw a policeman without trembling down to his toes and shifting his eyes away. Though the world looked nearly the same as it had before the mist, there was a sense that all of it was a fiction, an imitation world that hid a multitude of unsuspected unfamiliar things.

Keneally recognized at once what had happened. "If we are to go," he told his wife, "then let us go quickly." Because, though the lazy priest had died years before and no one had been sent to replace him, Keneally saw more than one villager pass by the church and glance yearningly at its bolted door. There was a force there, he saw, which if it weren't harnessed by one would be harnessed by another.

It would be necessary first, he realized, to eliminate the old woman who had kept him alive as a baby and brought him to his village and helped him to grow into a man, and who was only now beginning to realize that the sole purpose for her hundred and thirty years of life was after all to stop him from this overseas journey. She reminded the villagers of what she had told them before, that the boy had been fathered by a bull she'd surprised in the act of copulation with his simple-minded mother, but the people only laughed at her and said that it made no difference at all to them who his father was when it came to settling in a new country. She told them any fools that followed a maniac like that to the other side of the world were only looking for a worse kind of trouble than they'd ever found at home. She reminded them of the fate of Padraic Monahan who had left the village in sixteen forty-three to find a better place to make his home and had ended up as a castrated slave in some African king's place waving palm leaves over the royal head; when he escaped and returned to Carrig-dhoun his skin had turned black from the sun, his voice had gone screeching high as an old sea-witch, and his every breath expelled a cloud of hideous foreign flies that caused a sleeping sickness to plague the mountain cattle for two hundred years. When he walked back up this mountain road to kiss his grieving old mother and begin the wasted life of a burnt-out man, he told them all that a man had no business at all in leaving the piece of earth God had given to him, for there were things that happened out there in the world which had never been dreamed of in Carrigdhoun, things which would make the hardest-hearted of them lose his hair and his teeth overnight. And the kings of Africa were Christian gentlemen, she told them, compared to the savages of North America who made it their business to lure the honest Irishman to their doors in order to provide new and healthy meat for their cannibal pots. They were over there this minute, she said, howling and dancing and churning up a spell intended to cause this whole mountainside of fools to spend weeks of their life suffering on board a tossing ship in order to be eaten like so many mackerel the second they put foot on land. She predicted that, far from finding freedom there, if they weren't eaten by savages, they'd become the slaves of this monster-child as surely as Jems the Cripple had, and would curse themselves for not having the sense to listen to the warnings of Grania Flynn.

They listened, but they dismissed her words like so many flies. While she talked they went about the business of getting ready: some of the men travelled all the way to the city of Cork in order to meet with the officials about the business of emigration, the women scrubbed out the houses they would leave behind and mended clothes for the long journey, and Donal Brendan Keneally sat over a piece of paper moving numbers around and drawing shapes and heaving great sighs out of him as if this whole thing had become a burden thrust upon him and not a thing he'd asked for at all.

The evening before the departure, while Peter Scully gathered his courage up for his midnight visit to the sleeping Englishman, the villagers and the farmers gathered at the cross by Quirke's cottage and some attempt was made at singing and dancing. But it was a half-hearted affair and the uneasy people soon began to drift away to their own homes. Conal O'Sullivan who was an old man now and a widower, had one son living at home still, and two of his youngest daughters, but for this one night he brought his married girl Nellie with her husband Conal Ryan and their baby daughter home to sit at the fire and watch the turf clods burn and glow and crumble into ashes, and he brought his other daughter, Mary-Kathleen, who'd only recently married the widower-schoolteacher Peter Scully, home to be with them for the night, though he wished with an aching heart that they could have had their Nora with them, too, to sit through this long night in the cottage his great-grandfather had built high up on the rocks above Carrigdhoun where the cold mist rarely left them and the sharp wind never ceased. It took them all the night to say good-bye to the disappointed ancestors who cast accusing shadows in the room, and filed across in front of the gathered family, sniffing loudly to show their discontent.

The widow Donahue had her six living children with her by the bridge, including Mary-Delight who was the wife of Brendan Murphy now and the mother of five, and Mary-Dervit who was Brian O'Connell's wife and the mother of six; together the crowd of them knelt on her stone floor while the widow Donahue in a voice brittle as sticks sang church songs she'd been taught as a child in a language she never knew. Moriarty opened his bar to his son-in-law Seamus O'Mahony and the whole O'Mahony tribe — the doddering old Daniel and his wife Min who didn't understand what was happening to them, and the four bachelor brothers Paddy, Ned, Andrew, and Michael, who saw no sense in leaving any of Moriarty's stock behind for the weather to spoil, and made a valiant attempt to take it with them in their bellies. Their raucous partying could be heard far up the hill by Bridget Ryan who spent the night cooking bread to take on the journey while her ageing man Liam the one-eye Burke sat snoozing in a corner and their children cried over the family dog who would have to be left behind. Daniel Doherty sat alone in his darkened shop, touching his blacksmith tools.

In Quirke's cottage Jems the Cripple and Quirke's nephew Peter and Nell and Keneally were assaulted by a continuous flow of warning and pleas from the old woman, whose voice had taken on an edge of panic and whose eyes darted like birds about the room. At midnight Keneally said they'd listened long enough to her nonsense and led her outside for a walk along the mountain road. When he returned to the cottage, the dawn was not far off and the houses all up and down the slope were faintly visible, resting like scattered sheep among the rocks. In the doorway he told them it was time to leave, and by the time they had their few belongings piled on Quirke's cart, the others could be seen converging slowly on the cross from every direction. The mist sat like a grey ceiling on the roof of O'Sullivan's house and moved neither up nor down the whole time it took them to travel off the slope to the valley floor and out across the bogland and over the farther hill; not one of them was able to see the mountain top, but the clear light of the morning was bright enough to make the widow Donahue gasp and cry out for the great God to forgive them if it was a foolish thing they were doing. For miles and miles along the road the Burke children threw rocks at the small black dog which was trying to follow them.

As they were approaching the outskirts of Cork, a few days later, Peter Scully caught up to them on a wheezing horse and handed a sack of money over to Keneally. He leaned down from his mount to tell him that it had been necessary after all to kill the unfortunate gentleman, because the foolish man had developed the habit of sleeping on a bed whose leg was set squarely on the only loose board that gave access to the hidden money. Keneally said the knowledge was better kept between the two of them alone, and quickly spread out the coins on the floor of his cart to count them. It was more than enough, he said, and they would always be grateful to the man who had got it for them, but it would be a good thing just the same if Peter Scully would turn his pockets inside out and empty his sack of provisions in front of them all, because the temptation to keep some of it for himself was understandably irresistible and perhaps Peter Scully was not yet aware that from now on there would be no such thing as private wealth, only the wealth of the community, which would be protected and distributed by Keneally himself. They were safely aboard the ship before he began to refer to himself as The Father.

"I am the Father of you all, " he said, "and you are my children."

"Father, if you please," said Dervit O'Connell to her husband. "And his skinny wife barren by the looks of her! Father, if you don't mind!" But she told no one else what she thought and her husband knew better than to repeat it because they weren't very long at sea before they'd discovered what sort of man they'd followed. "Wisha, have you heard the latest?" he reported to his wife when they were squeezed together on their wooden berth one night. "The man is after telling your old one there'll be no more of her praying and singing allowed from this day. 'Tis a waste of good breath, he told her, to be talking to a god that's only a heap of metal in his pocket when she can talk to him instead." His wife sat up, snorting. "Do you tell me so? Would he be setting himself up in the religion business now, I wonder? Perhaps he has plans for us all to be bowing and scraping, and him with a history of sins that would be as long as your leg." The withdrawal of the church from Carrigdhoun had not necessarily meant the dying out of its vocabulary or its notions from the speech and thoughts of the inhabitants, particularly in the family of the Widow Donahue. "Hush now," said her husband, "or the others will be hearing you." But Dervit Donahue O'Connell would hush for no one. "Let him tell me to bow and scrape to him!" she said. "I'll only ask what the rest of ye are scared to set your tongues to, and that is: what did he do with the old one that raised him?"

"He ate her, sure." said Ned O'Mahony when she asked him. "And licked his chops."

"Can you take nothing seriously at all?" she said.

"Not a thing," he said. "Nor should I. For isn't it true we're all on a ship that will be sailing off the end of the earth?" His eyes popping. "A laugh, my lady, a laugh or two is all we have.

"Though it is said," he leaned in close to whisper mockingly, "that the moment before we go off the edge he'll tell his secret and save us all."

"What secret is that, you rascal?"

"Simple to tell, my girl. 'Tis only that all the while we've been thinking he's Donal Keneally from Carrigdhoun he's really the immortal reincarnation of your hero and mine the mighty Cuchulain."

"Now stop it, Ned," she said, and slapped her hand at him. "Stop that kind of talk or you'll be making me laugh."

"A terrible crime it is too, to laugh. But I tell you true, Dervit, he's bound to tell us he's your man at the tree, your man with the crow at his shoulder."

"Not Finn MacCool, you gossoon?"

"No, Cuchulain's the one, the only one. Our friend who led the armies, our friend whose presence kept the enemy frightened out of their wits, who even when he'd been fatally wounded tied himself to a tree to fight on his feet to the end and even to keep upright after his death, until a crow or bloody raven gave it away. A bloody bird on the shoulder told them the story, true, but it was too late by then, he'd made a hero of himself for certain. That's the one for me."

"A pretty story yes," said Dervit to her neighbour Peter Scully. "But there's nothing in it that reminds me of The Father. I wonder did he do his mother in? Is that what your Cuchulain was up to? Did he bury the old one that nursed him, I want to know? Is it a tradition of Ireland?"

"He was a fine one and no denying," said Peter Scully, "and could play the harp as well I've heard."

"The harp is it?" said Dervit O'Connell. "Could you catch *this* one at the harp now, and him more suited to the instruments of the devil? Could you catch our Donal Keneally plucking at the harps I wonder?"

"'Tis the custom for the heroes of every country in the world to play some instrument," said Ned O'Mahony. "They say the hero of the land we're sailing for had a fine hand at the harpsichord."

"Do you tell me so?" said Dervit.

"A fine big red-nosed Irishman named Sir Sean A. McDermott."

"Bite your tongue," said Dervit.

"May I die if it isn't so. Sir Sean A. McDermott, I heard all about

him. The whole country worships the ground that he walks on
and damned if he wasn't born in Macroom."

"Hold my hands for me Peter," said Dervit to her neighbour.
"For I'm bound to clout him if he carries on."

" 'Twas his father, pardon me, that was born in Macroom," said
Ned. "The man himself was spawned in a log cabin somewhere in
the wilds. Did his lessons by the candle light. They called him
Honest Sean for refusing to cut down a cherry tree no matter how
much the English bastards tried to force him."

"A cherry tree in the wilds?"

"Wild cherry. His father built the cabin in a nest of them. Cherry
trees as far as your eye can see, my girl, and every one of them wild
as a Dublin hoor. The boy came out of those wilds wearing a
raccoon on his head and shooting up the redskins right and left.
Right and left, I tell you. He made a fine great hero out of himself
for sure and marched himself straight as you please to the big
white palace up in Ottawa where he crowned himself the king."

"Will you stop it, Ned."

"King, I tell you. Elected king of the country by every man jack
and papoose that could get out and vote, and never once showed
up in parliament sober."

"An Irishman, did you say?" said Peter Scully.

"Have you heard that McDermott was a Turkish name perhaps?
or Hindu? Not a day sober but one, not a day sober but only the
day he was required to sign the papers that would send a railroad
train chugging its way across from one end of the land to the
other, from sea to sea. But look here my man, says he when he
reads the fine print of the matter. But look here, my man, and it's a
good thing I'm sober this day. For you cannot have a railroad train
chugging across this land from sea to sea, *a mari usque ad mare* as
they say, without first laying out some tracks for it to run on. And
with that your man from Macroom whips out another paper he
has hidden in his flask pocket, and a fancy quill he pulled from the
tail of a goose on his way in to work, and while the others are still
scratching their heads he signs an order for the tracks, every foot
of them to be nailed down to the ground with a golden spike."

"Golden?" said Peter Scully. "Golden, do you tell me?"

"I do. And do you think it's just any man off the street that's
good enough to hammer them in? Do you think he let them hire
your Englishman or Chinaman or your man from South Australia

to whang those goldens home? No, sir, he did not. Every one of those spikes was driven by an Irishman.''

"Lord save us all," said Dervit O'Connell. "Is that the kind of land he's leading us to."

"Golden spikes," said Peter. "The devil you say. A chain of golden spikes from sea to sea. And every one of them driven home by the hand of an Irishman. I wonder was it anyone from County Cork.''

"Maybe it was," said Dervit O'Connell, and winked. "Maybe it was Con O'Sullivan's uncle that disappeared in the time of the famine. He was a fine man with the hammer they all did tell me."

"Then that's your man," said Ned O'Mahony. "In this land ahead you're nothing at all if you're not a man with the hammer.''

"May we survive to see it," said Dervit.

Her mother the widow was the only one of the old people to survive the crossing. Con O'Sullivan died in his berth somewhere in mid Atlantic, singing "Wild Rover No More" while the lantern swung madly back and forth on its hook in the ceiling and all of his daughters and sons wailed and keened like winter winds around him. His last advice to them all was "Build your fences strong and high and you'll never have trouble with your neighbours.'' Moriarty lived only long enough to get a quick look at the lights of Montreal before he tumbled overboard and disappeared in the waters of the St. Lawrence River. On the train the old O'Mahonys, Dan and Min, who never did manage to understand what was going on but decided to go along with it anyway in case it should make sense later, caught chills and died within an hour of each other while they sped down the Fraser Valley upright and rigid in their seats, facing backwards with placid blank expressions on their faces and with fingers clasped into the quilt they'd opened across their knees. Seamus O'Mahony, who'd already had to leave his father-in-law behind in Montreal and intended to keep his own parents with him to the end of the trip despite their changed conditions, told no one when they died. And his brothers, when they found him sitting between the two stiff corpses, pretending conversation, agreed there was no point in stopping the train so close to the end of the line, and helped him keep the deaths a secret until they reached Vancouver. The bodies accompanied them across the strait, in coffins purchased from a city mortician, and were buried almost immediately in a small clearing not far from the water edge of the land Keneally had bought. No one had the energy left for a proper wake.

When they arrived on the island, the colony of weak, nearly-starved Irishmen moved through the town, on the wagons hired by Keneally, with eyes that rested somewhere far ahead and seemed to see nothing. But they were seen. Shoppers and merchants came out onto the verandahs and boardwalks to watch the emaciated immigrants pass by. "It's a funny thing," said one, "that the big bugger and his woman are the only ones in that whole bloody lot who look as if they'd seen a bite of food this year." But there was nothing strange at all about it, another said, if you recalled the last time you'd seen that big one on these streets. The former mayor, whose California holiday had helped him recover sufficiently to return to the town and open a dry-goods store, was arranging bolts of cloth in his window when the wagons went by. The intense gas pains which the sight of Keneally called up in his chest caused him to lock up the store immediately and go home, where his wife Myrtle put him to bed and sat dutifully by his side, embroidering the air with horrendous tales of the things that men will bring on themselves if they don't take care of their health. It was a grey January day and outside the window the rain fell steadily, as it had done for several weeks and as it would do for several more.

In the beginning, in the first year of the century, the Revelations Colony of Truth arrived on its land on January the sixth. They buried the old O'Mahony couple on the seventh. A day later, Mary-Kathleen O'Sullivan, the second wife of the schoolteacher Peter Scully, after weeping unceasingly since the moment of their arrival on the island, disappeared into the forest some time just before noon and was not seen again by any of them until she was found three years later and dragged back, with her little girl, to the colony. On the ninth day of January they began to clear the land for the first of the colony buildings.

In all that ragged company, only Jems the Cripple found the strength to cry out his dismay when they'd arrived at the land. The others were silently aghast or too exhausted to care. Gathered, huddled in the little clearing on the high sudden precipice above the sea, they watched Keneally out of eyes like dark smudges. "Jaysus," Jems the Cripple said, "the trees!" And all of them, who on their journey had felt themselves driven already to an incredible sense of smallness, looked up, up, at the giants that stood thicker and taller than the highest church spire they'd ever seen. And one by one, beginning with widow Donahue who had arrived in the last wagon and got out to stand by the wheel, beginning with her at the end and then the children and eventually the women and the men, they went down on their knees on the damp floor of fir needles and cones. "Mother of God!" someone said. "The trees!" As if they hoped that all of this was just one more mirage created by their conjurer-leader. For a while there was a silence among them then, in which they could hear the waves breaking against the rocks below and a lone seagull screeching in the wind.

Though it was only a little after noon, the sky was black and the heavy rain had already drenched them to the skin. When the widow Donahue approached and spat on the ground at his feet and called him Ananias, father of lies, it was impossible to know if there were tears streaming down her face or only rain, but there was no question that her eyes were filled with hate. "Make yourselves shelters," he told them, "But not under the trees. Make them out here on the edge of the cliff, for tomorrow we begin to bring those giants down." The villagers, who had no idea how anyone went about toppling a forest and lacked the strength or the energy to care, began to drag limbs and chunks of wood into the clearing to build shelters where a night's sleep would be possible, though Seamus O'Mahony took the time to comment that the forest had a smell to it that he had never smelled before, even in rain. "It goes sharp to the top of your head," he said. "'Tis a higher, sweeter smell even than the furze."

The question that ran from mind to mind in the morning, and from voice to voice all down the dripping clumsy row of shelters, was "How?" How was it possible to turn this forest into a piece of land where they could do the only thing they knew how to do, which was farm? "How?" Keneally said. "I'll show you how." And he rode off with the hired wagons into town. They waited on the spot for him to return, but day after day went by without any sight of him. Peter Scully and two of the O'Sullivan boys went into the forest to look for Mary-Kathleen, but they soon became frightened and returned. Food supplies were low. The possibility that Keneally may have abandoned them or been killed in town caused such a confused mixture of fear and hope that it was necessary for Nell to gather them around the fire and remind them that her husband was no ordinary man, nor was he an ordinary leader, that he was indeed The Father of them all and would not abandon them before his mission was completed.

When he returned, four days after his departure, he brought with him a team of white oxen, a wagon loaded down with bucksaws and axes and chains and springboards, and a long thin Finn with a vermilion birthmark on his face the size and shape of a large coin. The Finn couldn't speak a word of English, or of Gaelic, nor did he ever find it necessary to learn. He was a good-natured man who showed Keneally how things should be done, and then was content to sit back with a toothy grin and let the big Irishman boss the others. He taught them how to chop notches out of either side of the giant trunks, and to insert the springboards in them, how to stand on the springboards and with a two-handled saw and a bottle of oil cut deep into either side of the trunk, how to place the cuts so that the tree would fall exactly where they wanted it, how to trim the fallen tree of its limbs and use the team of oxen to pull it out of the forest, and finally how to use blasting powder to loosen the soil so that the stumps and roots could be dragged away and burned. He became so fascinated with the fiery-eyed leader and his band of hard-working people that even when there was no more need for him, he stayed on; he remained in the colony all through the clearing of the land and the digging of the well and the building of the circle of log houses around the well, and even the building of the House of Revelations, without ever learning to speak a word of their language. It seemed that instead of asking Keneally for a single penny of payment, he wanted as his reward only the right to eat with them and move among them and observe their work from the edges with a happy grin on his face. He watched everything with that same anticipatory smile, as if his greatest joy were simply to imagine what this crowd of misplaced creatures might be up to next, like a pack of monkeys or a lot of clever but mischievous children. He stayed with the colony for five years and did not leave it even to visit the town until at the end of that time he fell ill, and Keneally drove him in to the hospital and left him there. No one ever wondered aloud if he had died in hospital or gone on to somewhere else. It was as if he had been erased from their memories, or perhaps as if his presence had never been registered in their consciousness at all. No one had ever asked him his name.

The dreaded disease of fear, which had so successfully been

avoided by the people of Carrigdhoun for centuries until it began
like a cannibal growth in Nora O'Sullivan's womb, had during the
long ocean journey and the slow hungry movement across the
country become so deeply rooted in every member of the colony
that there was nothing their leader couldn't have done with them.
Because it was the nature of the disease to eat at the fibers of the
sufferer's self-esteem until he lost any desire to be healed, Keneally had only to keep his people so busy working towards the
immediate goals of shelter and food that they had no time to think
about anything else. He kept them working during the day, then
through the evenings kept them together while he painted glorious word-pictures of the civilization they were building, where
they would have a happiness and a freedom envied by all the
countries of the earth. In case they doubted his ability to create
this paradise, he continued to astonish them with more and more
incredible acts of magic, causing demons to appear and disappear, voices of the dead to speak from the mouths of the living,
logs to raise themselves and shift their position and lie down in
new and more convenient places.

The members of the colony were not encouraged to make visits
to the town, but Keneally himself rode in often, though he seldom
stayed longer than the time it took to gather all the supplies that
were needed by the colony. Even the briefest of visits, however,
was long enough to arouse an enormous curiosity about him
among the townsmen. Peter Krup, who had finally married the
last of his beautiful daughters off a year before and lived alone
near the railway station, refused to believe that Keneally had no
intention of renewing their previous friendship, and tried time
after time to get him up to the house. But Keneally only looked at
Krup as if he'd never seen the man before in his life and went
about his business with the air of a man who had descended, only
temporarily, from the clouds. When Gunnar Nelson saw him pass
by the door of the Paradise Beer Parlour he ran out and tried to
drag the big man in for a drink, to show the gratitude he still felt
for the saving of his life, but Keneally with a single hand knocked
the drunken man against the wall and continued down the street.
"You ain't natural," the fallen man yelled after him. "Living out
there like that, you must be crazy!"

And indeed that was the general agreement among those who
had tried to become friends and were rejected, that he was after
all a madman watching over a colony of madmen and oughtn't to

be disturbed. Others, who observed from a greater distance, accepted the madman theory without question, but suspected the whole business was more complicated than that and began to send out spies to report on the activities of the Irishmen. The spy system was hardly successful, though, because more than one of the most reliable of them gradually became absorbed into the colony and eventually forgot to return. A young miner by the name of Frank Turner fell in love with the eldest daughter of Dervit and Brian O'Connell and within a matter of weeks had become as much a part of the group as if he'd been there from the beginning. A short stocky youth named Enrico Manani walked out of the bush one day and begged Keneally to put him to work. Within a month he'd sent for his parents and his sisters, two of whom had been educated in Italy for a place in aristocratic society. Eventually the girls moved into the cabins of the O'Mahony bachelors and between them raised fourteen sons, every one of whom looked like their grandfather Dan O'Mahony, who'd died with his wife on the train. The eldest of these sons eventually left the colony, in the middle of the night, and became a world-famous singer. Whenever members of the press or television asked him at the height of his success to tell something of his childhood, he told them only that his mother had been Italian and he did not know who his father had been. He told them that any recollections he had once had of his childhood had been so terrifying that he'd driven them from his mind altogether before they sent him mad. But he still had vague memories of a single face, he said, which was so beautiful and so calm that it made him think of heaven. It was not the face of his mother.

The face he remembered was in fact the face of Nell, the sprightly girl from Cahirciveen who'd married Donal Keneally and become a kind of goddess in his god-play. Since the day of her hasty farmhouse marriage she had grown from girl to woman so beautiful that the people who saw her the one and only time she walked down the main street of town ventured to suggest that it was her beauty and not Keneally's power that kept those people prisoner. And not only beauty, either, but a calm and ethereal manner that novelists and maiden poets reserve for the sickly heroines destined for an early genteel death. The ex-mayor was overheard telling his friend the barber that if she put her hands on either side of his face as she must sometimes do to the small children out there, if she would do that and look into his eyes, he would die and gladly die and return to life so he could die again. "Wouldn't you know that goddam bastard would get a girl like that!" The ex-mayor was so overwhelmed by his infatuation that he composed a sonnet in the lady's honour, laying bare the anguish of his soul, but his wife found the rough draft in his wastebasket and even though it lacked the final couplet it was complete enough to give her what she needed to make him an attentive, loving, and most considerate husband for the remainder of their life together.

Hers was not the beauty of weakness or frailty, for she worked at the clearing of land and the building of houses as hard as any of the men, but it was a beauty of refinement so exquisite that the predominant feeling in a man who saw her was one of sadness, a strange hollow melancholy at the pit of his stomach, which was actually an awareness that the magnificent glimpse of her perfection could not be enjoyed because of the knowledge that it must somehow pass, even if it meant only that she would turn the corner or close a door. Her light casual manner gave the impression that she was completely unaware of her appearance and of its effect upon others, which was indeed the case. She never looked in a mirror, even before they were forbidden in the colony, and the attention she gave to anyone she talked to, however intense and concerned at the time, shifted so abruptly and completely and equitably to the next person as to give the impression that she registered no permanent opinion or impression of others at all. Like a queen among thousands of her subjects she passed among the few dozen of her neighbours as if they were faceless and nameless, and destined to disappear the second she moved away. Still, like the ex-mayor of the town, they would have died for her if she had wished it, worshipped her if she had wanted it, loved her if she had allowed it. For if Keneally had declared himself The Father, harsh and bitter and superhuman, she had, without even trying, become The Mother.

The fact that she found herself married to a messiah-monster seemed to have no effect upon her at all. That her husband sometimes spoke of himself in the third person, that he made tables fly around the room like moths and made dishes talk, that he allowed himself to be worked up into such a towering rage that he could beat Jems the Cripple unconscious time after time and hardly notice what he'd done, caused no more reaction from her than the normal day-to-day activities of any other man would create in his wife. Goddess or no goddess, she did willingly whatever he said and the hurts he caused she healed, the rebellious fires his inhuman demands would sometimes fan she quenched, the hearts that lay broken where his foot had trampled on them she mended.

When the schoolteacher Peter Scully began to brood about his runaway wife, and to blame himself, and to cry of the loneliness he was suffering, she arranged for him to move into the cabin of Mary-Delight and Brendan Murphy where there were four daughters to keep him from his depression. When Liam the one-eye Burke went swimming in the sandy bay and never came back, she consoled Bridget Ryan and their nearly-grown children with stories of the old man's kindness and gentleness that were only approximately the truth, but convinced them somehow that without him they had gained a far greater memory-husband-and-father than anything they'd had when he was alive. When Jems the Cripple, sitting on his coiled boneless leg, began suddenly to wail and to curse the day he'd been fool enough to follow Donal Keneally, and to bemoan the fact that he'd wasted what might otherwise have became a perfectly happy life, and to wish death and damnation on his hero betrayer, she moved him inside where Keneally would not be able to hear him and rocked him in her arms until he fell asleep.

Though she put up with her husband's rages and his orders, hardly noticing, she would have none of the great German shepherd he brought home from the town one day on a leather leash. He could let the big slobbering brute walk beside him in the fields and at the buildings, she told him, and call him "Thunderbird" and let him snarl at the people as if he intended to chew out their throats, but he would not bring it into the bedroom. So the huge ugly dog, who loved his master intensely and hated everyone else, spent his nights outside the bedroom door, growling softly at the sounds of movement and whispering within.

The dog walked between them as they supervised the construction of the final building together. Keneally had been particularly careful to design the settlement in the shape of a perfect circle on the top of the swell of land above the sea. The well was the centre, he explained, because it was the source of life for them all. The log houses for the colony families were built surrounding this centre, just as the ancient men had placed the stones in circles high in the mountains of Ireland. And because there was reason to believe that these circles of stone were places of worship once, where one carefully placed stone was the altar, the final house to be built, which was to be called The House of Revelations and to become the home of The Father and The Mother, would be on the sea edge of the circle, facing the rising sun. Sometimes centres of those old stone circles contained a buried pot of bones, he said, perhaps the remains of a child, but there would be no need here for that kind of thing, he said, because they were civilized men and saw no evidence at all of any god to worship.

Everyone worked on the house and it rose faster than any of the others. Unlike them it was not made of logs; huge timbers from the land were hauled in to the town where they were sawn into lumber and sent back in exactly the lengths and widths that had been ordered. Windows arrived on a boat from England, with leaded panes and unusual shapes, sometimes coloured glass. A special ship was sent up from San Francisco with cut Arizona sandstone for the fireplaces, and special gold-plated door handles and plumbing. A cabinetmaker drove up from Victoria to do the interior work, for he had had plenty of practice finishing the insides of houses to look like palaces for homesick Englishwomen and could handle the tools of his trade as if they were only so many extra hands he had been born with and learned to use when he was learning to walk. Furniture arrived from Toronto and Vancouver and Seattle and Mexico City.

For they needn't think, Keneally told them, that the thousands of giant trees they'd been cutting and turning over to the logging companies had been given away for a few pennies. And they needn't think that the load after load of their good healthy vegetables he'd hauled in to town had been merely tossed to the pigs. And they needn't think, either, that it had been necessary to spend all of Peter Scully's acquired fortune on the crossing. The fact was, he told them, The House of Revelations would be a monument to their success, and though it would be the place where he and his wife would live (for who else but The Father should be the one to see the sun rise first at the start of the day?) it would in fact belong to them all.

And there it is, The House, across the grass. You can tell how grand it must have seemed, when it was new, sitting out there on the edge with all those verandahs and gables.

It isn't hard to imagine them in there, crowded and crammed in for his big performance. You can see them come down the slopes from the fields behind, in their rags, backs stooped from the heavy work of the clearing and burning, the building of barns, the caring for the beef and dairy cattle. Heads down, kicking at the stones with their boots, they've come in from all over the colony, silently, to scrub up and wolf down some tea and get ready. You can see them come out of the doors of these cabins, all around the circle, step out into the courtyard and head silently across past the wellhead to the great staircase there and up the steps to the big oak door. No one speaks. They shout to each other in the fields, and holler orders, they gossip at corners all day, but now with the weight of this night on their minds they only glance at each other, families together, and — oh, maybe nod and make some kind of greeting.

Liam the one-eye Burke and his wife Bridget Ryan come out of that end cabin first, say, with their children. Old Liam, who will be drowned in the sea within a few years. Bridget is twice his size. She has her apron on; she takes it off for no one, but it is clean, always clean. Her big face is scrubbed shiny and apple-red. Moriartys come out of their cabin. O'Connells. O'Sullivans. Murphys. Peter Scully with a brand new bushy beard. All the O'Mahonys. Paddy, Ned, Andrew, Michael, gathering out at the bottom of the step, half-grinning at each other. Threatening even now to kick up some kind of trouble. But the silence of the others is dampening. Jems the Cripple leaning on his crutch; others stand back to let him go through first to the door. He is still, somehow, an outsider.

See how the widow Donahue is the last to leave her house. This tiny old lady has shrivelled to little more than bones. Toothless, without lashes or eyebrows, her face is the face of a wise baby. There is scarcely a hair left on her head. Like the crones of Ireland she is all in black: a black crocheted shawl is over the back of her head and hangs down to her knees, held together at her throat by a yellow band.

But this is no brooding tragic muse, no ancient hag of the stories. The widow Donahue turns at the door and gives Ned O'Mahony the benefit of a giant wink. This is not, yet, a colony of broken spirits.

"Do you know what it is the man will tell us here?" she says to Ned, daring him to answer. "Is it Cuchulain at last?"

It is said the dedication ceremony was his greatest show. The old Keneally had been left behind; the trickster, the magician, the orator, the prophet; he'd delivered his people to this new and promised land and was content to be their Father and Saviour. Kathleen Donahue played solemn music on the organ in the corner of the big room, and people when they entered were greeted by a gentle soft-spoken Keneally who pressed their hands between his and led them to a seat. When he addressed them, it was with his arms outstretched, to include them all, from behind the reconstructed black machine he'd assembled and dismantled a thousand times in his previous shows. This time a bowl of cat tails and pampas grass sat on top of it.

They say he spoke for an hour and a half. They say he began with a lengthy explanation of the habits of the neolithic men who seemed to have had some fondness for the circle as a symbol and must have spent whole lifetimes dragging stones up mountain-sides to build the mysterious monuments that decorate the coun-tryside from Glandore to Beaghmore, that he gave a quick run-down on the heroic and mystical feats of such men as Finn MacCool, Cuchulain, Brian Boru, St. Patrick, St. Brendan, Daniel O'Connell, and even Charles Stewart Parnell, all of whom were clearly intended to be understood as predecessors to their pres-ent leader, that he listed a catalogue in astonishingly minute detail of the task-by-task contribution of every adult in the colony towards the clearing of the land and the building of the houses and the construction of The House of Revelations itself, that he offered an intricate and completely incomprehensible explana-tion of his own role in the whole business, with vaguely worded hints in the direction of Moses and Elijah and Jesus Christ, along with all the previously mentioned worthies, and a distinctly am-biguous reference to humility and a willingness to serve, and that by the time he neared the climax of his speech his voice had transcended all possibilities of the human voice and came to them like the wind, from somewhere beyond earth, and was felt to the very centre of their bones.

They say, too, that nature did its best to co-operate. A wind came up from somewhere, bending trees, shaking the house. You could hear the screech of giant trunks grinding against each other. You could hear the squeal of nails wrenched in the lum-bered walls and the cedar roof above you. The water in the strait was churned up into waves that smashed against the cliff, and leapt upwards high enough to spray the windows and toss driftwood logs like sticks across the yard. A door flew open in the wind, crashed against the wall, and was forced shut again by someone whose face was streaming with rain and salt water and strips of kelp. Sticks and bits of limbs went flying across the floor. Dead pine needles clotted like hairballs in the corners. Keneally's voice rose above the tumult, to include it. Unimpressed, he appeared to be taking credit for the state of affairs outside as well as in. Terrified, Kathleen Donahue began to pedal the organ frantically, as if the instrument could not only spew out the confused and hideous tunes she was jumbling all together but could carry her away from this place as well. Her red face strained towards a take-off. He would be transformed, Keneally said, his voice suddenly heavy with importance. He would be transformed from flesh into spirit this night. He would, in fact, be dead. The organ music spiralled upward into a final impossible note that lay across the sudden silence like a clear metallic lid, though frightened Kathleen's feet kept pumping madly still and her forehead pressed against the elaborately carved wood of the instrument like a cyclist against the wind. Logs crashed on the verandah; men whimpered; bladders weakened; a light in the ceiling dimmed.

They say that Keneally stood behind the complicated black machine he had assembled out of pieces from his pocket and slowly faded, like a drop of colour dissolving in a pool of water, until there was nothing left to see but the flames of the fire in the enormous fireplace behind him. They say a gust of wind slapped against the house like a giant hand and that someone screamed, that one of the Moriarty men went out of control and threw himself down on the floor to lap up the sea water that had come in under the door, rolling his eyes at the taste of the salt and farting continuously like a bloated dog, that Ned O'Mahony barked out a laugh that stuck in his throat and nearly choked him, that frantic Kathleen Donahue, as if to make one more valiant attempt at escape, played "The Holy Ground" so fast the last notes caught up with the first, overlapped, and the instrument, out of control, played the whole song backwards by itself, over and over again until she stood back and kicked it solidly in its walnut face.

"He's dead," they whispered.

"He has risen, so he has, and left us mortals here below."

We have no way of knowing how they spent the rest of that

night, after his transformation, whether they sat there nervously waiting for something else to happen or went home eventually to stare at their ceilings and try to imagine what life would be like without him. Nor is it possible to guess what their reactions must have been when the next morning he was among them again, overseeing the work of the colony as if the ceremony had never occurred, except in their dreams. We know only that when she saw him there on the steps of The House of Revelations in the morning light the widow Donahue, struck by the first in a series of paralysing seizures which would eventually kill her, had a sudden and intense premonition that within the year Keneally would have clubbed his wife to death with a stone and buried her in a shallow grave far back in the woods behind the barns. She told her daughter Dervit about it, and Dervit kept it to herself until the disappearance of Nell Keneally a few months later, shortly after her mother had died, convinced her of the need to disclose the nature of the old woman's vision.

WADE

1

He could hardly avoid knowing what people thought of him. His scattered neighbours up and down the coast would make no secret of it.

"Not bad looking," the women accused, "but lazy. Wade Powers is lazy."

A paradox, apparently, or an aberration in nature.

"Half-naked most of the time, in that pair of ragged shorts, you can tell he thinks he's something."

Though it was left to the men to put their fingers on his greatest crime: "The bugger never *works*. Just leans back with that smirk on his face and lets the money come in." They were tempted to accuse the money of "pouring", but recognized that would be allowing him more than the evidence could justify.

Still, it was their suspicion that despite his lack of ambition Wade Powers had managed to achieve what appeared to be an ideal existence. And he said nothing to discourage them. He cared no more about their opinions than he did about the opinions of the tourists who came from all over the continent, from all over the world, to put money in his pocket.

When he built The Fort he was careful to choose a spot out at the end of a narrow spit of land, right out on the point beside a single twisted jack pine, where it could be easily seen from well up and down the highway. Copying a sketch he'd found in a history book, he built it out of rough timbers the thickness of railway ties, and put a high stockade fence around the whole thing so no one could get a close look without paying. Tourists coming in from the island highway drove first on dirt ruts across a field of sun-coppered grass, squeezed between two beaches for a

hundred feet of narrow road, then pulled up into the gravel
parking lot beneath his sign:

THE FORT
STEP INTO HISTORY

From outside the fence they could see the conical roof of the
bastion, but in order to see anything more they had to buy a ticket
from his mother, who sat with her enormous behind squeezed
into a wheelchair in the little ticket booth. When she collected the
money there was something a little actressy about her exaggerated hand movements, as if to give the impression that in another
country, where people knew class when they saw it, she'd be a
woman you'd notice. But she never spoke to the visitors, nor did
she ever accompany them back into The Fort. She sat in the little
booth Wade had built her and waited with a faraway look in her
eyes for the next carload to come churning up dust on the road.

Wade hardly spoke to the people who came to The Fort, either,
nor did he very often bother showing them through. He liked to be
around, just watching, sometimes leaning on the inside of the
fence with a piece of grass in his teeth like a gardener taking a rest,
or a casual guard. Why break your neck? Often he slid a glance at
the sky and laughed to himself, as if he'd just thought of something cruel, amused that tourists would so eagerly pay money to
see just about anything you wanted to charge them for. Even an
imitation. Women seeing this sudden derisive laugh checked their
hair with quick nervous fingers, or touched their throats.

A tall man, with dark coarse skin and a lot of hair, he could lean
with one shoulder against the fence and his feet crossed at the
ankles and look as if someone had just propped him up there for
the day. A long dark curve, a bent limb. He seldom wore anything
more than a pair of worn-thin jeans cut off high on the thighs,
though his mother told him he was a little old to be showing off
legs and chest like a brand new youth. But he liked to feel the air,
he said, he liked to be aware of himself. He smirked, smiled,
grinned, and ran fingers through the curled hairs on his belly.

Sometimes he did consent to show the people through. He got
some small pleasure out of taking them into the six-sided bastion,
especially in showing them the little damp-smelling prison to one
side of the ground floor. Barely large enough for a man to stretch
out in, it was a semi-circular space surrounded by big smooth
speckled beach stones cemented together, with a thick plank door

on iron hinges and no window at all for fresh air. People stepped inside, shuddered, and hurried out, letting their nervous eyes flicker over him. On the second floor he stood back to let them walk around, look out through the round cannon holes and admire the rusty old cannon he'd bought off a collector up north. And up on the third floor, which jutted out farther than the lower part and made a large, six-sided room, they ran from one rifle slit to another admiring the view, sniffing the salt air, imagining what it would be like to be holed up in here under attack, and marvelling at their own hollow voices under the rafters of the conical roof. If they asked for history he could tilt his head and look off to the side like an expert, as if he was trying hard to remember, and tell them a dozen stories so scary their eyes would pop: he'd read a lot of books and wasn't short on imagination.

But he would never get rich from it, even if it seemed an easy income. The tourist business wasn't so great as all that. Those neighbours who envied him, those who thought he had found the ideal existence, had more than income on their minds; he knew they were also thinking of the painter Virginia Kerr.

On the protected side of the spit, on the edge of the sandy beach that faced back to the island and away from wind, there were two small houses. They stood side by side, perfect twins—except that one of them was half-covered by a red climbing rose—each with a shaked gable roof, each with a shaded front verandah, each with a brand-new coat of yellow paint. A little gravel path lined with white-painted rocks went from one house to the other and then down the slope to the beach. Most of the time Wade lived in one of the houses and his mother in the other, but for two months every year he moved in with his mother and rented the other to Virginia Kerr, a university art teacher who came to the island on her summer vacations. Visiting her was one of the things he would rather do than hang around inside the fort all day with a lot of noisy tourists.

When she arrived she brought two wooden crates full of novels to read and a red bikini bathing suit to wear out on the beach while she was reading them. Rain or shine she went walking out along the edge of the sea every morning for an hour, looking at the fishing boats and the screeching gulls and the row of blue mountains across on the mainland; then she came in and spent the rest of the day reading her books or working on a huge door-size painting she wanted to have finished before she went back to school. When he visited she kept her bedroom door shut, kept him out in the kitchen to watch her paint (slapping on smears and shapes she said had something to do with what she could see on the beach, but which looked to him like nothing at all), and made him talk to her about himself and his runaway wife and the cross-eyed girl he had hitch-hiked to Winnipeg with one winter. Sometimes, though, she allowed him to take her walking back through the dying grass to the log shack that sat decaying on the thick wooded slope where his spit of land attached itself to the island's shore.

She wore a long flowered cotton dress when they walked. It was because she liked to hear it rustle through the dry grass, she told him, and because it made her feel more feminine even than the bikini. Her long hair, the rust-colour of dead pine, was usually clipped together at the back of her neck with something that looked like a green turtle.

He always knew the minute he stepped inside her house whether this was to be one of the days when they would go walking together. She might be reading instead of painting, maybe she'd be singing aloud with the book in her hand, and sometimes she would have a picnic lunch already packed and ready on the kitchen counter. She would look at him with an expression that seemed more like an idiot child than a university professor, and say, "I feel like a walk today, Wade, what do you feel like?" He'd laugh. Then he'd move in close to her and kiss the tiny scar on the side of her neck and tell her what it was he felt like. "What's the matter?" she'd say, "Can't you talk any of those tourist girls into going up to see your cannon?" And he would tell her not to mention cannons to him unless she had a certain thing in mind. But she said, "You don't think those women who pay money to walk through your fort are travelling all over the country looking for history, do you?" So he had to admit that when she was around there was no other woman who could affect him the way she could. Then, when he had admitted that, she would kiss his mouth, slip her tongue in like a quick electric shock, and tell him she felt like going for a picnic in the shack.

She did not, when he asked her, feel like going to the reception that followed the wedding of Maggie's son Forbes. She didn't know any of the people, she told him, and anyway he'd be expected to keep Maggie company. That loud lanky blonde would be enough for him to handle, she said, let him spend all his attention on her.

But she came, in the end, out of curiosity. To see what kind of people he got himself tied up with, she said, to see how the other half lived. Weddings bored her, but a good brawl might be fun, and who knows what interesting men she might meet?

She met plenty of interesting men, he noticed, though most of them scared her. She danced with a good dozen or more of them, and turned down as many invitations to share a bottle in the parking lot. And the reception, though it never quite developed into the brawl she'd hoped for (and which he knew Maggie was dreading) was exciting enough. Danny Holland wasn't a disappointment.

"I don't know what she ever saw in that man," she said. "Even when she was — what? — fourteen? He makes my flesh crawl."

Wade's opinion of the champion axe-thrower wasn't much higher, but he kept it to himself. People who wore themselves out having what they called a good time were just as mysterious to him as people who broke their necks working too hard. And Holland, on top of it, was dangerous. Though a stupid man, he was probably just intelligent enough to guess what people thought of him, which was probably why he enjoyed torturing Maggie.

He did not, however, pay her any attention at all at the reception. He must have recognized what Maggie had done to him, must have realized how she'd left him behind, somehow, and was not what he thought her to be. If he looked at her at all, Wade noticed, it was only with some confusion. He'd found Virginia Kerr interesting, for a while, until she told him that she was a professor of art, at which he visibly recoiled. The word "professor" would be like a bucket of cold water over his head.

Along towards midnight Danny Holland got noisy. Someone at the bar had offended him. Voices tended to hush so that his could be heard better. "Wow!" Virginia Kerr whispered. "Language!" But she couldn't see anyone who looked shocked, or anything but amused. Even the little man at the bar who was the object of all the abuse looked only surprised and not the least bit frightened, until the big logger's hand flew out and clamped down on the top of his head. When Holland pushed his face down into the punch bowl there were cries of protest, and someone grabbed at the arm to pull it back before the little man drowned.

Of course Holland objected to the interference. Fists flew. Grunts and curses came louder than voices for a while, and more than one body came sliding out onto the dance floor.

It was left to Madmother Thomas to put a stop to the fight. She'd been scowling and muttering around all evening looking for a chance to even things up with Holland, and here it was. She went outside the hall for a moment, to her manure-spreader home, then came in with a hammer and walked right across the floor, her little pink tongue flicking like a frog's at her lips, her eyes inviting everyone to enjoy this. She went up behind Holland, who was jumping on someone's back, stood on a chair, and hammered his head. Three blows from that nail-driving champion and he was out cold on the floor.

Virginia cheered as loud as anyone else, Wade noticed, and giggled with delight at the way little Madmother Thomas strutted around the hall afterwards, displaying her hammer, collecting congratulations.

"Though you looked rather silly when you danced with her," she told him later. "That little white head just reached your belt. And those rubber boots seemed to have minds of their own."

And the next day, which was the day the stranger arrived on the beach, she wanted to know if Wade had ever been in love with Maggie Kyle.

"Of course not," he said.

"Ha."

"For most of my life she was a pain in the neck. Like a cousin."

"But now?" she said, to the blue sky. "But now?" She might have been expecting a song, or already hearing one.

"I never see her, " he said, "except maybe twice a year."

And anyway, he might have added, that seemed often enough for her. She gave him no reason to believe she wanted more, or saw anything in him that hundreds of others couldn't see.

They were walking out on the beach. The tide was low, the edge of the water barely moving, trimmed with a lace of bubbles. The strait was laid out beside them in the low morning sunlight like a wrinkled sheet of pale plastic stretched from there right across to the mainland. They walked barefoot on sand, made hidden clams squirt up out of their holes, chased crabs until they disappeared beneath rocks. "The other day I read in a book," she said, "that most of us have forgotten how to enjoy ourselves. But oh," she said, and breathed in air, "how could anyone breathe the smell of the sea and not feel that here he is, enjoying life?"

Sucking his stomach in he was conscious of his shorts shifting on his hips with every step. "I don't think our painter likes teaching. I bet you hate going back to that job."

But "No," she said. "I like that too. And my painting. And everything else." She stooped and watched a cluster of barnacles fanning for food in a tidal pool. "Just look at those things," she said. "Nothing but that one arm ever sees the world."

"Hold on," he said. "Don't go feeling sorry for barnacles. Cut your foot wide open on one and see how sorry you feel."

When they had gone up onto grass, climbed up through the white tide-smoothed logs and the eel grass waiting like razor edges to cut flesh, the grasshoppers were busy jumping. The warm air was full of their clicking, and every step the two of them make in the long grass brought dozens up, straight up, leaping off in every direction. They climbed the hill (the dead-burnt grass slippery as a waxed floor under their feet; they could have slid all the way down to the bottom again just by sitting and letting go) and stood up at last at the top where they could see in every direction, even a white cruise ship moving towards Alaska along the opposite side of the strait.

The girl cried out, as always, and turned around and around taking it all in. She plunged her hands deep into the dusty puffs of needles on a scrub pine. "Look out!" she called, "I may want to paint you next," though she meant pine, not him.

Then she led him, running down the first slope and up the second hill and then off across the long field towards the firs, the quiet fern-scented woods, waiting for them, dark as an empty church.

Inside the log shack the dirt floor was grown-over with moss. The air smelled damp. A giant fir had pushed a heavy branch in through an open window and, over the years, had lifted up that side of the building, tilting the whole thing out of shape; Powers leaned against the door frame and watched Virginia Kerr visit every corner like a priestess before putting the picnic basket down in the coolest spot. She poked her head out one window, as if to see if the view had changed since the last time she'd been here.

She said, "I don't understand how a man can do nothing but run a silly tourist trap. The season here is only a few months long, and most of the time you just hang around weeding a few flowers, never doing anything much."

And he laughed at her. Running one hand over his belly, over the hair on his chest. She could say some things he had no answer for. Or preferred to have none.

"Well?" she said, and looked steady at him, like a queen entertaining a reluctant courtier.

"Sometimes I do other things," he said. "Sometimes I sell for a friend in real estate."

She laughed, too, and raised her arms wide, waiting for him to move. "And so you're not in love with her? So the *cousin* doesn't mean a thing to you."

But he went across the floor to her and stopped her words with his mouth. Then he kissed her throat and down into the neck of her dress. After a while she let him take the dress off and kiss her breasts and the insides of her thighs. To be naked himself, all he had to do was thumb down the zipper of his shorts and suck in his stomach. The shorts fell to his feet. She went down on her knees in the moss and soon he went down too and, impatient now, pressed her onto her back and spread her red hair out on the moss around her head like a circle of fire.

And yes, yes he would agree with those people up and down the island coast. This was close, he thought, this was close to the ideal existence, as close as he had any right to expect. But he had waited for it, he had earned it. It hadn't come easy, or only from hoping. For years and years it had looked as if it might never come at all.

2

One of the problems was that Wade came from an up-island family who all appeared to have more energy than they knew what to do with. Their purpose in life, it seemed to him as a boy, was simply to burn up as much of it as they could, as fast as possible. Work, work, work. They were scared to stop in case all that energy should pile up, unused, and overwhelm them. His father worked all day on the mountains as a second-loader for the logging company, and drove the crummy besides, and once he got home came inside the house only long enough to gulp down his supper before going outside again to work on what he called his stump ranch. In his evenings he cleared field after field out of the bush with a homemade pieced-together tractor — cutting, hauling, blasting, burning, planting—he looked after the animals that kept them in meat and milk and eggs, and he fixed machinery in the little workshop behind the garage. If he did anything else at all, if he even left the place, it was only to help a neighbour to do the same kind of thing.

Wade's mother cooked, baked, housecleaned the high old bay-windowed house ("when you live in a community of Finns you can't have the only floor people couldn't eat off"), drove her Hudson in to town for shopping, drove neighbour women who'd never learned to drive down to Netty Miller's shop for their hair permanents, and bottled the fruit and vegetables out of their own orchard and garden. When the supper dishes were done she threw herself into an armchair, stuck her legs out onto a stool in front of her to rest them, and read the newspaper through from beginning to end, every column. Then a huge sigh and up again to run baths, iron, bake some more, make lunches, and write letters to relatives in Ontario. He had the impression that she leapt out of bed in the mornings already in high gear—the house woke when her heels hit the floor, there was no need for alarm clocks—and went full-tilt at everything in sight until she flung herself back onto the bed at night and instantly died, as she put it, to sleep the sleep of the just.

Life is too short, there's too much to do, they told him, life is for living, standing still is dying. But Wade Powers, who arrived after a series of three boys and two girls who'd already thrown themselves into their parents' activities as if caught up in a whirlwind they couldn't control, only watched and wondered at their madness. Everyone smelled of sweat.

"You have to put effort into life, you can't just sit," his father said.

"Wade thinks all he had to do was get himself born," his mother said. "He thinks once he put out that little bit of energy he shouldn't have to do anything else except ride on the coattails of other people's work." She had a way of saying things as if it were the ceiling, and not he, that could be interested.

There was nowhere else to look for different models. Uncles and aunts were as bad, worse. Besides holding down full-time jobs in the logging camps or in construction, and pushing back the borders of their own stump ranches dotted all around the valley, they found time to squeeze in leisure activities that seemed to take up even more energy than their work—mountain climbing, hunting for grouse, deer, elk, and moose, to keep them in gamey meat throughout the winter, weekend matches of football or baseball or basketball.

For a while he thought he had found a few neighbours whose lives were more consistent with his instincts. The settlement had originally been surveyed into sections by the government and sold cheaply to returned veterans after the First World War, as a reward for their efforts on behalf of their country, and at the same time as an incentive to get that rocky part of the island settled. It seemed for a while to Wade, when he discovered who these people were, that they must have all decided once they'd done their bit for the country that they didn't intend to do another thing with their lives but sit on their rewards and attend Legion functions. Ageing men, slow men, serious men, they had time to smoke their pipes and talk. From the stories they told him he could see they'd worked so hard during those war years that they deserved a lifelong rest. And worse, on looking closer, he discovered they had hobbies that kept them more than busy: wood carving, gardening, hog-raising, fox-breeding. Some of them had turned their land into full-time farms. They, too, had let him down.

Nowhere in the adult world was there anyone he could identify with.

"Well what do you expect?" his father said, sucking on a tooth-pick. "People have to take what they want out of life."

"And we're very sorry," his mother said, "that we couldn't arrange for you to be born into a royal family. If you were a prince, maybe, you could have servants to do everything for you, even wipe your bum."

It was a hard lesson to learn, that you had to wipe your own bum in this world, and he fought it. Mahatma Gandhi was his hero, but only symbolically; he liked the idea of just sitting tight until eventually you got your own way. If he took a passive-resistance attitude to life maybe the world would eventually give in and deliver itself into his hands.

But teachers, apparently, had never heard of Gandhi, or misin-terpreted. "You've got to try, you've got to try, you've got to try!" they screamed at him. Not one of them even gave a reason. "You've got to try!" They jabbed fingers into his books, as if all he had to do was roll up his sleeves and go at it the way his father went at a new field he was clearing. Even the teachers smelled of sweat. "I hate to use this word about anyone," they told his mother, "but he's just plain lazy."

"Bone lazy," his mother said, and tightened her lips. "He would be still in his crib if we hadn't burned it." She tried to help out by inviting his teachers to Sunday supper or to tea, and by joining the PTA, but it didn't do him any good. *Wade has more than enough ability*, they wrote on his report card year after year, *but he won't apply it*.

"It's only an ugly mask you're wearing just to spite me," his mother said. "And some day I'll find a way of ripping it off you." But she became so involved again in the whirlwind of work which had spun her and his father and the other children and everyone else they knew into a frantic pace, that she soon changed her attitude and only stopped once in a while to remind him that people usually got what they had earned in this world and not a single drop more. If it was a mask, truly, then she'd never managed to get a single glimpse behind it.

People were a lot of fools, he decided early. Slaving their butts off like worker bees, and what did it get them?

One thing it got was a roof over their heads, they told him, and food in their bellies. Where would they be without *those*, Mr. Smart? Would he rather they were all living out on the road somewhere? His father had an image of the road as a no man's land, a narrow strip of world that was reserved for all the people who weren't willing to break their backs carving out their pieces of the wilderness or who didn't care enough about their families to put food in their stomachs. He was never comfortable driving, as if he were afraid that others would suspect him of being "out on the road"; he used the highway and the backroads only for travelling to and from work, and never once took his family on anything so useless as a Sunday drive.

"You'll be the first Powers ever to be out on the road. Living hand to mouth."

A Powers was someone who would give the shirt off his back, a Powers was the salt of the earth, a Powers was someone who worked his fingers to the bone, a Powers was someone who wasn't afraid to shed a little sweat, a Powers was someone who wasn't scared to get his hands dirty.

A Powers, the youngest of them said, was a sap.

For a while there was Grandpa Barclay, who was not a sap. He worked as hard as anyone else, but he wasn't afraid to stop and talk; he could talk with a boy without having that "got to get back to it" panicky look in his eyes. Wade's own grandparents had been dead since before he was born, so he had no compunctions about adopting Jackson Barclay when he found him, or about spending all the time he could down on the dairy farm where the big house sat under giant maples and a creek ran twisting in and out among the sheds.

Mr. and Mrs. Barclay had raised seven daughters who'd grown up and married loggers and mill workers and truck drivers and moved off in every direction, leaving the two of them alone on their farm where the island highway was met by a road that came up from the beach. He raised Jersey cows, which he milked in the big old half-empty barn and pastured out in the square green fields whose borders were blurred by the alders that had grown up along fences and in the drainage ditches. He was a white-haired man with veins close to the surfaces of his nose and stubby hands already freckled with brown ageing spots. He'd never miss a chance to tell a harmless joke on someone else, then hunch-up and give a big wink that pulled his whole face out of shape.

Sometimes he took Wade on his horse-pulled wagon back down a lane past the hay fields and the stump pastures to the woods where he was cutting alder. In the little grove, thick with the smell of blackberries ripening beneath the grass, Wade watched him throw his plaid shirt over a stump, swing the double-bitted axe in strokes that sent pink-white chips as big as books flying across the clearing, stop to wipe his arms across his mouth and take a drink from a lukewarm jar of water he'd propped up in the shade of a maple tree. When the blackberry smell had been replaced by the sharp sweet scent of the bleeding alder Wade couldn't resist helping a little, by stacking the lengths of wood, slowly, without rush, onto the wagon to be hauled back to the buzz saw behind the barn.

And the old man would stop, and help him, just to be able to talk. He'd come out to this place from the prairies in nineteen twenty-four, he told him more than once, from Alberta. He left a poor farm behind, after a long hard winter that had killed horses, killed cattle. He came west just to take a look, he said, just to look the place over, and then he'd gone back full of excitement with his suitcase jammed with giant maple leaves and pine cones to surprise his daughters. He was tired of breaking his back for nothing; this was the land for him, where nature gave you a little help. "Kate and the girls came out on the passenger coach, but me, I earned my way," he said. "I rode on a freight train, they gave me my fare for looking after a trainload of hogs. I slept right in with them, earned my way west to this place, where a man could earn a decent life, I thought, without breaking his back."

This, Wade thought, was his true grandfather. When they paused like two runaway kids to rest under an alder tree, sometimes the old man would put his hand on his neck, lightly, and know that that was enough.

But there were others, Wade discovered, with prior claim. Those invisible daughters, off living their separate lives, had produced real grandchildren for him, who weren't above showing up to claim him, and to put Wade in his place. One of them was a skinny blonde named Maggie Maclean, a year or two older than he was. She'd be seven then, or eight, when he first saw her. "I bet I know what you want," she said. "I bet you want to steal my grampa's horse."

"Shut up," he said. "You're a girl."

"I bet you just hang around to get some of their homemade ice cream. You're not a cousin. You're not even *related*."

In her family, as in his, being related was a fence: all the good-guys were in, all the bad-guys were out.

"Look," he said, and undid his pants.

"Blaagh," she said, sticking out her tongue and crossing her eyes. He might have been offering a bowl of fish innards. Yet she didn't run away, she stared at him until he buttoned up, feeling foolish, and got on his bicycle to start for home. The maple-cooled feel of the yard had been spoiled.

"How long are you staying?" he said. There was still the chance that this was a one-day affair, she could leave again just as suddenly as she'd appeared.

But "All summer" was her answer. And "Next summer too, my parents want to get rid of me as much as they can."

So she became a fact of life. Maggie Maclean was installed, queen, at the Barclay farm, from the first of July every year until the beginning of September. Dominion Day to Labour Day, from Parade to Fair. There was no escaping her. Maggie's mother, the only Barclay girl who hadn't married salt of the earth, liked to accompany her husband on beachcombing trips up the west coast and right on up to the Charlottes. There was no room on the boat for a long-legged blonde-haired girl.

Grampa Barclay, Wade was glad to discover, hadn't known what to make of her either. She was just as foreign to him. "If I threw her in the creek," he said, "she'd be still talking a blue streak when she came out at the beach, that one." He crunched down a wink that united them both in their uncharitableness. "You don't know what life is, my boy, until you've lived it in a house full of eight women." Though it was clear, from his tone, that he wouldn't trade, not for a dozen boys.

"You're a weird one," Maggie had told him once. They were sitting on the back step of the cream-coloured farmhouse, beside the climbing rose, while she podded peas. Mrs. Barclay came out and set the bowl down between them and said, "There, that ought to keep you two out of mischief for a while. Earn your supper."

"You're a weird one," Maggie told him. "You never lift a finger, you never help. In all the summers I've come here I never once seen you lift a finger to help anybody but my grampa. How come?"

Already the sharp bones were shaping the face that would make her some day a beauty. She scooped up a handful of fallen rose petals, bruised them with her thumb, and inhaled their odour.

"How come what? Why should I help? I wouldn't think you'd want help from a person that wasn't *related*."

"I mean how come my grampa? How come you'll help him?"

He didn't know, he told her. How was he supposed to know? Maybe it was because the old man didn't expect it. Maybe it was because the old man was really a kid, too, and managed somehow to make his work seem like a game, like playing.

"Your grampa slept with the hogs once, on a train. He slept with a bunch of snorting old dirty hogs."

"He did not," she said. "You're just saying that."

"He did too, stupid. You don't know anything, you don't even know your own family."

"He didn't sleep with hogs."

"He slept with a train load of hogs, that's how he moved out here, sleeping with the hogs. That's how bad he wanted to move out here."

"Well I wish he never moved," she said, and slapped at his fingers that were sliding down into the bowl of shelled peas. "If he'd never moved out here, I wouldn't be living here either, and we'd never have met *you*."

One summer she showed up changed. She was a head taller than he was and had sprouted bumps inside her shirt. She didn't want to play any more, she didn't want to help around the farm. "Well, what do you want to do then, besides curl up and die?" he said, and she said "Oh nothing."

In the next few summers "Oh nothing" usually turned out to be one of two things: talk or walk. If it was talk, it meant she wanted to spend the day telling him about boys this and boys that, how Billy So-and-So was so immature but he was cute, and Jimmy So-and-So would be a good-looking guy if he'd only shave off that fuzz. She told about the silliness of the boys in her school, a little two-room place somewhere deep in the bush, and how Marlene her friend had vowed to be the first one in the class to see Paris. That kind of talk made him sick, he told her, didn't she know anything that wasn't silly?

If it was walk, it meant strolling up the narrow gravel shoulder of the island highway, squeezed between traffic and a ditch clogged full of yellow-flowered broom. He hated the walks because he didn't know how to react to her. He didn't know where to look when she pranced herself out onto the highway, swinging her hips so that cars had to go swerving around her, honking their horns. And he didn't know what to say when cars she waved at screeched to a stop and older boys hung out the window to ask her if she wanted to go for a ride. "Oh I can't," she told them, and rolled her eyes. "I have to babysit my cousin!" The boys always laughed and told her to dump him in the ditch and come along anyway, but eventually they gave up and drove off.

"That's stupid," he said. "You could get into trouble."

"What a sissy," she said, nudging him with her hip. "And besides, haven't I got you to protect me? If I need it?"

"Sure," he said. Though he thought, sometimes, that she could go to hell for all he cared, before he'd do a thing to stop her.

A mile or so up the highway, at a crossroads, there was a little wooden shack built years ago as a school-bus shelter. Boards had been torn off, shakes had blown off the roof, words had been knife-carved into the walls. "Let's go in," she said, once, that final summer, "I bet it stinks in there."

Wade knew the corner. The school bus stopped here for someone, a boy, he didn't know his name. Someone with long legs and a big red face, thumping down that gravel road, jacket flying out behind him while the bus driver hammered on his horn. Whoever he was, that panting boy, he'd pretended every morning that he was not late, that the bus had come too early. No one had used the shed as a bus shelter for years.

Still, nothing had grown up inside. The ground was packed solid as cement, littered with Orange Crush bottles and old cigarette packages. There was almost no roof left, except slats and a few shakes, between them and sky. A long-stemmed dandelion, its furry leaves in a gap under the wall, came up the inside of the two-by-four plate and stuck its flower head outside through a

large knothole. There were other knotholes too, higher up, with
elaborate drawings built around them.

"Look," she said, "I bet they peed out of this one."

He was more interested in another, a great fat naked woman
that grew out in rolls and creases from around a long iron-shaped
knothole. She was humped over, as if she were trying to see back in
through the gap that had been knocked out of her body's centre.

"And that one," she said, "reminds me of home."

She was a foreigner, she'd gone over into another country
without him. She smelled strange. She was even, he saw, wearing
false eyelashes and make-up that looked ridiculous on her face.
She was no longer just the girl, the yappy brat who spoiled the
summer. There was a danger in her, something had happened;
there was something in her now that made the inside of his mouth
go dry. He didn't know whether he wanted to touch the pale skin
of those long bare legs, or to run.

She slid a hand down under the waistband of her white shorts
and pulled out a Players package. Lighting a cigarette she narrowed her eyes, hunched over her cupped hands as if there might
be a wind. And when she stood upright and tossed the match out
onto the middle of the floor to die its own death, she blew smoke
down her nostrils, two perfect white streams.

"You could've offered me one."

She looked at him, surprised perhaps that he hadn't slunk
away, or evaporated in the foul air. "Christ," she said. "Don't you
have your own?"

Of course he didn't. Because of course he didn't smoke. He'd
thought that she didn't, either, that she'd bought that package so
they could try it together. But he could see now, it was obvious,
that she was practised at it. She held the thing as if she'd smoked
all her life. His face burned. She made him feel like a little boy.

She crouched down in one corner, her back up against the
boards of the wall, her white thighs widening out under the
pressure. Wade sat down on the ground, against the wall opposite
her. "Your parents," he said, "do they *still* go away every summer?
All summer?"

"Those shitheads?" she said, and blew smoke out between her
knees. "Who cares what they do?"

"Don't they ever plan to take you with them?"

She looked at him as if he'd suggested something obscene. "Who wants to go with them?"

"But it isn't fun any more for you, staying with grandparents all by yourself."

She slid a look at the door, blew smoke down her nostrils, and picked a piece of tobacco off her tongue between two painted fingernails. "I can hardly wait," she said, "to be different."

"Different from what?"

"Different," she said. "Different from *them*. Different from me. Different."

There didn't seem to be anything he could say to that, so he picked at a piece of cracked board until he was able to tear a long thin strip away from the wall.

Suddenly she tossed the cigarette out onto the floor, to die beside the match, and stood up. She shifted from foot to foot, pulling down the legs of her shorts. "Let's make a pact."

His chest tightened.

He was sure he knew what she was going to say.

But she said, "We're not cousins, we're something better than cousins. Let's say we'll always tell each other everything."

He could only look. What was there he could tell this girl, this woman? What "everything" did he have that he could tell? She was a foreigner, something different, she was going to be beautiful. She was already almost beautiful. What could he tell her that she wouldn't laugh at?

"We don't really matter to each other," she said. "Not like real relatives. So let's say I can tell you everything and you can tell me everything, and I can ask you anything and you can ask me anything."

"Yes," he said, and stood up. He had no idea what she was talking about. It sounded like some kind of silly game. "Okay."

"Good," she said. "Now I can tell you this: I think I'm going to have a baby. I think I'm — you know — pregnant."

The Barclays kept her through the winter until after the baby was born. Grampa Barclay, when Wade visited, could only wink and make jokes about it, as if to tell him *Here's one more thing you have to put up with when you have a house full of women.* She took the baby back to Hed with her, back into the bush, where her disgusted parents had abandoned the house to her. When she returned, after that, it was for shorter visits, to share the baby she'd named Forbes with her grandparents, and sometimes to walk with Wade along the side of the highway, talking.

"If I called you," she said. "If I suddenly phoned you from Hed to say I was in trouble, that I needed you, would you come?"

"I don't know," he said. "I don't know."

"But we agreed," she said. "That day, we agreed."

"Yes," he said. "yes, I would come." Though he couldn't recall that their agreement had had anything of the sort in it.

But she never called.

She visited. She grew older, more beautiful. She had more babies and hardly noticed them. She worked, sometimes, in the General Store. And did housekeeping. She was what his mother called cheap. "Not a bit like the Barclays, I knew the girls well, you could never accuse them of being cheap. I don't know where that one came from, she must be a throwback." There were people, she said, and he might as well learn it now as later, there were people who chose to live as if no one had invented civilization. There were people who chose to ignore everthing that humanity had done to improve life over thousands of years. You couldn't do anything about them, she said, except feel sorry.

But Wade Powers didn't feel sorry for Maggie Maclean. If she'd called him, if she'd telephoned from Hed and told him something terrible was going to happen to her, he would be on the road in minutes, heading back in to the mountains. He didn't feel sorry for her, he grew more and more fascinated, and said so.

"Of course a person who doesn't think he needs to put any effort into life is bound to be fascinated by primitives," his mother said. "Only you're wrong, my young man, if you think that kind of life would be easy."

Never mind that, he thought. Because I'll show you. I'll find out a way a person doesn't have to break his neck to make a living.

But it hadn't been so easy to find. When the school teachers decided there wasn't any point in his wasting still more of their time, his father announced that anyone not going to school had to get out and earn his keep. Time, he said, to get a job.

"I'll look," Wade said. "I'll start looking for a job." It was something that could last for years if he handled it right.

"Don't bother," his father said. "Because I already found you one. Tomorrow morning you start your career as a logger."

Though he worked for the logging company he was never a

logger. He was helper to the company surveyor's assistant, and spent two months with a little stone-nicked axe in his hand, holding the assistant's steel tape, hacking small brush out of the way, and crayoning numbers onto stakes while they laid out the route for a new truck road around one of the mountain lakes. He fell into the lake more than once, lost his axe several times, chopped down a tree that nearly landed on the assistant's head, and scrambled up the sequence of number so thoroughly that a whole section had to be re-mapped, but he stuck with the job to the far end of the road before quitting. It was all a waste of his time and his energy, he said. And as if to prove him right, when he drove back to the lake a few years later to see what kind of road had resulted, he found they'd changed their minds about it. That even his stakes were gone, and all the brush he'd chopped down to make a clear trail along that line had grown up as thick as it had been before. There was no sign, even, that he'd ever been there.

"Break your back," he said, "and for what?"

He did not break his back at any of the other jobs which seemed to be forced on him by a world that couldn't stand to see him idle. He might have gone on driving a school bus forever if he hadn't discovered that when it broke down he was expected to fix it. The nicest thing about selling insurance, he discovered, was that he could take his time. No rush, he said, I'm my own boss. But as his own boss, he saw no point in holding down a job that brought no money in at the end of the month. Selling real estate, too, was like that. He could set his own pace. It was a job you could do with your eyes shut, you didn't have to know anything, you didn't have to lift a finger unless you wanted. But while his eyes were shut and his fingers idle, other greedier salesmen got busy and sold houses and land to the people who'd originally come to him. There was no point in even getting out of bed in the morning, he thought, if life was meant to be a competition, to see who could be the first to kill himself from overwork.

It wasn't until he hit on the idea for the fake historic fort that he began to see that it was possible, after all, to live the kind of life he wanted. When several of his mother's vertebrae were broken in the tractor accident that killed his father while they were clearing land together, he invited her down to sell tickets at the gate. She would do it, she said, but only if he allowed her to cook, sew, clean house, preserve, shop, wash, iron, keep the books, and pay the bills for him. If she had to be idle, she said, if she couldn't go on working the way she always had, then she might as well have been finished off under that overturned tractor. People weren't meant to sit around in wheelchairs, she said. She left him, often, in the long off-season, to visit his brothers and sisters and help them in their mad whirlwinds: spiralling up through careers, building families, building homes, throwing themselves into civic activities in order to catch other, lazier people up in the swirl too: but she always came back, content that they didn't really need her and convinced that somehow her example, if demonstrated in front of Wade long enough, would eventually impress him, even — she hoped — become contagious. "You can't imagine the content-ment," she said, "in throwing yourself into the bed at the end of the day, completely worn out, knowing that you've put in a good day's work."

He could imagine it all right, he thought, but by then he'd already spent thirty years trying to avoid it.

While he was still living on his parents' farm, driving a school bus, he came very close to marrying a girl named Maryann Klas-sen, the daughter of leading members of the Mennonite commu-nity a few miles up the highway. They had something he wanted, a mystery. He'd met her at school, a small pretty girl with long hair, and she gave the impression that there was a secret she knew, a something no one else could take from her. He wanted it, what-ever it was. "The religion of my family is called Work," he said. "I wouldn't mind trying something else." She told him that was hardly a good enough reason for a proposal, and he said would it help if he told her he loved her, and she said that was a start at least. Eventually she agreed that though no one else in the com-munity had ever married outside the faith, she couldn't see any reason why she shouldn't be the first, considering things. She had a wide mouth, red without the aid of lipstick, and a pink spot that appeared on either cheek while she was talking to him. Not even her father, he discovered, was against the match. He'd had daughters, he said, instead of sons, and could do with the help of a strong young son-in-law, whatever his faith might be. An extra pair of shoulders around the place, he said, one more strong back, would be a welcome help. But when Wade saw what was ex-pected of that extra pair of shoulders, that extra back — working like a Russian peasant on a "hobby" farm large enough to keep a

dozen families busy — and when he considered the hard disapproving looks which were directed constantly at him by the
mother, who spoke no English, he began to question seriously the
nature of his feelings for the daughter. He was not, after all, in
such an all-fired hurry to become a Mennonite as he'd thought,
no matter what spiritual secrets would consequently be withheld
from him forever.

He married, instead, an overdeveloped girl by the name of Laura
Schmidt, the only daughter in a large family of drunken thieves.
They lived in an old shack far up a dirt road, in a died-out orchard
cluttered with car parts and broken iceboxes and bedsprings.
Neither the old man nor any of the six brothers worked; they lived
off the results of "trades" they were always making with people,
exchanging one useless piece of machinery for another but always in such a way that they ended up with a little more than the
trade-partner had intended them to have. It was what the old man
called "stepping up in the world" and would eventually lead
him, if he lived long enough and logic was something you could
count on, to being the richest man in the district. Laura, too, was
traded off to Wade, though not in any way quite so obvious as the
bedsprings and car parts were traded. Without her, the old man
said, there would be one less mouth to feed: that in itself was a
profit. But in handing her over, he said, he expected to gain a
son-in-law who would lend a helping hand now and then, when
the volume of trade was too heavy for "the boys", and who
wouldn't be above sharing some of his liquor supply when the
police had been out in their yearly visit to smash up his still and
break all the bottles in his stock. Wade agreed to everything,
though he had no intention of doing any of it, because Laura had
thrown herself at him, practically begged him to marry her, and he
didn't know how to pass up an opportunity like that. As soon as
the wedding was over he moved south to build his fort and had no
dealings at all with his in-laws.

"You're a goddam fraud," the old man said. "But you don't
need to think for a minute you'll get away with it. Nobody out-
deals Montgomery Schmidt. Nobody."

There was hardly time for revenge. Within a month after the
wedding Laura, the bride, having found her way out of that drunken family, decided to keep right on going. She disappeared with
an American tourist who told her that in his California orange

grove there was nothing to do but lie around all day getting a suntan and thinking of ways to spend his money. How could she refuse an offer like that, she wrote later. Surely Wade would understand why she couldn't turn him down.

Oh, he understood all right, he wrote her. He understood only too well. But he couldn't see why she hadn't suggested taking *him* along too. Didn't he enjoy sunshine every bit as much as she did?

But what did he really care about that? The thing that really mattered, the thing he'd waited for all his life had happened. He had The Fort. He had those tourists so eager to part with their money. He had Virginia. Things were perfect.

3

On the afternoon of the day after the wedding, while Virginia painted in her yellow house, he walked by himself out on the beach, on the exposed side of the spit, a hundred yards out from the shoreline, just above the bed of green slimy seaweed that lay exposed and stinking along the edge of the water. He walked on rocks big as footballs, scarred with barnacles and limpets the shape of coolie hats, and whenever gulls came flapping down to investigate his movement he threw pebbles like bits of food and then waved his arms to send them screeching away. There was a dull ache in his groin. His stomach felt as if he'd swallowed fire. It was whenever he did too much thinking that he bloated up with gas, like a cow trapped on its back in a hole.

The figure coming towards him down the beach seemed at first to be vaguely familar, even at a distance. There was something about the loose hip-tilting walk he thought he recognized. It was a man, he saw, dressed in white pants and an orange shirt, but it was no man he had ever seen before. And when the stranger got close enough for Wade to see his face, he realized with a cold flush of shock that he was looking at an exact duplicate of himself. The man smiled, said "Hello" in a voice that sounded like Wade's voice, and then passed right by and kept on walking down the beach. Wade was too surprised to speak, nor did he make any effort to follow. He watched the man until he disappeared around the tip of the spit, out of sight behind The Fort.

At dinner he pushed the fat sausages around on his plate and tried to eat. His mother shovelled her own food in as if she were afraid someone would steal it, talking the whole time about a family of black people who came to The Fort today all the way from Mississippi. "Drove a big old red converted school bus," she said, "a whole pile of black faces looking out. It seemed like there was one for every window. And clean, I've never seen a whole family of kids all look so clean before, every one of them. Like little black dolls. I wish we had more black people in this country, they're so different from everybody else. Your stomach acting up again?''

Yes it was, he said. And she pulled his plate across the table and began eating off it as if she were the Queen of Somewhere at a banquet. That was how dainty she could be if she wanted, nibbling with just her front teeth.

"Was there a man went through today?'' he said. "Did you sell a ticket to a man in an orange shirt?''

She shrugged. "Who knows?'' through a mouthful of potato. "What did he look like?''

He couldn't tell the truth straight on. "Dark,'' he said. "Lots of black hair. Tall. He had white pants on.''

"Maybe,'' she said, though she looked dubious. "There was a lot of people today. Business was good.''

Business was always good. In the six years he'd been open there hadn't been a summer yet when tourists had failed to flock through. They handed over their money with an eagerness that made him suspect the only thing important to them was parting with it, that what they saw didn't matter to them as much as the desire to spend every cent they'd brought along on their holiday. The sight of tourists streaming off the government ferries onto the island had given him his idea for The Fort. They were just begging for him to take their money.

"Business was good,'' his mother said, again. "It wouldn't hurt you to hang around more. Show some interest.''

The next afternoon he went out onto the beach again at the same time in case the stranger should walk by. He knelt at the edge of the seaweed bed and listened to the crackling sound of hundreds of tiny crabs moving about beneath the rocks. He pulled in a piece of kelp, laid it out on the rocks, and stepped it off. Forty feet of stem, nine feet of leaves, and the Indians had known uses for every inch. He thought of Virginia Kerr in her house up there, painting that ridiculous picture and thinking she was doing something important. He recalled what it was like to be close to her, and to listen to her voice. When the stranger came walking towards him, Wade was so preoccupied that the man was almost past before he noticed him.

"Ah!'' he said, and stood up.

Yes, it wasn't a trick of light or imagination. The man was the exact image of himself. Even his dark eyes had the same flecks of pale green. Wade, excited, waited for him to notice it, too, and to say something.

But he didn't seem the least bit impressed. He smiled, said "Hello again, you must like this spot," and moved on past.

"Yes," Wade said. "I own that place over there, that fort there."

"Oh?" The man stopped, and showed his teeth, and rubbed the front of his shirt. He looked back at the stockade fence, at the top of the bastion showing above it, and raised one eyebrow. Then he studied Wade's face as if looking for clues to something. "A place like that must be a big responsibility," he said, which was not at all the kind of thing Wade might say.

"Look," Wade said, and stuck out his hand. "The name's Wade Powers."

"Yes," the man said, and held the hand in his grip for just a second, then let go. "Nice to meet you. Hope you don't mind if I take my walk along here."

Wade shrugged. "Nobody owns the beaches."

"True."

"And anyway, you're welcome here."

The man looked at Wade as if he had doubts about that. He looked again at The Fort. "I suppose I should have a look at the inside of your outfit there," he said. "Some day."

Wade watched his walk, his own walk, all the way to the point, and his knees felt weak. There was sweat running in streams down his sides. After a while he, too, walked to the point, saw the man walking far down the curve of the bay, and followed.

He followed the stranger nearly a mile down the beach, then up an access road to a campsite. The man went into a long house-trailer for a few minutes, then came out and drove away in a car paler than the sky, a silver-blue sedan that looked as if someone had tried to see how close paint could come to being invisible. Wade felt like someone who had just come through a museum where he'd admired everything there was, and then realized that he hadn't the slightest idea what any of it meant.

"Everybody has a double," he said, because that was something he'd heard his mother say at some time. He decided that when the man came into The Fort he would ask him why he hadn't seemed to notice how similar they were. Maybe he never looked in a mirror.

"Who says they have to look the same?" Virginia said, when Wade told her the painting she was doing didn't look like any beach he'd ever seen.

"It looks like somebody's insides," he said.

"Not yours I hope," she said, and gave him a look.

"You spend all summer painting a picture that's supposed to look like that beach out there and all you get is this. I could do better with a camera."

"Boy, you're touchy today," she said. "And all of a sudden you're an art critic."

He felt lousy. His stomach churned. He couldn't keep his mind off that damned man in the silver car. He had the suspicion that when he got around the corner the car and man both vanished into thin air, like a space ship. Not even Virginia Kerr in her red bikini could snap him out of it. "It's a waste of your time," he said. "I hope that's not how you teach your pupils to paint."

"Look," she said. "Don't you know anything? Can't you see what I'm trying to do? I don't *want* this painting to look like what you see when you look at that beach. You look with the eyes of a man who makes his living from cheating tourists."

"And you of course," he sang, "see with the eyes of an artist." He did a dance step in the middle of the room to show his opinion of artists.

But he'd spoiled it for today and she threw her brushes down. She turned the easel so the painting was facing the wall. Then she walked across the room and pushed him backwards into the sofa. "Damn you, Wade Powers," she said. "What do you know about anything?"

And sat on him.

"What good are you anyway?" she said

"Well, if you get up off my lap for a minute I'll just show you."

She laughed and moved off and slid her hand down inside his pants. "Show me what?" she said. "Show me this? What do you think I could make of this if I painted it?"

"Painted it?" he shouted. And stood up to drop his pants.

She locked the front door and led him through to her bedroom. "Don't notice the mess," she said. "Don't notice I haven't even made the bed today."

When he lay beside her, exhausted and exultant, he told her the reason he couldn't stand being over in that fort all day long was that the sight of tourists disgusted him. A bunch of fools was what they were, he told her, to part with their money so easily. They came into the place looking as if there was a real treat in store for them, and went out again looking as if something had just been added to their lives. They thought they were stepping back in time, living their own ancestors' lives for a moment, and didn't even suspect what idiots they were. They'd take pictures and go home thinking they'd been inside a real fort that was used once to hold off a howling pack of Indians. Or more likely, he told her, they'd drive on to the next tourist trap up the highway and forget by the end of the day that they'd ever been at his place. It probably wouldn't even bother them to be told what they'd paid for was only a rough counterfeit of the real thing.

"It makes me sick to see how stupid people can be," he said.

She told him the problem was he had too much time to sit around thinking. What he needed was a job. But sometimes he did get a job, he told her, sometimes he went out selling real estate just to get away. "It's remembering those stupid tourists that makes it easy for me to talk people into paying twice too much for things they don't even really want."

"Ha!" She slapped his bare buttocks and sat up. "When you talk like that I don't even want to guess what it is you really think of me."

The stranger, in his immaculate white pants and orange shirt, walked with Wade up onto the hill of grass the next day and sat down where he could see all up and down the strait. He said the little fort on the point of land didn't look like much beside all the rest of this natural scenery.

"It's a good spot, though," Wade said. "The highway follows the coast in both directions, people can see this point for ten miles coming."

"It's a good enough spot," the man said. "A nice spot for a park. You couldn't ask for a better proof." He took it all in with his moving eyes, following the spit from the stand of high firs down across the rolling field to the rocky point with its sudden wood tower. Then his gaze lifted and sought out a sprinkle of white dots, fishing boats, clustered far out on the water. "There's a handful of optimists," he said. "This time of day."

"This is the first summer I've seen you around here," Powers said. "Where do you come from?"

"From?" He raised an eyebrow. "Oh, nowhere." He dismissed the question with a brief gesture of his hand.

Wade listened to the air, to the grasshoppers. "Better proof of what?" he said.

"Proof?" the man said, and frowned to recall. "Oh, proof of things that need to be proved."

"I've lived on this island all my life," Wade said. "If somebody asked *me* where I come from I'd be able to point to a square inch on a map and say *there*."

"People are different," the man said. "Some are more tied."

"Yes?"

"To earth. To things. To themselves, to their own bodies."

Wade's bowels grumbled. Gas swelled in his stomach. "But …haven't you noticed anything strange?"

The man looked at him. "About what?"

"About us. About how much we look alike. We could be twins." A muscle twitched in Wade's eyelid.

"What?"

"Looking at you is like looking in a mirror."

"Good heavens," the man said. And laughed again. "What an idea. You must be joking." And lay back on the grass to stare at the sky.

Wade was afraid for a moment that he was going mad. He wished Virginia Kerr were here to see the two of them side by side. He wished he could get this fellow down where his mother could have a look at him.

"Look," he said. "How about coming down for a look at The Fort?"

The man shook his head. "Not today," he said. "Maybe tomorrow. When I get back."

"Back from where?"

"A man of God is a busy man," he said. "I'm on the road a lot, it's not very often I get the time to lie around like this."

"What?"

He sat up, shaking his head. "Oh, I don't mean preacher, not a minister. It was a silly thing to say, I suppose, but you see that's the way I think of myself, of us all."

"Then what do you *do*?" Wade said. He was beginning to think the mad one in this pair wasn't himself after all.

But the man was not listening. He was following, evidently, some idea of his own across the blank sky. "There's a woman," he said, "lives a few miles north of here. Most of her house burned down a while back and she's living in just the room that's left. She's expecting me."

"You're in insurance, then."

"Now the question is this: Can you really say her house burned down when there's still a room left standing? Can you even say it's the same house?" Suddenly he sighed deeply, and stood up to go. "I'll come down and have a look at your place there tomorrow afternoon."

After his mother had finished eating both their dinners again he walked over to Virginia's house and went in. But she noticed the sweat that had broken out all over his body, she commented on the way his hands were shaking, she even heard the rumblings of his guts. "You better go home to bed," she said. "You're in no condition for anything at all." He took a good look at her painting again, to see if he could recognize anything in it yet. But it still looked like nothing at all to him. And anyway, she told him, she hadn't felt like adding a thing to it today. She needed a rest from it, she said. He went back to his own house and crawled into bed.

He wasn't sick, he knew that. Yet he felt like a man in a fever. Something terrible was struggling to be born in his brain. He grunted and farted and sat up suddenly. He tried to read, and threw the book across the room. His mother banged on the door, calling out: "Wade, are you all right? Are you sick? Wade?" But he told her to shut up and leave him alone, nothing was wrong, he was all right, go on back to bed. He suspected that she stayed out there, just outside his door, for the whole rest of the night, listening, waiting for him to call out for help. He kicked and fought his way right into sleep and slept fitfully and dreamed that the stranger, hovering above his head in the silver-blue space ship, chased him all up and down this coast, all up and down every road and in every valley of the mountains, trying to suck him up with a gigantic vacuum cleaner. When he awoke in the morning the thing in his brain had been born, he knew what it was he was going to do.

"You stay here today," he told his mother. "I'll look after the ticket booth." She closed her eyes, recoiling from the shock, then squinted at him like someone trying to see through a mist. "Yes, stay," he said. "Do something here." And touched her once, on the shoulder, before going.

He put up a closed sign in the ticket window and walked back to Virginia's place. "I feel just fine today," he said, but she told him to go away and let her try to paint. Maybe tomorrow they could go back to the log shack for a picnic lunch.

"Tomorrow," he said. And knew that whatever tomorrow was, it wouldn't be the same as today. He went out onto the beach to wait.

The man arrived at the same time as usual, smiled at Wade as if just barely recognizing him, and walked ahead of him up to the gate of The Fort. He looked at the "closed" sign and at Wade, but Wade went through first and showed him in. The man said "Mmmm" about everything he saw: the flowers, the stockade fence, the weapons display. He walked into the ground floor of the bastion ahead of Wade and stepped right inside the prison just as everyone else did, and just as Wade knew he would do.

When Wade stood in the prison doorway the man was leaning up against the curved rock wall, looking back at him. "I wonder how many people have died in here," he said. "I heard once about a man who was locked up in one of these, down-island, a hundred years ago. After three years they let him out but within the day he was back begging to be let in again."

"I never heard of him," Wade said.

"I can't remember which bastion it was in. I guess it couldn't have been this one."

Wade put one hand on the clammy stones. "No. It couldn't have been this one. Nothing like that happened here."

"But still," the man said. "It would feel like a pretty small world. There'd be nothing in it but yourself. Or what you thought was yourself."

"They love this prison," Wade said. "The tourists. They all go in there and imagine themselves locked up. They think it's the real thing, that real people died here in it. Like you. And the funny thing is, it's not real at all."

The man looked up. "What?"

"I mean it's a phoney. There never was a fort here, not in this part of the island, no Indian wars or anything. I built this thing by copying a picture in a book."

"But the people think ... "

"They read the little brochure that tells them it's a replica and still they think it's genuine. Like magic, it fools them."

"Nevertheless," the man said, his head tilted in thought. "If you've offered it to them with love, if you're giving them this because it's the closest you can come to the real thing, and if the real thing is something you want them to have, then you're not really cheating them at all. They spend their lives being satisfied with reasonable facsimiles. This is no different. The important thing of course is motive. Any gift, offered with love, has some value."

"It's a business," Wade said. "It's my business."

"Then it's offered with contempt." The man sat down on the little bench where the curved outside wall and the straight inside wall met. "We're farther apart even than I imagined." He looked as if he truly regretted it. "I thought yesterday for a moment or two when we talked that it wouldn't be hard to find at least one point at which we touched. Tangent line and circle. But evidently I was wrong."

Wade shrugged his shoulders.

"Are you familiar with the woman who was burned out? Do you know her at all? She lives only a few miles north of here."

No, Wade said. He didn't know many up that way. He hadn't heard of anyone being burned out, but it could've been any one of a number of old ladies.

"She isn't old. She's young. She could still be in her twenties, I suppose, though it's not my business to ask. She was a mother — all three of her children died in that fire. Three little boys sleeping in the same bedroom; there was hardly anything left of them by the time the firemen arrived. They were all she had, her husband had left her years ago, they were her life; feeding them, clothing them, caring for them, loving them. Now all she has is that charred room she's living in, nothing else. A few clothes. A garden. The sympathy of neighbours."

"I told you I don't know her."

"I thought she would cry, I thought she would...well, you can imagine for yourself what a young woman in a situation like that would demand, who she would curse, how she would carry on. Well, there was only one thing she wanted from me, just one thing she said she needed me to find for her.

"What's that?"

"A child. She said she couldn't live without somebody to care for. She said the only thing she'd ever done that was worth doing was caring for those kids, and she couldn't stand the thought of living if she didn't have someone to love. I told her there was a whole human race out here, what was the matter with them?"

Wade sneered. "I bet that was a great comfort to her."

"These stones," the man said, feeling the wall, "did you haul them up off the beach?"

"Every one of them. And cemented them together. It took me a whole month to build just this bottom floor."

"I suppose if it were real there would be blood stains and filth around, and a lot of scratches on the stones. This looks too new and clean."

Wade stepped back and closed the big door before the man could continue. He slid the iron bolt to lock it and waited for the man to start yelling or pounding on the door. But he waited a long time, sweating, and heard nothing at all. There could just as easily have been no one in there.

He went out of the bastion and spent a long time making a CLOSED FOR THE SEASON sign which he nailed up on the outside of the gate. Then he went back into the bastion and unlocked the prison door. The man was still leaning against the stone wall, looking back at him with Wade's own face. He looked as if he'd counted on Wade to come back at exactly that moment.

"Look," Wade said. "This is a hell of a thing. I shouldn't have done that."

The man rubbed the front of his shirt and smiled. "Is this something you do to all your visitors?"

"Yes," Wade tried to laugh. "No. Of course not."

"I don't think you'd keep your business licence for long if you did."

Wade didn't know where to look. Could he ask a man to please stay there in the prison, to please hang around long enough for him to figure him out? Could he say *I want you where I can keep an eye on you*? "There's someone I want to meet you," he said. "Will you stay here just until I bring her?"

The man shrugged. "Better still, I'll go with you."

"No," Wade said. And again "No" as he locked the prison door.

Virginia was raging mad. "God damn you!" she screamed at him when he came in the door. "God damn you to hell!" And threw brushes on the floor, threw tubes of paint at the wall. "I can't see it any more, you've made me lose it!"

He moved a step forward, then stopped. "What are you talking about?"

"The painting!" she screamed, and threw a jar that went past his head and broke against the door. "When I look at the damn thing I can't see it any more, I see what *you* see." She began to cry.

"Look," he said. "You want something to paint, you come with me."

"Oh go to hell, Powers. Go...to...hell." She bared her teeth, backing into the bedroom. "Don't you come around me any more." She slammed the door. And hollered, "You just keep away."

"Please," he said. "There's something you've got to see."

He waited a long time before she came out of the bedroom. And when she did come out she was dressed in a tailored suit, something he'd never seen before. Her hair was tied back. She kept her eyes away from him, a little to his left.

"All right," she said. "Before I go. Show me."

He knew, before they even got to the bastion, what it was they would find. He wasn't even surprised that the door to the prison was open, though of course there was no way to unlock it from the inside. He stood a moment in the doorway, looking at the stone wall where the man had been. Virginia waited.

"Well?" she said.

"It's nothing," he said. "It's just that I thought I had found something."

She looked at him. "You wouldn't recognize it," she said. "With your eyes you wouldn't recognize it. What makes you think you would even recognize something if you did find it?"

He did nothing to stop her from leaving. He could think about her later. And anyway she'd be back next spring to start another of her paintings. While she walked across the fenced-in yard and passed out of sight through the gate he stayed in his home-made bastion, leaning against the open doorway to the prison, breathing the damp stale smell and staring at the wall of cemented stones. After a while, when there seemed to be nothing left for him to hear, he thought for a moment that there might be footsteps moving about over his head, treading the loose planks of the third floor, passing slowly back and forth across the bastion like the soft deliberate steps of a hunter. More likely it was nothing at all, a branch of the jack pine brushing the wall.

Then there was silence, perhaps total. Not even the splashing of waves or the low hum of wind in grass disturbed it. He might have believed he had driven sound away too, with Virginia and the stranger, that when he sent them away he had turned off some great switch supplying energy to the world outside.

For a moment he stood in the doorway to the prison and contemplated the possibilities of silence. Then he ducked out, chose sunlight, and heard the beginnings of life again. Tires whined by on the highway; a jet streaked eastward ahead of its own sound; seagulls screeched. He headed across the yard towards his car.

4

So it wasn't Maggie Kyle, after all, who was the one to take advantage of that vague childhood bargain.

"Gone?" she said. "That redhead?" Tidying up her wall of maps, pinning back the flopped-over corners of ageing charts, she listened to his tale as if she'd heard it all before and could beat the rhythm of it with her nodding head. Then she laughed. "Did she take the painting with her, or leave it to haunt you for the rest of your life?"

"I don't know, I didn't think to look. She could've stolen all my furniture and I wouldn't know it, I haven't checked the house out yet."

One of the problems with telling Maggie anything was that she sometimes missed the point, or pretended to, and burrowed straight for something you'd never thought of.

"I know his name," she said. "I'm sure I've heard his name somewhere. Something tells me. It'll come to me, just wait."

She put the breakfast coffee on the stove and told him to sit down while they waited for it to heat up. He sat at the wooden table in the middle of her kitchen, where he could see through the old library to the log cabin behind. There was a newspaper laid out in front of him, folded lengthwise down the middle. The price of sugar was going up again. *Slayer claims he was provoked.* London. Cairo. Seattle. *Oil Tankers Dispute Continues.* Nanaimo: *Drunken Vandalism Feared Again at Bathtub Race.* No mention of a visitor from Mars, in a space ship, who could unlock impossible doors. The cost of living was up. Strange phrase: cost of living. Like an admission ticket. His head ached. It seemed like forever since he'd last been here, in this house, but it was only a week. The place smelled of something, of something other than burnt coffee, it smelled sweet, like flowers. Her corsage was on the windowsill, stuck in the top of a water glass. It was Virginia Kerr who had reminded him, had told him to buy it. Get white, she said, it'll go with anything, and everybody likes roses. Week-old, now, they were shrivelled, and dry, and looked bruised. There must be other flowers, somewhere, that smelled.

Maggie stood by the stove, waiting. She probably hadn't combed that blonde hair today, nor had she any intention of doing so. She looked better, sometimes, when she just slopped around, and she knew it. There was a button missing from that plaid shirt you hardly ever saw her without. But for all the sloppiness about her, she was careful to stand where the light would hit her just right, and play up those cheekbones. He could almost believe she was pouting her mouth for him.

"I've only got rid of Madmother Thomas today," she said, and turned the coffee pot to encourage it. "She came back here after the wedding and stayed put for the week. She kept her old manure-spreader out by the well, I thought Julius would set fire to it, the looks he gave. Or push it over the cliff if he could."

"She deserved the week," he said, "after her heroism."

"And now she's gone," she said. And lifted the coffee pot to pour, ready or not. "I'm surprised you didn't see her on your way in. Off to lord-knows-where to drive other people crazy."

He looked down, into the deep ridges of the table's grain. Virginia Kerr said the old woman had worn rubber boots, when he danced with her. And kept her hammer hooked in her belt. She'd smelled of rubber too. Rubber and that dusty smell of dry hair.

"Oh, she had them all stirred up around here before she left," Maggie said. "Lily still hasn't come down from her bedroom where she's spent the week in a huff. Becker's in hiding. And sour old Julius was ready to commit murder."

When she put the mug of coffee down in front of him something felt heavy, for a moment, in his chest. He would have touched that perfect hand, if he hadn't thought she would pull away, or laugh.

"Bring your coffee out onto the porch," she said. "I could do with some fresh air."

"So the redhead has gone," she said, as he followed her out with his yellow-rimmed mug. "And the man drove a silver car and trailer. It'll come to me, something tells me I know his name. Something'll jar it loose."

She did not take him onto the verandah towards the water, but out the back, to the porch that faced onto the grassy courtyard and the ring of cabins. The sun was on his side, and shone down through the moving branches of the arbutus trees. The grass was littered with the fallen leaves, big and yellow and waxy. July was a messy time of year when you lived with arbutus, you just had to wait until they'd lost all that they could, and then clean up after them. If you left the leaves they grew brittle, and walking broke them into tiny flakes or even powder. Wade would leave his, Maggie would probably rake. Or get one of her freakish boarders to do it.

He sat on a canvas chair, carefully — it looked thin, probably rotten—and she perched on the railing to face him. "I'm thinking of getting Carla back," she said. He couldn't expect her to concern herself with his problems for long. "From those people in Victoria. It's not too late yet to be something of a mother to my youngest."

Maybe those who thought she was crazy were right. "Maggie, why should she want to come back? And think what a kid could do to this place, imagine what she could do to your old people. Especially any daughter of yours."

And anyway, what were they doing talking about her? It was typical, he thought, that she would get it turned around to herself. He'd come roaring in here because he thought she might be able to help him track down that stranger, that twin, with her trailer-park connections, and what did he get?

"And anyway," he said, "you're a rotten mother. You always were, you can't change that kind of thing overnight. Mother your old people, and those others, leave the poor kid alone."

"Oh, but I'm going on this retreat first, to get ready. I've signed up."

Hens cackled, somewhere in the bush beyond the cabins.

I don't believe this woman, Wade Powers thought.

He said, "Signed up for what?" She wanted him to ask, he could see by the look on her face. Eager to tell him.

"It's a two-week thing, on this tiny island out in the strait. If I was rich, or American, I guess I'd be hauling myself off to a psychiatrist, or jumping into a pool full of naked people. Or if I was European I could go off on a pilgrimage, and walk barefoot up mountains, and starve myself and expect miracles that will transform me. But I'm not. This is the best I could find. I've signed up for this session on a tiny island where we'll live like medieval monks or Spartans or something and learn about ourselves."

He laughed. "I don't believe it." It was the kind of thing she might joke about. He saw her walking around the edge of a little island, chanting something ridiculous and beating herself with a birch branch.

But she smiled a private kind of smile. "Cora Manson told me about it, she read all about it in the papers and of course she was shocked and disgusted. She didn't know we had such things around here, she said, she thought we were civilized here. And shouldn't someone do something to stop them?"

"A bunch of freaks and intellectuals," Wade said. "They'll eat you up. Or turn you inside out."

"But I thought *why not*? and got in touch. There's a psychiatrist and a minister of some kind and an expert in sensitivity training and someone who knows about religions."

"Will you have to fast?" he said, and hoped he was sarcastic enough for her. Sometimes she didn't catch things she didn't want.

And she didn't. "I doubt it, though there'll be someone to teach meditation. Transcendental meditation."

It was what people expected of Maggie Kyle. They would only be surprised that she wasn't doing something like going off with a guru into Tibet.

"If you're looking for a new direction ... "

"Oh, I've chosen my direction," she said, wide-eyed, across the top of her raised mug. "And I've cleared the decks. What I don't know is *how*. Maybe this thing will tell me."

And maybe it won't, he thought. It sounded like a cozy set-up for a lot of wild-eyed loonies. No place for a Maggie Kyle. But you couldn't tell her a thing, no one had ever been able to tell Maggie a thing. She had to learn everything herself, or go blundering on.

The house trembled, suddenly, the thunderous roll of feet cascading down a stairway somewhere inside. Then the big girl in the long skirt, Anna Sterner, came out the door. Seeing them there, seeing Wade looking back up at her, she shrank back, blushed, then slid along behind him to escape off the end of the porch. Half-smiling, nodding her head.

"Going somewhere, Anna?" Maggie said.

"Feeding the chickens." Without turning. The skirt swished-swished through long grass and out past the nearest cabin. The bare hurrying heels made a hollow thudding sound on the needle-cushioned trail. Then she was swallowed up in the woods.

Maggie gasped. "Horseman!" she said.

"What?" His coffee, nearly to his lips, splashed down his front.

"His name is Horseman," she said. "Don't ask me how I know, I can't remember. But his name is Horseman, I'm sure of it. Your mysterious stranger."

"What kind of a name is that?" He mopped with his handkerchief at his shirt, and the fly of his pants.

Trailer-park people, she said, knew other trailer-park people. If he was still on this island she'd find him. All she needed was a few minutes on that phone, stand back.

While she went inside for the phone book he found himself thinking of her on that island, with those psychiatrists or whatever. He didn't know who he felt sorry for, her for the disappointment ahead, or himself for envying her hope. But he knew he sure as hell didn't feel sorry for those others, the buggers that ran the thing, they had a cozy little set-up there if he'd ever heard of one. If they hurt Maggie . . . If they got her onto that island, wherever it was, and hurt her, or preyed on her ignorance, or screwed her up. It was the kind of place that Horseman might have come from, he wouldn't be surprised at it. Smooth, slick, so damn positive, someone with all the answers. People like that made his stomach rotten sick, he could puke on them; but somehow he couldn't keep away, he'd chase that bastard until he found him, if it took the rest of his life. There was no choice. Just to ask him some questions he hadn't even thought up yet.

Scrapbook

This book belongs to
STRABO BECKER

The House of Revelations
has always been full
of voices
you could go deaf
from listening
or join them
in their fever
while Donal Keneally
roars
like Rumpelstiltskin
from deep in his
foot-stomped
hole

CHRONOLOGY

1860?	Donal Keneally born, County Cork, Ireland
1883	First voyage to Canada
1898	Marriage to Nell Maguire
1899	Arrival of colony on Vancouver Island
1903	House of Revelations built
1909	Death of Nell Keneally and Christopher Wall
1910	Inquest, Keneally's "marriage" to Arbutus
1910-1920	World travels, periodic visits home
1920	Returned, without Arbutus
1921	Marriage to Lily Carruthers
1928	Keneally's death, break-up of colony

Coleman Steele
Hospital Road
Dec. 15, 1973

This is Cold Steele talking. Is that what you want me to say?
The address don't matter. My name is really Coleman Steele
but everybody always called me Cold Steele because I cut, see,
I ain't afraid to cut when I see something that needs cutting,
even if it hurts, and because I got these eyes that can look
like they're piercing you. Look. Here I'll show you. That's
how I got my name. But how is that little machine going to
pick up a thing like that? I must be losing my marbles. You
should've brought a camera too.

I'm eighty-four years old, believe it or not, and just take a
look at how steady that hand is. I was a boy, see, just a lad,
when that lot arrived and set up their colony, but I must've
been in my twenties before I seen any of them that I knew of,
I was busy with my own life and didn't have no time for
poking my nose into theirs. Well you don't think I always
had this here belly, do you, sitting out like a pan of raised
bread dough on my knee, I could get around in those days I
can tell you. Light on my feet? They told me I ought to been a
dancer I was so light, you know—one of these here fellows
that hippity hop on the stage—you know, like a jackrabbit
on a stove lid? Well I never took up no dancing, I'm going to
tell you, but I sure put those feet to work anyway. I was a
farmer. I hopped from leghorn chickens to hogs to dairy
cattle to beef, I tried 'em all. And built it all too, every board of
the house, every shed, every rail on the fence, I knew how
things were done.

And I'm going to tell you, that's what was the matter with
that bunch, they didn't know how nothing was done. They
should never've come. They should never've come in the first
place, all they did was take up good land another person
could've put to proper use, someone who knew how to do
things. Oh, I ain't saying they didn't make something out of
it, eventually, they learned like anybody else, I guess, and
made a damn good living off of it before they were through,
and before he got himself all tangled up in this trouble you

spoke of. No, it wasn't just that they never knew how to do anything when they came, though that was enough to make you bust your sides laughing when you heard about the things they did, see, the way they did them; no, what makes me mad is they never once stopped to ask what the rest of us had come onto this island to do. Just went their own way and to hell with the rest of us. What I mean is, did they ever ask what part of the world we come from, or what kind of town we wanted it to be, or what type of, you know, society we were building? No sir. They went their ignorant way. And I'm laughing. Well it's funny that's all. What else can I do but laugh? It's always funny when people get what they deserve.

I mean, they wouldn't've needed to ask very many questions to find out, would they, and then they could've copied the rest of us and got onto the right track. I could've told them myself, if they'd asked. But oh no, they had to do things their own way. Well what is the name of this province eh? And who is our capital city named after? And where do you think the head offices were, of the coal companies that opened this place up? And where do you think they sent to, to get the miners who started this town in the first place? And the farmers who followed like my father, where do you think they all came from? This is an English town, mister. Or was. The people who settled here knew what kind of life they were building, they had fine models at Home they could follow. But do you think that bunch paid any attention? The Indians went along with it. Why shouldn't they? And all those Chinamen they brought over to work in the mines went along with it, some of them turned into the best Englishmen of all. And there were other Irishmen who came over and weren't afraid to fit in with the scheme of things, doing the things that Irishmen are meant to do. But not old Whozzit, Keneally! He comes over here with his pack of sheep-people and sets up his own world like the rest of us don't exist, see, like the world stopped and started at the edge of his property. He was a King in there, like something out of the Dark Ages, and the fact that the rest of us out here were busy building a modern civilized society with decent values never occurred to him. And you may not agree with me on

this, but I'm entitled to my opinion as they say, I think that's
when everything started to go wrong. First thing we knew
you have people pouring in from all over the world, your
Belgiums and your Italians and your Ukrainians, pouring in
from all over the place, which is just fine with me, but when
they get here do they fit themselves in? No sir. They look
around and they see this one bunch that isn't paying any
attention to the rest of us and so they think it's all right for
them to do what they want, too. So I blame him for <u>that</u>,
mister, and it's no small matter. I blame that Keneally for
throwing it all off the track. Just look around at what's happened to this town and blame him for that. Drugs and sex
and socialism. None of it would've happened. You can't tell
me they have things like that in England.

Well, I wish you could've been there the one time I seen
him. Funny? I thought I'd bust! Look, I'm standing out in
front of the courthouse, see, like this, and this fellow comes
out. A tall man, with this red face and big ears like jug handles, thumping down out of that courthouse like it was on
fire or something and nearly knocked me over. "Hey mister,"
I says. "You watch where you're going!" And he turns,
swings see, like this, and hunches over, scowls at me from
under his brows like he thinks I'm a bug, or maybe he can't
see me at all and is trying to get me in focus. I didn't know
who he was. Well why should I? Did you think we had nothing better to do with our lives in those days than run circles
around him? "Oh I'm sorry," he says, just like that, all flustered, and "Some of them think that I murdered my wife." So
I says "Who are you?" and he says "Donal Brendan Keneally"
like it was a title or something, and of course I knew then
who he was and says "Well of course, it was nothing less
than what we expected of you." Oh, I was a fearless one in
those days I'll tell you. And laugh? I thought I'd bust. You
should've seen the look on his face. Like I'd clubbed him one
on the neck. He swung away and walked off in a huff but I
laughed, Lord I must've stood there and had a good laugh for
another ten minutes at least. I couldn't stop. I mean that's
what I said before, it's a funny thing when people get what's
coming to them. How could I help but laugh?

Mrs. Doreen Ryan Turner
Widow
9th Street
April 17th, 1973

I haven't got nothing to say to you.

It's an awful thing you're doing, digging up other people's pasts, rooting around in dirt like an old hog. Leave people alone to live their own lives, it's nothing at all to you.

I haven't got nothing to say.

My mother was an O'Sullivan, the last girl, Nellie. My father was Conal Ryan. My husband was descended from the Donahues, though his father come from the town here.

My husband was killed by the train, I got three kids, I work full time in a store downtown. Look, we lived in this house here for years now, you can come in and see how we keep it up, come on in and look around to suit yourself, but I haven't got nothing to say to that box there in your hand.

The past should be left alone. Leave people alone. Isn't there no privacy?

If you want to know what I think, I think it's cruel. It's cruel, and I'm sorry you don't have more sense.

Look, you're wasting my time. I got three kids to feed. Go find yourself some other hobby, mister. I haven't got nothing to say. Not a thing.

Mr. Henry R. Burke
Retired
Silverthorn Road
June 5, 1972

(Note: Mr. Burke's house, a one-room cedar-shake cabin, is got at by following a long torturous unused logging grade which burrows deep into the second-growth timber of Silverthorn Road. You know from the beginning that it is the right road—the mailbox has huge red dripping letters spelling out H.R. BURKE, POET AND REFORMER—but there are moments of doubt, where the alder between the tracks has grown man-high or where a dry-bed creek has gorged out a gully three feet deep right across. Burke is a tiny man, in

long johns, scratching at himself in the doorway. His hand
never strays from the handle of a double-bitted axe which
leans up against the wall of the house, in a pile of wood
chips.)

How do I know you're tellin' me the truth? What gives you
the right to walk in here like this uninvited?

Hell, I don't know you.

Sure I grew up on that place, I coulda owned it for Christ
sake, I coulda bought the whole shebang but what the hell
would I want it for? There was a man in here trying to sell it
to me a few years back now, a funny-looking bearded bugger
like you, but I run him off. You son of a bitch I told him, who
gave you the right to sell that land to me? I coulda bought it
long ago and not from you, neither. But I hate the place.

There's some stupid bitch owns it all now. Go ask her your
questions. Go ask her, she's the one bought it, living on it. I
don't know who the hell she bought it from, or how she could
afford a chunk that size but she's the one to answer your
questions. She owns it, let her answer for it.

She's got a lot of goddam Americans living on it. She's
probably an American herself. She looks like one. That's
what they're doing, y'know, selling the whole island off to
the Yanks piece by piece. Eventually they'll get their greedy
hands on all of it, every square inch. Except this. They won't
get this. They can run up their goddam flag over the whole
island if they want, and they will, but it'll never fly on this
property. I've had it with them bloody Yankees, just let them
try to get this.

So go ask the Yankee girl, she'll answer your questions.
You're probably one yourself.

Well how the hell do I know? You come in here asking
this, asking that, how the hell do I know you're who you say
you are? You wouldn't be the first American to come up that
road, I'll tell you, and you won't be the first going back down
unsatisfied. You got the sneakiest goddam ways of doing
your dirty work but I'm on to it all, I'm on to it, you'll not fool
me.

Go ask the bitch with the American trailers parked all
over the place. I know why they're there. They don't come up
for no holiday, I can tell you. They come up to buy, they come
up to sneak, and spy, and trick people, and steal, until they've

got the whole bloody island in their paws. That's what she's running there, y'know, that bitch. An American headquarters for an invasion. She oughta be shot.

I worked my ass off on that place when I was a kid, ploughing and hoeing, looking after the shitty chickens, but she's let it all go back, nearly all, to timber. You'd think nobody had done nothing to it. There ought to be a law that says a person has to be looked into before they can buy a big piece of land like that. To keep the Yanks out. And to be sure they're going to treat it properly. What the hell was the point of all that work, clearing land and cultivating it, if a stupid American spy-woman can walk onto it and let it all go back? What does she want, a Christmas-tree farm? They should kick her off it, her and her American friends.

I heard the Iron Bitch was there too now, living with her, but I don't believe it. That old whore couldn't share the house with nobody. Not unless she had a hundred servants kowtowing to her.

You'd think she was the Queen of England, the way she acted. More like the Empress of Russia. I saw her when she wasn't so goddam Queen-like, I'll tell you, with her skirt hoisted up around her waist taking a crap out behind a tree. Too bloody lazy to walk back to the house. And wiped herself with leaves. I hope she chokes on her own teeth, they should've shot her years ago.

I seen Her Majesty once, taking a stick to a little kid that'd splashed something on her. I wouldn't repeat the language. And then the next minute the old bag's walking around like a lady again, like she was bred or something.

But here, why the hell should I tell you that kind of thing? Go ask her yourself. If she isn't senile and drooling. Ask the old bitch to fill you in on the time I caught her with Billy O'Mahony. Ask her that. Ask her if she remembers Henry Burke.

But don't ask me nothing more. Why the hell should I tell you anything? I never invited you in here. You goddam Americans is all the same, sneaky as old hell, and I wouldn't trust a one of you for a minute. Way you go, with your plastic tape recorder. I haven't got no electricity anyway for you to plug it in. You're wasting your time.

If they'd've listened to me back in nineteen hundred and fifty-two your kind wouldn't be even allowed to step a foot onto this island. I walked the whole way down to Victoria to warn them, went right into the legislative building. But the sons of bitches kicked me out without hearing a word. Their spies had told them I was coming. And of course there isn't a one of them isn't paid with American money. Straight from Washington.

I know what you bastards are up to. First you'll buy up all our goddam land, then you'll demand the right to vote. And the first thing you'll vote for is joining up with your own stinkin' country.

Don't ... tell ... me! I know! You're not the first of them to come snooping around in here, hoping I'll break down and sell. I won't. No matter what excuses you make up for coming in here. You're a trespasser here, mister.

Go tell the Iron Bitch I won't sell. She's probably one of you, too. I know for a fact the bastard she married was a Yank, filthy rich bastard. Tell her Henry Burke won't sell, won't even talk about selling.

Tell her she can send all the spies she wants but she won't break me down. Ever.

And no sir, I will _not_ say one word about the inquest. That's no affair of mine. That's something else again, don't ask me about it, there are other people who might be willing to blab their faces off but not me!

LOCAL MURDER?

Police credit three local boys with solving the mystery of two missing persons yesterday. Staff-sergeant Mills reports that Bill Yon (12), Peter Stillen (13), and Greg North (12) while crossing private property north of town discovered a shallow grave which had apparently been disturbed by wild animals.

Upon further investigation the police uncovered what have since been identified as the bodies of Christopher Wall (22), son of Mrs. George Wall of this city, and Nell Keneally of the Revelations Colony of Truth. Both had been missing since April 10 of last year.

No further details will be available, Staff-sergeant Mills said, until an investigation has been completed. He would not comment on the possibility of foul play.

Editorial

There was a time when the people of this town could sleep safely in their beds at night, without fear of molesting and murder. Alas, this is no longer true, and unless the citizens stand up to demand the return of their rights, things are likely to get even worse.

It is no secret that in the history of our town we have had our share —perhaps more than our share—of petty crime and drunkenness. This is to be expected in any town which is a port for overseas merchandise situated adjacent to a Reserve. This paper has always tried to keep such things in their proper perspective and to report them fairly.

However, murder is another matter. Never before has this hideous crime been committed in our district, but now we wake up to dis-cover that not only do we have murder in our midst but murder so foul that no one from the youngest to the oldest of us can remain indifferent. It is to be regretted deeply that the police after all this time have yet to make an arrest or even to admit that they have a suspect. A murderer, ladies and gentlemen, may be walking free amongst us.

It is perhaps indelicate at this time, though no less pertinent, to repeat what we have said before on this page: that if this country had stricter laws governing immigration, and if this province had stricter laws concerning the ownership and use of land, and if this town had more say about what went on in the surrounding district, then perhaps we could all sleep more securely at night.

Dear Sir:
So the Master of Innuendo strikes again! With the lack of good taste and good sense so characteristic of your paper you've once again managed to display your ignorance and insult a good part of the community all in one blow.

I refer, of course, to your editorial calling for the return of our right to sleep securely at night free from fear of murderers and molesters. The slight on our Indian neighbours is forgivable, I suppose, because it is so obviously based on ignorance, but your comments on immigration and the thinly veiled accusation directed towards the Revelations Colony of Truth are malicious and perhaps slanderous.

I am not and have never been a member of the colony, nor do I have any more notion than anyone else of what their day-to-day life is like. But as a neighbour to these people I must protest that they have never been anything but kind and generous to my family. And as teacher for many years to most of their children I have observed them to be a most conscientious, hard-working, and well-intentioned group. Instead of casting unfair aspersions on them, we should be looking to them for our models. We could learn, I believe, a great deal about the spirit of co-operation and good will from them. If all our "immigrants" were as inoffensive as these, this would be a better country by far.

It is too much to expect an apology from you, of course, but it is not too much to expect that in the future you will think twice before making uninformed accusations against our neighbours.
Mrs. G. Newman

Dear Sir:

Insinuations again. This is my fifth letter to you on the same topic. Anyone I have ever met from the colony of "Immigrants" (they've been here for ten years, for heavens' sake, are they still "immigrants"?) has been far more of a gentleman than the anonymous writer of "Editorial" could ever hope to be.
(Mrs.) Edna McCreight

Dear Sir:

Please cancel my subscription to your paper.

I know this town has never aspired to literacy (preferring beer-parlour bragging to books) but I can no longer bear to see what you do to the English language.

Yes, there is murder in the district. It is the murder of grammar, logic, style, and good sense, committed with "Malice aforethought" by your writers.
John Nestor

Dear Sir:

I was embarrassed for all of us a few years ago when a series of editorials in your paper prompted a thorough, informal, and probably illegal "investigation" of a certain local group of citizens who have chosen to live apart from the rest of us. This "investigation", which was conducted by otherwise perfectly respectable and honourable leaders of the community, was unable to uncover anything "untoward, un-

Dear Sir:

Why don't you spell it right out? Like a lot of others living in this district I'm getting disgusted by the way foreigners come in here and think they can do anything they want without regard to our laws or our customs. I live on Northcove Road which as you know is quite close to where the bodies were found and living here I have heard things and seen things I couldn't repeat. I didn't think slavery was allowed in this country; I didn't think tyranny was allowed in this country; and I didn't think keeping people against their will was allowed in this country except by the police. Why hasn't anything been done? Now with this new development maybe people will wake up. My parents helped settle this town directly from England, they put their money, their hopes, and their love into it. I'm only happy that they're not here to see what is happening today.
G. P. L. Russell

natural, or illegal" to report.

I am embarrassed again today when I read your editorial which so clearly indicates you learned nothing from the previous experience and intend to go right on with your sly persecution. I only hope your readers have the good sense to ignore you, which is what you deserve.
(Mrs.) Anita Evans

Dear Sir:

Mrs. Anita Evans will be even more embarrassed when she realizes, like the rest of us, the type of people we have been harbouring in our midst, and when she remembers how she and several other local sob-sisters have defended a snake-nest of devilish misfits. Let us learn to see things clearly!
My Eyes Are Open
K. M. Tree

Copied from a child's notebook found in the old Northcove
School when it was being torn down in 1958, given to me by
Virginia Newman

Once upon a time a long time ago there was a beautiful
princess named Nell who was a princess of the kingdom of
Arland. She was so beautiful that every prince in the Kingdom wanted too mery her and other countrys to like England. But the beautiful gorgeous princess Nell was meryd to
a horrible Monster who took her a long ways away to live in
the bush. Insted of a castle she had to live in the scarry
forest. The Monster was meen to her and made her work
hard.
 Then one day the Princess Nell met a real prince who was
desgized as a miner and they fell in love but the Monster
would not stop being meen and let her go free so they had to
meet secretly in the forest and kiss!!!
 Then the horrible monster fond out and snuk up behind
them and bashed there heads in with something and beryd
them. This is a sad story.
  Mary Turner
  grade two

P.S. It is also true. My mother knew her!

Morris Wall
R.R. 2, Courtenay
July 3, 1974

When I come in to the house that day after work—I had a job
at a sawmill then, my first job—the police had already come
and gone but I didn't know and there was Mom sitting at the
kitchen table, sitting like this, you know, with her head sort
of down, and across the table was this neighbour lady, Mrs.
Preece I think it was, who was never far away if there was
trouble. Anyway she up and took off when she seen me, like I
was a ghost she was scared of, and then Mom just sat there
saying nothing until I sat down at the table too. "They found
Christopher," she said and I thought she would say down in
California or something so I said "Where?" I wasn't worried
about him because I knew what was going on, he told me
everything, and I just thought they'd skipped out and had
forgotten to write. So I says "Where?" and Mom she says
"They found him in a grave. He's dead," so I known right
away what must of happened.

All that day she just sat there all the time like this, with
her head down, sort of, and working her fingers together like
this. I made her a cup of tea because she always liked her cup
of tea and put it in front of her but she didn't even notice, just
stared like she wasn't really there, and I couldn't just sit
there and wait for her to come out of it so I went next door to
Mrs. Preece's to get the whole story but she just said "Let
your Momma tell you when she's ready, it ain't any business
of mine." I thought of going down to the police to find out,
but when I went back into the house Mom told me about the
woman, about the two of them in the same grave and it
looked like someone had killed them both.

Man, that was no fun I'll tell you, being in the same house
as her after that. She hardly ever left that kitchen table any
more, the next few days, just sat there staring and twiddling,
and the only thing she ever said to me was ask me did I know
what was going on, before like, before he disappeared, and of
course I said no just to keep peace in the family, because you
can imagine the hullabaloo if she ever found out that I knew
all along and didn't tell her and never stopped him from

doing it, as if anybody could ever stop Chris from doing
whatever he wanted to do. So I lied and said I had no idea
what it was all about and we'd just have to wait and see what
the police dug up, which was an unfortunate way of putting
it, because all of a sudden she broke, flew apart like something in her had snapped. She screamed and cried and carried on, Lord I couldn't tell you what-all she did, I had the
feeling if she had the strength she'd've pulled down the
house on our heads and ended it all for us, too. I'm telling
you, if I ever have to drive down-island now to catch a ferry
to the mainland I always get a funny feeling when I go past
the end of that street we lived on then, just remembering
how she carried on that day like a crazy person and I
couldn't do nothing about it.

The thing is I <u>knew</u>, and I felt guilty that I knew, Chris
used to tell me about it in the bedroom at night, you know —
not exactly bragging, but he knew a kid brother would be
impressed, and besides he didn't have any friends to share it
with, Chris wasn't the kind to have a lot of friends hanging
around, I was more the kind, he was the loner of the family
which I guess was what got him into the mess in the first
place.

Chris was good looking, and I'm not just saying that because he was my brother, I wasn't so bad myself in those
days, though you'd never know it now to look at this old
wreck I've shrivelled down into, but he was taller and
stronger and I guess what you'd call handsome. Once he
started working in the mine, of course, you couldn't tell what
he looked like, handsome or ugly, until he'd had a good wash
when he got home, and even then the pores of his skin were
still black, and his nails. But even after he'd washed he liked
to go for a swim every evening no matter what the temper-
ature was, he said it was the only way he could feel really
clean, swimming in the salt chuck, so after work — which
was plenty late in those days, our working day wasn't as
short as they are now — he used to hike out the highway
north and then cut down a trail through the bush to go
swimming in a certain spot where there wasn't anybody else
around. I told you he was a loner. Sometimes he never got

back until way after dark, he'd just get to dreaming about
something or start exploring. He said he didn't intend to
stay down a bloody mine shaft all his life and expected to get
out of here first chance he got.

Then he met this woman, this Nell. He told me he just
came up out of swimming and there she was, standing over
his clothes and looking at him. Me, I would've turned and hit
back into the water before I'd let a woman see me like that in
those days, but not Chris, he wasn't like that, he used to say if
you've got something the rest of us haven't seen, let's put it
up on a stump and throw rocks at it, he wasn't embarrassed
about his body at all. So he come up out of the water, like I
say, and there she was, this woman. He didn't say if she was
beautiful or not, though I found out later from somebody else
who'd seen her that she was — he only always just said he
come up out of the water and there was this woman standing over his clothes and looking at him. I thought he was
lying, you know how dreamers can do that, and it sounded
too much like one of those book stories to be true. I mean, in
real life when you meet a woman it's because somebody, a
friend, introduced you to her and after a while you get to like
her, or you work beside her for a long time without noticing
her and then one day you notice her or get so used to her you
can't stand being away from her. In real life nobody steps out
of the water streaming naked and finds a beautiful woman
standing there admiring you. Except Christopher. He wasn't
lying, and that's where they met every evening after that,
down at that little beach at the far end of the colony she lived
on, that colony of, you know, whatever they were.

In the early years apparently people used to refer to them
just as Those Irish, you know, because the title they gave
that place was too much of a mouthful to say, and more like a
joke. But they never kept it up long, because it was obvious
they weren't nothing like Irish at all, no matter where they
claimed to come from, we had lots of Irish around and knew
what they could be like — fine people, very fine people nearly
all of them — but those colony people had nothing in common with them. And of course after a few years there was all
sorts of others mixed up in there like a dog's breakfast —

Italians, and Swedes, and French, and Australians, Lord knows what-all—so people just got so they always called it the Colony, nothing else. A place where people disappeared into.

It wasn't exactly like a fairy tale or anything, not for Christopher anyway, because the first thing he finds out is that she's married and not married to just anybody but to what's his name, the leader of the whole works, Keneally. Well, when he found that out he says to me, Morris, I'm not going anywhere near that kind of trouble, not any more, I don't know how I can stand not to but I'm just not, I won't have anything more to do with her, she's dishonest anyway, not telling me right away before it was too late. He was an honourable kid, I guess, his intentions were right. But the next night, bang, he was gone again and never missed a night after that, except when he was laid up with something for a while, I think it was a cold or something.

The second thing that wasn't a fairy-tale story was that she was older, I bet she was twice as old as he was, beautiful or not she could've been his mother, and here she is fooling around with a kid that's never been in love before. I guess she got what she deserved in the end, though I can't say the same for Chris, it seems to me like she was the one ought to know better and he just sort of got sucked into it, if you follow me.

And mean. You wouldn't expect Chris to fall in love with someone who turned out to be mean, but he did. Some nights I'd hear him crying in his bed over there and I'd think, boy, if that's what being in love is like you can have it, but after a while he told me and it turns out she's just plain mean and spiteful to him, like they'd been married for a hundred years or he was her servant or something. Sometimes she wouldn't show up, or she'd make him—well, I'd rather not say some of the things, I think some things are just too private to be said and I am his brother after all, was his brother, and he's got a right to expect I wouldn't go telling everything, it would be humiliating, I guess. And things like that have always embarrassed me to talk about and I guess at this age I'm not likely to change suddenly, am I.

Poor Mom, all this time she didn't know what was going on. She thought he was sick and tried to make him eat more. She used to brag to the neighbours what a great provider her son was turning out to be — a working fool she called him — working all day like that in the mines and giving her nearly the whole paycheque instead of wasting it in the beer parlours like some other people she knew and wouldn't mention, while other people's sons were making nuisances of themselves and wasting their money and fooling around with women, but her Chris spent his free time out in nature, she said, a real loner and maybe he'd be a poet. You know what mothers are like, it's the same old story, they can't see what's happening in their own family though they sure know everything everyone else's kids have done wrong. And me, being the second son, well of course it was only hoped that I'd turn out to be half so wonderful as my big brother Chris.

Well, I'll tell you, she took it hard when he didn't come home that night. I just figured they'd finally taken off for somewhere together the way he was always threatening they would, and I wished him luck though I didn't envy him having to live with a mean older woman like that. But of course I couldn't tell Mom that, and all that night I heard her sitting in the kitchen, at the table, I guess, which was her favourite place, just sighing every once in a while the way she could when she wanted to make the whole world feel guilty, and then coming in to me and saying are you sure you shouldn't go out looking for him? By the time morning came she was all for going to the police, so I saw I had to tell her something, so I said listen Mom this is not going to be easy for you to take but Chris has been hinting about heading over to the mainland to get a job and I guess that's just what he's done. Maybe he wants to come back and surprise you. Well of course I couldn't mention anything about the woman, though I expected there'd be a great explosion come out of the colony any minute you could hear a hundred miles away, and sooner or later she might put two and two together. She was furious mad at me for not telling her, not telling on Chris before it was too late, and of course I had to

quit school and get a job in the sawmill so we could eat. I'd
never go down one of them mines, never, not if I was starv-
ing. Mom, she just watched the mail every day and got quieter and quieter as she gradually realized the son she'd
idolized had not only run away from home but wasn't going
to write her, either, not even to say send money.

Poor Mom, I often wonder if she'd've taken it as hard if my
dad had still been alive. He was killed in the mines, you
know, and that was one reason she never tried to talk me
into going down, she saw I was scared of it and I guess she
didn't want to lose the only person she had left. You know,
she lived to be a woman of ninety-seven before she passed
on, but I don't think she was ever quite right, you know, after
that day, not really.

That one day was the worst I guess, the day I came home
and the police had been. That was the blow that hurt the
most, discovering Chris had been dead all the time she'd been
cursing him for deserting her. And then on top of it finding
out about the woman. She never looked at a newspaper after
that, never went near the investigation, wouldn't talk about
any of it. You'd think there'd never been a Chris in the family. I was already used to her never talking about my dad so
this was no surprise to me.

One day I said to her, I says "Mom, did you ever really
believe there wasn't a woman in the story?" but she just
looked at me like she didn't know what story I was talking
about so I never mentioned it again. What was the point?
We'd all suffered enough on account of poor Chris, why drag
it out any longer?

I can't help wondering though, sometimes, what if he was
still alive, what would he be like? Sometimes I just can't help
wonder if we'd be friends again, now that we'd be old men
like this, I can't help wondering if we'd sit around and talk. I
guess it's natural.

Mrs. M. Wall
St. Joseph's Hospital
Comox
July 3, 1974
(since deceased)

Christopher? Oh, certainly I remember Christopher. I'm not
so old that my memory's gone, not yet anyway, in fact sometimes the things that happened away back at the beginning
of my life are easier to remember than the things that happened yesterday. My word, yes, I remember Chris, and I'm
certain a good number of other people do, too. If I wasn't laid
up in this hospital, if I was home with my husband listening,
I may not say, I suppose I shouldn't say this, but it makes me
mad to see how all his life he's sort of blamed himself, as if he
could have done something to stop it. And as time goes on,
every year Christopher becomes a better and better person
to him, if you know what I mean, and so he himself has
become more and more guilty. Well he's wrong, and I know
things, I could tell you things to prove it. Anyone with a
clear eye in his head could tell you it was that mother, she
was a real ripsnorter I'll tell you, it was her drove the kid out
of the house and into the trouble. She lived with us for
twenty-seven years so I could tell you things that'd make
your hair fall out but I won't, it wouldn't be fair to my husband. If it wasn't for her I likely wouldn't have to spend half
my life in and out of this place with one trouble and another.

And Christopher, I could tell you a thing or two about that
Christopher. He was not the angel his mother and brother
believed him to be. Not by a long shot. Oh he wasn't the
hellion either that you're expecting me to say, he wasn't one
of those perfect-at-home-but-devil-away types. He was a
brooder. You can say what you like about the "poetic tem-
perament" or "loner" or "dreamer", what it boils down to is
just plain old mean selfishness. He came hanging around
our house for a while, hanging around me though I was a
good number of years younger, my word I couldn't have been
more than fifteen, and when I showed I wasn't interested in
him any more he got real pouty and mean and started hanging around when I was with other people, saying things he
knew would upset me or embarrass me or make the other

people wonder what kind of person I was. Oh, he wasn't at all what you'd call a nice person. I guess that's why I liked my husband right away, he was so different from Chris, he'd never take offence easy or want to hurt you.

Not that I think Christopher did what some want you to believe he did. I guess we all know who really did it. But I just don't think it's right for my husband to go on blaming himself as if he'd sold Jesus Christ or something. Everybody has their own life to live.

Mrs. Elmira Harlow
McIntosh Avenue
August 5, 1973

Well, you know what happens to slaves once they get their freedom. They start scrambling as hard as they can to get to the top and grab all the power they can to wield it against the whole world. You wonder why you can't get more than a peek at the records of the coroner's inquest, why you can't get anywhere near any files on the whole business? Well, think about it a little. What happened to these people when they sprang out of that place in nineteen twenty whatever-it-was? They spread out all over this island and started climbing, that's what they did. There's been two or three mayors in different towns come right out of that place. Civil servants. Lawyers. I even know of one MLA. And you wonder why we have corruption. How could someone raised in a place like that turn out any other way? They want to get even, that's what. They want to have as much power as that old goat had over them, and they want to use that power against the whole lot of us. Ask yourself why you can't get at those files. Is some little secretary going to let you see the records that show her grandmother admitting on the witness stand that she was such a fool she let a madman tell her what to think? Is some lawyer going to put that kind of ammunition into your hands? No, those people have spread out, mister, and they're going to make sure you don't learn nothing. You can't tell me nothing about those people that'd surprise me. And I know you're not ever going to see those files. Not a one of them.

Mrs. Jackson Barclay
Courtenay
Sept. 3, 1975

Boys oh boys, sometimes I think this place is full of his
cripples, this island is just full of them, hiding amongst the
unharmed, a lot of crippled souls, but I don't understand why
you want to track them down. There are plenty of people
who settled this place without making a mess of it, I can't
see why you're so fascinated with the failures; my husband
and plenty of others we knew had a hard time of it some
years and it never got easy, but they were happy with what
they found here and willing to work and didn't try to turn it
into a torture chamber for other people. There are better
things you could do with your time, if you ask me, than
running around with that tape recorder.

I never met the man. Boys oh boys, I wouldn't want to,
though we stumbled into that place of his by mistake once.
We moved out here from Alberta a few years after he was in
all that trouble. Jackson had come out first, ahead of us all to
look the place over, he stayed with a cousin of mine in a
hotel they were running, up towards Campbell River. He
stayed through most of the winter, oh, it was a terrible winter we were having, the cattle died, the horses, I never seen
such a winter. Well! He came back with this story, you'd
think winter was something they never heard of out here. A
lot of rain, he said, and green, everything was always green
from one end of the year to the next, and he'd rented a place
for us, to get settled on, while we looked for a place of our
own. Oh, he handed that useless farm over to his brother and
in no time at all me and the girls — I had four of them then,
three to be born later — me and the girls came out on the
train while he stayed to come out with the furniture and
stock on a freight train later. I nearly cried when I saw what
had happened to my stove, the only good piece of furniture I
owned — all the condensation frozen to the ceiling of the
freight car melted when we got down to the coast and turned
that thing into nothing but rust. Boys oh boys, I just cried
when I saw it.

But that wasn't till later. When we stepped off that boat,
well, we didn't know what to do next. We never planned

anything ahead. There was more than seventy miles ahead
of us yet and here I was standing in the depot with the four
girls not knowing what to do. Then this absolute stranger
stepped up — good Lord he must've been rich — and told me
he had a taxi ready to drive him all the way up and would be
glad to give us a ride. Never entered my head to refuse. You'd
never do a thing like that nowadays, at least I wouldn't, you
never know what kind of nut you're getting mixed up with.
But I was young then, and it was a different world, seems
like, so I accepted the ride — I could see the five of us standing like that in the depot forever, feeling damp. It don't get as
cold here as it does on the prairies, I know, but when you
first arrive the dampness is every bit as bad. But this generous rich man mustn't have known his way around any better than I did, or gave his directions wrong, because boys oh
boys, before I knew it we'd gone off the highway and off down
that long windy road and into that place, that place where
you live, with my granddaughter, with Maggie. I thought
what is this man up to, what kind of game is this, but he was
as surprised as I was and started hollering at the driver
what was he doing? Here we were in this strange dead-end-
looking place, with everything scalped to the ground, all
bare, and a lot of log houses squatting around behind that big
house on the cliff, I never seen any place like it. What if the
driver tells us to get out, I wondered. I wouldn't have done it,
with all of those faces at windows, and people in the fields
stopped to stare. I wouldn't do it. And thank goodness it was
all a mistake. Good Lord, when I found out later where we'd
been, I nearly fainted, I'd heard of those crazy loons before,
and that Keneally. Boys oh boys, if I'd met <u>him</u> I'd've been
scared half to death.

Oh we had plenty of odd-balls on the prairies too, I can
even think of some we were related to, but would never admit to it, but it looks to me like you get more of that kind in a
place like this. Don't ask me why. And I'm not complaining.
Hard as it was some of those years, with all those girls to
feed and clothe, and Jackson not being the handy-man
pioneer type — hard as it got, we never had anything but the
finest people for neighbours and friends. That's what I mean,
there were plenty who came out and liked what they found

and did what they could with it and were happy and good to their neighbours, you don't have to think a man of Keneally's type was typical. My land, he was anything but. You know better than that.

We bought some of his dairy cattle when they were selling out, a few years later, that was the only other time we ever had anything to do with them. Six young Jerseys, we never had anything but Jerseys, that was Jackson's kind of cow, but I didn't like the idea. There'll be something wrong with them for sure coming from a place like that, I told him, better keep them in a field separate from ours for a while just in case. I don't know what I expected, but I had a feeling. But he just laughed. Jack never took any notice of superstitions or "feelings" about things, at least not about anyone else's feelings but his own. He brought them all the way up in the truck—I remember it was a Sunday, he took two of the girls along with him—he brought those cows up and turned them loose in our herd and I guess there wasn't a thing wrong with them because in no time at all I couldn't tell the new ones from our own. And the customers didn't ask which milk came from which cow. Jackson, he treated everyone friend or villain like they were put on earth to be his trusted friend, he was incapable of being suspicious or mean, and you knew he was usually right. He got taken a few times, and once or twice when things got rough there'd be people standing by to get mean, but he was a man who usually got back the friendliness he showed the world.

But those cows weren't all he brought back in the truck that day, not him. When he came back there was a young man standing up in the back with the cattle, all covered with manure and dirty as an old pig. "What's this?" I told him. "What's going on here?"

Well, you'd have to see his face, the way he could look pleased and guilty and childish all at the same time, the way he'd grin and shrug like there wasn't a thing he could do about it. "This is our new hired man," he says. "Sean Good."

"We don't need no more hands," I said. Sometimes I could shake him he made me so mad. No business head at all. "We're having a hard enough time already just keeping our heads above water."

He just took off his straw hat, ran his handkerchief around the inside of it, and slapped it back on his head. "Well, he's our hired hand anyway," he says, and winks at the girls as if to say <u>See, I told you I could handle the old girl.</u>

What happened was when he went down to get those cows there wasn't anybody left on the whole place except this one teen-age boy who was left tending them all by himself, it was completely deserted, and here was this boy who wasn't exactly what they'd call retarded nowadays or mental or anything like that, but he was certainly simple. The kind you wouldn't count on to tell the time, or remember a message, cross-eyed too and all sloped-down in the face. There he was, just sitting there, my husband told me, on an old apple crate in the pen waiting for him to come get those Jerseys. He helped get them loaded up, my husband said he coaxed them up into the truck like they were his own babies or something, and then he went back and sat down on his apple crate in the middle of the empty pen, swatting at the flies that circled his head.

So my husband said "Where's your family, son?"—he couldn't ever stand not to know if someone was being looked after properly—and it turned out his family had gone off he didn't know where, and it looked like he intended to just sit there by himself until somebody came along and did something about it. Well if you knew my husband at all it wouldn't take much to guess what he did, naturally he told that boy come on hop in, we got so many mouths at the table already one more won't be noticed.

Far as I could see, that boy turned out to be the worst hired hand we ever had—and, boys, we had enough of them, two even ended up as son-in-laws—he wasn't no use at all that I could see unless a cow got sick and needed sympathy, and I swear for years there my husband was doing the work of two men just so's he wouldn't have to admit the boy was useless and fire him, or pay someone else to take his place. The girls called him Simple Simon, but only when their father wasn't around to hear them. He would never allow them to make fun of anyone, not in seriousness, it was just something he wouldn't allow.

So Sean Good and those cows were all we ever had to do with that colony. But I'll never get over that taxi ride, and how close we came. It makes me shudder today just thinking about it. I never liked Maggie moving onto that place, and I told her, too, but she's fixed it up nice and I guess you might as well forget all the things that's happened on it. I've got twenty-three grandchildren now, and more than one of them's done worse than Maggie, believe me, and with less disadvantages to start with. I'm partial to family, can't help it—my mother was the same, if you weren't related you weren't nothing—but I don't think you have to be a relative to see what kind of stuff that Maggie's made of. Like her grandfather. It'll be up to people like her, made of that kind of stuff, to look after the cripples I guess, and heal them if she can. Boys oh boys, when I think of some things it makes me wonder.

Richard Ryburn
Instructor, Regional College
May 12, 1973

I have never believed for a single minute that those people knew what was in store for them when they got on the boat in Cobh or whatever it was called then before they started changing names around. I could never believe they'd fallen for all his hogwash and were putting themselves in his hands. The way I see it is this: here was a way out of an impossible situation—poverty and serfdom and persecution —and they would have followed him no matter who he was. All that hogwash he was supposed to have preached all over the country, if you could believe any of it, wouldn't have impressed them. To some he would still be that trouble-making kid they remembered. No, it must have been after-wards that he got his hold over them, when he saw they were grateful to escape that other existence and all worn down by the long trip—half dead most of them, even in nineteen hundred the journey wasn't so pleasant—and scared shitless, you might say, by the timber and what they'd heard of the wild life in this frontier town.

You don't believe any of that baloney they tell about him, I hope. All that nonsense they've spun into exaggerated tales to make him out some kind of superman or devil. It's just

because no one's been living here long enough to have any
heroes or villains of their own to tell about, so people go
around making up this ridiculous myth about him. He was
just a man, a creep too, like plenty of others.

There wasn't anything so special about the colony either.
There's been plenty of those around, you know, still are.
Hundreds. All the way from peaceful back-to-nature com-
munes to anti-social perverts to fanatical religious groups
just wanting to lead their own kind of life, to those really
far-out slave-mentality groups with drugs that think nothing of going out to kill off a few people. They're basically all
the same idea. There wasn't anything so special about this
one. People just want to make more of it than it was. It's a
fairly common phenomenon: when people feel that their
own lives and life around them is basically dull, they begin to
spin tales that will turn a slightly eccentric neighbour into a
mythological creature of epic proportions, and start to imagine life in the nearest exclusive group as exciting and per-
verse and perhaps dangerous. It's not uncommon, and
there's a whole field of psychological language related to it
which I won't bore you with now. It's important, I think, to
see things as they are.

So many pioneers to this island seem to have had some
tribal instinct to create even smaller islands once they got
here, separate isolated communities all over the place and
all of them failures.

No, I've never talked to any of them. Hell, do I look that
old? I've lived all my life in the States and didn't move up
here until a few years ago, when the College opened. It's a
nice place, I like it, a good place to raise kids. You people
aren't so different from us as you'd like to think you are, but
it's not so crowded here, and at least the crime rate so far is a
lot lower.

Dairmud Evans
Sunnyside Rest Home
January 15, 1976

(Mr. Evans insisted on carrying out the interview in The
Paradise Hotel where he'd been manager until his retire-

ment a few years ago. A nurse from the Home accompanied us.) He used to come in to town a lot, you know, between the time they found the bodies out there and the time they decided to call it murder by persons unknown. He had that sort of <u>waiting</u> look on his face, you know the kind of look I mean, and it was obvious he'd suddenly decided to be good and visible for a change. Maybe he thought people wouldn't gossip so much about someone they could see, or maybe he wanted to remind them he was just an ordinary grieving husband who'd been cuckolded and widowered both. He'd come in to town nearly every day on his horse, a big black something or other with his dog trailing behind, and he'd tie the horse up at the top end of the main street and walk all the way down past every store tipping his hat right and left until he came to the Paradise Hotel at the bottom, where I worked. It was not much of a hotel even then, I'd be the first to admit it, but it was a friendly enough place, and it gave him the opportunity to walk the full length of the downtown area. I think about that time we had a lot of carpenters in and out of here, they were ripping down the old-fashioned false front there used to be on the hotel and putting up a newer one, more modern.

This was before he met up with the Indian Princess. She was a beautiful girl, from some other reserve, not here, and he called her Arbutus because of her skin, it was that pinky-brown colour of the arbutus bark at a certain time of year. Her real name was Edna Bob or Edna Jim or something like that, you know the kind of name, but he called her Arbutus. A real pretty girl, too, he met her just outside the hotel one day, not long after this, but that's not the story I want to tell you.

What I want to tell is this. I was hardly more than a kid at the time, I'd just started at this job, working at the Paradise. And he would call me Mr. Evans, like I was an equal, even though he was so much older. And even though he wasn't a drinking man—he told me if you started to rely on drink, who knows what you might rely on next, and a man shouldn't put his faith into anything else but himself—he would sit at a corner table all by himself for an hour or so with this one weak drink and watch the others come and go and sometimes talk to a few of them but not for very long.

Not at first, anyway.

"Are you waiting for anyone in particular?" I asked him once, when this had been going on for a week or two.

"I am," he says.

"And will you know the man when you see him?" I said. He wouldn't have been the first man in that hotel to look square at a friend and think him a stranger.

"I will, Mr. Evans," he says, "I will. For it's a wee bit of a man I'm waitin' for, and him with a gimpy leg."

"Well a man like that shouldn't be all that difficult to see," I said, "if only he will show up in the first place."

"It should," says he, "be the easiest thing in the world. And we have an arrangement too, to be meeting in this place. I'll just wait so, if you don't mind, until he arrives."

I don't know why I wasn't afraid of him, like most of the others were. I'd heard tales about him that would shake you up. And there was the possibility that he was a murderer too. Maybe it was the soft manner of his voice, and his "Mr. Evans" and all that politeness. Or maybe it was that waiting look on his face. God knows, even at that age I'd discovered the minute a person starts waiting for something he's vulnerable. And here it was, naked, on his face.

He never mentioned the business that was going on to me, the police investigation and all that, except once. "They're out to get me, Mr. Evans," he said, and I said "Yes sir," because it was true. And I knew he didn't mean the police or anything, he meant the people.

Actually, he looked kind of funny sitting there by himself, such a big man with his red peasant face and those sticking-out ears. You couldn't really believe all those things they said about him. He looked too ordinary, for all his size.

Except once. Then I started to suspect there was some truth in it somewhere.

A couple of men were sitting there, at that table over there, arguing about something or other. One of them was a miner but the other hadn't worked for years, a fellow named Nelson that would never even look at Keneally for some reason or other, always sat with his back to him. Well, they were arguing away about something, these two, and an Indian couple came in looking for a room, you can see out into the lobby

from here if you lean just a little this way. One of the men
said something about the woman, you know the kind of
thing people might say, ignorant people, about smoked meat
and that kind of thing, loud enough for the couple to hear. I
don't think they even flinched, they must have been used to
it. But Keneally over in his corner there just rose up to his
feet roaring, his face the colour of blood, and his eyes bulging
like an aroused bull. For a minute there I wasn't even sure
what he was mad about, I must admit, it didn't strike me that
anyone had done anything so terrible as all that, it even
passed through my mind that he was going to throw some
kind of epileptic fit or something, or accuse me of putting
poison in his drink. Lord knows what goes flashing through
a person's head at a time like that. But he didn't give me time
to do much guessing. He hit across the room like a tornado,
hauled both of those men up out of their seats, right up in
the air if you please, and tossed them out onto the street like
they were a couple of old steaks he was throwing to his dog.
He told them it would be a sorry day indeed for them if they
ever came back to this hotel, and by George, I don't believe
either one of them ever did, even after he'd gone away. That
was the day I started believing what I'd heard. Or some of it
anyway.

Well it wasn't very many days after that that the little man
came in. Of course I recognized him right away. Short, squat,
hairy, with a bit of a limp. Well I don't need to describe him to
you, do I, I guess you know what he looked like, he could be
your mirror. I guess you can remember him better than I
can, though this would be a long long time before he met
your mother or had any ideas about fathering you. I should
mention that he carried a briefcase or leather bag of some
kind, maybe it was a suitcase.

"Mistah Beckah," he said to me. Oh I remember that terrible accent. He must have stepped right off the boat. Well of
course he had, but I didn't know that, quite yet.

"Mistah Beckah," he said. "And I believe there is a Mistah
Keneally expecting me."

Keneally, of course, had seen him and came rushing out
and pumped his arm up and down like they were old friends,
though I could see from the look on the little man's face,

from your father's face, that he'd never seen the other before in his life.

"We'll need a room, Mr. Evans!" Keneally shouted. "We've got business to attend to, and you must see to it that no one disturbs us at all."

And that was when the game began.

I'm a man who minds his own business, Mr. Becker. I have never listened in on the things that went on in these rooms, no matter how tempting it might be. Not to the time of my retirement as manager of the place. But that day there were reasons to pass up and down the hall, I suppose, and they made no effort to keep their voices down. I picked up this and that and this snatch of conversation and that outburst, and by the end of the day had a pretty good idea of what was going on.

Your father was a lawyer, of course, I figured that out, and Keneally had sent for him in case the worst came to the worst as they say, though I have no idea whether a lawyer from England would have been allowed to defend him in our courts, and apparently this man was the best there was.

But that was only a possibility. The real reason your father was here was that Keneally had somehow convinced him by mail to come all the way out from Ottawa where he was working as a consultant or something and to buy his way into the colony.

Late in the afternoon they both came out of the room and downstairs and went out, though Keneally asked me to reserve the room. I suppose they went out to the colony, to look it over, show it off, I don't know. Anyway, soon after supper they both came back in, in one big hurry, and went stomping up the steps and slammed the door.

I could hear the shouting down here. Words like "illegal" and "corrupt" and "false pretences" came exploding through the walls. Keneally shouted the louder of the two: Irish curses or whatever it was he used to yell, and "stupid little arse of an Englishman" and Lord knows what-all. You name it, they said it.

So Keneally stomped out after a while, madder than anyone I've ever seen before or since. I wouldn't want to have got in his way then, or been one of those people out there at his place when he got home. You could feel the whole hotel tremble when he shut the door behind him.

But the little man didn't leave.

Instead he did exactly the same thing Keneally had done before he got here, sat over at that corner table all by himself all day long, every day, with a waiting look on his face and just a bit of a smile. The little so-and-so knew his people, I guess, from all the experience he'd had as a lawyer. He just sat there waiting for what he was sure was going to happen. And of course he was right.

Two days later Keneally came in and sat down at the table and muttered something and Becker just shook his head and Keneally went stomping out again.

The next day Keneally came back and there was nobody in the room but Becker and me, so Keneally didn't worry about what he said, he just said it right out loud.

"You son of a bitch, you must be interested in buying or you wouldn't still be in town. You'd have gone long ago."

But the little man only grinned. "I intend to stay long enough to see them charge you with murder. Then I'll leave, happily."

And again the next day: "Look Becker, my people need what you've got to offer."

To this, Becker said, "I didn't get wealthy by throwing my money away on lost causes. Especially not when it would mean turning it over to a megalomaniac."

It must have been, oh, a week of that kind of thing before Keneally came in and laid it all out on the table the way I suppose the little man knew all along he would eventually.

It was a Wednesday. I remember because it was my mother's birthday that day and I intended to buy her a gift in the afternoon, but of course the stores were closed. Wednesday. A wet miserable pouring-down day in March. You know what it can be like, you'd swear you're never going to see the sky again or wear anything ever again but gum boots or see any colours again but grey and green. That kind of day.

Keneally was wearing, let's see, oh hell I can't remember anything but his face. He might have been a whipped child. Or more likely a child that was going to be whipped if this one last excuse didn't work.

Your father was in his usual place. By that time he'd taken
to playing solitaire with a deck of cards, humming to himself
and smoking a cigar. Some brand with a hideous smell. You
may recall what he used to smoke. The first few days he'd set
out some paperwork to busy himself as he waited, but by this
Wednesday he'd caught up, I suppose, and was just whiling
away the time with an old greasy deck of cards I used to keep
over there, down behind the counter. He never expected me
to pay him any attention, I'll say that. He wasn't one of those
men who can't stand being alone in here and expect you to
drop whatever you're doing, neglect your job, just to keep
them entertained.

Well, being a wet Wednesday, of course, there were quite a
few people in here. A lot of noise and smoke. Yet when
Keneally came in he didn't seem to care about the other
people. They could have gone up to the room and talked
there, but maybe he thought in all that noise nobody'd hear
him.

Well, I heard him.

"Mr. Becker," he says. "It's time for a little talk."

And I remember the little fellow just dipped his head, still
smiling as if to say he couldn't argue the point.

"Mr. Becker," he says, "it's a hard thing for me to say, but
the truth of it is my colony has a great need for money. We're
not so wealthy as some would want you to believe, at all. And
the sad thing, Mr. Becker, the sad thing of it is that all I have
left is the land itself, which is mine alone and mine to do
with as I please. Everything else is tied up in equipment and
stock. I'm offering that land to you, if you'll buy it. I'm thinking it's time for me to be leaving this place behind."

He laid the papers out on the table but the little Englishman did not look at them. He only looked at this Keneally.
And if I'm not mistaken, sir, he was doing then exactly what
I was trying to do in my mind, trying to reconcile this desperate whining man with the man of the legends. It wouldn't
work, I know, it never has. When story people become flesh
people we can't bear the evidence.

Well, of course, as you know your father was having none
of it. He folded up the papers and stuffed them into Keneally's pocket.

"A fine sort of man you are," he said, "a sorry kind of human, to turn your back on those people of yours. But you've convinced me of one thing, Mr. Keneally, and this is it. I'll stay longer than it takes them to charge you with the murder of your wife. I'll stay until I've seen you hanged for it."

Well, that was when I realized that the noise in the room had stopped long ago, and that every man in the room was listening. And watching.

But we were treated that day to one final display of the legendary temper. Keneally stood up, Lord I can hardly bear to recall it, silently up and silently across to the door like he intended to leave us forever. But he stopped and turned and I swear to God Mr. Becker that one of his feet pawed the floor, pawed at the carpet, and that his head went down, shaking like there was something on the top he wanted to get rid of. I can't tell you the noise, you wouldn't believe it, the most horrible noise from somewhere down in his throat or lower, my God it scared me to death! Then he went across that room again, knocking people right and left, and with his shoulder drove the table and your father into the corner.

The table split, they've still got it somewhere out in a back room, split right in two. And of course your father was lucky to get only a few bruises, he must have ducked down or something. Keneally, of course, did some kind of damage to his head that put him in the hospital for a good while. I believe he was still in there when the police and all those others decided to call the wife thing a suicide pact or whatever it was. On account of that cripple.

I never saw him after that. He never came back to the Paradise, of course, though I like to think he was on his way here when he met that Indian girl on the street. I like to think he was on his way to have a drink at the corner table, or maybe talk to me. I would be scared to death if he did, but it would have been nice, too. He spent a lot of time there. And I'd got to feel I'd become part of the thing, too.

I was kind of glad, too, when I heard he'd taken up with this Arbutus woman and gone off travelling, though I knew he hadn't sold the land. He never did sell the land, did he? The old woman, his last wife must have sold it after he died.

I don't know how he could afford to travel. Maybe the girl had some money.

Your father, of course, left as soon as he heard the verdict. And I don't believe he ever came back to this district again.

Cyrus Durrand
First Street
Feb. 14, 1972

I seen him when he come back, after he dumped that Indian woman somewhere. I seen him step off the boat. Christ, I couldn't believe my eyes, I never thought he'd come back, I never thought he'd have the nerve! But here he is, stepping off that boat like he expected a band to start up. King of the Island. And maybe he could've been, too, if this was another time. But there wasn't no band, I can tell you for sure, and there wasn't nobody there to meet him. Apart from me I'd say, hell, I'd say there wasn't nobody recognized him even. They'd forgot all about him. A town doesn't just sit around remembering one person or one incident all the time, y'know, I'd forgot about that bastard completely, and he might as well've been a brand new stranger for all the attention he got. The only reason I recognized him myself was because I used to own a little general store right out on the side of the road. I was just down hanging around the dock that morning, it was a Sunday and I liked to hang around where the boats were, see, and off he steps and the first thing I know he's asking me would I drive him out to the place, out to that colony place of his in Northcove, he'd pay me well. I could tell from the clothes he had on he had plenty of money, but that was nothing new, he'd always been a rich so-and-so with his pack of slaves, it made me boil when you think of how hard the rest of us had to work just to stay put, I came out here from Ontario and glad I did and I tell you I worked hard for every cent. But I drove him and his trunks out the road and right into the place—the only time I was ever inside—and dropped him off at the door, what else could I

do. He didn't talk much on the way out, just said a couple of
things, the kind of thing you might expect, like "The world is
a large place, Mr. Durrand, a much larger place than you
might expect," and "The thing that makes a place mean
something to you is its smell. I can tell that it's been raining
here without looking, for I can smell the pines now and it's
the smell of home to me." Oh, he was a big man. You can see
that I'm no shrimp. Never have been, but sitting beside him
on that ride out to the place I felt like there was a giant
beside me. I got the feeling he took up a lot more space even
than his big body seemed to. Anyway, when we passed
through his gate and were heading down towards the buildings he said, "You know, Mr. Durrand, it's a funny thing but
I'm not even sure that when I get home there'll be anyone
left there at all. They could have all left, for I haven't had
word in the past two years at least. I was tempted to ask you
in the town, in case, but then I thought I'll find out for myself
soon enough." And we found out long before we got to his
house. First, in the fields, people looked up and saw us and
started walking down towards the buildings. People came to
the doors of the barns and the sheds and the outhouses, took
a good look, and started down. Up off the beach, down out of
the bush, they seemed to come from everywhere. And then,
finally when we were there, housewives came out of their
houses, wiping hands on their aprons, to look. That cripple,
that old cripple that testified on the stand about seeing the
murder and nearly landed in jail for his trouble, he came out
on the porch. Eyes, eyes, eyes, just staring, Lord I bet there
wasn't a sound. I got out of there as fast as I could, didn't
even wait for him to pay me, if he really intended it. The only
other time I ever seen the man was a couple years later he
stopped at my store to pick up something, he had the last
wife with him then, that woman lives out there now with
you people, but he never gave no sign that he remembered
me at all. Never used my name or anything. He could've been
a different person altogether. That was the only time I ever
had anything to do with him, and I'm not complaining, the
less the better if you saw the mess he could get people's lives
into. The less the better as far as I was concerned.

Mr. Edward Guthrie
Island Highway
Campbell River
January 25, 1975

(Note: Mr. Guthrie deserves—and needs—some introduc-
tion. He is in his eighties, I suppose, a bachelor. . . . I gather
he's been a bachelor for thirty years or more. He lives alone
on a small plot south of town. A big man still, with plenty of
gusto, he tends to get very excited when he talks. His eyes
flash, his voice is usually a shout—as if I'm somehow at
fault for the crimes he is blaming on others—and the main
word of every sentence is barked out with special contempt,
spit-flying, while his arms shoot out this way and that as if
the air is full of enemies to be fought off. I couldn't keep him
seated near the tape recorder because he jumps up and acts
out the stories he is telling. Most of the time he addresses the
floor, his big head tilted down, seeing his audience there, I
guess, and never once looking me in the eye, and with every
one of those exploded words his arms shoot out sideways to
make him look like a hunched-over furious eagle. He laughs
at his own memories—a hee hee chewed up in his teeth—
and sometimes chooses not to tell what he is laughing at, his
sense of humour evidently as full of contempt as his sense of
drama. His pronunciation, which I haven't attempted to re-
produce, reveals the story of his life: he drops the h's from
his th's to say t'ing for thing, t'ought for thought, something
he must have picked up from his Irish father; he says "cam"
for "calm" and "crick" for "creek" from an Ontario childhood; and he says "bluff" when there's no cliff in sight,
picked up during a brief time on the prairies: all this though
he's spent his whole adult life here, on the coast, raising beef
cattle on a stump farm that he sold, recently, to "foreigners",
French Canadians, for just enough money, he says, to keep
him in beer for the time he has left. This is a much edited
version of our conversation, as Mr. Guthrie talked steadily
for fourteen hours—most of the time on topics which had
nothing to do with my quest. I haven't erased the tapes
though, which are numbered S-1 to S-14 in shoebox number
5. The interview took place in the kitchen of his little house

—where chickens and cats wandered in and out with equal freedom.) I'm going to tell you this and you're not going to like it: You're a fool and more than a fool if you believe one word anybody tells you about that Keneally. They'll make it up, they'll lie just to please you, they'll pass on what some other stupid bugger told them and call it gospel, and the truth is they don't know <u>nothing</u>. Nobody does. They only think they do ... (laughing) ... hell, look at all the years they've had to make it up or fill in the missing pieces of it out of their imagination. People will tell you anything, anything that comes into their heads, truth or lie it don't matter, just to get their voices into that box of yours. And don't tell me any different, because I know what I'm talking about.

So listen to this, I won't bullshit you, it's the truth. Keneally used to come up here, to my old stump ranch, whenever things got too hot or boring down there for him. Used to go fishing in what they call the Tyee Hole now, out in the strait, I seen him bring salmon in, hell, they'd be <u>that big</u>, long as a calf, and he'd get my wife Ella to bake it and we'd sit around and talk. When all that fuss was going on down there? in the newspapers? well I'd just laugh because what the blazes did those people know about anything? Maybe I was the only guy on this whole coast that knew what was really going on. I was just a young fellow then, just started, but we was friends.

You can't tell me nothing about the Irish. I seen them come in to the Ottawa valley when I was a kid, they come up the river with all their belongings and set off to hell and gone back into the bush. We watched them go through the town there, dozens of them at a time, setting out into the bush to hack out their farms, I don't know how the hell they did it, most of them never seen a <u>tree</u> before. They got into the logging camps too, later, and wasn't that something ... (laughing) ... when the Irish and them French Canadians got together! When it was just the French Canadians they'd treat you like the scum of the earth! They'd as soon cut out your gizzard as <u>talk</u> to you if they found out you wasn't one of them, but when them Irish moved in it was a different story to tell because they'd met their match, and after that you never had to worry as long as there was an Irishman around, he'd fight to save your hide even if he didn't know you. There was plenty of heads split open there and it's a wonder they didn't <u>kill</u> one another, the lot of them! And you can't tell me nothing about the Dirty Irish neither, which is another kettle of fish, because I know them, too. Seen plenty of them right around here and I'm not mentioning any names ... (laughing) ... hell, I'd hate to set a foot in their house. I seen one damn family, they was so goddam lazy, hell the old woman slopped around like a stinkin' cow, and dogs up on the table to lick out the plates, hell it made you <u>sick</u>, and then their men was no better than the woman, wouldn't lift a finger to work in case it killed them. I'm telling you this, and it's true, I knew one family with six boys and every one of them too lazy to cut a stick of wood for the fire ... I <u>seen</u> this, they put the goddam log in through the window with the butt-end in the stove and only had to move from their backsides long enough to shove it a little farther every once in a while! ... (laughing) ... There's more than one kind of Irishman, I'm telling you, just as there's more than one kind of anything, and I know what I'm talking about!

This far from home, with us, don't you think he'd tell us the truth? He never brought nobody else, only himself, and he never tried to impress nobody—hell, he knew he couldn't impress <u>me</u> with anything, and what good would it do him to lie? This far from home he'd tell the truth.

He did bring someone once. He brought the Indian one time, I think she was from somewhere around here, north of here, he brought her this one time but she didn't hardly say <u>nothing</u>. I thought she was stupid or something, the way she just sat there. You know. My wife, she tried to talk to her, Jesus I tried myself to get something out of her—just to be polite—but the best I ever got was a "yes" or "no" or a grunt. I never could see what he saw in her, but, hell, he wasn't the first I ever thought <u>that</u> about, what men see in some women has always been a goddam mystery to me. You can be sure there's no sense in it, whatever it is!

Jesus ... (laughing) ...

You'd think he was a kid, the way he treated her. Hell, the man was old, he must've been in his fifties. And she wasn't no spring chicken neither ... (laughing) ... I heard she left

a husband and a dozen kids behind when she took up with
him, up in one of them reserves, and I heard it wasn't the
first time she done it, neither. She must've been in her thirties at least, and I sure as hell wouldn't call her no raving
beauty. The best you could say about her was she was clean,
and knew when to keep her mouth shut. I told Ella afterwards she could've took a lesson from that. And the two of
them were always touching, always touching, it'd make you
sick I couldn't look. A man the age he was, he could've been a
grandfather, for Chrissake and here he was pawing at that
woman and giving her looks ... (laughing) ... It's a good
thing he never brought her back after that, I couldn't've
stood it.

Goddam women. That's what it was you know, always the
bloody women. If he'd've left the women alone from the beginning he wouldn't've got into none of that trouble. I told
him, too, but of course you can't tell a man like that nothing.
He couldn't keep his hands off them, he even started pawing
at Ella one time but I told him to keep his hands to himself
or he'd see the road. He just laughed, like it was only stealing
cookies or something, but he never did it no more, I can tell
you for sure. He just never grew up all his life. There's some
people just never grown up, no matter how goddam old they
get they're still kids and haven't learned a thing more than
what they started with. That was him, that was his trouble,
he never grew up his whole life, there's plenty around like
him, and I know what I'm talking about.

That time he brought her here I bet he wished he never
done it before they'd left. She sat there like a goddam mute
the whole time we was sitting around b.s.ing, never even
smiled when we told a rip-snorter of a joke, never cracked
her face except once just long enough to see she didn't have
no teeth missing, which was a surprise. Just sat there! But
then when they went outside for a bit of a walk before we all
hit the hay I heard her light into him ... (laughing) ... like a
hornet, kye-eying away in Indian and English and God
knows what-all at him, I don't know what he done or said
that set her off but, boy, was she mad. I figure she did the
whole weekend's worth of talking in that five minutes they
went outside, she must've gone up one side of him and down

the other and cursed every square inch of him ... (laughing)
... then I heard the SMACK and her voice stopped like a
stalled buzz saw, you know — sort of a dying whine — and she
never said another word again that I heard the whole goddam time they stayed. It didn't stop her from eating, she
must've shoved in enough food to keep a logging camp
supplied for a year, you'd think she'd never seen food. I told
Ella we better plant an extra field in spuds if he was going to
bring that rig with him every time he came.

But he never brought her again. He took her off to see the
goddam world or something. I got a card ... (laughing) ...
it's somewhere around here I guess, from Spain or some
bloody place like that. They was living in a goddam villa, for
cryin' out loud, though I don't know where they got the
money from because one thing I know for sure, he wasn't
rich like they made out. Hell, the guy was nearly bankrupt,
he told me. He didn't have as much money as I did. And she
sure as hell didn't have none. I heard they earned it as they
went, though I never learned what it was he could do, I never
did figure out what the bastard was good for, he always
seemed to me like one of them people that aren't no good
for a goddam thing, no trade or skill or education to speak
of, so I never figured out how he managed. It must've been
the women in his life, though they brought him more trouble, I'd say, than success.

He come up here once, between trips, by himself. Christ,
the man looked like he'd been through hell! That goddam
woman was ageing him faster than all that trouble over the
first wife did. "What's the matter with you, you son of a
bitch?" I says. "Can't you keep up with her no more?" ...
(laughing) ... But he never answered that, he changed
the subject: "How did your trial turn out, Ed?" he says.

Jesus ... (laughing) ... while he was away trotting round
the world having his fun and wearing himself out, old Kovic
the goddam Yugoslav that had property backed up against
mine slipped across the fence one night and stole my good
Hereford bull and butchered it into his deep freeze before you
had time to think! So I took the bugger to court. I told Keneally, I said, That goddam bohunk got up on that witness
stand and barefaced said Guthrie never had no bull. Every-

body knows Guthrie is a big goddam liar. He never had no Hereford bull in the first place for nobody to steal. Well, I stood up right there where I was with the judge, old pasty-face Miller, banging his hammer on the desk, and I pointed my arm like this at that Kovic, I said, I yelled at him You goddamed lying bohunk bastard! Your mother was no good; your father was no good; and you're no bloody good either. And I said, You liar, I hope you die! Old pasty-face threw the case out. You can't prove much with frozen chunks of meat anyway, he says, and why should he listen to a couple of cursing hicks. But that Kovic never had much time to do his laughing in because the so-and-so was dead within a month! Fell off his roof and broke his neck!

Old Keneally nearly split himself laughing. I thought if he don't stop he'll be the second man to drop on my account. Jesus ... (laughing) ... he laughed and laughed. "Ed," he says, "I wish I had your talent. I've made a few things disappear in my time with some tricks I learned as a kid, but I was never any good at long-distance killing." He said he could think of a few people he wouldn't mind trying it out on.

Well the next day I think I seen what he meant. We walked back into the bush so I could show him where Kovic's place joined onto mine and when we come back up to the house here was this car in the yard. A taxi. It must've been the first time any taxi ever come down my road. Ella was off staying in town with her sick mother so I thought maybe it was her coming back, riding in bloody style, and I'd give her hell when I got ahold of her, who did she think she was! But it wasn't her. The taxi driver came out of my house like he'd just left a parcel in it and got in his car and drove off right across in front of us without so much as a howjado. And when we went inside, here was this damn cripple sitting in a chair waiting for us.

"You see what I mean, Ed?" he says. "They hound me. No matter where I go they hound me."

I could've said it's your own fault for bringing that Indian rig up here, because nobody knew where this place was or where you went until you brought her. But I could see from his face there was no point in wasting my breath. Some people don't want to hear nothing.

"What you want?" he says to the little guy ... (laughing)
... just like that, like a bark, "What you want?"

Well it never took me long to see what a pain in the ass it
would be havin' a fella like that one trailing you around. A
slack-mouthed curled-up cripple. My Christ, I believe he was
older than Keneally, or just as old, you can't tell with some of
them people. Big hanging-open mouth; buggy eyes; grey hair
like a rat's nest. Jesus Murphy I said is that the kind you got
workin' for you down there? To myself, I never said it to him,
I could tell there wasn't no use saying nothing to him right
then he was too mad.

"What you want, Jems?" he barks.

Jesus ... (laughing) ...

And I swear to God this little bastard dips his head forward, like a bow. A grey-haired man. I thought maybe he was
going to fall forward off the goddam chair, I thought maybe
he was drunk or something. But no, up he comes again, his
bug-eyes blinking away, and says "If the Father will forgive."

"Holy Jesus," I says. "Keneally, what are you running
down there anyway?"

Well, son of a bitch, you wouldn't believe it was the same
man. "Guthrie shut up," he says. To me. The bloody old ape.
All of a sudden I was a dog to be barked at. "Guthrie, shut up."
The man's crazy, I think to myself, the man's as loony as
they say. You can't trust him a minute. Well, bugger you, I
think to myself, if you expect to go on eating my food and
sleeping in my house. Just bugger you. There's a certain
breed of man that can't be trusted, not that they make any
special effort to be like that, it's just that they're born that
way, one minute they think this and the next they think
that. It looked there for a minute like he was going to be
one of that breed. It's a kind you want to stay away from,
and I know what I'm talking about.

But getting mad at me like that only made him even madder at the cripple, like he blamed him for everything. "What
the hell did you follow me up here for?" he says. "It better be
important!"

The cripple started blubbering and spitting and trying to
get something out and finally he says "They want you to
come back right away. There's trouble."

"Trouble? What kind of trouble?"

So I'm going to tell you this and you're not going to like it, because it will spoil what you've already decided. That cripple, he gets all tangled up around his tongue and looks scared as old hell, I thought he was going to drop dead right there, but all of a sudden Keneally, mad as he was, went down on his knees and puts his <u>arms</u> around the guy. Like this! Just wrapped them around and pushed his face in against his little chest and says, Oh Christ, I can't remember what he says, something, and the cripple looks like he can't believe what's happening. Well, can't you imagine the shock.

Then Keneally got up on his feet again, steady, and I swear to God there was tears in his eyes, and he said, I remember this, he says: "In the end it comes down to just the two of us, Jems," which didn't make much sense to me at all, but might to you, and the next thing I know they're talking like I wasn't even there. I don't know what it was about, it could've been anything at all, something to do with that place down there and the people, I wasn't much interested then, I figured I seen everything now. This was the man they told the stories about? Maybe over in the Old Country all you had to do to get into legends was deliver a whole lot of blarney and pull off a few amateur tricks but I coulda told him around here the least that's expected is you'll have a fight with a bear. So I just went out to the garage and started up my old pickup and brought it up to the door ready to drive them out to the bus. You could tell it wouldn't take much talking on the cripple's part to have Keneally itching to get home and straighten things up. I never found out what the trouble was, maybe it was nothing, maybe they just didn't like him taking off so much like that and forgetting about them. People will do the goddamnedest things to get your attention if you ignore them a while, there's no end to the things people'll do.

I mind one old gal lived up the road, farther up the road, used to come hanging around talking to Ella. Her husband never paid her enough <u>attention</u> she said, so she said she wondered if he'd pay her more attention if she got herself a limp in one leg. Well, she started limping around like old gimpy the one-legged dog and he still didn't notice nothing

and the next thing she saw she couldn't stop, the leg got
something wrong with it that got worse and worse until
they had to cut it off. Her old man couldn't look at her at all,
after that, couldn't stand the sight of her. He took off and she
never seen him again.

People are the damnedest things, and more bloody complicated than you'd imagine. And they'll do anything that
comes into their stupid heads to get attention, anything at
all, and I know what I'm talking about.

Virginia Newman
Burgess Rd.
Sept. 5, 1974

I only want to tell you about one thing and that's all. I'm not
one of your great talkers, I'm not even a very good talker at
all, I think there's too many talkers in the world already, we
could do with a little silence. So I'll tell you just this one
thing and that's all, because you may be able to make something of it, I don't know.

My name is Virginia Newman, I live here in Burgess Road
and have done so for years, I'm older than this century, and
once long ago I taught school out at Northcove for several
years. Like most teachers I talked too much, far too much at
first, and then made it my goal to learn how to teach without
speaking at all. I never achieved the goal, but I have spoken
scarcely a word since retirement. An easy accomplishment
here in this basement suite where there's no one to listen.
Those who know me, or pretend to, consider me senile. I
don't know, I probably am. All the more reason for silence.

So I'll make this brief.

In those years that I taught at the Northcove school my
very best friend, who was nearly the same age as I was, was
a girl by the name of Hattie Scully. You may have heard of
her, her married name is Mrs. Thomas. Some people consider her a joke. They have a name for her, in the manner of
cruel children, I've forgotten what it is but I'm certain it is
uncomplimentary and completely without compassion. Hattie Thomas is no joke, Mr. Becker, she's a casualty. She has

spent nearly all of her life on the road, on some old farm
wagon, absolutely homeless.

I haven't seen her in several years, she used to stop by, but
the last time she came in here we could only look at each
other, after a lifetime we had nothing left to say. Oh yes, I
remember just as she left she said something, she told me
there was no point in coming again, she said if anyone found
the two of us in the same room they'd drop a net and drag us
off to the loony bin as she called it. One of us is as nuts as the
other, she said, and we'd best keep apart.

But in those early days she came by the school every day
for a while, when the children were being dismissed. Her
mother had made the mistake of trying to escape from the
colony, it seems, and when they were dragged back to live on
it, it was Hattie who paid the price. As a little girl, she told
me, she was never allowed to get through a day without
being reminded of her traitorous beginnings. Every morning
at a certain time she was expected to check in at the big
house, to Keneally, but she would never tell me what sort of
thing took place between them. Only that she went home
immediately after, as fast as she could go, to throw up.

She was eighteen before she got up courage to run away
from all that. And even then it was only as far as town,
where she worked as a housekeeper, I believe. But she came
back every single day of the week, every school day, to my
little school just off the edge of the colony a few minutes
before the children were dismissed. She did it for several
years, she took great pains to cultivate me as a friend, a close
friend. Oh, I was flattered, no one had ever wanted me for a
friend in my life, but I was never deceived, I knew what was
going on. She made my friendship for only one reason, to
have an excuse for seeing those children, for talking with
some and touching them, and asking questions about home.
And every day, when the last of them had gone off, I pretended not to notice the look in her eyes. Oh what a look! She
would give anything, I knew, to go back with them, despite
all the things that had happened to her. I was sickened, to
think of it, but I wouldn't tell her I knew why she was there,
I wouldn't risk losing a friend.

So I've never told her I knew why we were friends. And

after a while we stayed friends out of habit, when I wasn't teaching there any more. I wouldn't tell you about it, either, except that it doesn't matter any more, and I'd tell it to her face now if she stopped in. And I'm not telling it to give her an excuse. Yes, I believe she's a casualty, but I won't permit anyone to let a childhood be motivation for a whole life. She chose. Somewhere along the way she chose to be what she is. I won't give her an excuse.

And that's all. I'm rusted up. It's made my throat raw just telling this much. I've a clipping here somewhere, you can have it. My mother wrote a letter to the newspaper once. In those days she still believed you could help if you only spoke out. And—just a minute—somewhere around here I've got a child's story, a silly thing they found when they tore down the school. I typed it up; you may find it interesting. And you may as well have it, it can't do me any good.

And so there you are. That's all you shall get out of Virginia Newman. Where did you leave your coat when you came in? You're wasting your time with all this, because the best you can hope for is ignorance and prejudice. None of us will ever know what really went on in that place.

JULIUS

Julius Champney followed the low yellow steel railing which had been put there, presumably, to keep him from tumbling down the bank of grey boulders into the oily water of the boat harbour. To float like those bits of milk carton on the scum, or sink with the pieces of rusty iron and old cable. This had all been water in here once, they'd told him, he was walking on fill. An inlet stolen from the sea so that blacktop could be spread for the cars to park. What water remained had been laid out in a pattern of wooden floats, between pilings, where yachts and sailboats and small fishboats were tied up. A middle-aged couple in the stern of a small yacht stood up from the sizzle of their frying bacon to watch him pass, while they nibbled at toast, or something, and wiped their hands down the sides of their bright-orange shorts. Two rows over, a man with his hands behind his back paced back and forth on the float beside a scaly-painted fishboat, then suddenly stopped as if coming to a decision, and disappeared down into its interior.

A person had to get away, sometimes, from the Hayworth woman. With her old goat's face, and her voice that could nail you to the wall. You had to find other voices. Even imagined ones.

You could tell us
first
what we done

He was tired. Already. Getting too old for this. Still, you couldn't spend every day down on Maggie's float, or back in the log cabin. Not when time seemed determined to fly past, leaving you breathless. Books were becoming too much of a chore and tended, anyway, to annoy him. And the others were always busy, or pretending. Maggie would do anything he wanted, if he asked, but Julius Champney had never acquired the habit of begging for favours. It was much easier to catch the bus in to town and then walk up to the hotel for some coffee and a change of voice. Even if his legs protested against the effort.

Cars rushed by on the road this sidewalk separated from the sea-edge. Tailpipes fluttered exhaust. Children's heads bounced in back seats. Housewives off to shop, or taking this route to the other side of town where friends waited with coffee. Or to the bus depot. Trying to give some point to their lives, or fill them up. The blast of wind they slapped at him was enough to lift his thin hair, and once even to unbalance his step momentarily. The flare of his nostrils was all that he offered back, in contempt.

Taking his time. He had plenty of it. It was mid-August, the day would be long enough. Over there were the backsides of stores that faced to the main street. Tilted a little, some of them, fresh paint slapped over old boards, a concession to those who approached from behind. Oil smell, from the boat basin, from the cars, from the hot pavement: his lungs seemed filled with it. Still, it hardly erased the stink of the salt water itself, which was in the breeze and in everything. Even the people who lived in this place, he thought, would smell of it, if he ever allowed himself to get that close.

Some of them claimed Maggie Kyle had the smell of the bush on her still, pitch and the smell of mountains. They were wrong. Like everyone else here she was salt. It could not be avoided. You breathed it, it got into your pores. For a moment he could almost remember the scent of wheat, and of poplar bluffs at evening. Fenced in here by mountains and water, where you couldn't see anything, where you couldn't find lines that weren't crooked, you were trapped and had to absorb it.

When the walkway tilted uphill he slowed. Blacktop became concrete. His legs would ache if he pushed himself too hard. Old Hayworth always screeched that he was a fool, at his age, to take these excursions. As if he were finished, like her, and had only to lie down. Up past the customs house. To catch the Americans when they sailed in with their yachts. With the Stars and Stripes. A youth lounged against the wall, waiting for someone. His eyes, under the tangle of hair, followed Julius Champney past. What is the matter, boy? Do you think it won't happen to you? Do you think I was born this way, with these hands? Tourists with cameras milled around the little white Hudson's Bay bastion. Noisy children rode on the cannons, facing seaward. Up the steps someone yelled back "Have you got film, Charlie?" and others came out, blinking, into the sunlight. There were people in this town who claimed grandparents who'd holed up in that place, once, when the Haidas came south on a raiding party. After slaves. Except for the cannons, which were suspect, this was the real thing. Umbilical cord to the past. These tourists would drive north, though, and pay to go through that counterfeit one on the spit, and never suspect the difference. When they looked at their slides in the fall, one would be as meaningless as the other, just as much make-believe.

Mid-August. Though it was warm still, or so they claimed, he had three sweaters wrapped around his wire frame, and heavy wool pants. At his age he would be grateful to suffer from heat, he couldn't remember a natural warmth. Each morning this month he walked up the gravel road to the gate of the Revelations Trailer Park and caught the first bus in to town, where sometimes in search of voices he walked up this slope to eat breakfast in the blue-carpeted café of the Coal-Tyee Hotel. Hayworth, there, the Iron Bitch, became less than memory. And he could do for a while without Maggie's fuss, or the shy bushy stare of Becker. He submerged, rather, in the dizzying excitement of politics and gossip, the hurried serious talk of the businessmen and city officials over their gulped coffee. Sometimes he dared, even, to advise: "It would be madness to fill in the estuary for the sake of a larger port. Consider the wildlife you'd be sacrificing to economy, and the eventual effects."

But always, eventually, the businessmen took their voices with them back to their businesses. They had no need, in their hurried important lives, for an old man. Age, they felt, did not bring so very much wisdom that they could afford the time to separate it from the trivialities. Not even a lifetime as a surveyor, an engineer, and eventually a town planner was enough to offer, because any town he had ever had a hand in designing was stretched out along a prairie railroad. And the streets in this place, he was assured, were laid out for all time on a contour map, in England, more than a hundred years ago by a man who'd never set foot on the island. As if any man could draw proper lines on this ungovernable landscape.

A dark face watched him climb; an old Indian woman in a grey cloth coat standing by the back entrance to a hotel. She chewed on something, and grinned. She was there nearly every day, watching him. The long grey hair that hung over her shoulders was as familiar, now, as the wall behind her. She'd never spoken, only watched him and grinned when he looked at her and then, presumably, continued to watch him up out of sight.

He did not go into the hotel today. He was impatient for his voices. When the sidewalk had levelled out again, across from the triangular patch of flowers at the war memorial, he walked more quickly past the post office and then right on past the big front doors of the hotel and the windows of its coffee shop where pale faces watched him, down past all that to the little park beyond.

Two girls in jeans came up the steep trail from the seawall, up through the slant of green grass and flowers towards him. The slope was so steep at times that they made a chore of it, panting loudly and laughing, and flopped down for a moment to rest, giggling, before climbing up farther. Still, they arrived eventually at the top, and passed out under the hanging red-and-black dugout canoe to fade away, still giggling, down the street. The totem that faced their retreat, taller and straighter than any of the trees or shrubs that surrounded it, was a column of grumpy-looking Indians and bears, all resting their hands on the tops of their fat bellies as if feeling for a heartbeat that didn't exist. The expected thunderbird at the top was no thunderbird at all but more of a seagull. He didn't have the round white-ringed eyes of the thunderbird which would have registered something between alarm and fury, but rather looked upward out of human eyes, ignorant of life below, and clutched like the others at his own breast. Benches bolted to concrete slabs faced seaward down the slope, among beds of brilliant red-and-white petunias, and yellow marigolds and drooping leafy shrubs. Julius Champney, on the centre bench, was the only person in the park. This was the way he liked it, this was the way he wished it could always be. The sea below, as always, fascinated him, with its rhythms. And frightened him too, with its repeated assaults on the land.

It was a quiet morning. In the harbour the tide was full, smooth, nearly white under the clear sky. The long island which protected the harbour from the rougher movements of the strait looked like a floating tray of firs, a jagged-topped green platter that you wouldn't be surprised to see glide closer, or warp and roll if something should disturb the water. Near one end, near the harbour entrance, it tapered down to a low strip of land then swelled to a final hump, a sudden knoll crowned with a grove of

arbutus, which from this distance could have been black pieces of
coral with their naked spread-upright fingers. A few white government buildings hunched under the trees, and off the very tip a
lighthouse blinked. It was there, on that hump, that Champney's
attention was riveted. On a morning like this, in this quiet, it was
almost possible for him to hear those voices:

You could tell us
first
what we done.

The gallows, of course, had not been there for years. It had
probably been taken down immediately after the hanging. And
there was never, so far as he knew, a photograph taken, though
he'd made no effort to find one, or to search out a witness report.
He preferred to imagine a large elaborate wooden structure,
erected by a pair of carpenters whose hammer blows rang in the
ears of the townsmen across the harbour: a high platform of
newly sawn lumber, two tall sturdy posts with jutting beams and
angled supports, and two limp nooses. It was more likely, of
course, that it was a hastily-thrown-together thing, or perhaps
even just a tree, for the executions immediately followed the trial,
he believed, so that there would be no time for anticipation or
appeals. But Julius Champney on his bench could do what he
wished. And he wished, above all, that the gallows should be built
at the top of the knoll among younger, smaller arbutus trees, in
the clear view of everyone in town.

Here, in the park, he could hear them: the hammer blows, the
voices. It was as if he had been given a grandstand seat. Straining,
he might hear the snapping of necks. Now that he was alone, the
imagination which had never hesitated to take the elements of
prairie landscape and rearrange them into a flourish of streets
and buildings and parks, was free to play with the skeleton
elements of history.

But a sea-plane, coming in from the strait, landed on the white
water and moved slowly towards him, its motor idling, then glided
in to the wooden float behind the hotel. Two businessmen in suits
climbed out, walked up the steep ramp and along the high narrow
boardwalk, and disappeared beyond the hotel. By the time the
plane's motor was turned off a white seiner had moved out from
the wharves, its engines thumping softly, and had begun a slow
glide in the direction of the lighthouse.

Sea-planes and seiners, though, were not alone in the conspiracy against his solitude. Someone in a black heavy hanging-open overcoat and wool toque stopped at the entrance to the park, then started down towards the bench. He cracked sunflower seeds between his teeth, from a plastic bag cradled in one cupped-open hand, then swung his arm down to drop the shells behind him as if he believed a knee-high animal was following and taking them from his hand. He walked slowly, swaying, as if there was music somewhere which no one but he could hear, as if when he lifted a foot there was some doubt for a moment where he should put it down. When he sat, it was Julius Champney's bench he chose; he parked his rear end on the front-edge slat and leaned forward, as if the bench after all was only a prop to keep him from falling, and set his elbows onto his wide-apart knees while he continued to snap seeds. "Shit," he said, and spat a piece of shell which arced out and landed in the exposed red funnel of a large petunia.

The young man had brought a new smell to mingle with the perfume of the marigolds and the bland scent of petunias: rubber. For he was wearing a pair of green rubber boots, almost knee-high, with a strip of red around the large bulbous feet. He was dressed, in August, for the worst a winter can bring, impervious even to snow and frost, and the weeks of rain. Though this summer sun, Champney thought, may be something of a problem. There was, along with the rubbers, the smell of stale sweat.

The young man, who seemed unaware of the suffering he was likely to bring on himself, took in all of the harbour that was laid out before them and aimed a grin in the direction of Julius Champney who was tempted, almost, to move. There was the concrete promenade below, along the water's edge, which had yet to be walked.

"Jesus, man, this place is spooky."

Julius Champney's old yellow eyes blinked once and turned away. He was afraid they would betray pity, for the vocabulary. If it was spooky here, it could only be because he was the closest thing it had to a skeleton, or a ghost.

"I mean, look, it's not *natural* for the water to be that calm. You'd think some bugger had put a spell on it or something."

"Yes."

Then the young man added: "Don't this town ever wake up? Shit, it's nearly halfway through the day and you'd think it was the middle of the night."

"It's midweek," Champney said. Not that he owed anyone explanations. "A lot of the stores stay closed today. It's noisy enough, anyway, for me." There was the sound of machines somewhere, when you thought of it, and the steady run of traffic passing at the top.

The young man seemed satisfied, kicked with his green rubber boot at the pile of shells which had accumulated on the concrete between his knees, and only succeeded in scattering them. His head swaying, pleased, out on that long neck, looking for something. But it was Champney who was to receive the benefit of the grin. "My name is Corbett, David Corbett?"

There seemed to be some doubt, or an apology. As Champney was not in the habit of exchanging confidences, he chose to find fascination in a branch of a weeping willow which drooped over his end of the bench. An old man could be assumed to be deaf, or eccentric.

But the rubber boots were impatient. "I've been here, there, you name it. I thought of looking for a job here but I haven't seen nothing yet to make me want to stay. Do you have a name?"

Do you have a name?

The name of the murder victim was, apparently, Peter Brown. He was a shepherd employed on a ranch owned by the Hudson's Bay Company. And because he was a Company man, it was no small crime they committed, these Indians, when they killed the shepherd named Peter Brown. Even James Douglas, by the grace of etc., Governor, would join in the manhunt.

The identity of the killers seemed to be as certain, in everyone's mind, as the identity of the victim.

"Of course a name don't mean anything. I mean, what the hell difference does it make to me what your name is? It could be Mao Too Whommit, I don't care."

The young man had become tired of the sunflower seeds and put the plastic bag on the bench between them. He hauled a banana out of the thick black overcoat and held it upright in front of him, as if he was lining something up, or trying to figure out why it wasn't straight. For a moment Julius was afraid that he would be expected to watch the banana being played with instead of eaten. But his anxiety was rewarded with the sight of peel being stripped back, though he turned away from the sight of the white pointed meat disappearing.

He could have gone. There was nothing to say he couldn't leave now, and take an earlier bus. Julius Champney, though, had had a long life full of people who would ask him to leave, or disappear. People who thought if you were old, or a bachelor, or soured, there was no place for you. They thought if you wouldn't play their games, or laugh at the mad jokes of fate, or see their better sides (which they kept hidden, for the most part, from you), then you ought to have been drowned in a sack like kittens.

No. There is room on this bench for both of us, he thought. And ground his narrow behind into the slats. If he outwaited the young man, this David Corbett, there may be time yet for the voices. And he may as well talk, since there was someone to listen.

"That point of land, on that island," he said, "is where they hanged the two Indians." If he was not to be allowed to think of them in privacy then he may as well speak.

The young man seemed uncertain whether to squint at the island or glare at the old man. He settled for the round toes of his rubber boots. "Yeah?" he said. "I ain't surprised. They done worse."

"I believe it was the first jury trial in the colony."

The young man snorted. "And I suppose the jury was all Indians!" He seemed to find this extremely funny. His head, hanging out over the wide gap between his knees, shook the humour out of it. There was even the flash of spit flying.

"Of course I'm from the prairies," Julius Champney said, "where one incident like that is hardly remembered. There were so many, and more dramatic too."

"Yeah I heard. And they had more of a reason, there, to hate. Armies of white men laying tracks across the grazing land of the buffalo are more obvious than a few pockets of trading posts, in the trees. Hell, on this island you wouldn't even know you'd been overrun until someone built a supermarket up against your reserve."

"Or until you broke one of their laws."

The young man looked up at the totem, frowning. Perhaps he thought those grumpy faces were blaming him for something. "I never seen the prairies," he said, "though I want to. I been all over the States, I been to the Maritimes, but I missed the prairies. I just get a job here and a job there and move on. Seeing the world."

Champney hoped his sudden laugh didn't offend. "We all try to see the world," he said. "To cram it into our eyes and noses before it's too late. But it's always too late, and we don't know what to do with it anyway, once we've got it. And we never remember what reason we had for starting out."

For a moment he recalled a soft white middle-aged woman on the plane, flying, he believed, towards Amsterdam. "Soon now," she said, "I will have seen every country, which is my goal." Julius Champney was a little younger then, and still knew his reasons. "Why?" he said, and she puffed up like a contented cat, saying, "because once it occurred, there was no ignoring it. I was never one for leaving any job half done." Her husband, she told him, built apartment blocks. And how would he feel if he stopped building one a few storeys from the intended top, or neglected to put the plumbing in?"

"I've seen a lot of countries," Champney said, to the willow, "but it's done nothing towards holding off this time, now, when I'm sitting here on this island, with no love for it at all, and no desire to get off."

"Well I don't know anything about that." It seemed that a banana was not all that was hidden in that black overcoat. The young man hauled out a chocolate box, which he put on the bench between himself and Julius, beside the bag of seeds. But he did not open it. It was there, evidently, for some later purpose. "But how did you end up here, then, if you been so many places? I mean, why did you stop *here*?"

"You stop when it hits you that you've forgotten what you were looking for." There was more warmth in the sun than he expected, or hoped, and Julius Champney decided to risk a confidence. "It may surprise you that I loathe the ocean. And that I have little use for the type of people who move onto islands like this. Whatever their original reason might be, they end up the same. This is a place where people have two goals: to take life slow when it means helping out the other fellow, and to take it fast when it means grabbing a piece of the pie. Island people think they can make their own rules."

Even the island itself was that way, he thought: defying geometry. Straight lines looked ridiculous here.

The young man had not expected the venom and was uncertain what to blame his discomfort on. He decided on the boots again, and pulled one of them off to dump out a pebble, which bounced off the concrete and buried itself in grass. The toes, free, stretched and bent in the yellow socks before disappearing again down the rubber tunnel. "When I started school," he said, "the teacher told us never to sit all day in a pair of gum boots. She said it drew the eyes, weakened the sight. I had this picture of the rubber sucking all the strength out of my eyeballs down through my body and letting it drain out into the floor. I thought if I left them on I'd see the blackboard getting dimmer by the minute. I never did find out if she was lying, or if there was some truth to it."

"It's more likely she was worried about the smell." Not the most tactful thing to say, when you thought of it. Not with the rubber stink sharper in the nose than all those flowers.

"They tell you lies all your life," Julius Champney said, "without a thought to the consequences. They tell you anything that comes into their heads, if it suits their purpose. People will say anything."

Not even the woman on the plane was an exception. Somewhere over Labrador the sun sank behind the plane like a pink coin dropped into a slot, and then only a few hours later, out over the Atlantic, they encountered the strong blue sky of dawn. The woman whose husband built apartments right to the top fell asleep at the window, her lips fluttering with each breath, her perfect white hair motionless against the back of the seat. She might have been at home, she was so vulnerable, or so careless. Suddenly the sun painted her face a brilliant orange: the hair, the closed eyelids, the creased skin, the dark throat: a harsh unnatural orange, or copper perhaps, that you couldn't believe she didn't *feel*. But it lasted for only a moment, her goddess state, then the light thinned out and became the pale blue of morning and she was real again, a soft woman jet-streaking towards Amsterdam. When her eyes throbbed open and found him, to smile, there was no hint that she knew of her transformation. "I hope Customs is friendly," she said. "Sometimes they can be, if you hit the right one." Then before the plane landed, she gave him an address in Paris and invited him to stop by. But when he found the place, weeks later, and knocked, he was told her name meant nothing to them, they'd never heard it before.

"I'm going for a walk," the young man said, suddenly, and stood up. "There must be a public can around here somewhere."

Julius Champney was unaccountably relieved to see that the chocolate box and the bag of seeds had been left, as hostages, on the bench. And that the surface of the harbour had at last been ruffled, by a breeze, so that the water was bluer now, with wrinkles.

Suddenly a wild crab-apple bush exploded a volley of bushtits, which soared upwards then shifted, suddenly and all together, and disappeared into a tree. The bush, abandoned, shivered.

January, eighteen fifty-three. When the search party arrives at the cedar lodge there is no one left there but the old men of the tribe.

Lieutenant Moresby is perhaps, even then, subject to the ambition which will some day lead him to an admiralty, and has little patience to waste on the row of wrinkled expressionless faces that watch him from across the fire. Like his partner, Sansum, and like their party of French-Canadian soldiers, he is cold, sick of the snow, and cranky from the hunger that gnaws at his guts. The cold pork and soggy biscuits do little to soothe.

Through the night there is the crackling fire for warmth, and outside the snow has softened all sounds, even the rushing of the river. And there are no secrets divulged by the row of dark unmoving eyes.

But those who keep secrets can afford to be generous in other ways. Salmon and potatoes are shared freely. And in return the French Canadians offer songs.

The lieutenant-who-would-be-admiral is not diverted by food or song. Through the night his mind follows imagined tracks up slopes of snow, through timber stands, along rivers. And time after time he turns a river bend to discover the Indian at last, boxed in against the bank, frightened, and eager to give himself over to justice.

To justice, or to fate.

This young man must be having some difficulty finding a toilet. Not that Julius would know where to look. There was the hotel if he ever needed it, though an elastic bladder and iron muscles were something he'd developed in the travelling. Had to. You would burst, otherwise, in some countries. Or disgrace yourself.

Which reminded him: the plumbing in his cabin was strangled somehow, and must be looked at. He would tell Maggie about it as soon as he got home. A plumber would have to be called, to take it apart, or advise at least. The sound of pipes choking to death under your floor was intimidating.

You couldn't expect her to pay much attention, though, she was too busy chasing after this, after that, trying to improve herself, or whatever it was she was doing out there on her lush overgrown land. Tracking down that fellow with the silver trailer, for whatever secrets he had to offer. Helping Becker edit his stupid interviews. Pampering Lily Hayworth. Rushing to and fro. Everyone was always chasing after something. You couldn't convince them it was useless. They just wouldn't believe. You couldn't convince them that you were punished anyway, in the end, without ever being told why. That the searching only made it seem all the more cruel.

A woman like Maggie was wasting her life, looking. She ought to be satisfied with what she had; already she had more than most people were ever given: beauty, intelligence, a place to live, people who cared. She ought to relax enough to enjoy her special state in a world of people who lacked most of those things.'But she had her ridiculous plans, she insisted on *rising*, she insisted on *seeing*, as if she believed, still, that there was somewhere, ultimately, to go, something to see that would make some real sense of it all. You'd think she was that girl in the fairy tale, that mermaid, dreaming of legs.

Her ambitions were making a fool out of her. He'd warned her against that island retreat or whatever it was, others had warned her, too. But she'd gone, anyway, like a kid off to camp. She'd been flown, with a whole lot of weird-looking people, from that float down below, off to their tiny island up somewhere. Full of hopes for conversion, or revelations. Psychiatrists, ministers, experts at this and that. They would find her potential, they'd promised. They'd bring out the good that was in her. They'd show her how to get her floundering soul onto the right and proper road. He'd watched her, from this bench, when she took off. He'd seen her among all those others on the float waiting to crowd into the waiting planes, among three-foot-long beards and fat caftans and paisley jump suits and painted toenails and at least a dozen pairs of black glasses. At the last moment, when she'd been reaching out for help onto the plane and put her foot on the pontoon, she'd looked back up the slope to him, and smiled. He could've cried, for the ignorance. Or naïveté. But instead he only lifted a hand, nodded grimly and watched her plane taxi out into the harbour, speed up, and eventually fly up curving out over the little islands and eventually disappear. He was not there, of course, when she returned two days later, on a special flight, and was set out on that float with her baggage, like a sent-home discipline problem. She wouldn't talk about it. Those people knew too much for their own good, was all she would say, and "I was scared stiff from the minute I put my foot on that island. I didn't belong with those people."

Maybe you'll stop, then, he thought. But oh no, not her. There were the courses, first, that she insisted on taking: painting, of all things, in the park. When she ought to be making the beds, or baking. *The art of intelligent film viewing, a summer course for the truly concerned.* As if the local theatre would ever show a film that required intelligence, or concern. She'd bought a new set of encyclopedias she'd never be able to find in her living room mess, let alone read. She was considering courses at the college in town. And worse than all this was the volunteer work, the sudden need to have her fingers in everyone else's pie, gathering up merit points on the do-gooding scale. She'd gone frantic.

But worst of all, if you could bear to think of it, was the abortive attempt to undo the past. Julius Champney had scars, still, to show for it. Suddenly it had become important for her to be the mother she'd avoided being all those years, and Carla — poor surly Carla — had been dragged up from whatever foster home she'd been stashed away in, an adolescent presumably reconciled to her lot, to act out a ghastly two-week farce. She may have been fine, in her adoptive family, she may even have been a nice enough girl, though it was difficult to imagine. But living in the same house as her biological mother, even for two weeks, was more than she was willing to tolerate, or equipped to handle. The two of them fought for as long as they occupied the same room. Screamed at each other. The mother determined to mother. The girl equally determined to resist. A spirited hellion, more like Maggie than you could believe, the girl'd taken to throwing things without any distinction of value. A china cup clipped Champney's ear. At the end of the two weeks the girl ran away, presumably back to where she belonged, and left the mother heartbroken. For the rest of them to console.

So they all suffered, when the mad chase was frustrated or hindered. The woman just wouldn't see. He could save her the trouble, if she'd listen. He could prevent her from repeating his steps. He'd gone through it too, long ago, when the designs on paper had been no longer enough, when the new towns and villages laid out and growing were no longer enough for his signature, he too had gone looking.

There'd been that rock, that great two-mile hump of rock glowing like a huge orange loaf in the middle of the Australian desert. The aborigines told stories about it, of creation and a great falling from the sky. And there were caves, at the base, lettered with signs and blood-drawings, and the record of hopes. But it had become, after all, only a rock, and he was content to let the others climb it without him. On the life-line. Their noisy excitement on their return was more from relief than from discovered truths, he suspected, and soon transferred itself to other enthusiasms when the bus hauled them away.

Camel treks through the haunted valley of Mada'm Salih, barefoot climbs up Croagh Patrick, subterranean prowling down to neolithic wall paintings below the Vézère in France, trekking to Czestochowa in Poland, climbs to the top of the Statue of Liberty, queueing up to file through the tomb of Lenin, all these and more had been, in the end, as dry and fruitless as the desert rock. Finally they came to nothing, or nearly. It was almost as if he'd been better off back in his office drawing lines on paper, inventing his own patterns, shaping the low natural world into geometric blueprints and maps.

That crazy old woman with the manure-spreader was an example of what could happen if you didn't know enough to stop. Julius Champney could happily have drowned her, when she stayed for that week after the wedding, he could have pushed her down the well. She was sandpaper to his nerves. Madmother Thomas, with her pink little tongue flicking, as if at flies. *Son of a gun*, she said, *it's good to put your feet up in one spot for a while*. He thought she was settling in. He would move out, if she did, rather than put up with her nonsense. Hayworth was enough to endure, and Becker. He would not be able to tolerate that floating hair, or those bare muscled arms, or that bloody cheerfulness. *Son of a gun*, she said, *I could get used to this*. Just to tease him. But she'd gone off, after all, on her ridiculous wagon, to hunt down some other roads for whatever she was after.

But not until after she'd trapped him, behind Lily Hayworth's loom, and driven a finger into his chest. "There's a smell of something sour about you," she told him, "like an unclean dairy. And sourness in the muscles around your mouth. Can't you think of *nothing* that doesn't curdle in you? Are all your thoughts that vinegary?''

Forced. All of her laughter was forced. When she was unaware, or resting, she had the face of a victim, as if something had been beating on her for seventy years. Was the sourness of his smell any worse than the scent of bandages and iodine he could detect on her? Figuratively, of course. He saw her broken and splinted, wrapped in yards of white, hobbling.

Suddenly the young man was beside him again, angry, stomping his bulbous feet. "This whole town don't have a single public can," he says. "I had to ask permission in a bloody store."

Champney was alarmed at the force of his own reaction. "Public washrooms, like museums and opera houses, are the mark of a civilized people."

"Civilized? This place looks like it's been around a while. Long enough."

"But it leapt over civilization, which would embarrass it, all the way from frontier town to Disneyland. You'll find pornography shops and slot machines and periodic festivals of idiocy, but you'll never find an art gallery or, as you put it, a public can. They would ignore the paintings, and tear out the public plumbing."

The young man would rather sing, though, than listen to judgements. At the other end of Julius Champney's bench he sang a few lines from a song which Julius had heard on the radio. Suddenly, he stopped. "I got myself an appointment, for a job interview," he explained. "I guess this is as good a place as any to sit while I'm waiting."

His hand, which was resting on the chocolate box, had no intention now of lifting the lid. Only playing, fingering.

Julius Champney was horrified in advance at the words he was unable to choke back, despite the swallowing and the turning away. "Tell me, Mr. Corbett," he said, "Do you . . . do you believe in a God of any kind?" He couldn't credit his own audacity, and hoped that it wasn't clearly heard. "But then you must," he added "or at least hope to, or you wouldn't be on the move. You'd be satisfied to sit, somewhere, forever."

The young man could only look grateful that Champney had made an answer unnecessary. It was clear, from his busy fingers, that he wouldn't be able to count on the old man's sanity any more.

"I'm a freeze-dried Christian," he blurted. "It's only when I'm in hot water that the God-juices in me begin to thaw."

He laughed jerkily, at his own joke. Then stopped, abruptly, to watch a sailboat tilt dangerously, and change direction.

But Julius Champney had already forgotten the young man, and his own atrocious question. He had forgotten, even, to close his mouth, from which saliva threatened to spill. He had caught a glimpse of the face.

Of Siam-a-sit.

He has followed the river upstream, pushing up the icy shallows, climbing and stumbling other times up snow-covered banks, cursing, praying, holding his gun high to avoid the dampness of snowy limbs, of splashed river.

He has come, he thinks, far enough for now, and this place looks good enough for a rest. Under brush, under snow, backed up under a protective overhang, he can see downriver but not be seen.

The sound of water running is all that there is between him and silence. There is a temptation, after a while, to relax. To believe, even, that the hunt has been called off.

But the white man in the uniform has not called anything off and appears, now, in a clearing. He comes close, too close, but it is clear from his face that he is not at all sure that he's heading in the right direction. He listens, peers, thinks.

When the white man has given up, has turned to go back down the river, Siam-a-sit raises his rifle. Aims carefully at the hated back.

But there is only click *and again* click *and again* click.

Which the white man, who has trained his ears to hear everything, does not miss.

"Are you all right?" the young man shouted. His hand on Champney's shoulder.

"What? Yes. Of course." Although, truthfully, he was not all that sure.

"You do a hell of a lot of staring into space. And muttering to yourself."

Into space? Well, he was an old man, and should be allowed certain liberties.

We think you should retire early, they told him. Why wait until it's too late? Until you kill yourself with work?

"They told me to quit early, before the job killed me. Go on out to the coast, they said, to your sister. But when I got here they'd already put her in a nursing home. I'd forgotten, you see, that she was much older than I was, that she had already, herself, 'retired' while I was chasing around the world."

The young man made sympathy sounds in his mouth, pacing back and forth on the concrete; eager to leave, but unwilling to desert.

"It was only luck, a bit of luck, that I found that woman with her trailer park, and the empty cabin. I would not go back, and for a while there was my sister to visit in the home, on Sundays. Until she died."

His sister, Dorothy, had been as skinny as he was. A pair of beanpoles. At the end, she had shrunk to a few straws of bone and flesh, laid out on that bed. The white cover hardly bulged.

"Look," the young man said, and — desperate — picked up his chocolate box. "Look what I have in here!" But the box had knocked the plastic bag flying and seeds spilled themselves in a sudden gush across Julius Champney's lap and down onto the grass.

"Stupid!" he said, shouted, and stood so that the seeds would fall around his feet. "Stupid!"

Brushing, brushing, with his old hand.

"Look!" the young man said again. "Look what I have here, in my box!"

When Champney peered into the box he could see nothing, at first, but a mess of grass. Then, squinting, he discovered a stubby, greenish-brown thing, shiny or wet, lying on the grass. Like a damp cigarillo.

"It's a slug," he said. "A slimy slug."

"Not a slug," the young man said. "Look again." And held the box even closer to the old yellowed eyes.

It stretched, moved a little. Julius Champney could see, now, that there were antennae on one end, two long ones like horns, two short ones like bulging eyes. And down the side there was a tiny hole, a pin hole, that appeared to breathe. A slug, though perhaps not as slimy as some.

"It's a snail," the young man said. "It's a snail without his shell."

Julius Champney looked up from the box. The young man's face was only inches away, his breath smelling of the sunflower seeds. There was a row of blackheads along one cheek, under his

eye. For a moment, breathless, Julius Champney was afraid to ask:
"What happened to his shell?"

The young man was smug now, like a child with a secret. "He never had one. I found him just like this, naked, on a piece of grass by the road. This old box is all he has for a shell now, and my pocket. He travels with me."

Champney wondered if, after all, the young man was perhaps retarded, or otherwise simple-minded. After the confidences, the conversation, the spilt seeds.

"Do you really think," he said, "that a cardboard box, or an old black overcoat, can supply something that nature has not?"

"Look," the young man said, slapping the lid back on the box. "What's the sense showing anything to you? What's the sense telling you anything? An old man like you."

He was ready, apparently, to stomp off. The green rubber boots were angry, shifting. Their smell now, had completely erased the petunias and the marigolds.

Julius, too, began to walk away, down the sloping trail towards the water. His back, he hoped, was ramrod stiff, to communicate his disgust. That thing in the box, he was sure, was only a slug.

But the young man was unwilling to let go, to let him shake loose. He caught up, walked alongside, hunched inside that great flapping overcoat. "Look! You can't just sit around here hating everybody, hating this place! Hating me, for Christ sake, because of a damn snail!"

"You mentioned an appointment," Julius Champney said, "please don't miss it on my account." He had come to the railing now, and could look down in the clear shifting water. The rocks were speckled with barnacles. Crabs ran for cover.

The young man beside him looked as if he could rip the steel railing out of the concrete. "Stupid old goat!" he shouted. "For all your sourness you can't spoil it for anyone else."

Champney prepared a look which was intended to shrivel. But the frizzled beard was trembling, the blackheads aflame.

"You sit there and puke out your self-pity on me but you never once, not one goddam time, asked me one single question that *mattered*, about *me*."

"Because there isn't," Julius Champney said, "anything about you that matters. I can't even remember your name, and all that you've managed to leave of yourself is a mess of yellow spilled seeds on the grass, and their shells."

Though I did, he thought, I did ask you one.

A sea-plane pulling away from its wharf relieved the silence of its tension. As it gained speed across the surface of the harbour, its engine roar filled the head. Then it was above the water, lifting, lifting, and finally soaring up and curving out over the low island.

When it had gone, when its engine sound had faded into the other sounds of the harbour, the young man had left him, too, was thumping up the slope and across the top of the park. He passed behind the totem, behind the hanging canoe, and disappeared beyond the corner of the hotel. A hunched-over stomping fury of flapping coat.

But there was nothing in his absence, or in the slapping waves, or in the morning, to stop the raced-up thumping, or the visions that crowded.

If Maggie should succeed in her determined search. If Becker; if the cousin, Wade. If they should after all catch glimpses of whatever it was they were after.

Champney's hands, on the railing, were less than wire, were only flesh. Pink and hairless. Skin rubbed as shiny as old pants-seats by life. Far up the arm a small tattoo, an intricate pattern of overlapping rectangles, could only be imagined, or remembered, beneath all the sweaters.

If Maggie should succeed, or one of the others, where he'd failed.

Because it was necessary to believe that they wouldn't. As it was necessary to know slugs from snails, and to know that if one must fail then another too must fail.

If Maggie should see what he'd never been able to see, if she should actually manage to rise, as she insisted on putting it, and to glimpse that impossible view.

Here, somewhere, in this harbour, the trial had been held on HMS *Beaver*. Perhaps from this point he might have been able to see the white plumes of breath snatched from the mouths of the jurors, or the officers. Or the two Indians.

The two tall masts were naked, draped only with wires. No smoke rose from the smokestack which stood in the centre, above the invisible steam engines. The low flat-box look of the hull was relieved only by the yellow humps of the casings that concealed the two paddle wheels. It was cold, mid-January cold, and a light crust of frozen snow lay along the rail. On the deck, the men were dressed in their heaviest coats: the captain, the jury, the officials, Lieutenant Moresby, Lieutenant Sansum.

The two prisoners, who stood accused before this group of cold

238 / THE INVENTION OF THE WORLD

hurried men, were not sure where they should allow their eyes to rest. There was a suggestion of movement along the river's mouth, of canoes perhaps, and the one called Siam-a-sit thought that may have been his people, watching. His father. Waiting for the results of the trial.

And it was impossible to believe that in the cluster of houses around the Hudson's Bay Fort there weren't eyes behind the glass windows, curious. Or that those who moved on the docks had any other reason.

The charge was, of course, murder.

Of someone they called Peter Brown. A shepherd who was supposed to have been killed, they said, by two Indians.

The trial is in English. Though an attempt is made to provide an adequate translation, the long exchange of foreign mouth-sounds could be the yattering of squirrels to the ears of Siam-a-sit. Trying to follow it only produces a headache, so he gives it up and thinks of his rifle, which has betrayed him, and of the coming spring which, he is soon made to understand, he will never see.

From the island, too, the harbour appears calm. Lifeless. As if the whole place has drawn a deep breath and is holding it, for whatever time it takes for the execution to be over.

Nothing has come of the movement along the river mouth. Nothing has come from the white men, only more squirrel-yattering sounds. Nothing has come from the sky, except the promise of more snow.

On the platform, beneath the nooses, the flat chocolate eyes shift to the hangman, whose hands could be made of old rope. Throats, dry with fear, can only whisper. Cannot refuse to whisper.

You could tell us, first, what we done.

There was no record, anywhere that he had seen, which even hinted that the two condemned men, or one of them, said those words before the ropes snapped their necks. Nor was there anything in official records or in the newspaper reports to indicate that they said anything at all, or if they did, said anything that could be understood by the white men who were witnesses. At any rate, Julius Champney had no desire to consult documents, there was no reason to believe them any more reliable than himself. And the voices existed out of time, anyway, and belonged in the end only to him.

Fortunately, Julius Champney was alone.

It would be too humiliating to be caught like this, at this railing below the marigolds, with his old wrinkled yellow face gone out of control.

The Wolves of Lycaon

"When I saw he was determined to use that recorder thing on *me* I told him I don't sing any more and haven't since the day I met Keneally. Of course I'd lost my voice long before that, but I'd gone on pretending anyway, it took me to London and New York and Toronto. But I couldn't coax a note out of it now."

Not that she needed to tell Maggie a thing like that, or anyone else. They all knew that her voice, even her speaking voice, made the crows sound good in comparison. Some called it a heavy smoker's voice, which made sense at two packs a day, and somebody said she had the kind of voice some alcoholics can get, after a number of years. But it was age, she told them, the inside of her throat had only got as wrinkled and rough as her face. It was natural.

"He said if I sang he would tape me for the Museum of Natural History, like the song of the humpback whale. The so-and-so. But of course it wasn't my singing he wanted at all. So I said why should I tell anybody what's my own business? I can't even remember most of my life, so I'd have to make it up, or jar it loose, and I don't have any desire to do either of those. Leave things alone, it's safer. I don't want to remember Keneally at all, I only have one picture of him, our wedding picture, and when I look at it I could swear that I'm looking at strangers."

There were stars, she'd been told, up there in space, which had exploded, blown apart, and then sucked back in to their own vacuums to form dense tight invisible masses. They gave off no light, the scientists said, or any other kind of responses, they were black solid holes that were there and were not there, that could suck you in. Like Keneally, now that he was dead.

Even Maggie, reading a fat white book, wasn't all that interested. And why should she be? The lives of the people laid out in those pages she was turning were confined between covers, controlled. There was no threat in them. But Lily Hayworth didn't need to be told that the lives of real people around you were dangerous, once opened, because there was nothing as simple as covers or dust jackets to keep them in check, to stop them from going wild, and interfering in the business of others.

"I told Becker he wouldn't get a word."

He'd paced around her bedroom, humming and hawing, looking for a way to convince her. He'd fingered her books, her Robert Browning, he'd picked up the little black leather Bible. "A Bible, Lily?" he said. "You've been reading this?" No, she'd never read it, not through, she said. Like the other books, it was something of her mother's, who'd believed; but once in a while even now she read one of the psalms, to help her sleep.

A strange story, he said, if you'd read it. It has two beginnings. The first, a single chapter, would have us all made in the image of God, perfect spiritual creatures. Then someone else came along, started it all over again, and had us all made out of clay. The rest of the story shows a lot of people trying to get back to that first beginning, back before the mist and the clay. You get all the way up to nearly the end of the book before you meet the man who knows how to manage it.

Magic? she'd asked him, but he shook his head. Well, magic is what people want, she said, as no one could know better than the widow of Donal Keneally. Everyone put his faith in one sort of magic or another, or nearly everyone, though they had other names for it. Becker himself believed in the magic of the recorder, his electrical gadget; a few she could name still pinned their hopes on a "Second Coming". Some in a world government that would solve everything. Some in science, or medicine. Magic, magic. "It comes from the shock of discovering the limits that are put on us by this sack of bones we call ourselves, we go looking for some sort of magic to count on."

"I agree," he'd said. "But magic is what seems to defy the laws, or suspend them. There's nothing magic about something that was there all along, though hidden, like the underground roots of frozen grass."

Who would have believed it of Becker, talking like that? Funny, bushy-faced ugly little man. If he'd shave, or wear clothes that didn't look as if they'd come out from the bottom of a garbage dump, she would be tempted to pay attention. She had never, since the first day she met him, been able to take seriously anything that he said. He was more like a clown.

Of course, she could not know whether there was even worse ugliness hidden beneath the beard, and the clothes.

"I told him that when I met Keneally for the first time I had just come face to face with the fact that my singing career was over. I was in my thirties. I would have married him if he'd had purple skin and a pair of horns. The alternative was to live out my life with my mother, taking tea with her friends at the Empress, strolling through the manicured gardens of Beacon Hill Park. I chose marriage. And it was a marriage that has lasted up to this minute and will go on, despite the death and the second marriage and all the rest that you know about. Those others who escaped, though maimed, like your Madmother Thomas, at least got their souls back to call their own, in whatever shape. They weren't married to him. It will take more than what's happened so far to shake me loose from the man. If I ever give in and talk, if I ever let Becker's recorder run me to earth, he'll soon see that it's not over yet."

It was a November afternoon when he brought me up to this place, Becker, we'd been married the night before. Raining like the world was ending. The air was thick with it, when you looked out you could believe that you and all the world were under water, there was no sky. Rivers ran in the ditches. Wipers couldn't keep the windshield clear. You know the kind of day, when you think there mustn't be any other colour in the world except green and grey; even the trunks of trees have got soaked, and the green needle branches have swollen up silver with the trapped rain. Depressing. It's the only time of year that it's possible, here, to envy those other people, the ones in places where leaves die and take on flaming colours for a while. They have a longer, bleaker winter ahead of them, but for a while their world has a little more colour in it.

People when we passed through the town stood in the doorways of the stores just watching. There was no business, I'd guess, no one would go downtown shopping unless they had to, that month. The narrow cobbled main street winding up over the hump the town was built on was washed over by a torrent of rain water. The new stone and brick faces of the buildings were naked and streaming. There was a resigned settled-in look on the faces of the people, never the expectation that it would soon be over. And the interiors of stores, you could tell, with their weak lights burning in daylight, would be even gloomier than the outside.

What happens to light on a day like that, sunlight I mean? When it has to penetrate that thick white sky — who knows how deep that one solid lid of cloud is? — and filter down through the heavy falling rain and the swollen tops of trees. It's pale and weak — less revealing than moonlight — it makes me feel as if my eyes have lost the ability to detect any colours at all except that pale grey and that dull sober green. I want to dress in flaming reds and bright blazing yellows, but the weak depressing light seems to affect my will power, too, and so I don't. I feel thick and weak and washed-out and sad.

A bride, though, is not affected very much by weather. When he drove me out here I was too eager to get my first look at this place, to size up my new world and measure it against the legend. When he got out and opened the gate I can remember thinking: This is it, this is *before*, a few seconds from now will be *after*, I'm going in.

You'd think he'd've been excited too, bringing a bride home. Maybe he was, I don't know, you couldn't tell it by his face: he looked anxious, or annoyed. Impatient; there was that deep vertical crease in his forehead. Maybe it was the rain, maybe it was getting to him too, making him edgy. When he got back in the car, his face, streaming wet, was hard, and angry. Looking back on it, I wouldn't be surprised if he was mad because no one had magically known exactly what minute he'd be arriving home and run out to swing the gate open for us. Of course, there was no way of telling for sure what that man was thinking.

So we rattled down the gravel lane, down that road out there, down to this place. And of course, being at the beach here, it wasn't only raining, it was blowing too.

One of the first things I remember thinking when I got down into this place was *what have they done to it so that I feel as if I should keep my eyes always on the ground*?

For one thing, they'd cut down all the trees, anything tall that tempted you to look skyward. Oh, I know its grown back now, some of it, that's one thing you can count on here, but then the forest had been cut back to a solid timber wall that surrounded the place, and no spires had been left, nothing to raise your eyes. Even the sea somehow had lost its pull, it was only more flatness, even less varied than this land. You were conscious only of the earth, the dirt. The houses — except for this thing, this House of Revelations — the houses were all squat, dark, made of logs, as if they might have grown from the earth too, centuries before, and belonged there. There was nothing, anywhere, to make you want to look up higher. I felt, almost immediately, that I was expected to go around with my nose only inches from the earth.

This building, this big house, was barer then than it is now, before the arbutus grew up around it, and all those shrubs and vines. Then there was the circle of log cabins — where you live, and Julius — and those other sheds. All the original settlers had lived in them, twenty years before when they'd first arrived, but by this time only the childless couples, and the widows, had them. The families had gone off, farther back into the fields — what *was* fields then — and built themselves those other houses you can see falling apart if you walk up the bush a ways.

"What you've built here is a village all your own," I said, when I saw that circle of buildings. It seemed funny to me, a strange set-up, that circle. I was used to cities, remember, and straight streets, blocks of houses facing each other across parallel lines. Nothing in my experience had run to circles.

"In some cultures," he said, "the circle represents enlighten-ment. And perfection."

What education I'd got didn't run to mysteries and symbols, it dealt in facts and immediate realities. And I was eager to spoil it for him, to show I wasn't impressed. "Well what happened to your perfection when you got past the shacks? All the fields are squares, all the fences are straight lines."

It was an ugly sight, that first day, that first week, in the rain. Those brown log shacks, those pale fields, everything so dull. If I hadn't come through the rain to get here I would have believed the place existed inside a cloud, that the air was thick mist or solid water. Those people, whoever they were, out in those shacks and sheds and houses, could have been mermen. If it hadn't been for this house, not the way it is now, but like it was then, I would have demanded right away that we move in to town.

But not many women, not many women I know, could have resisted the house. It seemed old already, and posh, like it was built in some other country where they go in for a little class and then brought here. You'd throw most of it out nowadays, it was so cluttered you could hardly breathe, no bride today would put up with it for a minute. But I loved it. At least at first. That living room, it was full of good things then, a gigantic grandfather clock, velvet love-seats, thick satin tassel cushions, gilt mirrors, glass lamps and spittoons and china figurines, potted ferns, oh, let's see, yes, a beautiful big pump organ. He taught me to play it. In the evenings he didn't like to see me just sitting with a book, or God help me, knitting, he insisted I get up to that organ and *play*! "Sing!" he'd say. "Sing!" Teasing, and I'd say "You so-and-so," and he'd laugh. I never sang one blessed note the whole time I lived here then, as his wife. Not one note. At first it was because I knew I'd lost my voice, that I was terrible, and later it was because I couldn't remember the words of any songs. I just never felt like trying to remember them.

And the kitchen. You'd think I'd remember the kitchen, I used to spend most of my time in it. It wasn't that tile and linoleum thing Maggie's got down there now, with her fridge and electric stove. The floor was wood, oiled wood, oh I can't remember the rest, except that it was cluttered. I remember the big oblong copper tub I used to boil the clothes in, on the stove. And the clothes rack over the stove you raised and lowered with a cord. I remember because I nearly burned the house down once, when the cord snapped and the thing fell on the stove while I was out of the room. Lord, you should've seen me move when I came in and saw that smoke! But that's all I can remember about the kitchen. I don't have one of those memories, Becker, I'm not one of those people who can go tromping through their own past like someone with a searchlight, remembering every detail. I don't even remember half the stuff I tell you until it comes out and surprises me. About the rain, for instance, I wouldn't have remembered that about the rain, if it hadn't just come out. And not quite true, either, I don't feel like that any more. One season's as good as the next to me now, and green's as pretty a colour as any other.

A reservoir at one end of the stove, to heat the water. What do I want to remember the kitchen for, anyway, nothing ever happened there, except work. Oh yes, and the revolt or whatever you want to call it, they surprised us in the kitchen. But that wasn't until later, five or six years later.

You know what I hated, even then? In every room? Those smelly flypaper things you hung from the ceiling, those strips of sticky paper that uncoiled out of a tube and hung in the middle of the room clustered with fly bodies. It was better than the little tangle of black flies that would circle in the middle of the room forever if you didn't have one, but still I hated them. And he, he was so tall he'd catch his hair on them, it would stick. Lord, he'd get mad. He'd rip the thing off the ceiling and throw it on the floor but it'd get caught on his fingers and he'd dance around trying to get it unstuck. You ought to've heard that man curse. In English. In Irish. He could curse a thousand ways. But I always laughed at him. There was something funny about the way he'd get so flaming red and hopping mad at *things*, as if they had minds to decide they'd deliberately plague him. He got mad enough at people, God knows, but he got even madder than that at things. Or himself, for being their victim. I just laughed. There's nothing more foolish than a human being, with all he's got to work with, wasting his fury on inanimate objects that don't even know he's alive.

But he saved his anger for later. At first it was a real honeymoon, he was so attentive, and gentle. And we could have been holidaying in a Spanish villa for all I ever saw of the other people, somehow he kept them away. Oh I met Jems, of course, when we first got there. You couldn't miss Jems, fawning over the master, and slobbering. He lived in the second cabin at the time, Julius's cabin. And of course there was the girl who came in to help. Two girls. I can't remember either of their names. What a memory. Maybe it'll slip out when I'm not thinking, like all this other stuff. One of them was a Bridget. I would've called them all Bridget at that time, they were interchangeable. They never talked. Just "'Tis true, yes", and "Right away, missus", and if I tried to pry anything more out of them they'd just colour up like I was asking about their sex life, if they had any, or their underwear, and then they'd slip out somewhere and disappear. If they're all this shy, I thought, if they're all this *quiet*, no wonder no one ever left the place. Or hardly anyone.

I saw the others of course, some of them, but only through the windows. Out there in their fields doing their work, whatever farmers do in November, feeding their cattle. Or running from one house to the other in their gum boots. The women with their high-colour faces. I'm surrounded by a pack of peasants, I thought. It wasn't a word you'd use ordinarily on this island then. Well, weren't we *all* peasants? You couldn't live here and not be a peasant of one kind or another. But these were the real thing, real old-country peasants. It scared me. I saw them all through that rain, living in their cloud, going about their plodding business with their eyes hardly ever lifted off the ground in front of their feet. I imagined that they were incapable of seeing anything beyond their own bodies, their own clay. They might have had blinkers on, you know the things they put on a team horse, so he can't see his partner. They might have had no more opinion of themselves than a horse has.

"Circles and squares are very nice to represent ideas," I told him, "but you can't build your life on them. What do these people think, what do they feel? What keeps them here?"

He scowled at me. You must remember that even though I was heading into middle age myself he was getting pretty old and thought of me as young. Pretty old! The man was thirty or forty years younger than I am now! Wouldn't it make things a lot easier if people would just *be* a certain age all their lives? So you could say so and so was an old man. Or so and so was a pretty girl. But hell, no, they've got to complicate it all up by being *every* age at some time and you keep changing, too, to make it even more meaningless to talk about age. It's all too complicated, Becker, I don't know why you're even trying to do this. It won't mean anything by itself. And I've only got this one photograph of him. It's not very good either, you'd never know we wanted to get married. And you'd certainly never guess those two ageing people getting their picture taken could hardly wait to jump back in bed.

We didn't, either. Didn't wait. See those brand new spotless wedding clothes, he had them off us both — or all that was necessary — before we even left the photographer's. Old Littlewood his name was, and he was absent-minded. The minute he'd snapped the picture he turned around and started working at something else, forgot we even existed, so we ducked into the little back room. Trying not to snicker or giggle, at *our* age. And I remember, I remember I shocked him, Keneally I mean, it only just then hit me, I said, "They told me you'd have a sack of turnips between your legs, but you look normal enough to me."

Anyway he scowled when I said that, about the fields all being squares I mean. I wasn't supposed to think, or wonder. I wasn't even supposed to notice there were other people on the place besides us, I guess. "What do they think?" I said. "What do they feel?"

Of course the reason he didn't like me asking those questions was that they'd never occurred to him before. How would you feel if you suddenly realized that you'd never once wondered what went on inside all the people who surrounded you every day?

"If you want to know a thing like that," he said, "then go ask one of *them.*" As if one was the same as the next. And I could tell by the look on his face that he didn't believe for a minute that I'd do it. "They'll only tell you to mind your own business."

"Well, we'll just see about that," I said.

Well, I told you a crusty old woman didn't turn crusty just all of a sudden. What he saw in me, what he liked about me was *spunk.* We both had it. You don't marry a woman whose spirit has attracted you and then expect her to turn suddenly into a doormat. He knew very well I'd get out there amongst those people and find out what made them tick.

I don't like this, Becker. I don't like it. I'm listening to the sentences that come out of me and they don't sound like me. People have their own way of talking, everybody's different. You know how Julius always lays out his sentences in spaces, evenly. And you, whispering, as if everything you say is a gentle question. But *me*, I just talk like me until I start talking into that machine and start thinking about what I'm saying, and then it doesn't sound like me talking any more. Maybe it's because I can see it, laid out on a page, when you get at it with that typewriter of yours. Then I think, maybe that's the way I talked *then*, maybe people don't talk the same way all their lives any more than they look the same way all their lives.

"You old goat," I told him in the photographer's. "At your age you're expected to wind down a little, nobody would believe you still act like a young stud. You're supposed to be an ageing distinguished gentleman."

You couldn't call him any of those. There was nothing distinguished about that bony red face. Peasant face. It could never look distinguished. And he was too big for it, too, too solid. You can't very well look suave when you've got hands like a couple of bear paws. And there was no ageing to him, not at that time, he wasn't stooped or thickening, or even very wrinkled except at the eyes. From laughing, or squinting. And nobody knew better than I did that he was no gentleman, not when he caught his hair in the flypaper, or found out someone in town had cheated him, or discovered I didn't particularly like his hands all over me while I was in the kitchen, making supper. Lord, when I think of my father, who never lived to that age, but lost interest in my mother and all woman long before he died. When I imagine *him* acting like that!

But he was solid. I knew I had married a man. The legend had become flesh in my hands, and human, but when I looked at him I knew I was looking at a lot more than surface. He went in, deep. It would take me a lifetime, I could see, to sink far enough inside him to understand what he was.

"So if it's what they're thinking you want to know," he said, "then it's them you want to be asking, not me."

"I will," I said.

Well, I don't know if that's what I said, exactly. But I should have. Those are words of . . . commitment. The words of the wedding ceremony. Not just *I expect to*, but *I intend to and want to*.

But not tonight, Becker, not tonight. You'll wear my tongue out. Or my brain. What if I get to the end of this and discover I've been giving it all away, like someone unravelling a sweater, and there's nothing left of it for me? That spider-machine of yours will suck all the juices out of me and leave only a dry shell. I don't know why I'm doing this, I'd rather be sleeping. I'm tired, Becker. Don't you ever get tired? Are you doing all this so you'll have something to think about while you're throwing arm signals at cars coming onto the ferry, or are you doing it just to torture me?

"Thanks for the coffee but no thanks. That Becker has my stomach in knots, I wouldn't dare. Me, a coffee drinker too. I wouldn't dare, it would just come back up again. I only hope the cigarette supply down there doesn't run out, I must've doubled since he started up this thing, no wonder my stomach is sour, you'll be lucky if I don't burn your house down the way I've been puffing away, since he got started. Do you think it's right what he's doing, Maggie, do you think he's got a right to get me started?"

Not that she really cared what Maggie thought of it. What would a person like her know? A woman like Maggie Kyle could try to understand but her background was too different. Lily Hayworth knew a backwoods person when she saw one, they couldn't lose it. Logging-camp people had a mark on them, invisible, of course, but still there to the perceptive intuition. They just couldn't shake it. In the kind of place she came from, in the logging camp or whatever it was, they probably spilled their guts to each other every day, over morning coffee. They didn't wait until they were old, they didn't keep it all to themselves and then let a tape recorder gather it all up together at the end. Maggie Kyle couldn't hope to know what it felt like.

So she didn't look. You couldn't look when a person was standing like that, waiting, as if to say *Okay, then, tell me more of what it feels like*, you couldn't respond to that. She peered, instead, out the window. At the trees; it had rained sometime in the night, a summer shower. There was a certain time in the woods, just after a rain, when every one of the million needles on all the pines and firs was swollen with drops of water, so that if you glanced upwards towards the light of a grey, nearly white sky, the trees seemed transformed somehow, blurred, as if their outlines had grown a covering of fine fine hairs, the way a child's arm held up to the sun would have that blurred halo look.

"It's like looking at the sky through a giant silver cobweb," she said, and sipped at the coffee anyway. It could hardly make her stomach any worse. "There aren't many who would trust a man with a name like Becker. Especially when he's so ... homely. Ugly. But I don't expect anything'll come of it, he'll get it all onto tape and then he'll get tied up in some other hobby and forget all about this, he'll take up stamp collecting or something. I wouldn't be surprised if he lost the tapes, or burned them by mistake, or taped a radio programme over them. He's that type. Hiding in there behind all that hair and ugliness I think he's one of those busy ineffective little people who never get anything done."

"This is all the country you need," he told me, looking out over his bleak treeless colony, "this is all the world that anyone ever needs," and I thought to myself, that's a lot a baloney because you don't think I'm not going to get in to town and meet people or spend weekends in the city to do some shopping or go gallivanting around the world the way you did with the Indian, this is only a place to live, and I want one hell of a lot more than that, I want it all. All those years I was single I wasn't sitting around waiting for a Prince Charming to carry me off to a prison, I was building a career and travelling and getting involved with other people, and there's no reason I should give it all up now just because I've found someone to sleep with at night and put a roof over my head, no matter how many times you introduce me as a goddess to your dirty-nailed people and then laugh afterwards at their stupidity.

Damn it, Becker, I think he really believed it, that the place was all the world anybody ever needed except himself, he thought he'd provided everything on it that anyone could possibly want: a piece of land, a sense of belonging, enough work to keep you too tired to start worrying about anything, and food, even a sort of religion. That was the part I hated first, his speech-making; they used to all crowd into this house for what they liked to call a meeting but which always turned out to be just a chance for him to practise some of his silly magic or give a big speech. My Lord, he could make a speech, he could make the house tremble with the thundering sounds of his voice, he could roll out huge long lines that probably didn't make a bit of sense but sounded beautiful and throw in quotations from here and there, most of which I didn't recognize but some I did: things like "what though the field be lost" and "thou thoughtest that I was altogether such a one as thyself", rolling them out as if he understood them, using all the tricks you can hear politicians using if you listen close enough: commands and strange praise and implied insults and snatches of patriotism and promised hope and bragging and calls to arms and the deepest sincerity, it was all there. And the religion, I thought *how did you manage to knock all religion out of these heads, they're mostly Irish and probably Catholic*, but of course I found out that had happened long before, and besides not all of them were Irish in the colony, more had escaped than anyone in town ever knew about, just left in the middle of the night and disappeared somewhere, and in those twenty years new ones had come in, Italians and Frenchmen and Americans and Danes he'd gathered up on his travels or who had just got sucked in through marriage somehow and never got out. So the religion of the place, what he taught them, preached in his sermons, was not replacing anything else much and only, I discovered, reflected what most of the world believed anyhow, even if they didn't know it: "All the gods we need are in matter," he said, "in earth and wood and stones. All the mind we need is in our bodies, a magnificent brain. All the hope we need is in our hands, the ability to work. All the worship we offer is to ourselves." The Father of Life business was only ironic to begin with, making fun, though the irony had been lost a long time before, whether he knew it or not, and if all they worshipped was themselves they did it through him. They would have laughed at me if I'd said it, and denied it, but what they'd done was turn him into a breathing idol, he could have been a little fat gold statue sitting on the mantel over the fireplace. Maybe he should have been, then at least he'd have been consistent.

And then there were the speeches just for me. About his colony and how it would be held up as a model in the future and how he was trying to get the government to come in and have a look in order to set up others like it on the island. You shouldn't colonize a place by just inviting people onto it and letting them do what they want, he said, that way in fifty years they'll have ruined it all, you'll get people thinking they have the right to sell some of it to the others. You'll get people thinking there's nothing wrong with making profit from selling it. You'll get fighting and exploiting and waste. What the government ought to do, he said, is use his colony as a model to set up others. One of the things he was doing, he said, was training people here who could go out into all parts of the island, even the rest of the country, and be leaders of society, they would be able to use their experience here to help the rest of mankind to keep from ruining the earth. You just watch, he said, before long there'll be places like this everywhere you look. But I haven't seen much evidence of it, maybe you have, Becker, you get around more, there's those farms the hippies have started up back in at the foot of the mountains, but I don't imagine any of them use him for a model, and there was another colony around here not long after this one broke up, but it was a bunch of people waiting for the end of the world. Rich people from everywhere who came because this island was the only part of the world that wasn't going to end, but they got into a lot of trouble too not long after, and when they discovered they were literally slaves to a madman there were rebellions and murders and things. Keneally, though, wanted to go down in history or something, I could see, but you didn't have to be around long to discover he didn't have what it takes. He would like to have had the whole world looking at him in the same way those colonists did.

You should have seen him, Becker, it's a shame nobody ever

took a picture, I would've if there'd been a camera on the place but there wasn't and I never thought to get one. He'd get dressed up like someone out of the last century, a Southern Gentleman or something; he wore high boots polished by the cripple till you'd see the sky in them and a black narrow suit and some kind of silly hat like colonels or something might wear; you'd expect him to look a fool in it, a big peasant like him, but he didn't, he looked as if his body had been made especially to wear that kind of thing, he was straight, of course, and tall. And then there was his horse — sometimes a chestnut mare and sometimes his black stallion — and the dog, Thunderbird — a second one, to replace the first, which had died years before — who went everywhere with him. And his riding crop.

The first time I saw him in that outfit I laughed. Lord, Becker, I had a good laugh, my big sexy hero was a little boy playing dress-up. I thought, *What have I walked in on — a musical comedy*? Any other sixty-year-old man I'd ever known was busy counting his money or slipping candy to his grandchildren but I'd never before met one who was playing at — what? — Superman? Satan? Banana Plantation Owner? Whatever it was, it could have been harmless enough — you have to let people play their games — if the others hadn't believed in it.

You see, that was the only really sinister part, the only scary part — the make-believe. At least that was all that was left by the time I arrived. There was no slavery, people were free to leave any time they wanted, some had gone. And contrary to common belief, there was no religious fanaticism, only his irony and his devotion to material things, to earth. He owned the land and the buildings, the heads of families owned shares in the business, everyone shared in the profits. It was legal, moral, sane, I was disappointed. The only scary part was his play-acting, which would have been harmless enough in itself except that I discovered soon enough that nearly everyone else on the place was play-acting too. It was as if they'd said, okay, we'll let you pretend to be a dictator and a tyrant and even a superhuman legend, we'll even let you go so far as to act like you really believe it and treat us like dirt, if you'll let us pretend, too, to be filthy ugly creatures of the earth who can't see anything higher than our fence-posts. The whole colony was a stage for them, it wasn't the kind of play-acting you see kids up to, where they'll stop all of a sudden and break the spell with something like *Hey, you guys aren't playing fair*, it was more the kind of play-acting you'd get in a war, with grownups pretending they really believe they are on the side of right, and really believe there is some kind of sanity in the masquerade, and really believe there is no other way to handle things; *that* kind of playing. It scared me, worse than if all I'd heard had turned out to be true.

Oh I don't know all this from just watching. Or from listening to him. I got in there and talked with some of them. Mary O'Mahony became my friend, she was a granddaughter of the famous widow Donahue, and her husband Paddy was in charge of the beef stock I think, I can't remember. There's a lot I can't remember, Becker, you'll just have to take what you get. Mary lived up in that . . . , in that house they bulldozed down for the trailer park, it was a decent house, a good family house, they were one of the solidest families in the lot, I'd say, Mary was anyway, solid, a nice woman. She was younger than I was, but had that ageless quality about her the way a lot of them had, as if she was all ages at the same time. A shy girl, which was no surprise, she wouldn't look at me while she talked, only when I talked. Whenever she had something to say she said it to the floor, to her own toe moving around on her kitchen floor. She was only a child when they came over, she didn't remember any other kind of life, only what they told her. But some of it had gone in deep and hooked hard. She could tell me about the mist, for instance, as if it was yesterday, the great mist that changed the history of her people, she could trace the fear back to that. "Oh we was all meant to be timid, I suppose," she said, smiling at her toe. "We was cursed with our limitations."

"My God," I said, "do you know what they've done over there now?"

"Where?" she said. There was no place else for her.

"Back where you come from," I said. "Don't you read any of the papers? They've kicked the English buggers out! The people who stayed will be freer than the people who escaped."

But she saw no more connection between herself and the home of her grandparents than with the town, or the government of Canada. Her family was all that mattered, her Paddy O'Mahony and the little kids and her house, which she kept cleaned and polished like a work of art. She was scared of me, I could tell, because of who I was, married to him and coming from outside, but I could tell too that she liked me, after a while, and trusted me for the time being. She made tea for me when I visited and we sat and gossiped, and after a while she even began to show a little curiosity about the world I'd been in, she liked to hear about New York and Toronto, though they might as well have been fairy-tale places for all the reality she gave them. She had her hair cut, you know, like this, hacked off straight all around, but still she was pretty, she could have been pretty. Yet even sitting in that spotless kitchen with the gleaming floors and the clean white walls she looked as if she'd be uncomfortable as long as she was kept out of the earth, for whatever reason. As if her feet ought to be buried to the ankles in mud.

One day I was sitting at her kitchen table, you know like this, where I could see out the window, and we were talking about something, oh I don't know what it was, probably her pregnancy, I think she was pregnant again then, and I saw Paddy coming in down the lane, walking in from where he'd been out in the barn. A big man, I guess he was nearly as tall as Keneally, but stockier than Keneally was now that he was getting older, he came walking down towards the house wiping his mouth on his sleeve, you know how men do sometimes when they're just come up from taking a drink from a water tap, and then just as he was nearly at the step Keneally came galloping down the lane on his horse, the mare, I think, with that stupid big black dog panting along behind, Keneally hollering "O'Mahony, hold it there a minute" and pulling right up beside him at the front step where you wouldn't expect anyone to ride a horse. Poor Mary's face went red, she looked horrified, I expected her to offer to hide me some place, the way she looked at me, the way her hand kept playing with her lip, annoying the lip. Then Keneally was yelling at O'Mahony about something, giving him hell about something he'd just discovered in the barns and calling him this that and the other, I don't remember what, and O'Mahony I could see out there nearly as red in the face as Mary and not knowing which way to look. Then he looked by accident towards the window, his eyes caught mine in there, for just a second, and then all of a sudden he straightens up and tells the old bastard to go to hell. Keneally's hand came down *thwack* just like that with the riding crop and slashed the man across the side of his head, then he pulled the horse around and galloped off out of there as if there was nothing more need be said on the matter, and Paddy O'Mahony was left standing there in his own front yard holding his ear and knowing I was watching him through the window.

Then he just all of a sudden came in stomping, furious, and yelled at me to get out of his house. Mary was up, scared, trying to stop him, saying "Watch yourself, Paddy, think what you're saying, man," and grabbing a cloth to hold on his bleeding ear but he wouldn't take his eyes off me, just yelled "Get out of here! Get out of my house!" and Lord I was scared to go out—because the only door in the place was right beside him, I'd have to go past him to get out. Then he said "That man is . . . one of these days that man is going to go too far." And Mary said "Be careful, be careful" and he said "Go back where you belong, Mrs. Keneally, go back to your own house and please don't come here any more. And tell him something, tell him something for me, tell him this, that he can be lord and master around here all he likes, but he will never strike me again. And, Mrs. Keneally, tell him that . . . that if he ever touches Mary again, I'll kill him."

"*What?*" I said. "What are you talking about?" and Mary said "Nothing at all, he's only blathering, go home, please go home" but Paddy was getting himself worked up even more and would have hit me, I think, if there'd been a club handy or a stick. "Just tell him that. Tell him if he ever touches Mary again, if he ever comes around here bothering her again, I will kill him."

"I don't believe you," I said, but I could see there what he had done to them all, I could see it in Mary's face, the way he had let their timidity and fear fill them right up, and then he had convinced them somehow of their worthlessness so that all he had to do was treat them like that, remind them of it, and it went in deep, hooked hard just like the mist had done and they *believed* it, they believed what he saw in them, they believed what he reflected back to them, it never entered their heads to think of themselves in any other way. Except maybe Paddy, in his thick-skulled way.

But it was contagious after all. The disease the others had caught during the time of the mist or whatever the hell it was and which he had avoided all those years himself has finally turned on him. Because when I got back to the house he was there ahead of me, throwing up onto my kitchen floor, bent over and puking out his insides like he didn't have the energy or will power to move just the few feet to the sink or over to the outside door. "What's the matter with you? What's going on?" I said, and when he looked up I saw it was an old man there, an old trembling man. And I saw it in his eyes, sitting in there, the same way I had seen it in the eyes of the others. It was an old man who looked up at me, and full of fear. I had to put him to bed, I couldn't stop the trembling, no matter how many blankets I piled on or hot bricks I slipped under the sheets, or no matter what I said.

"Where were you?" he said, and I could have lied, it would be easy to lie, there were, oh, I don't know how many houses to choose from, or I could have said down on the beach. But I said "I was at Mary O'Mahony's" and left him, in the bedroom, to sweat out the rest of that day and the night alone.

But you see, Becker, you see what you've done, I can hardly breathe, my Lord you shouldn't let me get worked up like that. Turn it off now, I want to, I want to sleep. If I can, you bastard, if you haven't got me too worked up. Do you think that machine of yours will pick up the sound of my heart? Thumping hard, when you think of how long it pumps away in there without a rest.

Okay, you, Becker, look at me now, look at what you've done to me now, worn me so I don't even want to get out of this bed. Ever. A couple weeks back I was thinking of going outside onto the verandah for a little bit of sunshine, and now here I am in bed and no desire to get out of it. I could just settle back and sink right into this soft mattress, it feels so good I don't even want to move this old sack of bones around, it's too much of an effort. So don't expect much out of me today, I don't feel like talking, maybe it's just a bad day, maybe I'm just tired. Maybe I'm getting old! It's depressing, Becker, it's depressing the way most people you look at just go through their lives being themselves without asking any questions about it, they seem to be doing that and look happy enough just to let things be, but me, I lie here and start thinking about myself from the outside and the inside at the same time and I can't stand it, it makes me want to get out of here and be someone else. I don't know what I'm trying to say to you, Becker, I feel so rotten today, I just keep thinking of that tape gathering me up, winding me onto those little spools, and as soon as I think *What kind of person do I want that tape to hear*? then I don't know who I am, and it's so depressing I just want to sink back here and shut up.

And there's no sense telling me just be natural because by the time a person's got to my age there's a pretty good chance there's no such thing as natural, or it's buried too deep to come out. Maybe that's what life is, forgetting what's natural, or maybe that's what life *isn't*. Maybe our natural life goes on without us while we slap on layer after layer of what we think is life but is only pretence. Maybe you better just forget about me today the mood I'm in, you wouldn't want to trust anything I'd say on a day like this.

If you thought, every time you said a word if you thought about everything that happened in your brain and in your nerves and in your throat and in your tongue and in the air to make that word, you'd never be able to spit it out, you'd be a mute. That's what I mean.

Go ask Julius to tell his secrets. That'd be something. He wouldn't share the air if he had his way, let alone share himself. Ask Maggie. Or that Anna Sterner, even at her age she must have a past. And maybe she's old enough to have got a good look at herself and realize she doesn't know who she is. I'd like to know what Julius would say, though, that'd be something to hear. He'd refuse, of course, with a big sniff, but what if he didn't. Would he sound like a different person every day like me? Would he start to wonder who he was?

Lord, Becker, the trouble is I like it. It tickles me the way that little thing is gathering me up. And I get a kick out of knowing I can tell you any kind of lie and you'd believe it. I could tell you anything and it would sound like truth to you, you'd have to take my word for it. The best part is I probably won't be around long enough to contradict myself, or give the lie away, you'll just *have* to believe me. But I won't lie, I'd lie if it was just us talking here, you and me, but with that machine gathering it up I don't think I could lie. It already unsettles me just enough to think that after I'm gone that tape is capable of telling this stuff over and over again without me here to explain it or correct it, so I'd never be able to stand it, thinking this was an out-and-out lie recorded on it forever.

I used to think I could see right into other people, and know what they were thinking, I used to be able to see past a person's actions and know what really went on behind. I was usually right, too, it nearly always turned out I was right. It was scary. But I don't think it ever occurred to me to do the same to myself.

It bothered him—Keneally—that I could do that. He hated it. I don't know if he'd have preferred that I go on believing in the legend, I guess not or he'd never have married me, but he wanted to be the one to control how much I saw, how deep I saw into him. He hated it if he thought I saw further than he intended.

And I did. That day, that day that I told you about, when I told him I was there and had seen, he yelled at me. "Get out of here, woman," or something like that. He knew what I was thinking.

Oh, I didn't want to take over, I didn't want to take his place, not even when I saw what he'd become. I don't know who disgusted me more, him for being human after all, or the rest of them for letting him pretend he wasn't. For letting him get away with it. You can put any man in prison if he believes that's where he belongs. If he believes the filthy dirt floor is what he deserves, and the walls are there to protect him. I didn't want to take over, I didn't mean to take over, I would rather have chased them all off, told them to go face up to the world by themselves, I would rather have seen the whole thing disband. But things don't happen just all of a sudden, it's not as if you make a decision about these things and then they happen, things take place over a number of years and it isn't until you look back afterwards that you can even see what direction you were moving in.

My first concern was him. Let those others wallow in their dirt, they were used to it, they'd forgotten anything else, time and Keneally's brain-washing had convinced them of their limitations and I wasn't going to change that overnight. No, my first concern was him. Villain, god, demon, magician, con-man, call him what you want he was my husband and I could see what was happening to him, besides being human after all and getting old he was catching whatever disease he had set loose on the others, it was coming back on him now and he probably didn't even recognize it. I saw it sitting in there in his eyes the same way I had seen it sitting in the eyes of the others, and my only thought at first was to keep them from finding out or even suspecting. So I began to fill in, I let him show me how to go about running a huge ranch like that (though he never guessed then that that was what he was doing, teaching me) and learning how to get the most work out of everyone, what each person's weaknesses were, how each person's fears could be put to advantage. He didn't know that was what was happening, or at least he never let on that he knew, and I learned all I could as fast as possible so that the day could come soon enough when he would get up and look in the mirror and go back to bed, hiding under the covers, and I could go out and do what had to be done without anyone suspecting something was wrong.

Because even then while it was happening there were times when he was strong, when you could still believe that some of the old legends might have been true, when he'd maybe forgotten what he'd discovered — that he was getting old, too, like everybody else — and that he still believed in what he had done. Days when he would put on those immaculate clothes made somewhere in the Deep South or someplace for their colonels or plantation owners or something, but certainly not seen on anybody else around here, put on those clothes and the perfect polished black boots and go out amongst them like a dignitary, to visit the barns, to ride on his chestnut mare out into the fields, to stop in at the houses. Always, always the gentleman, even while condemning a man's work or ordering something to be done over again completely. Magic solutions to household problems. You'd think he had all the wisdom of mankind's history stored in his brain the way he straightened out the messes people could make of their feed-storage problems or butchering plans or vegetable gardens. You could easily have believed that he was simply the owner of a gigantic ranch and that all of those people were his hired hands. The cold edge of his voice was hardly ever necessary any more. He got his way without question. And then the days when he would invite them all to this house, all of them, they filled all the rooms, bulged the walls, so he could be the perfect host, the generous benefactor, and besides that an entertainer who could still work a few simple tricks to make their eyes pop out of their heads, he was always coming up with a new one, something weird and scary and full of meanings. He could rise to the heavens, on days like that, there wasn't anything he couldn't do.

And then in the mornings I would see it, sometimes, sitting in there in his eyes. But I didn't, it was never my intention to try to take his place. If I'd thought of it I would have known it was impossible, I just started moving in that direction without thinking because I could see what was happening to him, what was likely to happen. He'd fallen victim to his own vision, his own disease, as I imagine all those despairing artists do eventually. Like running up against a blank wall you've built yourself. I just didn't want everything to fall apart.

"Cheer up, Anna, the way I feel right now you won't have to look at this old face much longer, you won't have to come trudging up those stairs to wait on me. The way I feel you'll only have to pretend I never existed. It should be easy. As far as I'm concerned it's only a game he's playing, with his plastic toy, while everybody waits for me to kick the bucket. It's a way of passing the time. The summer must be nearly over by now, how long has this been going on?"

She knew why Maggie sent the girl up with the meals now. It was because she couldn't stand to see an old woman going downhill. She'd rather let that Anna Sterner do it. It saved legwork, too, if you were feeling lazy. Let the girl do it, the hippie.

Lily Hayworth had never needed to do much thinking to form her opinion of Anna Sterner. What there was of her. Shallow. A selfish sourpuss. It was what you expected to find, though, in this collection of losers. Dressed in what could have been her great-grandmother's skirts, what she could have had on when she stepped off the boat. The new pioneers. The only difference was when the real pioneers discovered they didn't like it or couldn't take the work they didn't have Maggie Kyle to go running to, to mother them. Lily Hayworth had no time for quitters, and that was a quitter if she ever saw one.

"She knows I hate her clam chowder, I can't stand it, with all those green stomachs, and the little white necks. Why does she make it? Doesn't she know that people don't eat hot soup in the summer, not even old women? Take it away, please, I'd rather have nothing at all, I just couldn't stand to think of those things floating around in my stomach, I'd gag. And tell her I'm sorry she broke both her legs, she'll know what I mean."

Of course, you couldn't expect her to pay much attention to an old woman when there was that cousin in the house half the time. Powers or whatever his name was. You'd think he was a movie star, all the attention he got, whenever he was here. She'd seen him; with that kind of competition an old woman didn't stand much of a chance.

The summer had gone by, or nearly. There was something in the air, something changing, she could tell even in here, in this stuffy overheated room. There was this consolation: they hadn't moved her downstairs yet, they hadn't got her set up in the living room or the downstairs bedroom where it would be more convenient for everyone in her final days. At least she couldn't be *that* close. Either that or they just hoped she'd disappear if they kept her out of sight like this, that she would just fade away and be forgotten.

"Tell her I'll use this old umbrella here. Tell her I'll bang on the floor with it when I need her in a hurry. I don't think I could make myself heard any more, all that distance, by yelling. Those stairs seem to get farther and farther away. Tell her I'll just bang on the floor with this umbrella."

"I don't want to talk to you today Becker . . . Take that thing out of here . . . No, don't touch me, I'm all right, I just . . . don't want to talk . . . Not to you . . . Please."

"What are you doing? What are they doing to me? . . . Look, I'm not . . . "

"Maggie. I couldn't . . . I didn't think . . . I would come out of that . . . Maggie . . . What would any of us . . . what would any of us do without . . . ? Child . . . Maggie . . . is Becker? Don't let . . . goddam . . . box . . . Maggie, the centre is . . . Maggie. Hold . . . hold . . . hold."

"Lord, your box must have thought it would have to starve. From now on. Nothing more to pull out. All the rest just, gone. You must have thought you'd be . . . looking for another hobby. The old hobby nearly . . . died. How long has it been? Since I talked. Must be weeks. Months. But I have no intention . . . of dying, Becker, not yet, I want to tell you just one more thing, that's all. But I have no intention of dying after it. Just stopping the talking. I'm sick of it. Just let me . . . catch . . . my wind here a minute."

Now, what did I want to tell? I can't remember anything. In this state of mind you'll be lucky if I don't start rambling on about Hayworth, they couldn't be more different, those two, but still they were both husbands. And betrayed me, one way or the other. An old person's mind sometimes gets onto a single track and can't get off it the rest of the day. Then the next day he wakes up on another track altogether. You'll have to help me, Becker, jar something loose. Maybe I should bang my head against the wall, shake things up in there. The way you bring air bubbles to the surface of cakes. Do they bring gold to the surface that way, tapping at a pan? Not that I have any gold to offer. Turn it off. Let me think.

Easter Sunday. It was Easter Sunday. They never made anything special of those days on the colony, even Christmas, one day was the same as the next to them, but I cooked up a something, probably a turkey and we had a few in for supper, Jems I think and the old people, the widows, I can't remember names, I can't even remember their faces, though I can still picture those old hunched-over forms around the table, some of them wearing black shawls they'd brought with them on the boat, old hags, you expected them to cackle or pull out a poison apple. I remember thinking what kind of company am I expected to entertain here, anyway, even on Easter Sunday? I thought of the kind of people my mother used to have in for dinner, those "finer people", thank God she wasn't still alive to know what I'd inherited. But it didn't seem to bother him at all, he sat at the other end of the table, behind the big brown hump of turkey, as if cripples and hags were his family. You could almost have believed that this was the way he liked it to be, this was the way he wanted it.

He was an old man. The big red peasant face and the huge hands looked all wrong, suddenly, on that thin trembling body. There were thick tufts of hair greying in his ears, and hairs growing on his nose he sometimes forgot to clip. He wasn't what he had been but he pretended, and it must have been easy for him with those old ones, the half-blind crones and that Jems. They wouldn't be able to see what was happening. I thought, if he pushes back his chair at the end of this meal and offers a bit of his magic, I'll scream. Their silly brainless talk would be enough to make him think of it, I half expected there'd be another God-machine constructed and demolished before my eyes, he was looking so confident. They could fool him into thinking that nothing had changed.

But I stopped that. I said, "Mary O'Mahony's baby is expected to die, there's something wrong with it, I think the heart." It was enough to remind him, to keep him from going off half-cocked and thinking he was God Almighty again, with his silly tricks and his speeches. He just said "Oh" and looked down and then tried to force some more turkey onto one of the old hags who was already nearly choking herself on what she had. She took it, I'll bet, and stuffed it in, even if she thought she would die from it; to her, Donal Keneally would always be the man he'd once been. The dog, that damn Thunderbird laid out on the floor by his chair, was enough to keep it that way.

And Jems. I could nearly have felt sorry for him if it hadn't been for the slobbering, if he was only a cripple. His devotion was, I suppose, admirable, I had heard what he did for Keneally. Before. Running the place for him while he globe trotted with that squaw. And even before that, with his story, to the police. About seeing the murder and being too scared to report it? I never believed it, I don't suppose anyone but a confused jury of old men ever really believed what he said about seeing some blackfaced stranger killing those two in the bush. But it showed something. Loyalty. He was old, too, as old as Keneally, and he had started out life ravaged. So you can imagine what he looked like by then. But I hated the slobbering, even my pity couldn't make me blind to that. They were a mess, the lot of them, I wondered what I was doing there, would I turn out like them.

I don't need to answer that, you can see it. Though I haven't succumbed to the shawl. I'll never wear black, I've always hated it. But the effect is the same.

So I said "Mary O'Mahony's baby is expected to die" just to stop any notions and to keep him down with his feet on the ground. I could swear it was gratitude I saw in his eyes, I don't think I'd ever seen it before, not from him, I'll bet he never said "Thank you" once to me in his life, not for all the things he ought to be grateful for, but here he was, when I cut him like that, looking thankful. Mary's baby was already dead, I knew that, someone came across to tell me that in the afternoon, it was only a few days old, I don't know why I didn't say it, there was more pleasure in it the other way ... I remember we were in the kitchen, afterwards, while he helped with the dishes. He was never afraid to help with a thing like that, he seemed to like it, maybe because it was a time we could talk. We talked better, freer, when we worked side-by-side like that than if we sat, facing each other, I was never very good at meeting people's eyes, even his, and there was some freedom in talking with your hands in the dishwater. We hadn't had the girls come in for that kind of thing in years, I couldn't stand them in the house, I always like to do my own work, look after my own business. So it was afterwards, in the kitchen, when the old hags and Jems had gone back to their shacks, it was dark, when I heard the first knock on the door.

It was Paddy O'Mahony, he didn't even wait until I got to the door, he just threw it open with a bang and stepped in. We never locked any of the doors. It was one of the things that was done on the colony, doors were left unlocked. He just flung himself in and stopped, like he'd known up until then what he was coming there for, but had suddenly forgotten. It must have been raining, I can remember his boots tracked mud in and a puddle spread out at his feet while he stood there looking at Keneally, and then at me, and then at Keneally. I thought maybe he wants one of us to go off for a doctor but of course that was silly because it was too late, he'd known about it for six or seven hours by then. It was something else he had on his mind.

But he couldn't spit it out, not right away. Keneally had always done all the talking, these people only listened. He had to sit down. Maybe he couldn't believe the sight of Keneally with a dish towel in his hand.

"What's the matter Paddy?" I said, I didn't see any reason why he shouldn't feel friendly enough to me despite the session we had, that day at his house. I had never gone back, I never did anything to make him mad, and I'd sent things across to Mary when the baby got close.

But he wouldn't look at me, he was looking at Keneally. "We want you to quit." Just like that. "We want you to quit."

And Keneally said, "Quit what?"

"Everything," Paddy said. "Quit everything and get out of here altogether. We want you to leave us alone. Isn't it long enough we've been lorded over like we was children? And can't we think for ourselves a bit now? We just want you to leave it all, go away."

If this had happened before, if it had happened even a year earlier, he would have exploded, there'd have been bloodshed immediately. No one had ever talked like that to him. No one. But he didn't explode, he didn't get mad yet, he laughed.

"The devil break your leg, you imbecile! Don't I own every inch of this place? Don't I own the houses you live in? And how is it now you are asking me to quit. How can I quit?"

Paddy was twisting his hands around, and biting his lip. There were two high spots of red up here on his cheek. Oh, you could be Keneally's son, I thought, the two of you are a pair. He said, "You could let us buy you out somehow. There's not a man left on the place but Jems that's willing to take another order from you. There's not a woman, either, that wouldn't turn her backside to you."

"Do you tell me so!" Keneally was rising, I could see the famous anger now, coming back. "You will leave my house, Paddy O'Mahony. You will leave my house. There will be a meeting."

Paddy jumped to his feet, oh I remember the sudden uncoiling of him. "There'll be no meetings. There'll be no meetings. Any meetings from now on will be without you."

"What's going on Paddy?" I said. "What are those people doing?"

"All of them are out there!" he shouted. "Every man of them!" He threw open the door and I could see them, some of them in the light that fell onto the ground from the kitchen window, but I couldn't see the others, not clearly, they were only vague figures out in the dark. And silent, as only those people could be silent. "And not a one of them will leave," he said, "until we have your promise, until we see the arse-end of you going off."

I wanted to say *not this way, Paddy, can't you see he's an old man now, that you could do it another way, quieter, and he wouldn't even notice.* I wanted to say *don't push, don't push him, he'll only have to fight back, but if you're smart you'll just ease him.* But I couldn't say it of course and there was Keneally with all his seventy years of being the grand hero having to listen to this kind of threat, so what can you expect. "Get out of my house!" he yells at Paddy and "Go on home where you belong!" he yells at the people out there, the silent bodies, and Paddy says "Not until", and stands like that in the doorway.

Then Keneally said "Sic him."

The dog had lain panting in the corner, watching it all, looking from one to the other, growling a little in his throat when Paddy got loud, just lying there. But when Keneally gave the command he just leapt, I swear he didn't even get to his feet, he just leapt straight from his place on the floor up in the air at Paddy's throat. Like a great, black, jet-propelled bird.

I'd heard it before, about the fight with the bailiff, about the fight with his dogs, about Keneally's hands, but I never believed it, I thought it was just part of the whole big lie. But he did it, Paddy did it, I saw his hand go down, disappear down inside that dog's mouth, down his throat, maybe, and grab something, the growling turning to choking to slobbering coughs and the black body was flung sideways against the wall and again against the stove and again down *crack* against the floor, I don't know if he broke his neck or strangled him or what but there wasn't a movement out of that dog ever again. It must have been old by then, it must have been — hell, too old for a dog — but there was still some strength in him, and I can't say I was ever sorry to see him die. I hated him. Except for what it meant to Keneally.

He could have stopped there, if he had been able to see what I could see in Keneally's eyes, he could have stopped there and he'd have won. We would have been gone by morning and the history of this place would have been a different history altogether, and you, Becker, would be living somewhere else. Still back in Ottawa, maybe, at that university. Or writing your book or whatever it is, about some other place. But he didn't stop, he wasn't smart enough to see that he had won, or wasn't content with only winning, maybe he wanted to relish it, too. Because within seconds he had Keneally too, was pushing was pushing him down out of the house and down the steps, that big bleeding hand clamped on the back of his neck, the other onto his shirt, pushing him down and then down in front of all those silent people, right down onto his knees, onto his face in the mud and pushed mud pushed gravel and mud into his face, into his mouth made him eat it made him ...

So I, so I changed their history, just like that, without even thinking about it, I shot his 30.30 off into the air, and then aimed it at Paddy and said "Go home, Paddy O'Mahony, go home to Mary where you belong and we'll talk, in the morning we'll talk."

I don't want to remember any more, Becker. I want you to turn that thing off, I want to stop. Because the next picture I see is the most terrible, I think, of my life. I don't want to remember it, I don't want to remember that face, when the others had all gone off into the dark without speaking, without even breathing you would think, and even Paddy O'Mahony had gone off, content perhaps that he had won something after all and maybe a little overwhelmed at the results, I don't want to remember that head still bent to the earth, then coming up, tipping up in the rectangular patch of light, turning up to me, I don't want to remember it.

"September? Only September? I would have believed it was Christmas I'm so cold. You could have told me it was December."

They could tell her anything they wanted, now, and she would have to believe it. The world had shrunk down to the size of her room. Nothing else mattered, nothing else existed except as bits of gossip they brought in like wildflowers or sea shells to offer her. Not that they brought much of anything, only the weather or sometimes the headline nonsense of famous people. Lily Hayworth would never accuse them of breaking their necks to keep her in touch with the world. If she'd been a caged canary they'd have told her more.

She recalled a movie she had seen once, years ago, where an invalid wife relied on her husband to keep her informed about the world, but he told her only lies, he was being unfaithful with a neighbour's wife and got used to telling her things that weren't true, and so went right on making up things about the neighbourhood and the city and the world. When he was killed, suddenly, and she was taken away by a relative to live somewhere else she discovered that she didn't know a thing about the real world and so withdrew into what the others called madness in order to avoid confronting the contradictions. Of course it had been only a picture and a badly acted one, but she'd often thought afterwards *how do I know that what I see is true?* and *what if people started telling me lies, would I be smart enough to see through them?* It was the kind of thought that she always shook off, immediately, with contempt, because of course she *did* know and because she had always had her head screwed on straight. You couldn't go around wondering things like that.

And now, when it could happen to her if they wanted it to, it didn't matter. There was little chance now that she'd ever be able to catch them out on any lies. And nothing they could tell her about the world could possibly make any difference to her, here in this bed.

Naturally she hated being in bed. Naturally she could tear up the sheets in her frustration, it was so terrible to be under blankets all the time. But she didn't have the strength to tear anything up, and she knew that if she'd had them move her downstairs when she could *see*, she'd have lost interest by the time she got there. Or be plagued by all the noise they would make. Voices and housework and dishes clattering, and feet.

"You see," Julius told her, "we have got you, now, where we want you. The holy terror has been run to earth."

He meant it as a joke, his kind of joke, but she'd never been able to see any humour in anything Julius Champney said, the way he laid out his sentences like measured pronouncements. She said "Haw haw" and pulled at the covers. "It wasn't Holy Terror they called me," she said. That may just be the only thing she hadn't been called, the only insult in those final years.

"No," he said, "but Iron Bitch, in the circumstances, seemed a little inappropriate."

"And rude," she said. "They never said it to my face. That had to be left for you." He stood, damn him, so that his head was between her and the ceiling light. He had no face. And she couldn't even pretend he had, she couldn't look that way, it hurt. He would think she was afraid to encounter him. Unless, of course, he was standing that way deliberately.

Nor was there anything funny in his "run to earth", not that she'd give him credit for using it deliberately. Perhaps, from where he was standing, he could see the mound. He hadn't, like her, had to watch it grow.

Then, suddenly, he sat on the chair beside her and had a face after all. Old, almost as old as hers, with those yellowed eyes. Sad sad Julius. At least she'd had the spunk to say bugger it! He only pulled in and grew sadder.

"They tell me you've been saying confession."

"What?" Her fingers stiffened around their peaks of blankets.

"To Becker."

The hands relaxed again, smoothed out the humps. "Oh that. Listen, you know me. It'll be a foggy Friday before I'll go out apologizing to God for my life. Or to anyone else. I've lived it, let it speak for itself."

He smiled. There was pleasure in this for him. "But still, I've read, there's this compulsion to . . . if not confess, at least divulge. Or acknowledge."

"Or plead guilty? Baloney. Listen, it's not even *my* life he's interested in. I'm telling him about . . . about Keneally. He's doing some kind of . . . research."

"Then he must have been lying. When he said you made him promise not to let the rest of us hear, or even talk to us about it, while you're . . . alive. If it isn't about you."

She couldn't follow it any further. It made her head hurt. Julius Champney was always doing that, giving her puzzles that couldn't be fathomed.

"Some people," she said, "just get to this stage and then stay there. I could last another ten years."

"Or more."

"But I don't want to. Oh, Champney, I don't want to kick the bucket, ever, but I've always been one to be eager to get on to the next stage. I hate standing still. Even if it means being scared, I want to be moving."

"Like Maggie, with her determination." One grey eyebrow lifted, he might have been making fun.

"If life was meant to be only breathing we'd stay in our cradles for eighty years and never move."

"Poor Maggie is the kind that would go chasing after shrines, or pilgrimages."

His riddles again. You couldn't have a conversation with Julius Champney. He wanted to make you suspect you were missing something.

"Not that it would help," he said. "I've tracked them all down."

If she could only force spunk back into these bones. "If I could get out of here, Champney, we could trade places. It's you who should be fading out, like this, not me. You started it sooner and I, I could go on. At least I had some fun while it lasted."

But she had nothing she could offer Julius that he wouldn't just use to feed his pain. She shut up. No one could ever say that Lily Hayworth, for all her talk, didn't know when to bite her tongue.

There were some people, she knew, that talking to only made

274 / THE INVENTION OF THE WORLD

worse. No matter what you said, they twisted it around to suit their own prejudices. She'd known enough of them, they'd let you say something and then they'd wink, as if they knew what you really meant behind it. Or they added it to their already long list of grievances against the world. It was because, she thought, they couldn't afford to admit that people smarter than themselves believed something different. If they did, they might have to change. That's what Julius was like.

Lily Hayworth, naturally, was careful not to do the same kind of thing. Even now. She wasn't afraid to listen to other people's ideas, she was smart enough and quick enough to understand exactly what they meant unless they talked in riddles, like some people, and she never tried to twist it around to suit herself. She could afford to let the world have some variety. What she wouldn't tolerate was the way some people refused to hear what was being said.

"Go away," she told him. "Go away. It isn't time yet to start a vigil."

Now Julius wouldn't come in at all. She could hear him, sometimes, in the hallway outside her door. He would come up the stairs, not easy for him, and then only stand there in his slippers. The floorboards creaked. Then he would sniff, as only he could, and descend. She was being punished, she knew; he would come in only when he was asked. She'd known dogs that had perfected the technique.

"So where is Becker? Now that he's got out of me all that I'll give, does he think he's left only a husk here, that can be ignored?"

Strangely, it hadn't done what she'd expected. Though the tape had pulled it out of her and gathered it up, she hadn't been left without. She'd been left with it all. It was as if, after all of those years of passing through time, forgetting the past as quickly as it became the past and ignoring the future, she'd been handed the whole thing like a full box. Your own life, stored in a pulpy brain, its own souvenir.

"Tell him I'm not dead, that I've levelled off. Tell him it isn't catching."

Sometimes she could swear there was the sound under her of digging. A steel bar clanged against stones, a shovel scraped up the dirt. She could even, in the night, hear the squeal of the unoiled wheelbarrow running up the planks, dumping. If she looked, if she had the strength to sit up and look, would the mound outside have grown?

She had been able to measure his descent, once, by the changing colours of the dirt on that growing mound. He had gone down through black topsoil, then brown pale sand, and blue clay, and washed gravel, and yellow clay, and grey stone, and black slivers of rock, down and down and down. Corkscrewing himself into the earth.

Maybe he was still at it.

"Becker you so-and-so! Sit down. No, you won't get another word out of me, not for the machine. That's as close as you're ever going to get to Keneally, sometimes I think it was closer than I ever got while he was alive, certainly it was closer than we are usually permitted to get to other people in this life. And your machine, that little black box, does it keep you entertained over there in your cabin at nights? Listening to this old voice like a dull saw, trying to hear things I didn't say. Don't you ever talk about yourself, Becker, don't you ever give anything of yourself away? Or are you only like your little black box, pulling in all the world and giving it back nothing more than itself?"

If she could have kept it from the others, she would have liked to have a light on in the night. Just a faint one, one of those little Christmas-tree lights with plastic covers they put in the rooms of frightened children. Not bright enough to keep her awake, or cast ugly shadows. But enough, perhaps, to hold back the sounds that stirred in the dark. But she couldn't ask, she couldn't have them knowing. Not even Maggie could resist telling the others and maybe having a laugh.

Now you've done it, she thought, now you're cracking up. Hearing crowbars and shovels, and wheelbarrows. Falling apart. Lily Hayworth was never a person to fall apart under any circumstances. They'd dished up plenty to test her, but she hadn't fallen apart for any of them. It was what Mama had called "character" and Papa called "backbone".

Timid old ladies could get away with it, it was even expected. Their second childhood, they saw goblins and bogey men in the dark, they were expected to be afraid. But the Iron Bitch had prepared no one for the possibility, not even herself. There would be no crybaby lights, not if she heard trains thundering through her room. Not if Keneally came upstairs from his digging and sat at the foot of her bed to watch her trying to sleep. Daring her, like Rumpelstiltskin, to say his name.

With his red eyes, and dirt-smeared face. Those big calloused hands had ceased trembling, now they had purpose again, and direction.

"What is it you're doing?" she said. "What are your reasons?"

He looked at her through the steam from the top of his tea cup, his face indistinct in the moving air. He liked tea, gallons of it, and never switched to coffee despite her addiction. There was always the coffee pot on the stove, but he waited for the tea, which had to be steeped just right. Down there in that kitchen, where Maggie would have the plates laid out now, in the evening, for breakfast. Down the wooden table.

"I can think of better ways to use up energy," she said. "And other people will be willing to dig your grave when the time comes."

It took her nearly an hour to get to the table. It was important not to waken the others. Maggie and, somewhere, that Anna Sterner. Julius was out there, in his cabin, sleeping. And Becker, dreaming of black machines and enough recording tape to wrap up the whole world and suck it in. The bones, the old bones, had no intention of going with her, and had to be dragged, protesting, through the dark. And breathing, during the descent, had to be pampered. Crossing the living-room rugs, in the faint light of dying fireplace embers, she could have sworn the place never used to get this cold. Then. Maybe it was the trees that had grown up around, they kept the place damp. Maybe the wind from the strait had wedged entrance-slits open after all these years of trying.

It was nearly the only piece of furniture that remained. Maggie had found it, somewhere, and resurrected it with sandpaper and coats of varnish. This was her only bow to the pioneers, she said, surrounded as she was by her white enamel and blue tile.

You could find as much of a marriage in the wood-grain of a kitchen table as in the sagging springs of a double bed. The ghosts were different but no less potent. You could see hands, moving, and read the mood-messages tapped out by silverware against china, and meet eyes that otherwise would avoid. Lily Hayworth in the dark didn't need to see, she could feel the worn-rounded edges and pass her hand over the surface of the top, she could sense the ridges of grain left between the ribbon-depressions which had been worn down by years and a million washings.

"Here I am, Keneally, you didn't know I could get so old."

But the sounds of digging beneath the house had stopped some time during her descent.

"Neither did I, Keneally. It wasn't something I ever considered."

People didn't put kitchen tables out in the middle of the room like this any more, they tucked them into a corner somewhere, or built them into the cabinets. With stools. But here, Maggie had put it exactly, in the exact spot. Sitting here, Lily thought, I could always see past you into the living room, the fireplace, if I didn't want to look at you. Or out over the strait. But you had to see me, or the blank wall.

She never tried to improve his table manners. A man in his sixties is too old to be told that you don't hang over a table like that, with your arms laid out like wings and your face down, with only the wrists moving. Mama would die. In those last years she didn't even remind him that it was customary, before sitting down for a meal, to wash the streaks of dirt off your face, and the black crescents out from under your nails.

He sat back. There were pine needles, she saw, in his hair. The conical mound, growing higher, had spread out, too, at its base, and one corner climbed the trunk of a young white pine, a survivor. Daily she could watch the soil move up the silver pitch-blistered trunk, watch the limbs disappear. Eventually it would be buried beneath this new mountain in her back yard, upright and suffocating, dying. While a five-needle cluster from its branches continued to ride in the thinning hair of its murderer, down into the deepening tunnels. She'd had hopes for that tree, it could destroy some of the bleakness of this ravaged place.

"Are you really afraid as all that?" she said. "Is it a place to hide?"

But he sat even farther back, the legs of his chair squealing on the floor, and wiped one long wrist against his mouth. His eyes were red-rimmed. Specks of dirt sat along the lower lids. He looked at the blank wall behind her, somewhere above her right shoulder.

"Do you know what you are doing it for?"

"Yes."

"It can't be to hide anything, it's not as if we've got so much money that we need to hide it from them."

He shifted his gaze to her, angry, and pushed up out of the chair. His clothes hung loosely on him, shapeless, as if there might have been only a skeleton inside. That great dirty head, those hands, and a skeleton. "Today I'll be working until after dark. Don't wait up."

"Does it matter? Down there does it make any difference if it's night or day to the rest of us?"

She sat at that table the rest of the days and watched him. The ashtray in front of her filled up and overflowed and had to be emptied into the stove and then filled up again. She drank coffee until it soured her stomach, then she sipped at it, even after it was cold. He worked well into the dark, and she turned no lights on for him.

From here she could hear his chopping with a pickaxe at the earth down under the house, and the scrape, scrape as he shovelled up the loosened dirt into the wheelbarrow. Then there was the squealing and rattling he made coming up the slope of the tunnel he'd built, up under the floorboards of the library. Then she could see him, eventually little more than a silhouette, or a shadow, stooped over the handles as he pushed across the boards he'd laid out on the living-room floor and out the door, across the yard, and up the planks he'd put on the slope of his mountain, up as far as he was strong enough to go, before dumping. Then down and across and back, the wheel squealing less on the return trip, his back bent over a little less. Across the living room and down out of sight beneath the floor of the library. Back and forth, with those long periods between while he hacked and scraped away down in the earth. Corkscrewing his way down to the centre of the world.

"Is there something down there you're looking for?" she said.

"Some places in Ireland," he said, "you can see these giant circular stone forts, high up a hump of land, where the people long ago used to live, or hide from invaders. Inside the stone walls and down under the ground there were tunnels, to escape, in case they were surrounded by the enemy."

"Is that what it's for? Escape?"

"No."

"Then what? What?"

She would be as red-eyed as he was, from the smoke. She didn't want to do anything else, just sit here at the table and watch him, listen to him. Weights in her body kept her attached to the chair. It was easy enough to make fresh pots of coffee, and she'd learned to roll her own cigarettes. In those months the top of the table was always littered with a mess of escaped tobacco strands. Thick crinkled shreds. If she cleaned it at all, it was only to scoop them into the sharp trough of a cigarette paper, roll them up, and set a match to them. Flaring up, sometimes that was all the light there was in this house.

She went out, sometimes, forced herself to go out, only to remind them she was still here, that one of them was still in charge. It was his land, after all, and his buildings, and he was still nominally the leader of the colony, though she had persuaded them to allow her to stand in for him. "Until he's well again," she'd said. "Then we can talk together about reorganizing this whole set-up." They hadn't liked it — Paddy O'Mahony had been tempted, she could tell, to spit at her feet — but they'd agreed to let her look after the business. Not one of them knew anything about the paperwork, not even Paddy knew about the finances. So once a day, if she could pull herself away from the kitchen table, she rode out to visit the barns, to talk with the young men who were feeding the stock and to check repairs that were being made. She walked out into the vegetable gardens and conducted meaningless conversations with the women hoeing the rows of beets and the girls picking beans.

She inspected the new slaughterhouse being erected up the slope. O'Mahony was supervising the job and got some pleasure, she thought, out of showing her through. The way he smiled, bragged, you might have thought she was only a brainless visitor he was expected to entertain, from some other country where barns had never been seen. But she wiped the smile off his face fast enough. "What the hell's the matter with you people? Look at those beams. That roof'll come down in the first snow. Replace those beams with bigger ones, or put up twice as many posts." Oh, she could feel him sneering at her, behind her back, she could sense the "Iron Bitch" being muttered.

"Damn it O'Mahony," she said. "If you think you ought to be running this outfit you'll have to do better than that."

The part that would hurt, she knew, was that she was right. He couldn't even accuse her of bluffing, or pretending. He knew very well those beams weren't heavy enough.

He never came near the house. No one ever entered it, not even Jems or the old women. Not one of them even asked about the mountain that was growing in her back yard, though Jems's eyes, like her own, watched the coming and going of the dirty stooped-over figure from behind the glass of his cabin window. She didn't want to think what suffering the old cripple must be doing, in there, in his cabin by himself.

Now in the dark of the house she thought that if this were space she were rocketing through, if this dark kitchen were her ship and time the space she moved through, she'd know that the imploded star had been found, not by its black nothingness but by the terrible pull of its suction. Was a man's destiny then, to blast a hole into space? Did Keneally after all, exist in all time as a lightless rupture? You're going in with him, Lily Hayworth, she thought, you've lost the control of your own direction. You're going in.

Yet she sat at the table smoking, and listening, then and now, as he went down deeper.

The mound outside, then, was growing. The rhythm of his movement in and out of the house became mesmeric; she was no longer able to tell how long he took between his journeys into air. He moved back and forth across her vision like a steady shadow machine.

When the first tunnel from beneath the library opened up into the deep round well-hole, he hacked steps out of the well's sides spiralling down, and then began digging again, another tunnel which curled out and down, circling under itself like a coiled spring. The process became slower now, of course, the dirt had to be dragged up the new tunnel then pulleyed up on ropes to the surface in buckets. Keneally had to unwind himself up the well-hole in order to haul each of those loads over to his mound. He had soon gone too deep for his sounds to reach her, and yet they did—the hacking, clanging, and scraping were as audible as ever. She knew that if he broke through to the molten centre of the earth she would hear the *thunk* of his crowbar and the boiling rumble of the liquid that would claim him.

Old, he had got old, he was slowing down. Sometimes he would sit at the table with her for hours, across the table, and never speak. The act of breathing seemed all that he was capable of doing. He would put out his hand, on that table, towards her, and it was all she could do to force herself into touching it. The giant hand, crippled into a claw now from gripping the steel bar, cramped by the ringing jolts of steel against stone, the giant hand was a swollen crucible of broken blisters, cracked bleeding flesh, and running sores. The black filthy crescents of his nails had become less repulsive to her in comparison. There were no moons in the fingernails, and the surrounding skin was ragged, shredded and cracked.

"You should let someone do something about that hand," she said, and her voice—from the smoke or disuse—rumbled low in her like a man's or a stranger's voice in the room.

Someone, she'd said, not *me*.

You should let someone do something about that hand. Who was there left to do anything for anybody? There was only this dark, and the two of them eyeing each other dully. *On earth the broken arcs, in heaven the perfect rounds.*

One day when she touched the hand he spoke. "They told me my mother had no memory." His lips were cracked and had to be licked before he could go on. "I never met her, she died in the stones when I was born. But the absence of memory would be a blessing, I think, and no great tragedy at all."

"Without memory what would we be?"

"Free."

"Like the turned-out mouse in the poem. A tree has almost as much."

"But it would be enough. A stone has enough for me."

"Not for me. I'll take the anguish thank you, for the comfort of knowing I'm alive."

A priggish answer, to a man who was surely making more than declarations. His mouth tightened and he wiped a sleeve across his sweaty face. Some of the dirt came away and that was the first time she saw the circles, the perfect red rings in his skin, as if someone had pressed the mouth of a small water glass hard against him several times. What? she thought. What is this? Ringworm? She'd had it once as a child, from playing with a stray cat. Her mother had refused to answer, when she'd asked if there were real worms in there, eating at her, or if it was only a fancy name. *Without a compass*, she'd said, *how do the worms know*?

"We don't have to stay here," she said. "We could go, anywhere you want. We could go back, to Carrigdhoun if you wish, or the stones. Maybe, if you unravel things right back to their beginning . . . "

But he pulled back, his red eyes quivering.

"At any rate," she said, "you'll have to do something, for *that*." She'd never touch him again, not while those rings were there; the curled bleeding hand would lie on the table untouched. A maggoty rat would be less repellent.

"If we'd had children," she said, "there'd be something. But I never wanted any. And anyway I was too old."

He looked down at his hands, in his lap. They might have been his children, the pain would be bad enough.

"Or if we'd made friends in the town."

He said nothing to that, only nodded, as if she too had become one of the children, to be humoured, and endured.

"Down there," she said, "do you think?"

"No."

"Not of anything? Not of your life? Or the colony? Not of us?"

"No."

"It's not possible," she said. "A person can't stop thinking. You *have* to think."

"Wrong," he said. "most people never start. There's a difference between thinking and reacting. Down there the only difference between me and the shovel is that I would automatically jump back if the roof started to cave in, and the shovel would not."

Anyone else, she knew, would have forced a doctor on him long ago. Not for the hands or the rings, for the life that was burrowing. Sucking in on itself like that exploded star. But how was it possible for someone else to witness only this and give it a name and a treatment, as if it were a temporary aberration and not part of a whole life pattern? Should a doctor, or a psychiatrist, be permitted to put patches and Band-Aids on a life that had been plummeting like this from near the beginning? It was only natural that he should screw himself into the earth, after the fall.

But natural was never taken as an excuse and wouldn't be for her. There was nothing natural in the way she only sat at that table, listening. Wives did not do that, even when they knew it was the only sensible thing. Yet there were some things that mustn't be tampered with, you had only to shift the angle of your vision. *On earth the broken arcs, in heaven the perfect rounds*.

When he stood up she saw that he was shaking, trembling. That great dirty head bobbed on his neck like a heavy flower in wind. His back was no longer merely bent forward, it was hunched-up and hooked, as if his skeleton had plans to roll itself up. The only strength left in him was the strength of what burned in his eyes.

"Don't go back down," she said, "not now. Not without a rest. You look too weak."

He turned at the doorway, nearly invisible in the dark. "Maybe so. But at least whatever strength I have is my own." He made no sound at all moving away, and then there was only the soft *fft* of the library floor closing.

Thus, with his borrowed words, he disappeared. And now, in the kitchen darkness, shivering at the cold, she heard other echoes from somewhere else. While he scraped in his tunnels, like a gynecologist scraping a womb, deeper and deeper, she heard the clatter of footsteps on boards somewhere, a stage, and the clanging of metal: *Turn, hellhound, turn*. A voice like a beating drum. *Turn, hellhound, turn*. A play somewhere, she'd heard it in a play. And below he was turning, in the forty-six years since his death he'd been turning, in her mind.

It had begun as only a shudder, it might have been only herself, in the cold air. But it was as if the earth itself were chilled. It came up from below like a bubble of air escaping, without sound, the slightest tremble; it began deeper and came up a second time like a shoulder nudging the underside of the house, a rocking impatience; then it sucked back and came up a third time, growling and belching, loud, and rattled the windows, shifted the coffee cup on the table. She imagined the surface of the dark ground outside the house rippling in circles of waves that spread out from this centre like ocean waves driven back by a surfacing whale. Above the growl, coming up, was the clearer sound of a human scream so loud and long she was forced to put down her cigarette and clamp both hands over her ears.

There were people in town who would tell her they'd heard it, that even after the earth had settled it went on. They thought it was another collapse in the mines, they said, and that the scream was the alarm siren that was blown to alert the rescuers.

There were no rescuers here. She continued to sit at the table. The quaking might have been confined to her own body, the scream to her head. When the colony men came banging on the doors she let them hammer away until they pushed the doors open to get inside. She let them tear the inside of her house apart, looking for the entrance to his tunnels, but they never found it.

"Becker, you . . . " she said, now in September. The black silent walls absorbed the sound. "Becker, you bastard."

Out on the strait there was a wind, and the tide had come up high to bash driftwood logs against the cliff. Arbutus trees would be bent with the weight of rain, she could hear them shake in the wind and loose their load all at once, thundering, on the ground, then become still again to collect more. On a night like this she could have gone walking, once, it was a night full of movement and life.

She had no grief then or now. These cigarettes were more real than the settling of earth, the smoke had more substance than a scream.

"Becker, you . . . "

She brushed a hand against her face. It felt as if it were covered with dirt, from having her nose rubbed in it. Her neck ached, as if Becker's hand were there, clamped and pushing. Becker, who was asleep, in his own cabin. Not suspecting the black powers of his little plastic machine.

"Becker! You . . . Becker!"

But she wouldn't tell him. Even if he rose from his bed and came over. Even if he sat up at the sound of her voice and came hurrying across the wet overgrown courtyard dragging his overcoat and his plastic box, even if he came panting and rain-dripping into this room, leaving mud tracks from his bare feet on the floor and sat across the table from her where Keneally used to sit and pushed the little buttons on his machine she would not tell him a word of it. She would tell him, instead, about the wolves of Lycaon. It wasn't much, but it was as close, now, as she dared to come, and for a while it would make him suspect there was meaning after all in her vision. Not that she had any intention, ever, of commenting on its truth.

PILGRIMAGE

1

Green hedges and fuchsia. Wind, rain, and drifting banks of mist. The drive south to Carrigdhoun did nothing to improve her state of mind, she was in no mood for acting like a tourist. When Maggie Kyle had landed in Ireland with Donal Keneally tucked in her purse—or all that was left of Donal Keneally, a cylinder of ashes— she had no intention of having a good time, she'd just as soon have stayed at home where she belonged. Chasing down this wet winding road after a village that may not even be there, or may never have existed at all, made her uneasy, and vaguely guilty. People she knew did not fly halfway around the world to scatter ashes, or hunt up villages you couldn't even find on a map. Miles and miles of stone fences, snaking up rocky slopes and boxing in fields hardly larger than pens. If Wade shouted "Just think of the work that went into those!" one more time she would scream. Or leave him stranded with his rocks, by a dripping hedge. Him and Becker.

The sudden grotto was no help, the little picket-fenced triangle of flowers and brilliant white madonna, miles from anything but scraggy growth and naked hills and this greenish wet road. *Pray for the donor*, it said on the fence, but that only made her think of poor Lily Hayworth, who was paying for this silly excursion from her grave. Who'd never seen this place, or wanted to. She'd seen enough of the world, thank you, she said, it was somebody else's turn. Maggie had a sudden memory of the old woman down the well, laid out in her nightgown like a pale dropped moth on the clay ledge. And later, in the hospital, smelling of plaster. *Pray for the donor.* Someone who'd tended the real flowers in summer, up here in this lonely wind, and brought the sealed plastic bouquets in fall. Poor Lily, poor Lily, poor Lily. The flowers on her heaped grave would be colourless and rain-beaten by now, in the bald uninteresting city cemetery. Not even a tree, in that island of forests. You could only hope she'd found whatever it was she was after. She had already, it turned out after her death, settled all of this sort of business in her will, even planned this trip for them.

Green hedges and fuchsia. The sweet throaty smell of bogs, and turf smoke. Solitary cyclists, streaming wet, tipped their hats in greeting but eyed you suspiciously, as if they expected you to veer suddenly and knock them flying.

With Wade driving this little rented car that was not impossible. He kept forgetting which side of the road he was supposed to be on, and had no idea how much clearance was needed on her side of the car; she gasped when he whizzed by within inches of the hedge, or nearly swiped the cars parked along the edge. While she strained over the map, trying to make sense of the crooked lines, he didn't expect sense at all, he followed the road, wherever. When it forked, as it did often without signs, he simply kept to the wider choice, it didn't matter to him if they drove forever in circles. It was all a lot of nonsense, he said. When they climbed, suddenly, into thick white fog he hardly slowed, the faster they got through it the better; when they found themselves in what looked like someone's yard, he kept on going past sheds and pens, it was road again soon enough, there were no surprises. If he didn't slow down, Maggie told him, they'd have gone right on past where they were going before she'd even found themselves on the map. Becker in his smelly overcoat only grunted from the back seat. His eyes, when she glanced back, were wild with trying to take everything in. Somewhere, out there, he expected revelations, to make sense of his hoarded research.

Ireland looked on her map as if it had dragged itself up out of the sea at its south-west corner, and was moving still, with a lot of pointed streaks and dribbled islands left hanging out behind in the Atlantic. It was one of these narrow peninsulas they were heading down, on one of the few roads the mapmakers had bothered to record. Carrigdhoun was out there somewhere, they could only hope that somehow they would know it when they saw it. There were tiny dots along the road, with names, but none of them was anything she'd ever heard of before. Nor were the names of bays and headlands any help.

"There's not much point in looking at this thing," she said. "I'm beginning to think it was cooked up in someone's imagination, without them ever coming to see what the place is like."

"That's possible," Becker said. "Are there laws that say a map has to conform to reality?"

A family riding a two-wheeled cart behind a donkey all raised their hands in greeting. The old woman, who seemed to be the largest of the cluster, gave them the benefit of a gap-toothed smile.

"I suppose they have their Madmother Thomases too," Becker said. "Casualties of something or other. Like everywhere else."

"Why not?" Maggie said. "This is where your friend the madman came from, don't forget, or what are we doing here?"

With Lily Hayworth a fresh bruise on her mind she didn't need to be reminded of that other old one, wearing out the island roads in her squeaky wagon.

Driving down, they met very little traffic on the narrow paved road, but what they did meet seemed determined always to come at them directly down the middle of it, as if they weren't there at all, forcing Wade to swerve suddenly and dangerously towards the high wall of hedge along the side. Little black Morris Minors, battered and old, rattled down the road so fast that they looked as if they were trying to get somewhere before they fell apart. Heading for church, probably, it was Sunday. Young square-faced men with black curly hair and both hands gripped to the top of the steering wheel. In the front seat there was always the older woman, the mother, grey-haired and sometimes black-shawled. As they flashed past, Maggie caught glimpses of the old men in the back seat, tiny hawk-nosed wrinkled faces, caps flat on their heads. They'd had their turn at driving years ago, apparently, and now only watched the scenery unroll. Green hedges and fuchsia.

For miles, sometimes, they seemed to be driving down the bottom of a chute, with nothing at all to see but the high solid wall of vines and tangled shrubs that grew house-high and nearly vertical along either side, trimmed smooth as a cement bank. Gate gaps, flashing by, gave only glimpses of hayfields, or a slate-roofed house, or a pile of ruins. Then, suddenly, there would be nothing. The road, like a greenish ribbon, rolled out across miles of flat soggy ground, bogland, with no houses or fences anywhere in sight, just the low green spongy growth, dotted with flowers like daubs of white cotton, and sometimes a high heap of turf bricks stacked in the shape of a giant loaf.

Houses, when they saw them, were all the same, or nearly: perched up on higher ground, alone and bare among rocks and scraggy growth, white or sometimes blue, with smoke rising from the chimney and shredding out level across the valley as if there were an invisible ceiling not far above the roof. Most were two storeys high, plain, built of stone or concrete blocks, she couldn't tell. A few had low stone walls around a tiny front yard, with the ruins of a flower garden black and drooping, and a black dog laid out in the driveway with his nose on the ground between his paws. The only cows they saw were solitary animals, off by themselves on the top of a rocky hump. Standing around like statues, they looked as if they had nothing else to do with their lives but pose. Escaping flies, she thought, or watching for a break in the weather.

"Look out!" yelled Wade, and slammed on the brakes. Rounding a corner, they found the whole road clogged from hedge to hedge with sheep. A road-wide, hundred-foot-long, dirty white mattress moved towards them on dainty feet. A man at the rear, swinging a long switch, frowned heavily, as if he couldn't understand how a thing like a car had got out on the road in the way of his sheep.

"Just sit tight," Maggie said, and put a hand on Wade's arm.

"What else can I do?"

The sheep parted, passed down either side of the car. For a while they were surrounded, stranded in a bouncing flowing sea of backs, each marked with a long streak of blue paint; a symphony of bleating. The farmer, last to pass by, touched his cap but didn't look at them.

"Wet day," Maggie said, leaning out her window. The man might be able to give directions.

"Yes. 'Tis," he said, but did not look. His frown moved out ahead of him, as if already prepared to meet the next anticipated nuisance; his knee-high rubber boots kicked through a pattern of black trampled droppings. His dog gave them more answer, at least stopped long enough to eye her up, his long tongue panting, before moving on past after his work.

But Wade was no more inclined to gossip than the farmer was. As soon as the way was clear he pushed his foot to the floor. The car leapt forward before Maggie had time to pull her head inside.

"When I think of the money wasted on your ticket," she said.

"It's all of it wasted money," Wade said. "This whole scheme of Lily's is a stupid waste."

As if she needed to be told. If she'd stayed at home she could have enjoyed her misery in private, or nearly. Instead of going off on this ridiculous trip to carry out Lily's whim she should be home, facing up to the fact that all her high-blown plans had come to nothing, that nearly everything she'd tried had failed; she should be packing up her things to move back into the bush where she belonged. And she just might have refused the trip altogether, too, despite her guilt about poor old Lily Hayworth, if she hadn't discovered that her misery was bringing out the worst in everyone around her. Some people accused her of being miserable for the same reason she wore plaid shirts and hooted like a chokerman and drove like a logging-truck driver, to evade the responsibilities of the beautiful woman, to hide. She got no sympathy from them, not that she wanted it.

Others who had been intimidated by her usual nature suddenly found their courage when they saw her unhappiness: she was barraged by a series of men determined to cheer her up with the only thing they had to offer, sex. One of them, a fat red-faced car salesman from Texas, snuck down through the bush from his trailer to tell her he had just the thing she needed, but his leather-skinned wife followed him down and told her that what he had was a case of the clap, which nobody needed. Men offered you sex, the woman said, the way you offer a whining bitch a bone; as if it was all that was needed to start your tail wagging, or at least to shut you up. Maggie agreed. She would go on this trip, she decided, to escape the people who were determined to force her to be happy.

"It's your own fault," Wade told her, "for being so noticeable."

And she couldn't argue that. She'd always been one to let it show. It was because she had got fed up, when she was a small girl, with having to take her feelings down under that west-coast shack so nobody would see them or hit her for them or get into a fight over who was to blame for them. She had determined, one summer day when she'd bumped her head on the floor joists, that from then on if she was happy the whole world would be forced to witness it and if she was miserable the whole world would suffer, and to hell with the consequences. It was only in looking back now that she realized what the consequences were: her happiness intimidated people, her unhappiness brought out the worst in them.

She'd done a whole lifetime's worth of thinking under that shack and out walking along the beach in those days. All she could think about was getting out of there, getting up into the mountains where she could see the whole island and pick out the right kind of life for herself. And when they finally did move out, she was so excited she could hardly breathe. The narrow gravel road snaked along the edge of lakes, followed streams, clung to the face of rock cliffs, twisted up narrow valleys, and rose finally to a steep mid-island mountain which had to be crossed by climbing a long series of dangerous switchbacks cut like knife-slashes up its face to the very top. And there at the top the midsummer sun, which back at the coast had bleached out the bay in a pale haze, seemed to come at them nearly level from behind and gave the world more colour than it needed: the roadside bushes were an unnatural gold, the mountainside of rock and scrub was orange, the burned-over timber a field of silver hairs. Looking ahead to the confusion of pink and purple mountains still to be crossed, or passed, realizing that even from here she still wasn't high enough to really *see*, she was certain that the something inside her that wouldn't let her rest, that wanted her to keep climbing higher, was really an extra instinct she'd been cursed with. Other people either didn't have it or didn't pay attention to it. Maybe she was a freak.

Through those years in the logging camps and finally in good old abandoned Hed, she'd done her best to ignore it, the way someone else might try to ignore a festering toe. If she kept it hidden it might die by itself, or maybe she'd wake up some morning and find it was never real, only a dream. An extra arm could have been handled more easily, even an extra head. But an extra instinct was a quiet torture. Through the confused years of growing up, through the long string of men, through the births of her children, even while she discarded them like so many unwanted pups she was aware that some day that thing in her would have its say, would refuse to stay hidden. And when she finally broke out of Hed, when she finally moved down to the east coast of the island, bought the old colony, started looking after her collection of people, it was with all the wild exuberance of someone who'd just decided to indulge in a secret vice before the eyes of the entire world. The instinct had been freed. Who cared where it led. She would trust it, follow it, she would climb—my God, she thought, she would soar — until she was able to understand all there was to understand about the universe and be all that she was capable of being. There was no end to the preposterous plans this instinct could devise for her, once given free rein.

She knew people said it was a good thing her parents had turned their backs on her years ago. If a daughter who was a loggers' whore was an embarrassment, a daughter with notions about improvement and ascent would be a mortification. What they dreaded most of all, of course, and expected, too, was that any moment she would start bringing God into it, or turn religious, or go off to study with some crazy guru in India. People who let their feet leave the ground for even a moment could be counted on for every sort of madness conceivable. The horror and fascination with which they watched her convinced Maggie that she wasn't the only one with this instinct; that in there somewhere they all had it, but had learned better than she had to suppress it. People are never so horrified as when they see others doing what they'd like to do themselves. This conviction was all the encouragement she needed to make a display of herself.

So she indulged her extra instinct like a sweet tooth, or a passion for pickles, publicly.

When she'd hauled herself out of the bush and set herself up a new kind of life on the old colony, she'd made no secret of it. The whole world, it seemed, had witnessed her attempts to keep Danny Holland out of her life. When she decided to bring Carla back, and prove she could be a mother as loving as anyone else, she made no secret of it. And half the town knew when she flew off to that island of shrinks and miracle-workers. The problem with that, she discovered too late, was that when she failed it was bound to be in front of an audience. An old woman falling down a well while chasing after a dead man was hardly something that could be kept quiet. Nor was the screaming match with her daughter Carla in a doctor's office. Nor was it possible to keep the news quiet that Julius Champney had suddenly gone off and signed himself into an old folks' home. Confronted with all this public failure, Maggie Kyle did the only thing she could think of: she suffered, and suffered publicly. She was nearly as bad as Cora Manson. Obviously, she thought, she'd been wrong to trust that instinct.

At least it had stopped raining here, she could leave the window open a little, get some fresh air into the car.

Oh she had to admit it was beautiful. It was a beautiful country. Any other time she could really have enjoyed this, thrown herself into it. But not now, not with so much uncertainty ahead.

And besides, she missed her trees. It was all bald and lumpy, any bush she could find was only a bit of scrubby stuff here and there, growing on the tops of hedges, or close to buildings. Maggie Kyle could not be comfortable without real timber close at hand, trees that soared above, so high their lowest branches were above your reach. She liked to have the feeling she was snuggled in among the giants, cuddled up against a mountain. If she were here for long she'd feel naked all the time, exposed, a lonely thing wandering around on a bare and knobby planet. It had always been her need, when things got bad, to head into the timber for comfort. Here, she would have to spend her life huddled under a hedge or crouched beneath a scraggy shrub.

And huddling and crouching were hardly postures for a woman like Maggie Kyle. She would walk upright, thank you, as long as she was able. And she would stay close to trees that permitted it.

"I should be able to get a decent price for the place," she said. "Now that the house is fixed up, and the trailer park is bringing in money." It might even, she thought, bring in enough to set her up nicely, up the coast someplace where she could work only when she felt like it.

"People running away," Wade said, "usually take whatever they can get." It was typical of him to say that. He hadn't said a pleasant thing since they'd left home, she couldn't even remember why on earth she'd invited him to come along. He had no feeling for other people.

"Maybe one of my rich Americans could buy it," she said, just to get even. "They have more money than they know what to do with."

Becker leaned ahead, behind her ear. "I believe you capable of doing it," he said, "if you don't get over this snit. But you'd be sorry afterwards."

And who asked you? she nearly said. It wasn't her idea to have him along, it was Lily's. Becker will never be satisfied, she'd said from her hospital bed, until he's absorbed it all. Take him along. Well, she'd brought him, you couldn't deny a dying woman, but the sound of his pen scratching away at his notebook was more than anyone should have to take.

"I'll do what I want," she said. "It's my place."

"It is that," Wade said. He flashed his smile, and looked as if there were leaves he had to peer through, to see her. He kept that imaginary screen between them always. And made it clear he knew how childishly she was acting.

He stopped the car now, to ask directions of a woman and a young boy who'd come out onto the road from a gateway. Behind them a series of buildings leaned on each other; at one end a roofless shed of loose unmortared stones of every size and shape, in the middle a thatched open-door place of grey stones with gaps plugged unevenly with clay or mud, and at the other end a whitewashed slate-roofed house, with a half-door and two windows, a chimney. The successive generations didn't tear down and build, apparently; they sidestepped. A donkey grazed by the gate, its front leg tied to its back with a length of rope. Maggie didn't want to think about how poor these people must be. It got too complicated.

"Eh?" the woman shouted, and leaned closer.

"Carrigdhoun. Do you know it?"

She was a big woman in a shapeless dirty housedress and overshoes, leaning on a crooked stick. Her mouth had sunken in around her toothless gums. The boy, when she flung a string of words at him, grinned and looked down as if he knew they were only leading up to a surprise meant just for him. They looked, to Maggie, as if they belonged in some nineteenth-century movie.

"Nivver heerd of it," the woman yelled. She put a rough hand on the sill of Wade's door and slid a look at Maggie and Becker. "Is it down this way now? Or is it somewhere else you should be looking?" Her grey hair floated like crinkled wires. "Noo—I nivver heerd of Carrigdhoun."

"It's all deserted now," said Wade. "Maybe you know of a place where the people all pulled out and left for Canada."

She moved back and laughed. "Sure now you're joking. It's any corner of Ireland you could be telling me about." She looked at

Maggie as if inviting her to join in laughing at Wade's stupidity.

"In that case we'll just keep looking," Wade said. "When we run out of land we'll turn around and start back."

"Well God bless," the woman said, and bowed back a step. Her walking stick tapped a hole into the gravel, as if in search of a solid footing.

"Thanks," Maggie said.

"For nothing," the woman said. And already her eyes were set on something far away, far down the road. The boy lifted a hand shyly, to wave. He was still waiting for his surprise.

In a tiny village of colourless buildings, the road which had narrowed to a single car-width was suddenly filled with people. In the open doorway of a grey, thin-spired church a priest with hands folded together in front of him talked excitedly to an old shawled woman. Other women stood in clusters everywhere, talking, with arms folded, scrubbed faces smiling, eyes constantly shifting to watch the children who played on the road. A number of men stood in one huge huddle of black suits and caps around a youth on a bicycle selling newspapers. Through an open door, Maggie could see the dim small interior of a bar, clogged solid with suits and red faces. People smiled at them, nodded shyly, as if to say *You too, whoever you are, are included in what we know.* But they did not move aside for them. Wade nudged the car through, slipping the clutch, twisting in and out of groups, brushing against clothes, touching the brakes at the sudden movements of children. Maggie felt like someone who had ridden a car into the middle of a living room full of people; they seemed to have no idea that she belonged there, that this pavement they treated like the foyer of their church was part of the road that came from somewhere, that led somewhere. Yet there was not a flicker of annoyance on any of those happy, holy faces. They accepted this intrusion, they seemed ready to absorb the intruders.

"It must be nice to be so sure of things," Maggie said.

At the far end of the crowd Wade pulled over to the side of the road, against a building, and got out to ask directions. In front of the car one tall heavy man in a shiny suit, leaning a shoulder against the pale gable-end wall of the building, looked steadily at Maggie out of a wide calm meaty face. And behind him, a shorter man with a face like a round red dish and one eye drooped or blind or just unused leaned against the same wall and watched her just as steadily. They talked to each other, without ever once shifting their gaze away, like one person behind another on the seats of a tandem bicycle. When Wade came back and the car pulled away, neither head turned to follow; they continued to talk, she saw, and to look off in the same direction, as if there were a common goal somewhere ahead they were approaching together.

"They may be sure of their soul's destination," Wade said, when he returned, "but they haven't any idea where this Carrigdhoun might be."

"You know what we're going to find, don't you," Maggie said, once they were out flying along the road again. "We're going to find there's no such place and never has been. And then we're going to go back to Kealkill and find out that at the top of that hill there aren't any stones at all, no stone circle or anything else, just a few cows. We'll go home feeling like fools."

"They exist," Becker said. "The stones and village were two things that *weren't* lies."

She glanced down at the newspaper she'd borrowed from the woman at the B & B in Ballylickey. That Mrs. O'Sullivan. "Something to read if you get lost," she'd said, laughing. Maggie had started reading at the house, skimming through, but had given it up and folded the pages back. A lot of advertisements, they looked much the same as she'd find at home. Job openings and cars for sale and houses for rent. One thing, though, was unfamiliar.

LOURDES / PARIS
SHRINES OF FRANCE
BY SEA / COACH
11 Days from £ 107
First-Class Hotels
Spiritual Director

"Listen!" she said, and read it aloud. "This is something old Julius would enjoy. A pilgrimage. I should tear it out and take it home to him."

"He's been to all those places," Wade said.

Becker leaned forward from the back seat. "He's been everywhere."

"Still," she said, "he'd get a laugh. In his old folks' home."

"His big orange hump of glowing rock," Becker said, and snickered. "He didn't even climb it. He wouldn't have believed anyway, he never expects to believe."

Poor sour Julius. He hadn't even come downtown to see them

off. "You're letting that old woman make fools of you all," he'd said on the telephone, from his new room in the Harvest Years Home, or whatever it was. He would sulk until they returned.

Mrs. O'Sullivan had been just as disapproving. She'd nearly fainted when Becker told her why they'd come: "To scatter a dead man's ashes at the stone circle above Kealkill."

"Oh dear dear dear dear dear," she'd said. "This is not a country that goes in for cremations, as you might have guessed."

They spared her the supporting details: the well in the middle of the circle of buildings, the tunnels that cork-screwed their way down into earth, the men she had hired to dig out the crushed skeleton, the reports she had to make to the police and the government people, the arrangements with the crematorium on the mainland. Mrs. O'Sullivan was just not prepared for the grimy details.

And when they said they would drive down to find Carrig-dhoun first, she told them they'd never find it. It had probably never existed.

But they did find it. A shopkeeper confirmed it. "Carrig-dhoun?" he said. "This is Carrigdhoun."

"This?" There was nothing else, only his tiny store, with the small-paned windows and the clutter of cans and fly-specked signs. A single gas pump stood out at the edge of the pavement. Cars, stopping for gas, wouldn't even have to leave the road. Around it there was only mountainside, and mist.

There'd been a village here, once, he said, talking to Wade. He avoided looking at Maggie. If they peered about in the weeds, he said, they'd find the remains. But the people all had gone long long ago, no one knew where, and there wasn't anyone left. His father had built this shop, for passing motorists, but it was a bad spot to have a business and he was thinking of moving up to Cork. He had two sons in Maynooth and a daughter who was walking out with someone. As soon as she left home he had his eyes on a little flat along the quay right in the middle of Cork city. It was his dream to spend the rest of his life within the sounds of the noisy morning haggling of the Coal Quay market. And to take his pint each day, he added, in Oliver Plunkett Street.

"So there," Wade said to Maggie, gesturing into the thick white mist, "is your village."

"Can we poke around?" Maggie said, to the shopkeeper. "Can

we prowl around a bit back there? To see what there is. We've come a long ways to see it."

"See it so," the man said, still not looking at her. He indicated to Wade with his wide-apart hands that all of it was theirs if they wanted it. "There's more still, up the hill. If you wish to drive your motor up that boreen you'll come to some standing buildings. The old church there was used in the time of troubles as an orphanage. The fadder told me this hillside then was loud with the sound of weeping children."

A pleasant thought. In this mist it wouldn't be hard to imagine them still.

"Thanks," Maggie said. "We'll drive up."

"God bless," the man said to Wade.

They drove farther up the slope, in the thickening mist, on a road that was little more than two paved tracks with grass growing down the middle. Short gnarled limbs brushed against the side of the car. Once, Becker had to hop out and lift a few rocks out of the way. Eventually they came to a cluster of ruined buildings and parked the car.

"Hell," Wade said, "I don't even want to turn the engine off. Think what it would be like to get stranded up here."

But he was talking to himself. She'd gone off, already, into the ruins. And Becker too, with his notebook open. The world for him was a catalogue of details to be listed, or sucked in. The two of them with their noses pressed against the world would miss what Wade could see from the car, that this whole wide mountainside was a place to make your flesh crawl. The pale green rocky slope, slanting up, faded back into the white mist with salt-and-pepper stones like silent shapeless things the size of sheep or cattle, stretching back to nothing, to disappearance. There was no sound at all, not a breath; the air was a cold damp thing he could feel, by holding out his hand, around his fingers like damp cloth. The stone fences, waist high and nearly white, and fallen here and there into shapeless piles, formed a giant woven mesh laid against the earth, defining fields the size of front lawns and lanes no wider than the car and yards around the buildings only large enough to turn around in. And with all those stones piled high like that, the ground was still cluttered with the larger ones, the stones that were too heavy to move. The nearer buildings were only fallen sheds, the houses and barns were back up at the top of the narrow lanes, almost invisible, blank and colourless shells of cemented stones, window-holes like black blind eyes, roofs caved in or bared to rafters. It was impossible to imagine anyone ever living here, or believing in this place. It was impossible to think of people in those houses waking up in the morning and looking out on *this* and knowing that they'd be working in those fields, among those rocks, the whole day long. To be wrapped in this mist would be like living in the cold, damp, frightening world of fantasy all your life, you'd never really be sure that anything was real.

Though Maggie climbed fences to get at farther sheds, Wade walked up a narrow lane until, looking back, the car had taken on that same veil of unreality. "What the hell are we doing here?" he said. But there was no one to answer.

It wasn't something Maggie would stop to ask. She was busy up there, dragging herself from one piece of rubble to the next, not even bothering to enjoy any of it. Wade, watching her, didn't know whether to pity her or envy. What was she after?

Whatever it was, he was scared for her. In the old days, when she was content to live the kind of life her circumstances had defined for her, there'd been no risk. A cheap and vulgar girl, by some standards, she'd grown into a type he recognized. There were plenty like her around, in every settlement, in every camp, it was a pattern. Content, they grew into certain types of middle-aged women, hard, perhaps, and bitter and tired, but recognizable. Maggie Kyle, with her determination to buck the pattern, had taken a risk, there was a chance of failure.

She would not, no matter what she threatened, go back to what she had been, if she failed. He was sure of it. She'd never survive. A jet taking off either succeeded or crashed, it couldn't reverse and gently slide back onto the runway. That was what scared him, that was what made this whole trip seem so dangerous.

Chasing after ghosts, galloping through stony fields, racing down roads that couldn't be found on maps. He'd gone crazy, he was sure they'd all gone crazy. This mist, clammy on his face and damp through all the layers of his clothes, was the thick white sea of insanity. Or distortion, anyway, and fantasy, clinging and gathering in watery drops on his skin.

"Maggie!" he yelled. "Let's get out of here!"

Becker, walking the top of a fence, looked up suddenly like a startled animal.

Wade could hardly believe he'd given up his summer's end at

The Fort to come along on this trip. The season wasn't even over. Back home the weather was better than it had been all summer and the Americans were still streaming through: some of them on their way back down after a summer of camping in the mountains or following the coast down from Alaska, some of them just on their way up, getting ready for hunting season, eagerly imagining the dead deer they'd have strapped all over their trucks on the return trip. All he had to do was lie back in the sun, getting brown, and watch them come through. Some days all the payment he needed was the kind of smile he got from their long-limbed daughters, or even the wives; if he hadn't needed to eat they could have kept their money. It was enough for him just to watch. Or almost enough. He liked to talk, too, when one of them looked interesting enough, and find out all about the kinds of lives they'd left behind. By now he could've put together a thousand-page book on the weird ways you could get rich if you lived in the States. It was a perfect set-up, he was crazy to leave it.

But the fact of the matter was he didn't have much choice. For Maggie, by acting for so long as if she were unaware that he even existed, had got him so he'd do practically anything she wanted, though she didn't know it yet. And wouldn't get to know it, either, if he could help it. Wade had had more than his share of women who'd guessed at how much he depended on them and then used that knowledge to turn his life into hell. Once they found out, you were finished, you couldn't even recognize yourself any more. Without even making a show of it they led you around like a bull with a ring in your nose, and the worst of it was he couldn't help liking it. When he thought of the things that Virginia Kerr, that redheaded painter, could've done with him if she'd wanted, he could only shudder. Women. If they were all removed from the face of the earth it would be a safer place, but he'd have to kill himself. What he wanted to do, his mother said, was get married again; marriage would give him time to think of other things. She was nuts, of course, he liked things the way they were.

It was just that Maggie kept him waiting so long. After that stupid agreement she came up with in the school-bus shed, there was always in the back of his mind the possibility that some day she would holler for help. The fact that it took her more than twenty years to do it only made it worse. She'd been there, in the back of his head, all that time.

And then she'd called him up that morning, with her hysterical story about the old lady falling down the well. He'd rushed down to her place, assuming that he'd know what to do when he got there just the same as anyone else would. When you were asked to help, you helped. But by the time he got to her place the ambulance was already pulling away with the Hayworth woman and all he could do was stand beside Maggie while she stared at her own reflection in the small round dusty surface of the well water, far below; and when he stayed with her in the waiting room of the hospital while they waited for some kind of news, she hardly knew he was there and all he could think of to say was "Let's get out of this crummy place." And now that they were over here, to scatter ashes of all things, there still wasn't anything for him to do but drag along. He couldn't for the life of him see why she'd called him.

Her self-pity was the worst. The last thing you'd expect from Maggie Kyle. Where was her old hoot and to-hell-with-it? A woman like her only looked silly with her jaw dragging on the floor. He'd noticed it first in the hospital while they waited, her wailing about how she'd got up that morning and found an ashtray full of cigarette butts on the kitchen table but couldn't find Lily Hayworth anywhere until Becker came in and said she was down the well. Laid out flat at the entrance to Keneally's tunnel, as if she'd fallen straight from sky. Like a moth flattened. Oh boy, was she feeling sorry for herself then. You'd think she'd been accused of murder. If you knew how ugly you look, he'd wanted to say. But only complained, instead, about the waiting.

As if a hospital wasn't already bad enough. He walked out to the corners of that room, to the elevator doors, to the gift counter, to the big glass doors that opened onto the parking lot. The air conditioner was so loud you could be in a plane or something, with that steady powerful motor hurtling you through sky. Throbbing. And the whole room, of course, was a damn pretence, which made him even madder; with its rubber plants and its brown steel-and-plastic furniture it could have been the lobby of a decent hotel or theatre. Except for the brick mural, of white mice and test tubes, to remind you that behind the walls you could expect just about anything. And of course there was that damn woman across the room with her red swollen eyes staring into nowhere, like a dummy propped up there, while two small boys ran toy cars back and forth on the carpet around her tucked-back feet.

You couldn't disguise a hospital. And Wade hated them all. It was where people went when they lost control. He knew what hospitals were for. They built them to scare you, they built them huge and high among ordinary houses to say: *Just in case you think you have control.* It was easy to remember his tractor-mangled father delivering his life into the hands of doctors and brisk nurses. But he didn't panic, not in that waiting room with Maggie, all he could feel was annoyance — that he couldn't stand being cooped up in the place and that he couldn't figure out what it was she expected him to do.

He'd tried to draw her attention to the mural on the wall behind the woman's head. It was a puzzle of geometric shapes, in flat bold colours. From the upper right-hand corner a yellow sun, painted up to look more like a giant eyeball, sent black lines radiating down over the whole wall like thick roads on a map, passing through prisms and lenses, dividing, outlining squares and triangles, circling jars and white mice and fish and skeleton leaves, down across bubbles and atomic patterns and mortars and pestles to a tiny black Bible in the lower left corner. He must have stared at it for half an hour. But when he tried to get her to look at it she'd only got cranky, and started to blame herself again, and told him that mural was exactly what she didn't need right now. If she took it seriously, she said, it was just one more thing to convince her she'd been a damn fool to try any of the things she'd tried, that she had no business trusting her instinct in the first place.

Now she appeared at the door to one of the falling-down huts, gesturing for him to come over. "Look," she said. "Come in and see this."

I can't, he wanted to tell her, I can't believe in this place. But he went in anyway through the low open doorway, ducking his head to keep from bashing it open on the long stone lintel.

There was no roof, there were no doors or windows, only the grey walls of mortarless stones: one narrow room, and an opening through to a second, even smaller. Not much to get excited about.

"Can you imagine my house," she said, "or your own, with stinging nettle and blackberry vines like this, growing inside? Or your floors covered with cow shit and sheep marbles. Smell it."

He smelled nothing new, only the same damp sweet odour of the furze or whatever, that seemed to hang everywhere in the mist.

"The stones," she said, "these walls. Can you imagine these

being all that separated inside from outside? All that made *home* separate from *world*?"

"This is only a shed, for Christ sake Maggie. Cows or donkeys would be kept here."

"This was a house. Look, it had to be a house! Over there in those weeds I found a broken plate."

Right or wrong he only wanted to get out of here. "Come on," he said. "You've seen enough. Let's go."

"We'll have our lunch first, thank God for Mrs. O'Sullivan and her bag of fruit. We'll have a picnic."

"Here? In this place?"

"Here or anywhere else we'd still have to eat it in the car. It's wet, wet, wet, everywhere you go. Too wet to sit." She laughed, or nearly laughed. Then, suddenly, she scowled, a mock scowl, at him. "Of course it's nothing to me if you can't get over that Horseman."

"What?" He couldn't believe it. She struck out, that woman, at the damnedest times, and with the most unexpected weapons. "What's that?"

"It only just hit me what's the matter with you. Hell, you've been grouching around ever since we tracked him down. You didn't like what he said about you, about hiding your real self. It's been grating on you ever since."

"Don't be stupid."

But when she'd left him alone in that crumbled shed he couldn't help but think of that damn Horseman. And her bloody cheek in suggesting that it mattered to him. She'd gone too, that day, she'd heard what he said, but this was the first time she'd ever mentioned it.

She'd gone with him down along the waterfront, south of town, through the Reserve and past the lumberyards, along the windy road above the river estuary clogged with log booms and naked pilings and floating skeletons of trees, to catch him paying up his bill at the trailer park, ready to leave.

"Horseman?" he'd said,

"Yes, that's my name. And you, you're Powers, from that counterfeit fort."

"That's right," Powers said, "The Fort. But look, Maggie, look, couldn't he be my twin?"

"Your twin?" the man said, and raised an eyebrow at Maggie, as if they shared a secret. "Mr. Powers," he said, "you're just as phoney as that museum of yours. You're your own twin, Powers, but you've hidden the true one. Buried him. Locked him up, maybe, the way you tried to lock me up."

"What the hell?" Wade said, appealing to Maggie. "What the hell is he talking about? What kind of crap is this?"

"Excuse me," Horseman said. "I've got to be going. Don't you think, Powers, that it's time you took responsibility for what you really are?"

A lot of garbage. He'd pushed it right out, hadn't thought of it again since they'd left the bugger to go his own way. In his stupid silver trailer. The man hadn't passed through his mind again since then, until Maggie dragged him up, now, for her own reasons. Maybe it had been bothering her, maybe she hadn't been able to shake off the pompous ass as easily as he had. People like that ought to be locked up, the world didn't need them.

And he was not going to think of him here. Not now. He went outside, and instead of heading back down to the car, walked uphill, farther up into the mist, crossed field after field of wet grass, climbed over collapsed fences and thick hedges, until he found Becker sitting on a cement sarcophagus in the middle of the ruined church. He was running his fingers over the slimy weather-worn letters carved into the top, his foot resting on the rusted metal railing that surrounded it.

"Donahue," he told Wade.

There was no roof. The two gable ends of the church stood up like trowel blades thrust out of the ground, moss-covered and wet, and one of the long walls had buckled out and fallen to a pile of stones. The floor was a thick lumpy carpet of grass, or moss, shot through with spikes of dead flowers. From here he could look out over a half-buried graveyard, a confusion of fallen headstones and shrubs and mounds of dead limp grass. Trust that crazy Becker to be drawn to a place like this.

"Donahue," Wade said. "Does that mean I've got to believe everything I've ever heard about Keneally? A grave labelled Donahue?" He sat on a pile of stones and laced his own fingers together. It was as good a place as any to rest.

"The reason most people at home would find Maggie Kyle less interesting than Keneally," Becker said, "is they think they know how to handle her, what slot to store her in, so she can't cause them any trouble; but they don't have any idea what to do with Keneally. As long as he was out there, unreckoned with, unlabelled, he was a fascination and a threat. You couldn't be sure how much reality to grant him. Evil is always like that. Even after it's destroyed itself right in front of your face, you still aren't sure if it was something to be scared of or not."

Mutter away, Wade thought. You could never understand what Becker was getting at. Instead of listening, he became more interested in the mist, which was pulling back now, as it probably did every day about this time. At first it seemed to be merely thinning out, diluting in the air, but soon the space around the church was clear of it and he could watch the ceiling slowly rise, slide back up that slope, peeling back over minutes — perhaps half an hour—past fields and stones and farmhouses and barns, up steeper slopes of ridged mountainside to the top, which was a dark gentle arc across the sky, and then above that too to sit, like a lid, over the valley. Everything seemed to have moved closer, gleaming wet. Bushes along the lanes were blooming yellow flowers. Cattle, a handful of black and white cows, grazed in the fields above the barns. They'd been there all along, unseen, silent.

"Did you see that happen?" Becker said to Maggie when they got back down to the car. "Did you see that stuff roll back? Everything looks different now."

"But not much better," Wade said. "It's still the bleakest-looking place I've ever seen."

Becker looked frantic, as if he just couldn't stand that they were unable to see whatever it was that he wanted them to see. "It's all gone back. There isn't anything here that wasn't here before, before the people came. The stones have been reorganized a bit into shapes but nothing new that was added has remained. There's beauty in that. These fences will fall down some day, the world will grow right up through the ruined houses. It's alive, underneath everything it's *alive.*"

"Stones and moss and scrubby bush," Maggie said.

"But green," Becker said. "A blinding green."

"Green or bloody red," Wade said, "what difference does it make? Let's get back on that road, get out of here. If we're lucky the engine may not have rusted up. If we're luckier still the road going back will seem shorter and straighter than coming down was."

There was nothing in Maggie's face to make him think she'd been impressed by anything they'd seen, there was nothing to indicate she wasn't as determined as ever to be miserable. She didn't even look back up the mountain as they drove down the slope to the valley and then along the curved depression of the valley, on the narrow greenish road going north.

When they had to admit, eventually, that they were lost, when every narrow road they tried only got narrower and eventually died out somewhere in a bog or linked up with another apparently aimless road that made no sense, she was in danger of getting crankier even than before, and could hardly bring herself to be civil to Wade when he stopped to ask for help from a woman sitting in the grass with her back against the hedge, smoking a cigarette. And when the woman, who quickly squashed her cigarette and ran fingers over the perfect white braids on the top of her head, had to admit—her enormous blue eyes anxious at her own inadequacy — that the way back to the main road was too complicated for simple directions and insisted they come into her house where her husband would help them, Maggie only snorted and looked the other way.

But she showed signs of thawing, inside the little house, when the woman rammed bricks of turf down into the firebox of the kitchen stove and made them a cup of tea, and when the husband, an eager toothless Kerryman who told them, in a swinging tipped-up musical accent filtered through a low gargling voice, of a lifetime they'd spent in a dozen different parts of Ireland, as drapers and as farmers, and of the dozen children they'd watched go off into the world to be nurses and engineers and teachers, all over the country and in England and even as far away as India. By the time they got back out into the car again, an hour later, heads spinning with the repeated directions, loaded down with fresh milk and potatoes and cabbages for Mrs. O'Sullivan to serve them at their tea, and sent on their way with a chorus of *God blesses* and *Come agains*, Wade was sure that something in Maggie was beginning to change at last, like the working of yeast. Her single familiar hoot of pleasure when they discovered they'd been only a mile or less from the main road all along, pleased him so much he burst immediately into his own laughter and forgot, once again, to drive on the left side of the road.

2

"Shouldn't we be doing this in bare feet?" Maggie said. "Shouldn't our feet be bleeding?"

She got all the answer she expected from Wade, a growl. She talked him into parking the car below in the village, in front of a garage where a couple of youths were pulling an engine apart, and though he'd done what she asked, it was only—he said—to let her find out for herself how foolish she was. Going up past the little shops, and the houses where women behind curtains watched them pass by, he refused to talk. But when they stopped by the church and saw, high at the top of the hill, the reflected light from what could only be a high flat stone, he said, "If those people knew what you were up to, they'd laugh their heads off. That thing could be a mile away, and all uphill."

"Then stay behind," she said. "Sit in the car, or go in the pub and drink something. I'm going up."

Becker rushed on ahead, his big overcoat catching at the top of his boots, his flat cap rolling with his gait. He could imagine it better, he said, if he was alone.

The sun was shining, just as Mrs. O'Sullivan had promised, though this late in the day it was on the verge of disappearing for the night behind the hills at their back. "We have long evenings, here in Ireland," Mrs. O'Sullivan said, at tea, "and you may discover that our evenings are often the best part of the day."

But she hadn't, for all her friendliness, been easy about the ashes, or the trip to the stone circle.

"You'll not find it," she'd repeated. "I know that village well, and no one's ever mentioned the stones. They won't be able to tell you."

She'd been right, too, about that. The boys at the garage had only looked at each other and shrugged. A man stepping out of the bar said Yes, he'd heard of the stones, there'd been people searching for them years ago, but he'd never seen them himself, and couldn't be sure which road they ought to take. A short fat woman with a brilliant red face cocked her head like a chicken to listen to the man, then gasped air to add her own opinion. "You can't tell a t'ing by them signs," she said, and chuckled. "The Borde Failte people make them in their factories, in Dublin or in Cork, and put them in the ground whenever the urge comes upon them."

But Maggie, while the woman spoke, had turned and looked up the only road that led uphill. Beyond fields and farms and clumps of bush, on the clean flat top of the mountain slope, something tall reflected sunlight. "Thank you," she said, "we'll try this road, anyway, and see where it takes us to."

"Where it'll take you to," said Wade, "is into bed for a week, with aching legs and blistered feet. You're a fool, Maggie Kyle, to try it."

How many times, she told him, had they laughed at the American tourists who were content to see the Island from the windows of their cars, or campers, flying sixty miles an hour up the highway. So let's not do the same, she said, let's take it slow, let's *feel* it.

"Feel it," he said, and looked away.

"They know the stones are there," she said. "They see them every day, from their own windows and from the street, but they don't want to share them. They were hoping we'd just go away."

"A good idea," he said. "They can't imagine a good reason for going up, and neither can I."

"But you'll come, anyway," she said, "to see what you can do to spoil it."

The road, to avoid the steep grade, cut sideways across the hill, rising slowly along the bottom of a large field. A man on the lower side, pretending to cut back the fuchsia hedge around his gateway, stood watching them. He grinned, when they greeted him, and scratched at the fly of his pants, which was held together by a large safety pin. "A fine day," he said, though he looked as if he had his doubts. "'Tis, yes. A fine day altogether when you think about it." Limbs dropped from the snick of his shears, then were gathered into his arms.

When the road divided, the strip of pavement splitting into two narrower strips, they turned onto the one that headed directly uphill, a steep climbing grade, where Becker had already gone on ahead of them. It went up straight for what looked like a quarter mile, between two high rows of bleeding fuchsias. A tunnel, nearly, with Becker burrowing on ahead, his coat flapping.

But nothing could hold her back now. Maggie Kyle going up was a force to reckon with, she could feel it in her legs. Those long legs stroked a rhythm beneath her, carried her up. If she had a voice, if she could sing, she'd fill this tunnel full of echoes. Becker ahead was singing his forest song, his rather song, she could hear shreds of it floating back. But Maggie Kyle could better that, she could out-rather him, if she only had a voice, if she knew the words to what she meant.

The ashes, swinging in her bag, brushed back and forth across her thigh.

"You walk," Wade said, "as if there are broken bodies dropping off behind that you want to get away from. Slow down or mine will be next."

"Shedding," she said.

"What?"

"But not you," she said. "It's not you I want to shed."

She slowed down, for his longer but lazier legs. They could climb poles, they could carry him straight up a fake spar tree, to ring bells, but they balked at bell-less slopes.

"Tell me," she said, "why you came."

"I don't know," he said. "You asked me to."

"No, tell me the truth."

"To see you make a fool of yourself? Or to be there when you fail."

"You'll have to try harder than that. I believe it's fear, you've dragged along after me out of fear, and a little bit of hope."

"The truth of it is," he said, "I'm as foolish as you are."

"But you hadn't the courage to let it show."

"Don't understand me, Maggie. I'll be damned if I'll ever let you understand me."

Though his grin, returning, didn't forbid her from trying.

At the end of the long straight stretch, the road turned, and they were faced with a steeper grade still, through leafy trees instead of shrubs. It demanded to be climbed in silence. They moved up, side by side, putting all their effort into their legs, whose muscles protested at every step. After the next turn they passed a farmer's gate, a driveway leading down to house and sheds and tractor and standing cows. A dog looked up, suddenly, from his paws, and watched them pass. The road, damp now and pitted with potholes, coated with washed-down mud, twisted through low-hanging branches, nearly level, then turned suddenly for the long last steepest climb of all, along the face of the bare hill. Edges of pavement, broken away, were half buried in mud, or sat in caught brown puddles. Becker, far ahead, nearly to the top, took one step, rested, took another step, rested. He turned, looked back down on them, raised a slow hand in greeting, or benediction. He was not singing now.

"To do this every night after supper," Maggie said, "would be a constant reminder that you're really alive. Every muscle knows you're alive."

But only for the week it would take to kill you," Wade said. Laughing, he took her hand. From here, the farm below seemed less than real, the village a cluster of toy buildings.

"Don't look," Maggie said, "not yet. Just keep climbing. Save the view till the end."

The road ahead of her feet was enough to look at. Grey cracked pavement, rising up, a steep artificial strip of tarmac laid against the face of the hill. Climbing stairs would have been easier. They grunted and sweated the last hundred yards, legs almost numb, having given up their protests as a futile thing, hands slippery in one another.

"When we get there," Wade said, "I only want to lie down." Panting, he sounded ready to do it now, and here, on the clumps of sod and stone along the side of the road.

The road reached the top at last, and levelled out suddenly to go lolloping off across miles and miles of lumpy green plateau, winding and rolling and dipping off as if wild with freedom after that climb.

"There it is," Maggie said. "What we came for."

To her left, on a flat apron of land at the very edge of the plateau, the stone they'd seen from below stood up high behind a ring of ragged brush. That single stone was all she could see from here, but when she moved ahead a step a second one beside it appeared, a little shorter. Both of them were no thicker than a wall, or a heavy door, but as wide, perhaps, as this road.

Becker, standing on the roadway, grinned. He might have been playing host. He'd buttoned up his coat against the wind which,

Maggie discovered, soon chilled the sweat she'd worked up, dried it off, and burrowed deep for bone.

"But we're not there yet," she said, and leapt the shallow ditch. A wire fence, pushed down into vines and stones and mud, was easily stepped over. She set out across the spongy ground. Heather and moss and grasses, it felt like the uncertain edges of swamp at home, where cows' footprints sink deep and fill up with mud.

She was as far as the ring of brush—another ditch to jump, and this hedge to push through — before she realized that she was alone. Becker and Wade were a hundred yards behind her, sitting on a bank beside the road.

"Go alone," Wade called. "We'll come later, when we're rested."

"Come on," she said. "You can rest here, at the stones. Come look at these things!"

"Go ahead," Becker said. "This part you should do alone."

She would rather have huddled together with them, against the wind. It had found rare corners in her, and frozen them, it had identified her skeleton for her, head to foot, a brittle rack of icy twigs, separate from flesh and colder than flesh could ever be. But she went ahead, anyway, into the grassy circle, huddled into herself, to get it over with. Had she made all that climb, after all, only to be chased back down by wind?

Behind the two giant upright slabs she walked past an oval bed of ordinary whitish stones, a deflated rock pile, she thought, fallen in on itself. Puckered in the centre. It looked pitiful, as if it had been something else once and been reduced to this. But there was nothing pitiful, or pitying, in the stone circle itself, if four big blocks of rock could be said to form a circle. They were closer together than she'd expected, there was only room between them for muddy cow trails to cross, but they looked as if they'd grown up, four large blunted teeth, from beneath the earth, and as if their roots went down for miles. A small black sign nearby, on a metal rod, said this was a national monument, and something else, then repeated it all in Irish. It gave nothing away beyond that, no hints, no clues to the magic. Only a plea to respect the place, to leave it alone. The tallest stone, burning up sunlight, made a mockery of that request. What could anyone *do* to it? How could you help but leave it alone? How could you not suspect magic here, somewhere, even if it was only in the wind?

Or in the immensity of the vision they called up, of the men who planted them here, for whatever their reasons, on this edge of the world's top, where they could worship their gods without losing sight of an enemy's approach.

But if there was magic here it wasn't in the stones, it was in the command they had of the earth, which fell away below them and ringed them round as far as she could see. *Dominion* was the word that nagged to be said. Dominion over the sun, even, whose fire had already sunk beneath the hills but whose rays like horizontal bands of light streaked out of cloud to cross the valley and find themselves absorbed in stone. Absorbed and then thrown out again, against themselves.

It was too immense to be experienced alone, without crying, or mistaking the cold for fear. She called to the men.

The view from this edge was too wide to be taken in all at once, it was like seeing the whole world laid out and not knowing where to look. Ocean and mountains and valleys and church spires and roads and patchwork farms and animals and moving cars. To the right, to the north, hills like giant blue and purple domes pushed against each other, folded and fell, crowded across the top end of the valley. Down the valley, which was a long sharp gash slanting like a pried-open chute to the sea, the silver road ran loose and lazy, disappearing behind clumps of trees, swinging up around farms and their little white houses, twisting along the hedges, nipping past grey ruins of houses and one crumbling tower of a castle. Along the opposite slope, farms climbed up as high as they dared, laid their green and blue and yellow fields, framed by darker ruffled hedges, right up nearly vertical and then stopped so that the rest of the hill, a wide expanse, was only a dark green patchy dome freckled with sheep.

"And down there, those are oil tankers," Maggie said. Like floating factories they sat out in the silver bay, waiting.

Becker was so excited he forgot to open his notebook. Maggie was not going to remind him of it; let him see this with his own eyes, for himself, for a change. His greedy face gorged on the view, crammed it in, stuffed, and went back for more. "Pilgrims to the valley of Jehoshaphat," he said, "reserved stones for themselves to sit on at the last judgement."

"But listen," Wade said, stepping back from the edge, "you came here for a reason."

"Yes," Becker said. "For Lily. The ashes, Maggie."

She had them, in her bag, but she wished now that she hadn't. To dump them over the stones, into the cow manure, made it all into some kind of game.

"Maybe we could just leave the urn here, bury it somewhere. That'd be good enough."

"Not good enough," sang out Wade Powers, who was enjoying himself at last. "You made a promise. You took money on the strength of it."

She took the long narrow cylinder out of her bag and looked at it. "I'd rather just bury it, or leave it somewhere. If we made a ceremony out of it, or something, that would be like admitting we believed the stories, the lies about him."

"No ceremonies," Becker said. "Just dump it, scatter them. By morning the rain will have washed them into the ground."

Wade's face flushed. "You can't really act as if you believe it, that his life really began in this circle, that he was thrown up out of the earth. It's just something you were silly enough to agree to."

Becker took the cylinder from Maggie's hands, the greed she'd seen at the edge of the cliff still there in his eyes. "Myth," he said, "like all the past, real or imaginary, must be acknowledged." He took the lid off. "Even if it's not believed. In fact, especially when it's not believed. When you begin to disbelieve in Keneally you can begin to believe in yourself."

Maggie turned away until he brought the cylinder back, lighter now by a few ounces, and put it into her hand. "When Hugh of Lincoln made his pilgrimage to Fécamp," he said, "he chewed off two relics from the finger of the Magdalen."

She dropped the thing into her bag, out of sight, and stepped over to feel the heat of the largest slab. "These things are real, Wade Powers," she said. "So real that no one ever knows why they're here or how they got here. Think of your bastion now and compare."

Her own mind shuddered, like a struck bell, at the possibilities. She couldn't think for long about such things, she needed something she could hang onto. Her map. It rattled and flapped in the wind, twisted away as she tried to open it.

"Maggie, what are you doing?"

"I just want to see, I want to have a look at this thing, see what all that valley is."

"Get up off the grass, put that thing away. You spend more time looking at that paper than at the real thing."

Deliberately, Wade put his foot, his shoe, in the middle of her opened-out map, covering whole counties. She stared at it, at the shoe. He had small feet for such a tall man, and shoes that seemed too flimsy, too shapeless, for him. This was like a child's shoe, plain and worn-over and scuffed, with water stains soaked into the sides, a white line like the edge of an alkali lake, like a child who has walked through puddles, playing. For a moment she wanted to touch it, to put her face down, to feel the childlike shape of it in her hands. She was tempted to brush the mud away, with her fingertips.

"I'm sorry," she said.

"Get up, Maggie. What are you saying? Get up off the wet grass."

She let him pull her up again, into the wind. His face appeared stricken. His eyes, she could see, were unable to understand.

"What's wrong?" he said. "Is there something wrong? Why are you crying?"

"I'm not crying," she said.

"There's something wrong," he said. "You *are* crying. Did I say something?"

"Yes. No. I said it. I've been saying it all along. As if I couldn't be accused in return."

"What are you saying? Maggie? ... " He looked worried. His hand touched her shoulder, fell away, then came back to rest there. "I can't follow you, Maggie. There's too much, you have too much feeling in you for me to follow, you've always had."

She brushed a finger lightly against his cheek, as if the tears she felt were *there*, to be wiped away. He continued to stare at her face, looking for answers there that she didn't have.

"This damn wind," she said, shuddering suddenly, and trying to laugh, "it makes me cold right to the bone—I half expect to see your friend Horseman sneaking around behind the stones, he had the same kind of effect on me."

"Horseman," Wade said. As if the name had a taste he was unsure of.

"You believed him, didn't you? About the buried twin."

He looked at her, both surprised and trapped.

"You hated it, but you believed him."

They looked at each other for a moment. He slipped his hand inside his jacket, to rub his chest, then pulled it out to look at it as if it had appeared, on its own, from somewhere else. Becker with his little black notebook laid open in the palm of his hand, like a gift slice of bread, or a wounded bird, came across the grass towards them.

Then Wade said, his own eyes shifting away towards the stones, "Yes, I believed him." He said it with shame, and turned to leave.

"I don't think you do," Becker said. They both turned to him in surprise. He closed the notebook by simply folding up his hand, like a teacher who had come to the end of a story he'd been reading, and knew the last line by heart: "I think you only believe part of it, the part you hate. Both of you."

Somewhere behind them, on the wind, there was a new sound. Turning, they saw far, far back across the lumpy plateau, the small black speck of a car coming towards them. It came humping over rises and falling suddenly into dips and disappearing behind rocks; it came bouncing unevenly nearer, its motor roaring un-used on downhill slopes and growling in the strain of the climbs; it came zig-zagging closer, growing bigger, moving first one way across the full width of the plateau and then, larger, moving the opposite way across; it came sprouting arms, suddenly, bare arms that waved madly from windows, and voices high and raucous, shouting, yelling, above the increasingly noisy sound of the motor; it rounded the final curve, came up the final slope, going fifty or sixty miles an hour, came yelling and screaming, waving bottles and papers, spouting steam from the grill, belching blue coiling clouds of smoke behind, slowing suddenly, screeching, at the very edge of the drop. A bottle, arcing high in the air and then down, smashed exploding against the tallest stone at the same moment the car went over suddenly, dropped over the edge, and turning, roared shooting down the first steep broken section of the road.

"My God, look," Maggie said. "Look at them go down, look how high we've come, look at how high we've come."

And high above the Strait of Georgia, in a twin-engine pontoon plane, Wade still clenched his hands against the expected plunge. The water below appeared hard and brittle, like wrinkled blue metal, stretched out to catch them all when this rickety crate flew apart, as it was bound to do sooner or later, and dropped them like spilled toys.

He felt sick. He wished they had taken a ferry this final part of the trip. If it hadn't been for Becker with his big ideas, wanting to save time, they could be safely moving across the surface of that water, like humans, instead of pretending to be birds.

Maggie glanced at him periodically. She knew how he felt, but he could see she was too excited herself to sympathize.

"Swallow," she told him, and laughed. "You can bring it up when we're landed."

And Becker was busy in his notebook again. Scribbling. It was never enough for Becker to enjoy a thing, or even to suffer this ride, he had to record it too. And still you never knew what went on behind all that bushy hair, behind those eyes. He opened only to pull in, it seemed, never to let anything out.

Nuts, Wade thought. We're all nuts.

"When we get home," he said, "all I want is a bath." And made a face. He smelled sweaty, and stale.

But she didn't hear. "What?" she said, and lost interest. She stretched her neck, to see everything out the little window. "Fishing boats," she yelled. "Sailboats."

"Does that girl know we're coming?" he said.

"What?"

He leaned closer. "That girl. That Anna. Does she know we're coming? Will she have the coffee pot on, and a deep hot bath ready that we can leap into together?"

"Who?" she said, pretending amazement, "You and Anna?"

"It's about time you had someone to scrub your back."

But he couldn't think of that now, not here. There were some images he just couldn't permit himself at this time. Though she was no help, putting her hand on his knee. He could hardly avoid a picture of Maggie Kyle stepping out of the bath, her long limbs streaming.

He knew now what it was he wanted, why he'd gone on that stupid trip.

"There were a hundred and forty-four of those little stone beehives erected along that Dingle Coast," Becker said, "by the monks."

"Oh shut up, Becker," Maggie said, and flipped his notebook shut.

"Erections?" Wade said.

He leaned his face to the glass again, to watch the midget boats below them.

There were other ways to approach the island; those big blue-and-white government ferries didn't control them all. There were plenty of people hauling bodies back and forth. Minds, of course, were less easy than bodies to drag away; they stayed, where it was safer. The ferries and planes and barges and tugs and freighters could do only so much.

And people got onto the island however they could.

Grandpa Barclay, he remembered, arrived on a barge.

After riding that freight car of pigs all the way out from the abandoned dust farm in Alberta, he crossed the strait in the same barge that carried his furniture. A forty-foot plank-built scow pulled by a little tug. He'd had to swim out to it first, he said, when it left the Vancouver pier without him. Then, cold and wet, he huddled among the mattresses and chairs, watching the mainland fade back, the continent recede; then found himself, in the rougher water of the open strait, in the midst of a school of killer whales going north. Snorting like horses they rolled forward at the surface of the water, passing within feet of the barge, their great black hides gleaming wet, their tall triangle fins arched with each surfacing like a rotating arm, or knife-blade. Eyes, he said, glared at him. White throats threatened. He had never been so scared in all his life, he told Wade, though he was assured later that he needn't have worried. Killer whales liked to put on a good show, when there was an impressed audience. The storm which came up and tossed the barge around was no help; he'd weathered storms before, though never on the sea. But it was those huge snorting bodies that frightened him the most, so much so that when the tug had pulled him close in to the island pier at last, he'd leapt out prematurely, lost his footing on the pier-edge, and fallen into the water. After all that trouble, he told Wade, how could he ever move anywhere else?

And he hadn't. He lived on that dairy farm until old age drove him in to the closest town, where he passed his time talking with the other old-timers on the sidewalk across from the Royal Bank. At his funeral, high up the hill outside the town, Wade sat in his car while all of Maggie's relatives huddled in a sudden hailstorm around the grave. The mountains across the valley remained in sunlight through it all, green and startling blue, and seemed to have moved up closer so that it was possible to see roads and gravel pits and ski runs and logging claims chiselled into the slopes so sharply that he felt he might have reached out and touched the scars. It was the only funeral Wade ever attended, except for his own father's; he couldn't see any sense in them, as a rule, unless there was something you felt you needed to say, or think about.

He had plenty to think about, now. His head would burst with it before he was through. There was a list as long as your arm, of things that had to be faced, and chewed on. But he would face them tomorrow, chew on them then, when he wasn't trapped in this flying rattle-trap and his head wasn't throbbing with pain.

What he needed, first, was that bath. A long, hot, up-to-the-shoulders bath. Even if it had to be alone. He'd be damned if he'd pay—what?—a dollar and a quarter to splash in that O'Sullivan's tub, it was too cold in that house of hers even to take his clothes off. So he was itchy, and sweaty, and he stank. He hated to get close to Maggie, in case she noticed. Wherever they went — his house or hers—the first place he was heading was the bathroom. A good hot bath, a sleep, and life could continue. But not until.

Becker wrote in his notebook, which lay open on his lap. His pulse raced, as if there were a deadline to meet, or someone to snatch the book from his hands.

Approaching the island . . .
Wade pretending to snooze. Like a lizard on a hot rock he basks in
— what? — relief? exhaustion?
A high pale colour-drained sky above us. Emily Carr clouds —
weak crinkly radiator-slats. As if the clouds have been raked away
by an unsteady hand, leaving thin furrows. Sun poised lemon over
Mount Arrowsmith. Fish boats, pleasure boats, below us like
specks of white confetti on all that wide stretch of crawling blue.
Maggie will talk the log off our tattooed pilot if he lets her. For those
flashes of white Mediterranean teeth. This might have been noth-
ing more than a weekend in Vancouver. Three crowded weeks,
looking back, can seem telescoped down to no more than that.
Aeroplane inadequate symbol for transcendence. On the contrary,
it makes you more aware than usual of your bones, and flesh.
Maggie happier. Words only nibble at reality, don't really touch it,
can't really burn through to it. Symbols not much better. If words
won't do, and symbols fail, maybe only the instinct, some kind of
spiritual sense, can come close. All we can trust. Maybe all our lives
that instinct is in us, trying to translate the fake material world we

seem to experience back into pre-Eden truth, but we learn early not to listen. Instead, we accept the swindle, eat it whole.

Learned strange lesson in Canadian history from a Cork man on a street in Skibbereen. "If Wolfe hadn't defeated Montcalm," he said, and touched two fingers on my forearm. "If Wolfe hadn't defeated Montcalm and brought the open Bible to the land, your country by now would have become as corrupt as South America."

Back to editing Lily's tapes tomorrow.

In the pretty little seaside village of Glengariff the hawkers leap out onto the road as if to strike you or your car, waving their arms, you think there must be some terrible accident ahead, around the corner. But it's only that they're competing for your business; they want to take you in their boats to the garden island of Garnish. "Boat to d'island!" "Take ye t' Garnish!" "See de flars!" In traffic lulls they fall back, talk in clusters, or lean against posts: all but one, a young man with black curly hair, a yellow shirt, a sway-back strut —he makes of it all an uninterrupted symphony. Between cars he sings ("I coulda danced all night, I coulda danced all night") he walks, he waves his arms, he struts, calling into open windows "Och, yer brakin' me harrt!" "Y'don't know what yer missin'! Could you be honeymooners now? 'Tis a great beautiful island for honeymooners." He weaves in and out among cars, caravans, buses, donkey carts, sometimes sucking in his stomach to pull back from moving traffic, never ceasing. Asked him if this wasn't a rather dangerous way to make a living. Should've known better. "It don't matter at all! The man in d'white hat, see him, dat one is our ondertaker." Like the Fahan monks in their cliff-edge beehive cells and the drivers of the black Morrises and nearly everyone else on that rainy green island, he seems eager to be ushered as hastily as possible into another world. A contrast to the people on this island ahead of us, who think they've already reached it (and found it wanting) and won't — most of them — even imagine anything better.

Thank God no one expects me to adopt the Glengariff technique for drumming up business for the B.C. Ferries. Not needed. No real competition. And anyway, who needs more visitors?

Descending. The streets of this town, laid out by some Englishman who'd never seen the place to look as if they radiate out from the hub-centre of the harbour front. Could as easily be seen, from up here, as a web.

"When this thing falls apart," Maggie said, "think of us as you're drowning and remember we're all on your conscience."

"My plane won't fall apart," the pilot said. He spoke with an accent, a thick man with a mat of black hair on both arms, a tattoo nearly hidden in the jungle of his wrist. "This is a good nice plane. The mechanic, he is checking it over every trip. Every day I fly this distance, at least twice. It is a good nice plane."

If this was a good nice plane she'd hate to ride in a less. Strapped in beside her, Wade had the faint greenish tinge of the Irish roads about him, particularly his face. "Think of home," she said, "and solid ground," but he only turned his eyes up and rested his forehead against the shuddering window.

On her lap, the big grinning face of a wild-haired hurler with a missing tooth beamed up from the back page of the newspaper. The note from Mrs. O'Sullivan was still tucked somewhere inside.

> *Won't be home when you leave — tea at the hospital! Take the Press with you, something to read on the plane. Do come again. God bless.*
>
> *Maire O Suilleabhain*

The pilot, with his neck stretched to follow some movement on the sky far above, sucked at a tooth. "Do you live on the island?" he said.

"Yes," she said. I did, and I will again if you'll get me there safely. "And you? Do you live there, or on the mainland?"

He looked surprised that she'd asked. "I come here, to the good life, I come to this island from my own country in nineteen hundred and sixty-two. Come live with us the good life, my wife's relatives they say, where you can get a good job and take it easy."

"And you like it? You'll stay?"

He pondered this, scratched his wrist. "No, I am not staying. My wife, my children, we move across to the mainland soon. Or East. I got the good job you can see, I can take the life easy. But it is not the good place to live. If you want a repair man he say I'll come tomorrow for sure, but he don't come tomorrow or next week; when you phone him again it is Oh yes, I'll come tomorrow, for sure. Maybe he comes, maybe not. In the stores they say, Oh we sorry we don't have, and you ask when will you have and they say Who knows, maybe next month, maybe you better try someplace else. I will try someplace else, to live, the peoples here are too slow and lazy, they all want to be lying on the beach, or loafing."

"Maybe that's because they all came here for the same reason you did."

"Maybe so. But it is not good to be always waiting while some person decides if he feels like doing his job."

Wade looked at her and grinned. His sympathies were clearly not with the pilot.

"Bullshit," he mouthed silently to her.

She mock-frowned at him and turned away again, laughing.

Something in him had been released, she knew, though she couldn't be sure what. Something in him had settled, or flown.

The first, smaller islands were clearly visible now, across the front of the harbour and fitting into each other like pieces of a puzzle down to the left far out of sight. They appeared to be solid timber from here, floating forest. She had to peer hard to see any signs of civilization at all. Buildings, wharves, roads, were scattered, hidden by trees.

"My God," Maggie said. "Things look different."

"Yes," the pilot said. "And now look at your island, see what you think of it from the air."

The high snowy mountains were still a jagged wall across the world, even from up here, pale blue and scarred and fiercely steep, but the rest of the island, the nearer slopes, looked like nothing she'd seen before from the ground or on her maps. The town was only a small scar, a concentrated black growth on the edge, everything else like the little islands seemed to be timber still, a great irregular carpet of treetops, unevenly pierced by narrow inlets and cut through by lakes. The people, all the people that she knew down there with their cars and their houses and their roads, had been buried, or hidden. They crawled around presumably, beneath the bush, hardly mattering.

"It is a shock to me every day," the pilot said. "When I walk on the streets or drive on the pavement I see only the lines and things that people have tried to put there, but when I get up here, in my plane, I see the real island. It is there, still, all the time growing up through."

"It must've looked like this when Captain Cook arrived, it's hardly changed."

The pilot laughed. "Cook did not see it from a plane, but yes, yes, you are right, it hasn't changed. That's what real is, that's what true is, it can be hid but it can't be changed."

3

It didn't take Maggie long to announce her intention. The minute she saw the Bug Wagon parked down the street from the Coal-Tyee Hotel she told them: she wasn't going home. They had walked all the way down to the old van, across the street from the little harbour-side park, before Wade and Becker realized that she meant what she said. They could do whatever they wanted, she told them, but don't expect her to go back to the Revelations Trailer Park, or that House. Ever.

Wade dropped his suitcase. "Don't be ridiculous," he said, but with more weariness than command. When he was as tired as this, and still throbbing, you could threaten to slice your own throat and he'd only hope you would do it quietly or wait until morning.

Becker, of course, was alarmed. She had surprised him while he was congratulating himself on the success of the whole crazy trip.

The late-afternoon traffic had slowed down, bumper to bumper, to move through this part of the town: cars, campers, motorcycles, station wagons, buses, crept along the layer of blacktop that had been laid out over the cobblestones, past the jumbled succession of rejuvenated old buildings an insurance office, a body-repair shop, the big hotel with its modern ground-floor face and its nineteenth-century top storeys, the plain grey cement post office. Drivers, impatient passengers, stared ahead. Maggie gave them all they deserved, a quick glance.

"I'll pay for your taxi, if you want, but I'm not going back. I've still got a long way to go tonight." And if the look on her face didn't convince, there was the mean eye, beside her, of the bug that refused to die.

"You're being stupid," Wade said. "And childish. And selfish. Damn it, Maggie, you make me mad sometimes."

But a perfect eyebrow only twitched at his words, no more than if he'd touched her. It took more than accusations to shake her kind of resolve.

"Speak to Becker," she said. "He'll understand. He engineered the whole thing. If I can trust the one instinct, after all, then I can trust the other, too."

She rammed the key into the lock, twisted, turned it both ways, unlocked and locked again. If she didn't hurry, if she didn't get out of here, they would begin to pressure her. Wade with his tired confused anger, as if she'd just wakened him out of a deep sleep. And Becker with his crestfallen eyes.

The engine, too, was in no hurry to shake itself out of its three-week rest. It whined for so long before starting and she had got herself worked up into such a fine fit of panic that when Wade threw up the hood to look inside, she hammered the horn and blasted him away. The engine caught, finally, and roared. Blue smoke curled forward and surrounded the van.

Becker, by this time, had turned away and started back towards the hotel. But Wade was not so easily shaken. Even when she'd started moving away he ran beside her, hammering on her window; when she had moved out into the street, he leapt up onto the hood in front of her.

She stopped. "I don't care if you take me home or not," he shouted through the glass, "I'm going with you anyway."

So she let him inside, and warned him that she was in no mood for talking, or listening, and he told her he had no energy left for either and only wanted to know where she was headed. If it was going to be a long way, he said, he would sleep. If it was a short distance, he'd try to keep awake.

"But you're crazy, Maggie," he added, and slid down to sit on his back. "You're crazy as a loon." He put his knees up on the dashboard, and dropped his head down onto his folded arms.

They drove north, mostly north, for more than two hours. They moved slowly at first, out of town; down around the highrise apartment block and across the bridge and out past the string of service stations and take-out restaurants and motels that stood where until recently there had been the high old houses and flower gardens of the town's pioneers. They did not glance at the road that headed downhill to circle the bay and then go twisting out past the Revelations Trailer Park. They did not glance, either, off to the left where the hospital could be imagined if not seen behind houses and a few taller trees, nor did they look at the street that led off to the old folks' home. Faster now, on a widened highway, they passed a long series of sprawled-out new-car lots and the long wall of wrecked cars piled ten high, and passed between the two sky-reflecting lakes. Faster still, the hood flapping and shuddering, the tires whining, they roared up through roadside stands of timber and gouged-out subdivisions and trailer sales, out into country, and farms, then dipped down to follow the edge of the strait, a thumbprint bay, where the broken barnacled posts and piles of rubble from an abandoned sawmill lay in the beach gravel and the lace froth of the water's edge, passed a long line of freight cars thundering south on the tracks, and swelled up again to the top of a hill to snake through a village where a woman in a blue-flowered dress stopped walking on the shoulder to watch them go by. In the mirror Maggie saw her turn, a thick woman with her hair in rollers, to waddle stiffly away on her short white legs.

North. She needed no maps for this journey. They sped uphill again, shuddering. North had always seemed uphill. A few leaves were turning, just beginning to turn, it was October. But there'd been no frost, even the sumacs in someone's garden hadn't got any of their redness yet. And alders were nearly as green as the spring. Clumps of pampas grass thrust giant white feathers at the sky, and had no notion yet of the rain that would clot them, or the snow that would eventually bring them down. The Bug Wagon whined north, crossed the tracks, slowed down through the resort village where late-season tourists were coming up off a windy beach to wander through the little stores, or to dine in the big old-fashioned hotel below the road. Maggie slammed on the brakes at the stop light, revved the motor while she waited for it to change colour, then leapt ahead. She was a good driver, she could drive anything; Danny Holland had taught her, in a Kenworth truck, and told her she was a natural, she could drive anything they could make. With one elbow out the window, her hands gripped on the top of the wheel, she drove, had always driven, as if there were sixty tons beneath her, and fourteen wheels, and a load of logs behind. Trees, telephone poles, gate-posts blurred past. With her window open she could smell the firs, the giant firs along the road, with their long pitchy cones.

At Qualicum Beach they stopped, parked nose-in at the curb beside other cars, and went inside a tiny restaurant for coffee. Through the windows they watched children, fishermen, old ladies with dogs, walk out across the wide level expanse of white sand. Most were in summer clothes, but with jackets against the chill. It was evening, and the shadow of the hill across the road and the long-spiked shades of the trees had crept far out on the sand. By the time they had got out onto the road again and on past Wade's Fort, and up into the high dry pine country, snaking back and forth across the tracks, and slowed down through a settlement of houses and service station and general store and big community hall surrounded by cars, the sun had gone down behind the mountains completely, and what had been green was now bluish, the high scars of logging had faded, the snow peaks were pink. At this time of day you couldn't pretend it was still summer. In all that way they had passed only one pair of hitch-hikers, two boys, where in summer there would have been hundreds along the gravel, sitting or crouched or even lying down, heading for the west coast and the freedom they expected to find there.

Maggie Kyle rolled up the window, pushed her foot to the floor, and mentally ticked off the landmarks as they flew by: Swiss chalet. Goat pens. Snag swamp. Oyster beds. Log-booming ground. Ferry to Denman. On the left, the old false-fronted store where the Flying Dutchman was captured after shooting a policeman, empty and boarded up with scraps of plywood, its broken dusty windows giving back only a dim reflection of the car flashing by. On the right, the black dead-end snout of the abandoned coal-loading wharf, which rose gently on a long ramp of dirty slag and died suddenly, above the beach, like a changed intention. Oh, she was getting into home territory now, or closer, something in her could burst into song. Sharp turn, in the town, down across the bridge, along the river, uphill past the cemetery, the golf-course, the narrow farms, the big old weather-blackened barn of Grampa Barclay's dairy. She braked, farther on, and turned off the highway, followed a narrow paved road twisting back towards the mountains, through farms and timber and abandoned logging company town, crossed the river and burrowed deep through second-growth fir and cedar swamps, right back inland on loose washboard gravel, turned suddenly and again crossed a river, this time on a high bridge without railings where the planks thumped and shuddered beneath them. The light was faint now, she flicked on the headlights. Something was tightening up in her chest. The road straightened out, and cut through dusty isolated farms with old car bodies and junk in the yards, past the wired-shut gate of the Jimmy Jimmy Arts and Crafts Commune, past the high water tower to the final bleached-out tiny shake house in a dead orchard.

Maggie pulled up in front of the sagging picket fence and yanked on her hand brake.

"What the hell?" Wade said, straining. He knew the house, but his eyes fighting up out of sleep refused to believe. "What are we doing here?"

"This is my house still," she said. "I still own it, it's mine."

"It's a shack," he said. "It's a dump, a pile of junk."

It was nearly white, in that orchard of black gnarled apple trees and wild sprung-up alder — the dirty white of weathered bone. She'd forgotten it was only a plain square box like that, up on short posts, with a painted pyramid roof which was moss-slimy and dark, and that it had a sagged-forward little porch roof on the centred front door. It looked like a joke, or something a kid might have drawn. The metal chimney pipe was still standing, though bent, and both of the narrow front windows were unbroken, which was a wonder, but someone had torn her Keep Off sign from the clothesline post and a few of the front wall shakes were missing — black patches in all that white, like missing teeth. Maggie Kyle sighed, uncertain what to do next; she didn't really want to stop looking, as it got darker around, and the thick stand of trees at the back faded out altogether into a solid wall of black. She'd had four kids in that house, once, though she hadn't kept any of them for long. Four kids and God knew how many men and a husband, for a while.

"It looks to me like the whole thing'd fall on your head if you ever tried to open the door," Wade said.

But as if to prove him wrong, the two windows suddenly filled with light, a pale light which she mistook for a moment for the reflection of headlights, perhaps, coming from some car behind her. But it was not a reflection, it threw patches of light out onto the ground, and a tree, and drew her attention to a high wheeled contraption that had no business at all being there.

"What's that?" Maggie said, though she knew already what it was.

Wade, squinting at shadows, took a moment to see. Then he started to laugh. He threw his head back against the seat and laughed until the van rocked. "That's Madmother Thomas's manure-spreader," he said, and laughed again. "That crazy old biddy is living in there!"

Maggie got out of the van, leapt over the fallen gate, pushed her way through the grass that had grown up between the slats of the boardwalk, and hammered on the door. She wouldn't get mad, she promised herself, she wouldn't act like a bitch, though she was tempted. She'd find out, that was all, and make arrangements to send the old bag away and see what had to be done to the house.

But it wasn't Madmother Thomas who opened the door. It was a girl, a young woman of eighteen or nineteen, with a frizzed-out halo of blonde hair.

"Who the hell are you?" Maggie said.

It was the shock.

The girl looked frightened; her hands fluttered at her chin, and fell again to her skirt, where they held on. She wore round wire-rim glasses and a long skirt, the kind of thing Anna Sterner wore, which could have been found in her grandmother's trunk. Behind her, a hissing coal-oil lamp hung from a hook in the middle of the ceiling.

"This is my house," Maggie said, trying not to sound rude. The girl was obviously scared, and too small to be much of a threat. "I didn't expect anyone to be here."

The girl stepped back. "Come in," she said. "Please come in." Behind the glasses her blue eyes were too large, stary, as if she'd practised holding them wide like that, to look pleasant. There were pimples, Maggie saw, on her chin.

And before the door had closed Wade, too, had come in. He looked around the little room and threw himself into a chair. His long legs, splayed out, reached nearly across to the opposite wall. Maggie had forgotten how small this place was, like a playhouse for kids. After what she was used to, she'd bang into walls here every time she turned around.

"We've been here for a year now," the girl said. "We didn't know, that is, nobody told us there was an owner, or that anyone would care." Her voice, barely above a whisper, was a thin childlike sound. Too eager, Maggie thought, too desperate to please, to be nice.

"We?" Maybe this was one of those hippie dives, crawling with weirdos.

The girl stood, careful not to bang her head on the lamp, but made it clear that she wanted Maggie to sit in the only other chair in the little room. Two auction-sale chairs, a cheap formica table on a braided rug. They'd even slapped new wallpaper over the old, or Maggie guessed they had, she couldn't remember white brick and ivy, it wasn't her taste even then. There was a little wood heater hooked up to the chimney, over in the corner. It wasn't any heater she remembered; hers had been brown, and sat on an asbestos pad. She didn't want to think of all the entertaining she'd done in this room.

"Well, you've got it comfortable enough anyway. Warm." Though it smelled; they wouldn't do much about the sour damp smell of the rotten boards, like pee, and old apples.

Sitting down made her feel at a disadvantage, with that little Miss Innocence standing up there by the light. Maggie stood again, climbed over Wade's legs, and poked her nose into the kitchen. As bare, nearly, but there were signs that someone was living here. Jars on the counter, and dirty dishes, a coffee pot on the stove. Her old stove, rusted up, they hadn't even polished the rust off it. There was no one else in the house, though, as far as she could see.

The girl insisted that they have coffee, now that they were here. She was just going to have some herself, she said, it was already made. She brought out old chipped mugs for them all, and leaned back against the wall, sipping like a bird at her own. "Oh," she said, suddenly, remembering something, and apologetically handed a can of cookies around, flustered, rattling it at them like a beggar's collection tin.

"You're barefoot," Maggie said. She wished immediately that she hadn't, but the sudden sight of those toes, peeking out from the skirt, alarmed her. Bare feet on *this* floor, on this old cracked worn-thin linoleum. She could remember her father laying it out, it must be twenty-five years old, and cheap. No one ever walked barefoot on it, not with the drafts you could get from under the house. She'd never put any of her kids down to crawl, the wind from under the door was enough by itself to give them pneumonia.

"Yes," the girl said, almost a giggle, and looked down. The toes disappeared. "My name is Carrie?" she said, a question, as if she'd be willing to take it back, change it, if Maggie objected.

Wade pulled in his legs, sat up. "Well what do you do here, what kind of place is this to live? Where are your parents?" He sounded like a stern uncle.

"This is my house," Maggie said. Why did she feel so old? And big. This girl was as young as Forbes, another generation. And she looked scared again; she was hiding here, or expecting to be hauled away.

When the back door squealed open the girl went into the kitchen and, after a moment or two of whispering, came back into the front room with a boy by her side. He was in bib overalls and boots and had frizzled hair much like the girl's, and looked tremendously pleased — like an old man — to find company waiting for him. He shook Maggie's hand, his head nodding, grinning; then he shook Wade's hand and moved back to put his arm around the girl.

"This is Craig," the girl said.

Craig was more talkative than the girl. Whatever she'd whispered to him in the kitchen hadn't bothered him a bit, he was eager to play host. He'd been out in the garden behind, he said, digging carrots and spuds for tomorrow. It was great soil, he said, and he'd grown a marvellous garden, he would give them some vegetables to take home with them. Organically grown, there was no chemical fertilizer on these. The two of them had moved up here from Victoria, he told them, he had brothers and sisters spread all over the place, with jobs, and one who'd become an engineer and was building bridges in Ceylon or somewhere and a sister who was a nurse on the mainland. He and Carrie didn't plan on a family that big, he said, though they wanted children, some day, if they could afford it, they both loved children. And gardening; he intended to have that whole backyard in garden next year if he could, he'd never run into such wonderful soil before, there was no end to the things he could grow. Some day he would have a truck, and haul produce into town to sell, or to a farmer's market somewhere, maybe they could make a living that way. We don't want a lot, he said, only enough to get by.

Before Maggie or Wade could say anything to stop him he'd brought carrots in from the kitchen, to show them how large, and potatoes as big as his fist, and bigger. Then he'd dragged a box of them in, and set it by the door. They could take it, he said, when they left. Just wait and see how good they were, they'd be surprised you could grow things that tasty in here, where you didn't expect decent soil.

But they're only children, Maggie thought. They're hardly more than kids. And so sure, so goddam sure. There was not a flicker of doubt, or hesitation, on that boy's face. He was young enough to believe you could drive like a bulldozer straight for your goal and there wasn't anything could stop you, or knock you off the shortest route.

"I came here," Maggie said, "because ... " She couldn't say the rest, it would sound so foolish. "But you don't seem to understand that the house belongs to me. It was my father's. I lived here for years."

Though she couldn't be sure, now, that it was really the same place at all. Or even the same world she'd lived in then.

Whatever the girl had whispered in the kitchen had apparently not got through to the boy. His face fell, flushed. Obviously he felt like a fool. He looked at the girl, and at Wade, who was no help, who said, "It's the truth, I'm afraid. This lady not only owns the place, I believe she intends to throw you out on your ear. Or move in with you." The prospect of either one apparently struck him as funny and he aimed a good laugh at the ceiling. "She's strong as an ox," he said, "and would be a good help with a hoe."

"Mother of God," the boy said, softly, and went back into the kitchen. When he came out, he was drinking a glass of water. "Is this a joke?" he said. He looked at the girl, who turned away and went to the window. "I mean, Christ, is this some kind of rotten joke? What is it? Do you mean it?" There were beads of water across his upper lip. His eyes were wet. "Are you shitting me or what?"

"That was Madmother Thomas's rig outside," Maggie said. "Where is she?"

The boy looked at the girl, suddenly relieved. "Then it was a joke," he said. "You're a relative, or something?"

Maggie hooted. "Of hers? Hell no, though I might as well be I suppose, by the looks of things. That old crow isn't related to anyone. Where's she gone? She's never very far from her wagon.''

"She's sick,'' the girl said.

The boy ducked his head, his gaze somewhere down around the toes of his boots. He explained.

"We brought her in here, oh, it must've been a month ago. Weak, and wheezing. I found her out in the woods, and brought her in. She's been in here ever since. A bit stronger, but too weak to get out. We had the doctor out once and he said there was nothing serious, but she needed rest and warmth.''

"She's back there now?''

"She is.''

"Well let me see her.''

But the boy stood in the doorway, blocking it. "I'm sorry,'' he said. "But I'm not going to let you go back there.''

He nodded to the girl, who slipped under his arm and disappeared through the door off the kitchen. When she came back she was smiling modestly, almost as if she were pleased with herself. "Yes,'' she said. "She's awake. She said Maggie Kyle's hoot is enough to wake the dead. And she told me, she said tell that woman to haul ass in here before I get up off this bed and get her myself.''

The boy took the lantern in to hang on the doorjamb so they could see in the back bedroom. The old woman's wild white hair had disappeared against the pillow, there was only the little round face, with those eyes, and that tongue that flickered pink on her lips.

"You old crow!'' Maggie said. "Hiding out here, of all places!'' In this dump, she nearly added. In this dark, damp, rotten old box of a room.

"I knowed you would come,'' she said, grinning. "Eventually. But you sure took your sweet time about it.''

"We came the long way,'' Maggie said, and swung Wade a look. "They got me side-tracked a bit, by a few thousand miles. But you — what are you doing here? What's the matter with you?''

The little tongue flickered. "The matter with me?'' The two tiny hands gathered blankets to her throat and held on, as if they'd threatened to drag her out of that bed. "There's never been anything the matter with me, except in this screwy old head.'' The blankets, pulled up from the foot of the bed, revealed her little black rubbers with the fur trim, which peeked out, their sharp pointy toes side by side aimed at the ceiling. "Gawd, ain't it awful!" she said.

"What? What's awful?" The smell was awful, that was one thing, the strong stink of pee, and old-lady smells. Feet, those rubbers. Was she determined to die with her boots on? Or only prepared to escape?

The old woman slid a look at the eavesdroppers, motioned Maggie closer. "What's awful is this: I'd be out there still, on the road, living the only kind of life that I'm used to, if I hadn't listened to nature."

"What?" What had nature to do with this place? With this cold narrow room, with these V-jointed walls?

"Headed into the bush, heeding the call—in a hurry too, I was running—and fell off a windfall down into a big root-hole and couldn't get out. This young man found me, two days later, and brought me in. Craig." She looked at the boy and winked. "But it'll take more than a hole to finish me off, I'll be out of here in no time at all."

She looked so pleased with herself, as if she was glad this had happened so that she could prove there was nothing could hold her down for long.

"My old lady taught me something when I was a kid, before they dragged us back to that colony. Whenever they kick you in the teeth, she said, just tell them *pog mahone*, it'll make you feel better, especially if you know they don't understand it. And you know, in all my life of being kicked around I've never yet said it to anyone? It's a comfort just knowing I've got it." Her eyes checked again, to warn of the eavesdroppers, her voice dropped to a whisper. "Come here." She put her hands on either side of Maggie's face and pulled her close. "*Pog mahone*," she said, and rolled her eyes. "Means kiss my arse." She pursed her lips at the joke, shook with the laughter that rumbled through her, and spread her hands in a gesture of total innocence, or helplessness.

"But indoors?" Maggie said. "It must drive you crazy surrounded by walls."

"Well, I'll tell you Maggie." Her hand dismissed the others, motioned them away. "The thought just came to me all of a sudden one day *What does it matter? What does it matter if I look for the place or not?* and once I'd thought of it I couldn't shake it. I mean, think, suppose those old Wise Men that followed that star,

remember? Suppose one day it was this star and the next day that
star? How long do you figure they'd stick at it? As long as I have?"

Maggie looked at the eyes. They were screwed up, pleased with
their cleverness. Ready to dance.

"I don't know," she said. "I wouldn't be surprised if they'd kept
it up all their lives. Some people, once they get an idea stuck in
their thick heads ... "

"Ha!" The old woman's hands clapped together, then grabbed
Maggie again and pulled her close. "That's what I thought to
myself. And as soon as I can get out of this coffin I'll be on my way.
Not that I'm complaining," she said, and held out a hand to hold
off hurt from the couple in the doorway. "These two've been real
good. In fact everywhere I go people are good to me. And like a
fool the most I ever take from them is some water for the donkey
and a place to park my rig. I been thinking it wouldn't hurt me,
now and then, to move inside for a while with some of them, and
be comfortable, take advantage of their hospitality. There's no law
says crazy people aren't allowed to be pampered a little, now and
then."

"You get sneakier every year, old woman," Maggie said. "Why
don't you spit it out? Say what you really mean."

The tongue flickered. The eyes made a tour of the room. "Do I
need to?"

"She's been waiting for you," the boy said from the doorway.
"She told us there was someone who would come, eventually."

"I heard her tell me that," Maggie snapped. Don't push me.
Don't push me. They would run your life for you, all of them.

Even Wade, who was close, had wrapped his arms around her
from behind to breathe on her neck. "Remember the pilgrims to
the valley of Jehoshaphat," he said, and laughed. "And good old
Hugh of Lincoln with his mouth full."

She elbowed him away.

And said what had to be said.

In the car, later, she let him drive, and rested against him. It was a
black night. The headlights cut a road out of it for them, a bright
moving corridor of light laid out on the gravel ahead. There were
no lights in Manson Hed's tower, or in the old Arts and Crafts
Commune, or in any of the first farms they came to.

"I can't believe you didn't expect to find her there," Wade said.

Believe what you want, Maggie thought. The Bug Wagon smelled of fresh earth, the potatoes and carrots and beans and onions that boy had forced on her, and smelled of Wade, too, his slept-in clothes. She was tired, good lord she was tired, she couldn't remember feeling like this before.

She did not sleep, however, she thought of the young couple in her house, saying good-bye at the door, leaning into each other. Play-acting their own grandparents, it couldn't be cornier, but it was real, they were real, and what was it they'd said as she left? *Peace? Bless you?* Turned her away from her own house and saddled her with one more responsibility at the same time.

Well, she could handle it, she couldn't heal them all by herself or cancel that monster's damage alone, but she would do what she could. She closed her eyes and felt Wade's hand resting lightly in her hair, and travelled south in her mind, ahead of the van, down past the bays and the oyster leases and the log booms, down through the little settlements and the farms and the resort villages, down under timber and dark sky and occasional lights, to the House of Revelations where it hunched in her second-growth forest with a single light burning, where Becker would be waiting, by the fireplace, for their return.

Second Growth

Becker tells you this:

Believe what you want, trust me or not, this story exists indepen-
dent of both of us. Donal Keneally is dead. His story has returned to
the air where I found it, it will never belong to me, for all my
gathering and hoarding. It is more than a year since Maggie Kyle
left his ashes at the stones above Kealkill, and wept there for her
own life. It is a year since Madmother Thomas abandoned her
wagon to the rain and the weeds at the side of the road and set
herself up in the House of Revelations; it is nearly a year since
Julius Champney found the Harvest Years Home too indifferent to
his constant complaining and moved back into his little cabin in
our circle; it is half a year since Wade Powers tore down his Fort
and set out on a cross-country hitchhiking tour that would last for
three or four months while he looked for himself under bridges
and behind museums and in parks; it took nearly all of that year for
Maggie Kyle and Wade Powers to recognize what anyone with any
sense looking on must have known from the very beginning.
  This is the true story of what happened when they finally admit-
ted it.

The first Saturday in November had been a clear, cold day, without rain. At seven-fifteen when Maggie Kyle came out of the House
of Revelations, a yellow moon shone down on the strait, paving a
wide corrugated track across the water. She was alone. The others
had all gone ahead, as she'd insisted, to wait at the church. A taxi
sat idling at the bottom of the verandah steps. No Bug Wagon for
her today, she would arrive in style, for a change. She wore the

same pink dress that she'd worn to her son's wedding, though cut off this time at the knee: she did not want to look like a bride, she said, but she did want to look sexy. She was still, as she liked to insist, one hell of a gorgeous dame.

In the back seat of the taxi, with her bouquet of white chrysanthemums laid out beside her on the leather and her two white gloves laid limp and useless on her lap, she watched the faint receding edge of the strait slide past her on the left, weak waves idly licking at driftwood logs, abandoned seaweed black and shimmery on the gravel beach. The taxi shuddered up the washboard slope of her own narrow driveway, past black-leafed alders scraping against the windows, clusters of seed-cones breaking off to catch in the taxi's windshield wipers, past seedling firs along the edge pushing up to fight their way through alders, past a barn skeleton nearly buried in brush, its gable end and gaping door less than a stone's throw from the edge of the road, heavy and stark in the moonlight. Under the large painted sign across her gate the taxi stopped and the driver spoke something into his radio set and raised a finger in greeting to a carload of nuns that whizzed by. They drove slowly at first, through the rows of ugly new houses in the subdivisions that were growing up on the rest of the colony land, the stain of splashed-up mud from their unfinished yards still visible like a high-water mark on the white stucco walls, blue-and-yellow SOLD signs still nailed to the single trimmed-up fir left standing at the front of each; and farther along, the larger, lower, landscaped houses of people who could afford to build at the water's edge, where they could see from their huge plate-glass sliding windows the clusters of red and blue and yellow fishing shacks like piano boxes huddled together on the little rock islands in the bay, colourless now in moonlight but still visible. They turned sharply inland and passed a row of new houses she'd seen built up around one-room cabins which, presumably, existed still somewhere inside like the pearl's grain of sand, then passed fields and silver fence-posts and a parked large Volkswagen van with a smaller Volkswagen van welded onto its top, and dipped down to the water again where the biological station was lit up like a giant checkerboard lampshade and out in the bay a government ferry, on top of its own brightly-lit inverse reflection, moved slowly out towards the strait.

The taxi driver reported nothing especially unusual. Brides, he said, usually went to church with their fathers, it's true, but this one, it was easy to see, needed no one to give her away. A woman like that, he said, wasn't given; she gave or she didn't give but she couldn't be given. Alone in the back seat she was silent for the first part of the ride, then asked him to stop by the cemetery where she stood, for a few minutes, over a grave. "Your father?" he said, when she returned, "Your mother?" But no, she told him, it was an old woman, a very old woman, who hadn't believed in the last wedding and would not, if she knew of it, tolerate this one. Please hurry the rest of the way, she said, the kind of people she knew only fidgeted and started to sweat when they had to sit waiting in church. The taxi driver, a fat man with a neck that bulged over his collar, had a special weakness for weddings — he'd had three of his own and married off five of his daughters, crying his eyes out through all of them — and had asked his boss for permission to stay and watch this one. When he'd taken the bride to the door of the church, his arm hooked out for her to hold onto as if he were her father, too, or an older brother, when he'd delivered her to the red-faced men who waited there on the steps in their suits, he was already crying. "I've seen hundreds of brides," he said, mopping with a big white handkerchief at his eyes, "but the latest one always seems to be the most beautiful one of them all."

The ushers agreed. It was their job to escort the bride down the aisle, one on either side. But if he didn't mind, one of them said in the foyer, it would be appreciated if the taxi driver would hold back the noise of his crying, he was making it difficult for them to hear the sound of the organ. The fat man turned away and stuffed his handkerchief into his mouth long enough for the ushers to get their signal and start their long slow journey down the sloped aisle.

People, crammed into the wooden pews, stretched their necks to see Maggie Kyle; they couldn't believe it was happening. Pressed over against a wall, Danny Holland put two fingers into his mouth and blew a whistle that rang in their ears like a sudden siren; though a ripple of subdued laughter ran through the crowd in the church, the two red-faced ushers and the bride didn't miss a single beat of their organ-measured progress, nor did any of them look anywhere but straight ahead. It was the longest walk in the world, reported one of the ushers, who suffered from embarrassment whenever he thought people were looking at him, but it was worth every agonizing moment to be able to walk with a woman like Maggie Kyle, and to see the great look of rejoicing on the groom's face. Nothing could spoil an experience like that.

No, nothing could spoil it, agreed the people who sat in the front pew. They were not the closest relatives customarily found in the front rows at weddings, but simply the people who had arrived first, in a bunch, and frightened the ushers into letting them crowd down front where they could get the best view. Not even the mother of the groom, who came late, of course, in her wheelchair, and demanded in her loud hog-calling voice that they move back and clear out a space for her to park, could spoil it for them. (She had to be content, in the end, to wedge herself in front of them with her knees nudging at the back of her son's legs.) A wedding, for them, was a show, better than a movie, more exciting than any play, and the price — a Woolworths gift, wrapped and appropriately ribboned on the back seat of the car—didn't have to be paid until after, when they'd know whether it had been worth it. And a wedding where they knew everything about the bride, absolutely everything (Oh, they could tell you, there wasn't anything they couldn't tell you about Maggie Kyle, they said, her life was as easy to read as a newspaper column!), a wedding where the bride's life was their business was the most fun of all. Here she comes, they thought, pretty as a picture (some said beautiful) trying to look like a bride with *her* history. You could smell the pitch on her still, if you thought about it, you couldn't be sure she wouldn't let out one of her logger hoots in the middle of the ceremony. Up and down that front pew, on either side of the church, ran the same thought: she was still bush, for all her airs, it took more than a wedding to turn a loggers' whore into a lady. They were town people, all of them, and town weddings tended to be rather ordinary and predictable, so they never missed an opportunity to attend a country wedding where there was more chance something interesting would happen. No, nothing could spoil it, they agreed, not anything at all unless the whole thing turned out to be quite commonplace and uneventful. Not one of them so much as batted an eyelid when Cora Manson of the Tasty Bakery fainted dead on the floor, right across the aisle in front of the approaching bride, and had to be hauled up and crammed back into her seat by the sweating ushers. And they knew they were not going to be disappointed when the poor little redheaded woman fell out again, behind the bride, and stumbled back up the aisle with a pink plastic pig flapping against her chest.

When the bride and groom came out of the church, married and properly blessed and able to breathe at last, the weeping taxi driver pushed them into the back seat of his taxi, roared away spraying gravel all over the people on the church steps, and drove like a madman five or six miles up the gravel road before he could make out, through his sobs, what the bride and groom were yelling at him: that they hadn't intended riding in the taxi at all, that he was taking them in the wrong direction, and that they'd left the bride's bouquet behind on the ground in front of the church where he'd knocked it out of her hand. The poor fat man slammed on the brakes, stopped the car under a maple tree, and took the keys out of the ignition. A man in his condition, he admitted, was unfit to be driving a bride and a groom; a man as emotional as he was had no business at all behind a wheel, he was a menace on the roads; a man like himself with a heart condition, a nagging wife, and five sponging sons-in-law ought not to be working at all, especially at his time of life. He would not, he said, drive another inch. But he would, he said, hand the keys over to Wade. "This is ridiculous," said Maggie Kyle, the new Mrs. Powers. "Someone's done this on purpose, someone's buggering everything up. This is the worst wedding I've ever been to." But the taxi driver, understanding at last that he may in his eagerness have actually spoiled the wedding for the bride, was so stricken with remorse that he tossed Wade the keys, got out of the taxi, and started walking down the road in the direction of the mountains.

Everyone came to the reception, which was held in a barn-like hall, a community hall, at the back of a baseball park. Everyone came, everyone was there and waiting before the bride and groom arrived. Wade's mother was there, of course, making sure the serving girls didn't put too much wine in the glasses, and all of Wade's brothers and sisters were there, with their husbands and wives, and their children who wrestled and raced in the middle of the dance floor. They'd had to leave their businesses, their work, these brothers and sisters, in every part of the province, and there was a frantic guilty look in their eyes, but they consoled themselves by imagining that a wedding was an excuse to make business contacts and to cultivate customers. His uncles were there, talking machinery and land in the foyer; his aunts were there, talking grandchildren and recipes by the door to the kitchen. All of the Finns and all of the Mennonites and all of the descendants of the veteran settlers from Wade's home district were there, to see what kind of a bride he'd managed to catch this time, a lazy boy like him. His first wife's drunken father and thieving shifty-eyed brothers had shown up at the last minute, sliding in behind others, uneasily suspicious that they might not be welcome. All the loggers who worked with Danny Holland had flown down to see Maggie married, as had everyone who'd known her when she lived on the west coast, and everyone who'd lived near her in Hed —including the whole of the Jimmy Jimmy Arts and Crafts colony and Craig and Carrie from Maggie's shack — and all the loggers and their wives from Camp Fourteen and Wolf Lake and Boxer Inlet and Crum had driven down in their campers, which they'd rigged out like bars and had parked in a row with their back doors facing the door to the hall. Julius Champney was there, and Anna Sterner, and Madmother Thomas. People from the town had driven out. The mayors of several towns on the island, with their wives, and more than one elected MLA and several judges, lawyers, doctors, and businessmen from all up and down the island had come, though none of them knew either the bride or the groom, but because—as everyone else there suspected—they'd all lived on the Colony of Truth in their earlier years and couldn't be blamed for wanting to wish the best of luck to the colony's newest residents. Mainlanders had come across, and sat silently along the wall benches, wondering what to expect. Victoria people had driven up, and sat together near the punch bowl, with their backs to everyone else. The premier of the province, who was unable to attend, sent a representative, a little freckle-faced man who shook hands, before the evening was through, with every person in the hall, including the lieutenant-governor of an eastern province who had flown in at the last minute and had to leave for his plane as soon as the cake was cut. The Prime Minister of Canada was rumoured to be in the crowd somewhere, but the Queen of England had disappointed everyone by accepting an invitation elsewhere. A photographer from a famous magazine took a picture of Wade reading a telegram from the Irish government and inadvertently caught, in the background, Cora Manson flapping her pig in Danny Holland's face. Holland, as everyone could see when the picture was published, was not enjoying it.

During the first hour of the wedding reception people ate. Long, paper-covered wooden tables sagged under the weight of the food that had been laid out for them: bowls and bowls of potato salads and tossed salads and strange-looking salads found only in foreign cookbooks, and platters of turkey and chicken and ham and beef. Wade's eldest brother, who was in the process of changing his ranch into a tourist resort, butchered his entire herd of white-faces for the occasion and threw in four of his neighbour's hogs. Cora Manson had closed down her shop for the week preceding the wedding in order to devote her full time to baking the tons of fancy cakes and pastries and bread-rolls it would take to satisfy that hungry mob. Her swollen feet ached, and she'd put on ten more pounds from sampling her work, but it was worth all the torture, she said, when you knew at the end of it you could sit back and watch people dig in. She'd spent the day of the wedding in the hall, directing the setting out of the food, and it was her excitement over this, rather than the marriage itself, which accounted for her fainting in the church. When the bride and groom had arrived at the hall at last, and got themselves sitting down behind the big cake, and everyone else had rushed to the tables and thrown their legs over the benches and leaned into the food, she let out such a sigh of contentment and pleasure that a huge crepe-paper bell hanging from the ceiling started swaying in the force of expelled wind and dropped straight onto the pointed head of a magistrate who wore it like that for the rest of the evening. "Ring me, I'm a bell," he told everyone, and swayed his buttocks like a clapper, causing screams of laughter to surround him wherever he went.

The crowd was so large and the place settings so close together that for a while there were several skirmishes as people fought for elbow room. But the talking died down, and all movement but the movement of hands and mouths stopped as food was consumed — or inhaled, as Cora put it — and for a while the only sound was the sound of knives and forks clanking against china and the sound of a million teeth chewing. Little ladies with small stomachs and big ladies with girdle-pinched stomachs, faced with all that food, did the only thing possible: stuffed as much into their mouths as they could until it hurt, and then started filling up their purses, their pockets, and their hats, for later. Those who were incapable of eating without laying their arms out on the table and bending their heads down inches from their plates decided to wait until some of the others had finished and, hopefully, moved away. But the food was disappearing at such an alarming rate that they were forced, against all their instincts, to eat upright and rigid like everyone else.

So much food was consumed that some women were overheard saying that they didn't intend to cook a thing for their families for the rest of the month of November; so much food was consumed that it was calculated it would take four life-times on an ordinary working man's salary to pay for it; so much food was consumed that supermarkets in town, alarmed at their depleted stock, sent emergency telegrams to their mainland offices for truckloads to be sent over by Monday morning; so much food was consumed that the hospital staff, put on alert by the doctors who were attending, had extra help assigned to the emergency ward the whole night; so much food was consumed that the cost-of-living figures for the west coast were thrown out of kilter and had to be ignored for the rest of the month.

When the bowls had been emptied and filled up and emptied again, when the platters had been cleaned off over and over again, when the last crumb had been eaten from the last plate of cakes and gallons of coffee gulped down, Mrs. Annie Muldare from Upper Saltair, who sat closest to the kitchen door, exclaimed in a voice that could be heard in every corner of the hall, "I'm so full I could die!" and did. She fell face-down on her plate and expired, with an enormous burp, and nothing that was done by the internal-medicine specialist from Victoria or the throat specialist from Vancouver or the travelling foot specialist from the East could revive her. She was carried out, past rows and rows of stunned and bloated guests, who, determined not to let anything spoil a wedding, agreed that if you had to go, there were worse ways, and pushed back their benches to see what the bride and groom were doing.

"Maggie and Wade!" they shouted, "Maggie and Wade!" and clanked their spoons against their glasses until the bride and groom stood up in front of everyone and kissed. Everyone clapped, to let them know that they hadn't eaten so much or so well since they didn't know when, and to say thank you. Everyone, they agreed, was stuffed, which is what weddings were for. Everyone, that is, except Danny Holland who by some accident of fate had found himself sitting at the end of a table that ran right up against the bar and had spent the time, while people were eating, drinking the whole bowl of punch. When the bride and groom kissed, instead of clapping like the others, he pulled the starter cord on the chain saw he'd hidden under his bench, swung it up over his head, roaring and belching blue smoke, and let out a wild yell of delight. Then he turned and, before anyone realized what he was up to, cut a door-size hole in the wall, right through to the ladies' washroom. The battle that followed, it was generally agreed, was all the fault of a man named Herbie Purkis from Beaver Cove: when the hole had been cut in the wall he was upset, it seemed, that for one startled moment the whole assembled crowd was given a flashing peek at the creamy white buttock of his surprised and fumbling wife.

The second hour of the wedding, therefore, instead of speeches and dancing, was spent in what was later called the best damn brawl the island had ever seen. It was for this, more than for the food or the drink, that Maggie and Wade were to receive a flood of thank-you cards so enormous the local post-office lady would threaten to quit her job. It was for this that the first Saturday of November would be set aside, from then on, as a day of special significance: men who normally forgot their own wedding anniversaries would take their wives out to dinner on this date without ever having to be nagged at; women who had eliminated their own birthdays and grown tired of the commercialism of Christmas became misty-eyed on this date and thanked goodness they were alive; children who hated school and had to be pushed out the door every morning leapt out of bed on this date and rushed to the classroom in order to exchange memories with others who had been there. It was better, they said, than a World War II movie, though this was an exaggeration: no one at the wedding had been killed. On the other hand, it might be argued, no one in a World War II movie had ever danced the two-step with a ghost or been pounded unconscious by a short fat redheaded woman wielding a plastic pig.

The first words of the battle were Herbie Purkis's: "That's my wife!"

The second were Danny Holland's: "That's your fault, not mine! If you'd surprised her like this *before* you were married you might have had more sense!"

The first blow of the battle was struck by the red-faced wife. She stood up from the toilet, yanked up her pants and dropped her dress, stepped through the newly cut doorway, and slapped her husband's face. "Go get him!" she cried. "You coward! Go get the crummy bastard!"

The second blow of the battle was not struck by Herbie Purkis, nor by Mrs. Purkis, nor was it struck by Danny Holland whose chain saw idled at his side; it was struck by Maggie Kyle Powers, who let out one of her famous hoots, stood up on the bride's table, and threw the top layer of her cake — three feet in diameter, complete with plaster bride and groom — straight at Danny Holland's head, but missed. She began to shout out that *this* was going to be one wedding that wouldn't end in a brawl, that *she* expected everyone to act like proper society, and her *husband* and she both wanted them to have a good time without resorting to violence. But her throwing of the cake was vastly misinterpreted, and while she was making her position clear the crowd, who could not hear her, was shouting: "Atta girl Maggie!" and "Go gettem girl!" and "There's the old spirit again!" and "Christamighty, this is more like it!" If the bride could throw cake, they understood, the least they could do was throw dishes and furniture.

Danny Holland, alone, was no match for the barrage that was heaved at him. But he was not alone for long. The loggers from Camp Fourteen and Wolf Lake and Boxer Inlet and from Crum had all, luckily, brought their own power saws in their booze-filled campers, and rushed to the side of their friend, armed, with motors revving and trigger fingers itchy at the clutch. They formed a long line of ready men, weapons poised, faces eager, teeth clenched, shoulder to shoulder down the full length of the hall. Their wives lined up behind them, murder in their eyes, armed with beer bottles and purses. "Go get those sons of bitches," they snarled, and nudged their husbands forward.

The people of the town, rewarded now beyond their dreams, had no weapons handy so dramatic as chain saws, and had to resort to all they'd brought, their wits. They hurled insults, like hand grenades, which exploded in the air above the loggers' heads. They flung elaborate comparisons and dire predictions, they tossed innuendoes and shreds of gossip and unsavoury speculations about the manner of their opponents' births. They raised their prices, they cancelled appointments, they cut off supplies. They voted to a man to pressure the government into closing all roads to the north and the west, and to take positive steps to have all the unsettled island turned into a national park, and to refuse to buy lumber, paper, or cardboard boxes. They promised, especially the wives, to drop poison into every planeload of supplies flown in to the camps and to cut the brakelines of all the logging trucks. But an orchestra, hastily assembled on the stage, began to play some loud and thumping music, which, coupled with the motors from the chain saws, made it all quite laughable. When the bride's son, Forbes, began to dance with his pregnant wife in the middle of the floor, as if to say he knew there was no danger there, the people from the town saw they had a choice to make: to join the visitors at their own game and go after them with chairs and legs wrenched off tables, or to admit defeat. They chose table legs and broken beer bottles and smashed plates and ballpoint pens and shoes. When Cora Manson gave the call to attack — "Cut out their gizzards!" — they advanced.

Those guests who were uncommitted, because of their occupation or place of residence, feeling left out of the fun, now decided to join the side of the saws. They threw themselves into the midst of everything, and disappeared in a confusion of shouting and wrestling and scuffling. The visiting loggers, who discovered themselves suddenly left out of the battle, went mad and turned their weapons against the hall. They sawed tables into pieces, they cut up benches, they cut holes in the walls and carved designs on the floor, they reshaped toilet doors into deer and store-room doors into bear, they sawed the steps away from the building and cut huge elaborate air-holes in the roof. So preoccupied was everyone with the excitement of the battle that it was likely that this one little bushy man, hiding under the bar-table, was the only person to see the ghost of Donal Keneally move palely through the crowd, dragging his three chained wives behind him, and then dance, to the terrible music, with each of them in turn, while the other two, forced to follow, watched all that happened out of sad uncomprehending eyes. It was only Julius Champney, gone home early in disgust, who refused to believe any of it was possible. Nor would he believe, he said, that it was Maggie and Wade who stopped the battle in the end, before anyone got seriously hurt, by expressing their feelings for each other so vehemently in word and deed under the flower-bedecked arch that a pale warm eerie glow radiated from them over all the crowd and stopped them dead in their tracks, full of awe, to contemplate the nature of their own actions. People fell, where they'd stood, in heaps on the floor. Both horrified and amazed at their own behaviour, they either escaped into sleep or hid their faces in shame.

During the third hour of the wedding reception, while most people were too exhausted from fighting to move, the freckle-faced man who said he represented the premier of the province, and who had been hiding behind the piano for most of the battle, working his way through a case of Scotch whiskey, stepped up onto the stage and—standing unsteadily among beer bottles and flowers and torn decorations — delivered a speech. What price justice? he said, and whither Love? What man hath seen a greater pair than these? What man hath seen a nobler pair of hearts? The roomful of broken furniture and spilled food and collapsed and panting people swayed and tipped dangerously before him. But he went on. He represented the government, he said, which meant he represented the whole electorate of the province. And he was here to tell them, proud to say, that it was people like them, like you and me, who make this country strong. What we needed he said, and what the whole electorate knew we needed, was a whole new breed of people like — he looked at his monogrammed serviette—like Maggie and Wade, and like the kind of wonderful people who'd turned up, turned up he said in this godforsaken drafty dump of a hall, to wish them well. You are the salt, he said, of the earth. You are the lights, he said, under the bushel. You are the strength, he said, of the land, he said, and the land shall ever be strong. But the beauty of his own words stuck in his throat, he began to feel faint. When the amber stub of a broken beer bottle sailed through the air towards him, it missed, not because he had the presence of mind to duck but because by the time it got to where his head had been, he'd already fallen face-first off the edge of the stage and somersaulted onto the floor, where he lay flat on his back, spread-eagled, with his head resting squarely on the fancy bottom layer of the wedding cake. The thrower of the bottle was Danny Holland, who came forward across the hall, weaving between bodies, tripping over chairs, slipping on pieces of salad, to crawl up the stairs on all fours and then stand up slowly where the little man had stood. That little fart couldn't make a speech to save his ass, he said, because the little fart was a goddam government man who didn't know nothing. Well, he, Danny Holland, down from the bush, axe-throwing champion of the island, did know something and could out-speech that little fart any day of the week. And since he, who had more manhood in his little toe than all the rest of these bastards put together, and since he had been the one, don't forget, who had been the first to, been the first to ... He eyed up the bride who, sitting in a pile of debris, eyed him back with a vengeance, and found he had forgotten what he'd come up here to say. It didn't matter he said, because they all knew this one thing for sure: you can't beat a goddam wedding for fun.

It was left, after all, for Wade Powers to make the speech of the night, which he did from the top of the bar-table, with one foot planted firmly in the punch bowl. He spoke for an hour and a half. He began with a high-flown tribute to his bride, starting with fifteen minutes in praise of her beauty and going on through all her most admirable qualities in embarrassing detail, ending up with a declaration of his own unworth. He took them all, then, on a word tour of every room of the House of Revelations where they would, he said, be living. He gave them a brief half-hour run-down of the history of the Colony of Truth, as he knew it, or as rumour had it, for the benefit of those, he said, who had been asleep for the past hundred years, or had only just moved to the country. He challenged any man in the hall to battle, if battle was what they wanted. He challenged God to produce a man, anywhere on this great earth, who was happier than he was at this minute. He ended his oration by quoting a poem, which he apologized for, realizing that this was not a poetry-reading crowd; nor was he a poetry-reading man himself, he said, in fact he hated the stuff. But he'd come across this thing in a book of Lily Hayworth's and had memorized it in case the day ever came when he needed to know a line of poetry or two. What better time, he said, than at a wedding? "What was good shall be good, with, for evil, so much good more: On the earth the broken arcs; in heaven, a perfect round." That was all. He didn't know what it meant, he said, but it had made him think of a rainbow, and that reminded him of a pilot who told him once that a rainbow, from up in the sky, was a full circle.

And now, he concluded, didn't they think it was time they opened the presents?

The people roused themselves, those who had fallen asleep with their heads in their neighbours' laps as well as those who had sat up enthralled through all of his speech, got themselves up off the floor and off the benches and up out of the coat cupboard and the cubicles in the washrooms and the storage rooms behind the stage, down off the windowsills and the ceiling beams and the loft over the kitchen, in from the steps, in from the campers, in from the baseball park, all the way in—some of them—from out on the gravel road, to watch the bride and groom open the huge pile of gifts stacked ceiling-high on a table at the back of the stage.

But "I can't!" Maggie said. "Just look at that pile! I can't face it."

And "Let Cora do it!" someone called, and the hall threw back a hundred times "Let Cora do it, let Cora do it!" Children on the floor called it, clean-up women in the kitchen called it, men at the bar called it.

So Maggie and Wade sat on the only unbroken chairs, under the decorated arch, while Cora Manson behind them opened parcel after parcel, called out its contents in a loud voice, and tossed wrapping paper and ribbons onto the floor. There were pillows and sheets, she said, blankets and lamps and tablecloths and ashtrays, there were toasters and irons and mixers and blenders, plates and cups and bowls, there were pots, pans, jars, vases, glasses, toilet seats, and towels. Bedroom slippers, baby diapers, pepper shakers, oven cleaners, window washers, cheese cutters, pie servers, ice crushers.

Her voice went up higher with excitement. She tore the paper off, tossed each gift aside in a frenzy to get at the next. A subscription to *Maclean's*, a trip to Hawaii, a bucketful of bolts, a crate of Japanese oranges, a carton of cigarettes, a box of candy, a chair, a table, a stool, a bed, a book, a pen, a photo, a car, licence plates, serving spoons, road maps, garden rakes, a side of beef, a pound of coffee, a book of matches, a tin of peaches, a promise of peace. A painting. A shrub. A bird cage. A ring. A bird. A radio. A record player. A television. A calender. A cupboard. A holiday. A load of gravel. A chain saw. A rowboat.

Cora's hands flew. Gifts, opened, were barely seen. She screamed out the words. Junk mail. Thirty acres. Twin grandchildren. American oil tankers. Bad television programmes. Tax

notices. Insurance premiums. Advertising. The French language.
Surprises. Suspicions. Celebrations. Revelations. Meditations.
Weddings. Funerals. Elections. Rising prices. Hollow promises.
Special deliveries. Television commercials. Disapproval. Free
samples. Hope. The bomb. Crime. Ecology. Faith. Charity. Life.
Truth. Grief. Despair. Tantrums. Psychology. Biology. Lethargy.
Jealousy. Reconciliation. Inspiration. Sentiment. Rage. Patience.
Joy. Torment. Excitement. Serenity. Criticism. Regret. Relief. Re-
joicing. Complaining. Tedium. Beauty. Grace. Forgiveness. Fash-
ions. Laughter. Courage. Cowardice. Danger. Desire. Wonder.
Worship. Pride. Immortality. Humility. Friendship. The right to
vote. The right to complain. Speeches. Overpopulation. Food
shortage. Restless youth. Badly-treated Indians. Disappointed
immigrants. Passion. Retirement. Neglect. Loneliness. Love.

Reeling from the shock of such an incredible display of wedding gifts for a couple who'd been married once before and
already had enough to set up housekeeping without anybody's
help, the excited guests barely heard the last words Cora
screamed out at them, and were not quick to notice the stranger in
the doorway. They exclaimed, poked at the gifts, rescued cards
from the tossed-aside paper, hugged the bride, punched the
groom on the shoulder, congratulated each other on knowing
such a fine and important couple. Even the orchestra, amazed at
the litany, forgot to start playing again for the dancing and only
looked vaguely at their instruments as if they didn't know what to
do with them. It was the piano player who saw the stranger first,
and hammered on middle "C" until he had everyone's attention.

Almost immediately there was total silence. Breaths were held.
No one moved. The stranger in the doorway didn't look like a
stranger at all, he looked exactly like the bridegroom. He was even
dressed in a black tuxedo, exactly as Wade Powers was, and for a
moment they thought it was only Wade playing games with them.
But the bridegroom, too, looked as shocked as the rest, and put
out a hand to keep his balance. The stranger started across the
hall towards them, nodding to the right and to the left, smiling at
the women, helping himself to a pickle, kicking aside a crumpled
serviette, stopping to tickle the chin of a little girl, winking at Cora
Manson, who had unaccountably started to cry, and then held
out both of his hands to Wade Powers. Maggie stood up, beside
her husband, ready. Then the stranger led the bride and the

groom, the new man and the new woman, out of the hall and into his long silver vehicle parked at the door. No one ever saw the stranger again, though he apparently drove the new couple all the way back to their home at the House of Revelations.

And if, as Becker will tell you, with borrowed words, pulling you closer, rolling his eyes in the direction of the House, *if they're not dead nor gone they're alive there still.*